False Impressions

Ace Bryann

Dare To Dream Books—Bruce Twp, MI
ISBN: 979-8-218-34329-3
Library of Congress Control Number: 2024900869
Title: *False Impressions*
Author: Ace Bryann
Digital distribution | 2024
Paperback | 2024

This is a work of fiction. The characters, names, incidents, places, and dialogue are products of the author's imagination, and are not to be construed as real.

Dedication

For Michelle, RIP

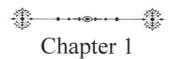

Chapter 1

Present Day

The music thumped in the background of the upscale club. The top-shelf liquor poured freely and beautifully dressed people danced underneath dazzling lights. The clientele here were the rich and famous; celebrity sightings were common in this luxurious hangout spot in New York City. It was the kind of place where connections were made, hook-ups happened, and a deal could be sealed. The club space was massive and almost every inch of the sleek, ebony black bar was occupied as well as the dance floor. A corner staircase to one side with a velvet rope in front of it indicated the entrance to the secluded VIP section which from the second floor, one could overlook onto the entire scene. It was quieter upstairs, where intimate conversations could actually take place over the pounding of the bass music. As always, the atmosphere was one of laughter, frivolity and mischief.

Even in such an environment, the young man seated upstairs in the back corner leather-clad booth wore a look of complete boredom as he picked up his crystal glass full of expensive amber colored liquid and took a small sip. He then turned to his right as a lazy smile crossed his handsome face. Leaning into the beautiful blonde seated next to him, he placed a hand lightly on her half-covered thigh, a curl from his dark brown hair falling across his forehead.

"Why don't we get out of here," he murmured. "My place is much cozier." She reached up and gently pushed back his thick hair, tangling her fingers in his curls in doing so.

"Oh Nic," she purred and giggled, "I promised my friends I'd meet them here tonight. Besides," she added, a pout now on her face, "I've only had one drink. Won't you be a sweetheart and get me another glass of champagne?"

He sighed and removed his hand. Sitting up straight, he glanced over at the maitre d' and made eye contact, signaling that he wished for service. If he had known Heather was so high maintenance, he would've stopped taking her out. Honestly, didn't she realize he could drop her in an instant and have any other woman in this club? It had been already two weeks, he had taken her on numerous expensive dates, and still she refused to sleep with him.

As the maitre d' approached their booth, he glanced at Heather. She was certainly stunning with a tight figure, long honey blonde hair, large, heavily lidded blue eyes, and full red lips. But he was deciding that she was no longer worth his effort. He just had to get through this evening as quickly as possible, then he'd be able to move on.

"Another glass for the lady," he told the maitre d', who nodded, then left promptly.

He raised his whiskey glass to his lips and took another sip, but a sudden loud squeal next to him made him choke, causing the liquor to burn. Snapping his head back toward Heather, he looked on in annoyance as she rose quickly to greet her friends who had just entered the VIP section: two more women and a man. *Fantastic,* he thought grimly, *more freeloaders.*

Shifting to the edge of the booth to make room for the newcomers, he placed a fake smile on his face as Heather scooted back in next to him and began to make introductions. He soon tuned out their voices, (he didn't really care who her friends were), and let his gaze wander back to the VIP entrance. His eyes widened slightly as he caught sight of who had entered behind Heather's friends. He grimaced as he overheard the maitre d' gushing over the man and his companion.

"Mr. McKenzie, we are honored to have you here this evening."

He watched as the maitre d' escorted Gregory McKenzie and a pretty redhead to a table on the other side.

Seeing the famous CEO of one of the most powerful companies in the country, Land Corporation, made him scowl, and he continued to observe Gregory McKenzie with both envy and resentment.

"Nic, aren't you listening to me?" Heather's voice called his attention back, and he suddenly realized how nasal it sounded. He raised his eyebrows at her expectantly. "I was saying how nice it would be for all of us to spend the weekend somewhere warm, like Palm Beach," she repeated. "Don't you have a place down there?"

He had to swallow to prevent himself from laughing at her. Did she actually think he was going to spring for a weekend vacation for her and her friends when she wouldn't even put out for him? Clearly, she was only interested in his money.

"Not anymore, darling," he replied through white, clenched teeth that bore a false smile. He spoke the truth, which hurt, as he downed the remaining whiskey in his glass, realizing that if he was going to get through this night without losing his temper, he needed many more rounds. She had hit quite a nerve with him without her knowing it bringing up his Palm Beach property, which he sold a week ago to pay off debts.

"Sir." The maitre d' reappeared, which seemed to be perfect timing, and he passed over his now empty glass.

"Where's my champagne?" Heather whined, "and they'd like to order drinks too." She gestured to the others in the booth.

"Sir," the maitre d' repeated however, ignoring Heather, "I would like to speak to you privately."

The young man blinked up at the maitre d' who held his gaze with an urgency. Deciding it best to do as suggested, he rose to follow him. Once out of earshot back towards the entrance of the section, the maitre d' turned to face him.

"Sir, I regret to inform you that your credit here has been declined," he stated matter of fact. "I've been instructed to ask you and your party to leave at once and you will receive a bill for any outstanding debts." Unseen due to the dim lighting, his face became flush at the maitre d's words.

"That's impossible," he replied quickly, "there must be some mistake."

The maitre d' held his stoney expression. "No, sir, there has been no mistake."

"Don't you realize who I am?" He snarled.

At the young man's arrogance, a cruel smile crossed the maitre d's face. "I know who your *brother* is, sir," he said, "unfortunately *your* name doesn't mean much these days, and rumor has it you no longer have the financial backing you once did."

He glared at the maitre d' calculating his next move. If he was escorted out, he would never live down the embarrassment. What was accused of him was true, of course, he knew he was headed for financial ruin. But his image was so far still intact, and if he were to ever recover in this city, he needed his reputation. His gaze moved passed the maitre d' and fell once again on Gregory McKenzie.

"If I settle my obligation here this evening, will my party be

3

allowed to stay?" he questioned as he met the eye of the maitre d'.

"Sure," the maitre d' gave a mocking smile, indicating that he did not believe for an instant that were possible. "Why not. You have fifteen minutes."

He turned and headed back to his booth, however once out of view of the maitre d', he made a sharp left straight toward Gregory McKenzie. As he approached the table, the CEO looked up at him. The smile he held while chatting with the redhead faded quickly as recognition appeared in Gregory's eyes. Without waiting for an invitation, the young man took a seat at the table across from Gregory and the redhead. She looked at him inquiringly, and he could tell she was trying to place his face, as though she knew who he was.

The two men eyed each other in silence for a moment, and Gregory raised his eye brows in anticipation that the other speak first. The young man chuckled.

"You've mastered that poker face well, Gregory," he stated, "my brother would be so proud."

Gregory didn't respond, only adjusted his glasses. At his words the redhead's eyes opened wide, now understanding why the young man seemed familiar to her; she knew his brother well, and his resemblance to him was evident.

"That makes one of us he would be proud of," Gregory finally replied with an even tone. He turned to his companion, "April, this is Nicola Landino," he said as he gestured back to the young man. "Nicola, please meet April Blackburn."

Nicola held out his hand to April and she placed hers in his in a greeting. "Enchanted," he murmured, looking directly into her green eyes.

The young man was indeed charming, and his reputation of being a playboy was well known. Gregory, however, was not amused by any flirtatious attempts towards his date. He was quite protective of April; they had been together for some months now.

They had met in North Carolina where he worked for the former CEO of Land Corporation, Nicola's older brother, Derek Landino. When Derek moved the company back to New York City, he had resigned from his position naming Gregory as his successor. Although he was ready and eager to run the large enterprise in New York, Gregory realized he needed April in his life too, and when he asked her, she had agreed to move to be with him. Although just barely 30 years old, Gregory took his position and his relationship seriously and maintained a high level of success on both sides.

April retracted her hand, and Gregory leaned back extending an arm casually behind her shoulders across her chair.

"What do you want, Nicola?" he asked.

Nicola opened his eyes wide in innocence. "I merely spotted you across the club and came over to extend my greetings," he said smoothly. "Do I need a reason to say hello to a friend?"

Gregory now folded his arms. "Because it's you, yes," he answered. "Now, I'd like to get back to enjoying my evening, so why don't we just cut to the chase. You came over here for a reason. Otherwise, you wouldn't dare show your face to me considering your estranged relationship with Derek—which is your own doing by the way. So I'll ask you again. What do you want? Money?"

"My doing?" Nicola asked in astonishment ignoring Gregory's question. "He took away my legacy! A legacy he didn't even want. He left me with nothing. And why? Just out of spite."

Gregory laughed out loud at Nicola's declaration. *So immature*, he thought.

"It was his birthright, not yours," he reasoned. "True, he didn't want it, but he took it out of your hands because he knew you would suck at it. How many times did he try to talk sense into you? How many times did he try to get you to grow up? Make you understand the responsibility you both had. He had hoped that you would have risen to the challenge, but you refused to change. So Derek did what he had to do, in the best interest of his people." Gregory took a breath to calm his rising anger. "He is the rightful monarch of Calina, and you are what you've always chosen to be: a washed up prince."

Nicola winced slightly at his born-given title. He didn't like to be reminded of his heritage, especially since his brother had declined the throne to him only to change his mind. He resented Derek immensely for taking away his opportunity at something great— to be somebody. He had never even been given the chance to prove himself worthy of running the microstate of Calina. Derek had just assumed he'd mess it up, and so therefore took the power for himself.

"He did it for greed," Nicola sneered. "It wasn't enough for him to own the most powerful corporation in the US, no, he had to rule a country too. But, nothing is ever 'enough' for Derek. He's living the life of a king and meanwhile I'm struggling to make ends meet."

5

Gregory shook his head sadly.

"It's clear you know nothing of your brother, or what he's been through. The life of a king, you say? Were you living under a rock when his name was being dragged through the mud and he was being shot at causing him to almost lose his life? Do you have any idea how many people in Calina itself would like to see him dead? That country is buried in serious corruption and Derek is tasked with digging it out. Is that what you wanted?" The CEO looked Nicola in the eye. "If Derek hadn't taken the throne and left it to you, there's no doubt you'd be dead, Nicola."

Nicola opened his mouth to respond, but Gregory did not let him. He waved his hand in dismissal.

"You say you are struggling," he stated, growing tired of this argument. "Why don't you just tell me what you want."

Nicola sighed softly, realizing this dialogue was not achieving his purpose. Gregory was his only hope. He knew he was running out of time, and he needed to switch tactics. He nodded reluctantly, casting his eyes down to the table.

"I am struggling," he repeated, "I didn't realize how bad it was until recently, and I'm in a bind tonight."

Gregory raised his eyebrows. "Tonight?" he asked astonished. "You mean, you can't pay your tab?"

Nicola shut his eyes briefly, it sounded so much worse hearing it out loud. "No," he admitted quietly, "they're threatening to throw me out." He looked up at Gregory with pleading eyes. "I'll be publicly humiliated."

As Gregory sat in silence for a moment, the maitre d' spotted Nicola.

"Mr. McKenzie, I am so sorry," he said rushing up to the table. He turned to address Nicola, "sir, I've asked you to leave our establishment, now I must insist."

Nicola gave a defeated nod and prepared to rise.

"Actually," Gregory interrupted, "Mr. Landino is my guest tonight." He looked from Nicola to the maitre d', who's expression had turned to shock. "Please ensure that he and his friends have everything they require."

The maitre d' sputtered. "Yes, sir, absolutely." He looked back down at Nicola with an astonished gaze.

"Could you please see to the needs back at my table?" Nicola flashed the maitre d' a dashing and triumphant grin revealing the dimple in his left cheek.

"Of course, sir," the maitre d' replied tightly. Then, excusing himself, he turned and walked quickly away.

Nicola watched him as he crossed the section back to his booth, then turned back to Gregory, the smile gone from his face.

"I owe you," he offered.

Gregory remained serious. "Yes," he replied simply, "you do." He paused. "I'm only doing this out of respect for my mentor. I feel the Landino name has been through enough, and Derek doesn't need any more bad publicity." He met Nicola's gaze. "He will know of this exchange."

"I understand," Nicola replied stoically. He stood from the table and buttoned his suit jacket. "Thank you, Gregory." He looked at April, "a pleasure meeting you." He gave her a smile and a wink, then turned to rejoin Heather and her friends.

Walking back, he knew he had dodged a bullet. This had to be one of the worst and most embarrassing nights of his life. Begging for money from Gregory McKenzie? He suppressed a slight groan, adding Gregory's name to the long list of people that he was now indebted to.

It was a little after 2:00 a.m. when Nicola returned to his penthouse apartment in Manhattan. Ironically, after spending thousands of dollars of Gregory's money on her in expensive booze, Heather had hinted at coming home with him. But after this evening, Nicola had decided he was no longer in the mood. So, he returned home alone. As he stepped off the elevator and approached the door, he saw a note tacked to it from the owner of the building: a notice of eviction.

"Damn!" He muttered under his breath, ripping the notice off the door and entering the apartment.

The apartment opened up first into a spacious kitchen, modernly designed in tones of pale grey, stainless appliances and white cabinetry. Nicola slammed the notice down on the granite countertop and walked straight to the side bar. As he poured another whiskey, he eyed the eviction paper. He knew he didn't have the money. He'd have to move. He downed the drink in one gulp wracking his brain about who could possibly help him.

Only one name came to his mind.

He shook his head in stubborn defiance. Approaching Gregory had been bad enough, and he had only done so because he was conveniently there when he needed him. But he just couldn't bring himself to stoop any lower.

As he picked up the decanter his cell buzzed. He replaced the decanter back on the bar counter and pulled his phone out of his jacket pocket. Incoming Call: Private. Fear flooded through Nicola as he accepted the call.

"H—hello?" He answered. There was a brief pause, then a gruff voice.

"Time to pay up, Nic," the disembodied voice replied.

Nicola's heart was pounding. Had it been a month already?

"I, I'll have the money," he said quietly.

The voice sighed. "Oh, Nic…" it trailed off in a heavy silence. "We don't believe you anymore."

"Come on!" Nicola cried, unable to hide the panic from his voice. "I'm good for it! I just need a little time." He held his breath.

"You have 48 hours," the voice replied, "then, we're coming for you." The phone clicked off.

Nicola stared at the screen, his breathing labored from fear. How had he gotten here? How had it gone this far?

With absolutely no pride left at all, he knew he only had one choice. Phone in hand, he wandered over to the plush living area with an enormous view that looked out over Manhattan. Apparently he would stoop lower…

He sank into the leather sofa facing the view and opened the contacts on his phone. Still in disbelief that he was about to make this call, he scrolled to a name he thought he'd never have to talk to again and hit send. His call was answered on the third ring.

"Derek… it's Nic… Yeah, I'm uh… I'm in trouble. I need your help."

Chapter 2

1 Month Ago

Christine Dayne shifted uneasily in her chair. Still recovering from her unfortunate run-in with a bullet to her back, she continued to strive for comfortable positions in which to rest. It had been almost a month since she had been shot, the bullet itself having been meant for her fiancé, Derek Landino. She had thrown herself in front of him in an effort to shield him from the fire, but her efforts were in vain as he had also been hit in the shoulder. Both of them had nearly lost their lives that day, and the incident, as well as other events leading up to it, still haunted Christine causing extreme post-traumatic stress along with night terrors. Her eyes glazed over as her thoughts turned once again to that day; the day that very vividly replayed itself not just in her waking hours, but also in her nightmares.

"Are you ok?" Derek's voice broke through her reverie and she focused on him where he stood across the room. His face held concern, and she forced a smile. She was supposed to be keeping him company while he packed, not that she was doing a great job at holding up her end of the bargain.

They were in his hotel suite in New York City, a massive, luxurious room, fit for a king, overlooking Central Park. Because that's what Derek Landino was: a king. A monarch who ruled over a small, microstate in Europe called Calina. And she, Christine, had agreed to marry him. They had been in New York now for almost two months— Derek's stay having been prolonged because of their recent injuries. But now, he was anxious to go home and to the country that needed him.

She met his gaze as he looked at her intently waiting for her response.

"I'm fine," she assured him. He furrowed his brow, knowing that she didn't sound convincing, but he turned his attention back to his suitcase, attempting to keep things orderly but failing with his dominant arm still sling-bound. A slight frown crossed her face as she watched him struggle, again feeling guilty at his injury. She realized that she would have done anything in her power to have protected him, she just hadn't been fast enough. She stared at him, the man she loved deeply, feeling charmed by his grace, even with his temporary handicap, he still held presence and power.

Struggling slightly, she rose from her chair. Grabbing the cane leaning next to it, she used it for stability as she made her way slowly over to him. She reached for the shirt he was attempting to fold.

"Why are you doing this?" she asked quizzically. "Don't you have 'people' for this?"

He gave her a grin, the dimple appearing in his left cheek. "Sure I do," he replied, "but if my 'people' were in here packing my things, we wouldn't be alone." His sapphire eyes twinkled as he watched her finish folding his shirt neatly.

She met his eyes and her breathing hitched in her throat as a deep longing for him came over her. By now, she should be used to the way he affected her, but she knew she never would be. He was tall, had broad, muscular shoulders and a strength in his arms and chest that was unyielding. His hair was tousled, raven black, accentuating his olive tanned complexion, and he always seemed to have a constant five o'clock shadow adorning his strong jaw. His piercing blue eyes were famous, and he was adored by women everywhere he went.

But Christine didn't love him simply for the way he looked. She loved him for his integrity, his strength of character, and his passion for making a positive difference in people's lives. This is why she agreed to marry him, even if it meant giving up everything she knew to follow him to Calina. This is why she risked her life for him, knowing that even with her pain and torment, she'd do it again a thousand times over.

Now that she was near, Derek abandoned his feeble packing attempts. He reached for her face with his hand, running his thumb lightly across her cheek. Her lips parted slightly, and Christine felt the tension mount with a fury as he brought his mouth down on hers. Her need for him swelled and she couldn't help but grip the front of his shirt, bringing him closer. Her movements were still limited, and she could tell through his kiss that his desire for her matched her own, but Derek was very careful not to hold her too tightly for fear of causing her pain. He broke the kiss, a smile playing on his lips.

"I wish you'd stay here with me," he told her, "I promise to keep my hands to myself."

"Hand," she corrected him, smiling back and raising an eyebrow at his own limited capacity.

He laughed in response. "Either way," he mused, "I hate the idea of you staying at that facility. I know you're still recovering, but there are more than enough resources to make you comfortable here."

She gave him a grateful smile. "Rehabilitation has been important for both of us," she countered. "Don't worry, I'm being well taken care of."

Feeling weary from standing, Christine sat down gingerly on the corner of the bed, using her cane for support. Derek sighed and gave up the argument.

"Well," he replied, winking at her, "it's only just for this last night anyway. The car will be by early tomorrow to pick you up. Our flight leaves at six." She just nodded, and he turned away, striding back into the massive closet.

Traveling with him back to Calina made her nervous. Not only was she moving to a foreign country to begin a life in which she knew nothing about, she had personal motivations for maintaining her distance from him these past several weeks. Blaming her need for solace on the injury rehab, she had as well been able to hide her need for psychological therapy. Embarrassed about her inability to control her PTSD and night terrors, Christine had not shared her torments with Derek. As a trained and once practicing psychologist herself, she found it ironic that she was now in a position of needing treatment. She thought she had begun to get her symptoms under control, but once she and Derek became engaged, her nightmares worsened and have continued to do so. She could only conclude that the more time she spent with him, the closer she was to him, the more likely she was to lose her mind. Moving to his country; living with him, terrified her. Once she actually got to Calina, she didn't know what she was going to do. What would he think of her when she woke up screaming in the middle of the night?

Derek emerged from the closet, tossing a suit hanger onto the bed.

"The flight's about eight hours," he continued, throwing her a cautious look. "When we land, there's going to be press, Christine," he paused, "lots of it."

She met his eyes. She was no novice to the press having dated him

11

during his infamous run as CEO of Land Corporation. And in recent months, Christine herself had found her own fame as a successful and highly sought after oil painter in France. But even if she was used to it, she still didn't like it, and Derek knew that. Also, this would be much different. She was entering a new world, a royal one, and here on out, there would be no escaping the limelight.

"Do you think they'll ask me questions?" she asked him, almost with a timidness to her voice. "I don't speak Calean."

"Yet," Derek finished for her. "Don't worry," he said in a reassuring tone, "I'll do all the talking. But expect to be introduced to the people." He flashed her a winning smile. "I'm sure they will be anxious to meet you. Not only are you their future queen, but you saved my life as well."

Christine's eyes widened at his words. The expectation scared her, and she felt unsure about her reception from the people of Calina.

"What if I'm not good enough in their eyes?" She stared at the silk comforter unwilling to meet his gaze.

He took the space next to her on the bed, and reaching for her chin, he lifted her face making her look at him. "You are more than enough for anyone," he said quietly, "and regardless, you are the woman I love."

"But, I'm an American," she protested. "Does that matter? Am I even *allowed* to marry you?"

Derek laughed softly in response. "This isn't medieval times, Christine," he said, amusement filling his eyes. "I can marry whom I choose. And in time, you will become a citizen. In time, Calina will feel like your home."

Her large, hazel eyes misted over, wanting nothing more than to believe in the comfort he offered. She leaned toward him allowing her head to rest against his chest.

He stroked her chestnut brown hair lightly, wishing he could just remove the doubt from within her. Christine had always struggled with her insecurities surrounding his position, but he couldn't help but sense that there was something deeper troubling her. He wrapped his one arm around her shoulders and pulled her in closer, tighter against him. Now that she was back in his life, he couldn't bear the thought of losing her again. He could only hope that she would once again open back up to him. In the meantime, however, he knew she was harboring some secret that she, for some reason, seemed afraid to share.

It always starts the same way. She was running up steps, her vision seemed blurred. The steps were white and stone, and it felt like there were a million of them. She looked around her, as if in slow motion, yearning to see into the mass of people. She finally spotted him through the crowd, more toward the top of the stairs. Why were there so many stairs? Her legs felt heavy. Would she ever reach him? Finally, as she got close enough, she called out his name. He turned, startled at first, but as he moved in her direction, she could see the sweet relief on his face. She shouldn't have distracted him. She knew that now. If only she hadn't called out to him then, he wouldn't have been exposed. But all she could think about at the time was getting to him. She was within reach of him, and her heart clenched, knowing what was about to happen.

There was a scream, a shriek, and a scuffle. She turned toward the commotion behind them down the stairs just a second before he did; he was still looking at her. She moved instinctively in front on him, shielding him, turning her back on the crowd as a shot rang out, then another. She felt the bullet pierce her back, left of her spine, and she immediately fell into him. As he caught her in his arms, that's when she saw it: the blood. Gushing from his shoulder like a dark ruby fountain. She knew the bullet had hit one of his main arteries—he had minutes to live. She'd never see him again. She'd never get to tell him how wrong she was, how sorry she was. She heard weeping, a painful cry emerged somewhere in her mind as the bloody image dissolved, replaced by the laughing face of a woman with pale skin and long, dark hair: Courtney Metcalf. The crying turned into a raging scream.

Christine opened her eyes. It was now eerily quiet, and she was shaking, every muscle in her body twitching from an extreme tenseness. She was cold, damp from the sweat which now soaked through her tank top and shorts to her skin. Without looking at the time, she knew it was close to 1:00 a.m. This was always the time she woke up. She closed her mouth, her throat dry, realizing it was frozen open from screaming—she had been the one crying and screaming. Trying to regain her bearings, she hugged her frigid arms and looked around. Where had she wandered to this time? She never woke up in bed. If she was lucky, she only made it as far as her bedroom door,

13

but other times, she found herself out her door and down the hallway of the rehabilitation facility. Tonight she was still in her room. As she turned to limp slowly back to her bed, she heard a light knock.

"Christine?" Pamela, her private nurse, poked her head into her room. "You ok, dear?"

Pamela had been working with Christine since she had come to the facility. She knew about the night terrors, the anxiety, and the PTSD, and had been the one who recommended the psychologist Christine had been seeing over the past few weeks.

"I'm ok, Pam," Christine replied wearily, grasping the bed for support as she made her way to it.

Pamela entered and offered Christine her arm to grip onto, helping her back into bed. "Is it still getting worse?" she asked Christine quietly.

Christine sighed and nodded sadly. She thought back to the visions from her dream. She had never seen Courtney's face in them before now, she always woke up right after the shooting. As terrifying as Derek covered in blood was to Christine, seeing Courtney's laughing, haunted face was far more disturbing.

"What am I going to do?" She whispered more to herself as she shuddered at the vivid image in her mind.

"It'll pass," Pamela replied reassuringly. "Can I bring you something?"

Christine shook her head, disliking the idea of taking medications, and her pain was tolerable. She didn't share her nurse's confidence, and she wondered again why these dreams would continue to heighten in terror for her. They were occurring more frequently, the imagery was more alive and real, the dreams themselves were changing to include more traumatic events.

Being with Derek should make her feel whole again, safe. Why was it the more time she spent with him, the worse her dreams became?

Anxiety grew in her as she thought about how in five hours, she'd be on her way with him to Calina. She should be happy and excited about beginning this next phase of her life, not terrified that the man she loved would discover she was going insane.

———————————

Having been unable to fall back to sleep, Christine now found herself exhausted as she exited the facility four hours later. She stifled a yawn as she slowly made her way out the back, still using her cane for support. The flag-bearing limousine was already waiting for her, parked right outside the back entrance in hopes of drawing less attention. Due to the hour, she didn't expect there to be a crowd, and she was delighted to see there was no press. Or if there were, they were hidden.

For her first appearance to the people of Calina, she had decided to wear a pale pink skirt with a matching cropped jacket. The suit was made from a luxurious fabric that breathed easily, and the style accentuated her curves, while still maintaining a conservative and modest feel. The color was chosen specifically for its femininity and complimented her tanned skin and chestnut hair.

An attendant escorted her down the short sidewalk towards the limo, then opened her door. Derek was already inside, and she slid in next to him.

"Good morning," he greeted her with a smile while handing her a take-out cup of steaming, black coffee. His eyes slid over her, appreciating her attire. "You look beautiful," he murmured.

She accepted the cup, returning his smile.

"Thank you," she replied, grateful for both the compliment and the coffee, and she inhaled the aroma. She glanced at him, noticing he held no cup of his own. "Still no black coffee, huh?" And she smiled knowingly at his dislike of what he referred to as "regular" coffee. He made a face in response. "Snob," she said with a small grin as she took a sip. He laughed lightly and gave her a look of feigned astonishment.

The limousine pulled away from the facility, making its journey towards the airport. Christine took another tiny sip of the coffee, glancing up across from her. In doing so, she caught the eye of the only other occupant in the back of the limousine, Derek's personal security guard, Vincenzo Costa.

Costa was a senior member of the King's Guard, and it was his duty to protect the king—at all costs. Therefore, he rarely left Derek's side. Christine was used to Derek having a side-kick of sorts. Before he took his position as monarch of Calina, his personal assistant, Gregory, had never been too far away. Christine liked Gregory, he was approachable and down to earth; amiable. Costa, on the other hand…

His dark eyes were always set like an eagle's, alert and pensive, always looking for something. Christine had never seen him smile, and his stature and black suits made him appear intimidating.

She had no clue what he thought of her, and she briefly wondered if it would bother her if he didn't like her. She decided that it would. After all, Costa had already proven he'd give his life for the king. When Christine had thrown herself in front of Derek that day to shield him from the gunfire, Costa dove into the crowd at the gunman, tackling him to the ground. If it weren't for Costa's quick actions, there would have surely been more shots fired, killing her and Derek both. As such, Christine felt it was important she was in the good graces of Derek's most trusted guard.

He met her eyes as she glanced at him offering him a small smile in greeting. He did not return her smile, only lifted his eyebrows slightly, further instilling in Christine the notion that no, he did not like her.

Feeling slightly disappointed and now a bit awkward, Christine inhaled deeply and turned to Derek, who had pulled out his phone to make a call. The party he rang clearly didn't pick up and he left no voicemail. He grimaced as he ended the call, and Christine could tell that whoever didn't answer his call would be very sorry for that later. He continued to brood staring at the phone in his hand, which was out of character for him.

"Is something wrong?" she asked, concerned.

He clenched his jaw and took a moment to respond. "My brother," he said simply.

Christine furrowed her brow slightly. She knew that Derek and his younger brother, Nicola, did not speak. She kept quiet, waiting for him to add more information.

Derek sighed. "I was hoping he would have, by now, seen past our disagreements," he began, "but it seems his pride won't let him. He won't return my calls. Maybe I should just take the hint." He turned to look at Christine, and she could see the emotion in his eyes. "After all," he added, "I didn't even hear from him while I was in the hospital."

Wishing to comfort him, Christine placed her hand gently on his sling-bound arm. "No one could blame you for being angry with him," she said. "It should have been him reaching out to you, yet you continue to try to contact him. You've done more than your fair share to try and salvage that relationship."

He nodded slowly. "I know you're right," he replied, "it's just…

he's my brother. We've never really seen eye to eye, but how he was raised really wasn't his fault."

He fell quiet, and Christine could tell by the thoughtful expression on his face there was more he wanted to say about that, but didn't, and she knew it was best not to push him.

"I was really hoping to clear the air," he finally added, "but that's probably because of my own guilt." With a last glance at his phone, he tucked it away in his jacket. "We'll be at the airport in a few minutes," he said now, changing the subject and looking back to her. "How are you feeling?" Before she could answer, he continued. "I want you to know that the gravity of your situation and what you're giving up isn't lost on me." He looked intently into her eyes. "What you're doing means the world to me."

At his words, Christine couldn't help but let some of her fears melt away. Maybe she could get through this; as long as they were together. Meeting his gaze, she suddenly wished they were alone. She couldn't think of how to express her emotions, both her fears and her love for him in words, and the urge to embrace him was becoming painful.

As if on cue, and reminding her of his presence, Costa cleared his throat. Christine blinked, the sound pulling her from the moment.

Derek smirked and glanced up at Costa. "Don't worry about Costa," he said, as if reading Christine's mind in connection with her concerns about the guard's attitude towards her. "He doesn't talk much, but I promise you, he does have a personality."

Her eyes opened wide at Derek's quip, unsure what Costa's response would be. But Costa merely raised an eyebrow at the monarch.

"I hope you're familiar with Derek's dry sense of humor," Christine said, speaking to Costa now, then she turned to Derek. "You should apologize," she hissed.

Derek's grin widened. "He's familiar," he replied.

The limousine slowed, pulling up towards a private jet at the airport. Christine peered out the tinted window at the plane, her stomach flooding with nerves. The unknown holding within it just as much excitement as it did fear for her. As she looked around, gathering her things, preparing to exit the limousine, she didn't notice Costa's slight smile in her direction.

Chapter 3

Taya Mariano smoothed out her navy suit jacket and pencil skirt as she made her way toward the entrance of the airport. The monarch was landing momentarily, and as a member of parliament, she was expected to be present. Not only was she expected, she was eager. As a newly elected member, just within the past few months, she had not yet been able to hold an audience with His Highness, given his recent prolonged stay in the States. She was not anticipating to be able to have a private conversation with him today, but she was most anxious to hear him address the people in person when he landed.

Curious about the new ruler of their small, intimate microstate, Taya wanted to hear for herself his message and make her own judgements. The temperament surrounding Derek's reign amongst the people was mixed. He was undeniably popular, but the older traditionalists in the community held reservations. Taya had yet to make up her mind, but craved information.

Born and raised in Calina, Taya was very patriotic with regards to her home. She loved the sense of community, the deep-seated traditions, and nestled between Italy and France, close to the Swiss border, the microstate held a unique culture, unlike any other. The people pulled societal inspirations from their surrounding neighbors, but made it their own, including the food, government, and even language. Although its citizens knew and used Calean, a dialect consisting of mostly Italian, everyone also spoke fluent French, Swiss German, and English.

Even though she was happy to see signs of much needed change in Calina under Derek's leadership surrounding the country's economy, she was hesitant to jump on his band wagon of blind support. Some relief had been provided to the people, but there was still a long road ahead toward rebuilding their country. Taya wasn't quick to believe that what Derek had been able to accomplish in this short timespan was sustainable.

In addition, she feared Derek's innovative and forward-thinking reputation as an entrepreneur would be too much for their little country. Like many, she wondered if his true intentions were what was best for the people or himself. She knew that in order to sell a product, or a business, it had to look good first. She only hoped that Derek wasn't making them look good just to sell out in the end. Was he committed here? Or was Calina just to be used as a stepping stone for greater wealth?

Then there was the matter of Calina and its relations with the European Union. As a standalone country, Calina has always abstained from joining or collaborating. The members of parliament and the prime minister had always shared a consensus of pride over their independence. But, Derek seemed to think otherwise, opening negotiations with the EU in terms of securing arrangements for protection and economical benefit. No one in Derek's position before him had been willing to do this. Joining the union would mean a reduction in the authority of the monarchy as a whole, and although the alliance would free Calina from the economical vice-grips of corrupt power players still operating in the country, Taya wasn't sure if she agreed with this change. What could it mean for their future? Or could it cause the potential demise of the microstate altogether.

She walked quickly toward the gate in which the king was to arrive. She had already passed through internal airport security, but she was running behind. The other members of press and parliament that were to be part of the welcoming committee had already been escorted out to the private landing area.

She approached the exit leading to the outside platform. Through the windows, she could see the small crowd gathering awaiting their monarch's arrival. Making haste, she began to pass through the exit door when a firm hand grasped her arm, halting her.

"Just where do you think you're going?"

Taya opened her forest green eyes wide at the security guard who had snatched her arm, perhaps a bit too tightly. She glanced down at his hand, her mouth set in a straight line as she turned to face him. He was of average height, about 40 years of age with a slight receding hair line. But his shoulders were broad, and he puffed out his chest slightly. She met his dark eyes and he let go of her arm.

"I'm Taya Mariano," she replied stiffly. "I'm a parliament member and I'm expected to be among those to greet His Highness when he arrives."

The guard all but snorted at her explanation. "You?" he exclaimed, "a member of parliament? How old are you, 22?" He looked her up and down, unashamedly taking in her long blond waves, red lips, pale skin, and lean figure. "You look more like a crazed fan hoping to glimpse the king. Did you really think your 'parliament' story would fly?"

She narrowed her eyes at him in response, not appreciating his disrespect of her in the slightest. She was truly 31, but she knew she looked young. And not seeing how that even mattered, she wasn't about to argue the moot point. Still, that was no reason to question who she said she was in such a way. With a scowl now on her face, she dug into the baguette bag over her shoulder and pulled out her ID along with a pass she had received allowing her to be present.

The guard looked over her credentials then raised his eye brows in surprise. "I apologize, signora," he stated.

Taya crossed her arms. Oh, she was "signora" now, was she?

"Please, go on through."

She forced herself from rolling her eyes as she took back her ID. Not wishing to waste any more time, she shook her head slightly and turned to push open the exit door.

She made it out onto the platform and had taken her place amongst the other government representatives just as the private royal jet had landed and was taxing to its designated stop. It was a clear day, warmer earlier, but as it was nearing evening, there was now a slight chill in the air.

As the jet engines died down, light chatter began amongst the crowd. The press was huddled together off to one side, each of them vying for the best angle. Taya tried to tune out the jabbering behind her as well as the camera clicking, and she kept her eyes focused on the jet as she now saw several members of the King's Guard make their way towards the door. They took their places, lining up on either side, creating a pathway from the plane to a podium.

The first to emerge from the plane was Vincenzo Costa, whom Taya knew to be the king's personal body guard. Behind him was Derek Landino. A hush fell on the crowd as Derek de-planed and there was a slight uneasiness amongst the people when they caught sight of his injury. But the monarch smiled brilliantly and waved with his good arm, his apparent charm never ceasing to impress. The crowd applauded in response, and Taya noticed that he then paused by the bottom steps, looking back towards the door in anticipation. A woman appeared, and Taya could only deduce it was Christine Dayne, whom she had read about extensively in the news. The masses became quiet again as Christine made her way down the steps carefully, grasping onto the rails as much as she could for support. She was clearly struggling with the steps, and it was Derek himself who met her halfway, allowing her to take his hand and lean against him while he helped her down the last few. The sight was rather endearing, and Taya glanced at the press who seemed unable to click their cameras fast enough.

Behind her, Taya heard a slight grunt.

"The American, no doubt."

She heard a man whisper. She blinked, intrigued by the reaction and strained to hear the hushed conversation.

"They're engaged," his companion replied lowly. "She's going to become our queen."

"It's absurd," the first man replied indignantly. "I don't think he cares at all about safe guarding our culture, and now he's going to marry an American!"

"She can't be all bad," a third voice now whispered, "she did save his life."

There was a slight pause and Taya almost didn't catch what the first man said next.

"If DeGrassi had seized power…"

Her heart began to pound at the name in which he spoke: DeGrassi. The rivalry for power between the Landino family and the DeGrassi family was well-known, not just in Calina, but in Europe, and it spanned back generations.

She tilted her head to try and make out what the man said next, but it was in vain. The prime minister at that moment had made his way up to the podium to greet and shake hands with Derek who had now taken his place behind it. There was too much applause for Taya to hear anymore of the conversation behind her. She tried to focus her attention toward the podium, but she was rattled, and she couldn't prevent her mind from wandering to past events.

It was Marco DeGrassi who initiated the revolution 32 years prior, plotting against the monarch at the time, Luciano Landino, Derek's father. It had been easy for Marco to gain support, with Luciano's reign practically running the country into the ground, a situation that still caused suffering for Caleans to this day. The plot ended up resulting in Luciano's death, and the remainder of the Landino family was forced to flee to the United States. Once Luciano was out of the way, however, Marco showed his true colors and had immediately begun to petition for power. But he was met with resistance, and with good reason, as the people saw in him the same qualities as the former tyrant king.

Marco settled on the ability to influence the government by being placed within parliament. Although he was not king, and with no king named, many looked upon him as the ring-leader of sorts, and it was Marco who had helped elect the appointment of Luca Mattia, the current prime minister. Hoping that Mattia would do his bidding, Marco continued his on-going appeal for power, however never gaining enough support to pull it off. To his great dismay, Mattia had other plans and sought to restore the Landino family. By bringing Derek, who was technically in line for the throne, back to Calina, Mattia was able to secure the wealth and resources that came with him.

With the return of the Landino's, Marco knew his days in control were numbered. Derek was already a powerful and successful CEO, running one of the largest and most influential corporations in the United States. He had a reputation for being shrewd, clever, and honorable, and he would not cater to the corruption which existed amongst the Calean government. Derek's dismissal of Marco and several others within the walls of power was swift, and did not go over smoothly. It wasn't long before history began to try and repeat itself.

Along with others, Marco sought once again to overthrow the king and had developed an assassination conspiracy. This time, however, the monarch had the backing of the people and his confidants, and Marco's attempts at an uprising were extinguished quickly, causing him to be apprehended by the King's Guard. He was tried and convicted of treason and ultimately executed.

Taya was surprised to still hear amongst those in government a sympathetic view toward Marco DeGrassi. She supposed there were those who believed that since the revolution, he should have been named king, or at least prime minister. He did have some support, after all. But among most Caleans, the DeGrassi name was considered a black mark, something you didn't want to associate with.

Members of the family still lived in Calina, Marco had children: a son and a daughter. Enzo, Marco's son, was still a prominent member of the community due to his wealth and connections. He was, in fact, a business and entrepreneurial powerhouse, and someone who would have much to lose if Calina joined the EU. But everyone knew Enzo would never secure a place in government. He was someone one kept in company out of necessity, not desire, and he had a ruthless reputation. It is rumored that Enzo DeGrassi shares his father's visions, and although it is never spoken of, everyone, including Taya, wondered if he sought revenge against the new monarch for his father's death.

The eruption of applause and cheers around her snapped her mind back to the present and she realized with frustration she had missed Derek's address. *Damn*, she thought. Damn DeGrassi, whom she chose to blame for her distracting train of thought.

If she were going to serve the government and the people to the best of her ability, she needed to gain more access to the monarch and uncover his plans. She had been made aware that in certain circumstances, parliament members were allowed to stay at the palace. With the impending conference to discuss EU relations and her own newness to her position, Taya felt she could make a case for just such an occasion.

After the "welcome home" reception at the airport, Christine now found herself once again in the back of a limousine. Sitting beside Derek, to his left this time, his hand covered hers on the seat between them. She felt drained, physically from a lack of sleep, but also emotionally. As Derek had predicted, there had been a mass waiting to greet them. Not just press, but government officials as well. She had felt awkward and out of place standing next to him during his speech. Actually, she had been able to do little more than lean on him. Standing still was difficult for her and continued to strain her back.

She didn't, of course, understand a word he had said, and the whole time she felt on display. Considering all she could do was smile, acknowledge the crowd at what she felt were appropriate times and wave, she was glad it was over.

As if reading her thoughts, Derek turned to her.

"You were amazing today," he said, his voice low. "They loved you."

Christine scoffed.

"No, they loved you," she replied, trying to hold a smile on her face. "I don't even know what you said or what was going on."

Derek brought her hand up to his lips, brushing them over her knuckles lightly. "I know this will be a huge adjustment for you," he said softly. "But, you're not alone. I'll be here by your side, and you'll feel more comfortable soon."

She locked her eyes with his. Even in the dim lighting of the limousine, they shone like sapphires. How could she tell him that it was him being by her side that was triggering her mental anguish?

The limousine slowed, and Christine immediately peered out her window to glimpse the palace. She had been only once before, during Derek's coronation, but this was different. This time, she was journeying here to live. To make this her home. As they passed through the gates, she couldn't help but feel a strong sense of being overwhelmed. Subconsciously, she gripped Derek's hand tighter.

Derek glanced down at her hand. He knew she was scared. He suppressed a sigh, a slight sadness filling his eyes. He wanted her to be happy. Could she be happy here with him? Knowing that there was something preventing her from being completely open with him, he had been hesitant to address it with her, almost afraid of what she may say. What if she was deciding she couldn't handle this lifestyle after everything that's happened? Was her love for him enough to overcome her fears?

He had lost her once, and a scowl crossed his face as a brief thought of Courtney entered his mind. He was glad she was dead. Studying Christine's profile as she looked through the window, he instantly knew he'd never recover from losing her again.

It was dark, well into the late evening as the limousine halted in front of the palace's main entrance. An attendant opened Christine's door for her, and offering her a hand, he helped her out of the car, offering her her cane. Derek followed her, and with his appearance, the attendant then stooped into a bow. Derek nodded at the attendant, then placed his hand around the small of Christine's back to lead her inside. As they entered the main hall, with Costa following closely behind, several other guards and palace employees were awaiting their arrival. Once they had all acknowledged the king's presence with a bow, Derek guided Christine toward two women furthest down the hall.

The first was a middle-aged woman, who was somewhat severe looking. Her black hair held strands of grey and was pulled back away from her face. Her brown eyes were sharp, and her face held a serious look. The woman standing just to her left was younger in her early twenties. She was blond and blue-eyed and smiled brightly at both the king and his bride-to-be as they approached them.

"Christine," Derek said, "This is Signora Irena Nucci," he introduced gesturing to the first woman, "and Signorina Olivia Cardelli." While Olivia gave a slight curtsey in front of Christine, Irena stood straight with her hands folded in front of her.

"*Buonasera*," she said rather curtly, then she looked at Derek and gave a nod of her head, "your pending nuptials are highly anticipated, signore."

Derek cleared his throat at the comment, which he knew would make Christine feel uncomfortable. He assumed it was due to all the recent trauma she had faced, not the mention the constant physical therapy, but she didn't ever seem too eager to discuss their wedding details, including the date.

His eyebrows came together as he glanced at Christine attempting to gauge her reaction, but she was only smiling politely at Irena.

"Irena is head of the palace domestic staff here," he explained, "she will ensure that you get settled in. Olivia," he now gestured to the younger woman, "will be your personal attendant, should you need anything."

Christine's eyes opened wide at this revelation.

"I don't think I need a personal…" she began, but Olivia cut her off, eager to please.

"Please, Signora," she protested, "it would be an honor to work with you." She smiled again, and Christine saw a sincere look of enthusiasm on her face. She immediately liked Olivia and she couldn't help but return her smile.

"How could I refuse then," she replied, and Olivia beamed.

Irena cleared her throat, and when she spoke, she spoke to Derek. "Where shall I instruct the attendants to bring Signora Christine's belongings to, your highness?" she asked. It was a heavily loaded question, and Christine blinked.

The fact that Irena did not automatically assume that Christine would be sharing the king's chambers gave her a glimmer of hope.

Christine studied Irena's conservative attire and surmised she was very traditional. She and Derek were not yet wed, and therefore, it would not be proper for her to stay with him. And if she slept elsewhere, it would give her more time to control her psychological instabilities.

"Is a room on the third floor in the East Wing acceptable?" Irena now suggested.

Before Derek could reply, Christine interjected.

"I'm sure wherever you think I belong would be most adequate," she said kindly, "you would know best."

Derek narrowed his eyes slightly and gave Christine a quizzical look. Not wishing to make the situation awkward, he consented to the arrangement with a slight change.

"The West Wing of course," he answered looking at Irena now.

"Yes, Your Highness," she said, "there's a beautiful room at the end of that hall with a balcony overlooking the garden." She turned to Olivia, "Olivia, why don't you take Christine up, and the attendants will meet you there with her things. You can then help her get settled." Olivia nodded, but Derek wasn't through.

"Actually Olivia," he said, now turning back to Christine, "I need a word before we all retire for the night." His expression was unreadable, and Christine hoped he wasn't too upset.

"Of course, Your Highness," Olivia responded with a bow of her head. "I'll wait here."

Derek took Christine by the elbow and steered her further down the hall. His tone had made it clear he wished to speak with her in private, and Costa remained behind with Olivia.

Turning the corner, he led her into a lounge room with velvet sofas, ornate rugs and a large marble fireplace. Once inside, he shut the heavy, wooden, double doors behind him. She turned to face him, anticipating the questions.

He stood silent for a moment, studying her. Then, striding toward her, he reached behind the back of her head, pulling her to him and captured her lips in an intense kiss. The passion took her breath away and fueled within her a hot desire only he could produce. She kissed him back eagerly, relishing in the feel of him and coming to the halting realization that it had been too long. She needed him. He broke from her and met her gaze.

"Do you want to be here with me?" he asked quietly. His question was direct, but that was Derek's style—always to the point.

She glanced down, feeling guilty for making him feel this way. She had been foolish to think that she could hide her hesitations, and it was wrong to keep him in the dark. But she just couldn't bring herself to tell him about her torments yet. She was too afraid they would get worse if she did.

"Yes," she replied, looking back up into his eyes. "I love you, Derek, I want to marry you." She immediately saw relief cross his face. "I'm sorry I've been distant from you," she offered.

He took the cue. "Why?" he asked. Before she could answer, he continued, "you know I don't care about formalities, right?" His eyes flashed with desire as he wrapped his good arm around her waist. "I want you with me."

She sought to put him at ease while maintaining her plan for distance. "I know," she replied, "but, my reputation here is of concern. I'm an outsider. There are high expectations, and I want to be respected. Isn't that important?"

He sighed, consenting. "I suppose it's best," he held her eyes, "for now."

She smiled, feeling a tiny weight lifted.

"I just want you to be happy, Christine," he said, reaching up to caress her cheek.

"I am happy with you," she said softly, knowing that she owed him some kind of explanation. "You asked me once if I could be patient with you, I just need that from you now." She paused, "these past couple months have taken a toll on me, emotionally and physically. I just haven't digested all the adjustments yet."

She chose her words carefully, hoping to give him the insights he needed to put his mind to rest so he wouldn't worry, but not alluding to the depths of her torments so he asked more questions.

"Of course I can be patient," he replied, then he kissed her again tenderly, but firmly on the mouth.

Pulling away from her before either of them could get too heated, he grabbed her hand to lead her back to the entourage in the hall. "Come on," he said, "it's been a long day and you need to get some sleep."

"Derek," she said suddenly, a thought occurring to her, "why the West Wing and not the East?"

He turned and smiled. "My room is in the West Wing," he said simply. "At least you won't be too far away." He turned again to exit the lounge, and Christine followed him slowly.

Yes, she thought, she did need some sleep. Unfortunately, she wouldn't be getting any.

Chapter 4

1 Month Later- Present Day

Having secured permission to stay as a guest for the time leading up to the impending conference, Taya paced slowly inside the main palace foyer. Her heels clicked on the marble tile, and she folded her arms across her chest examining the interior.

As with most European royal structures the Calean Palace, which was built in the mid-18th century, was architecturally structured in the neoclassical style. Taya admired the smooth, classic lines and symmetrical use of marble columns which lined the corridors. Unlike other palaces of grandeur, the Calean Palace was smaller and offered a warmer presence, although still nonetheless elegant and luxurious. The colors used throughout consisted of rich burgundies, earthy browns, and accents of cream. She appreciated the massive crystal chandeliers which hung overhead, however, the overall glamour of the palace was understated and not laden with gold trim. As spacious as the palace was, it felt welcoming; as though it were someone's home.

Parliament held congress in the Calean Palace, and it was residence to not only the monarch and his family, but also to the King's Guard, the soldiers sworn to protect the king, and the palace staff. It was common for it to play host to prestigious out of town visitors, government diplomats, ambassadors, and on occasion, members of parliament itself. Although the prime minister did not take residence at the palace, he was often present here, frequently staying on as a guest. His visits were less frequent these days since the Landino's had been reinstated and moved back.

Once Taya had entered the grounds on her appointed arrival date, passed through the gates and security, she had then been received by a guard and a staff member at the entrance. After her purpose had been stated, she was instructed to "please wait here," while her accommodations were confirmed. Fifteen minutes had now passed, however, and Taya was beginning to wonder if she was forgotten about.

She heard sure footsteps echoing across the floor around the corner. Confident that someone was finally coming for her, she straightened her jacket. Her eyes grew wide as Derek Landino himself appeared and now strode toward her.

"Ms. Mariano, I presume?" He greeted, stopping in front of her.

Taya quickly bowed her head. "Yes, Your Highness," she replied, in shock that the king was personally seeing to her arrival. Should she question this? Her heart began to pound as it dawned on her that perhaps he had uncovered her reasoning for coming and was going to now deny her request. But before she could ask, he explained himself.

"You are a new parliament member, is that right?" he asked. She nodded in response and he continued, "I wanted to personally introduce myself to you, since we have not yet had the pleasure of meeting. I thought before you were settled, we could chat first," he paused, "why don't you accompany me to my study? The prime minister is due soon, but I have a few minutes."

Taya gaped at him for a split second before composing herself.

"Of course, signore," she replied, daring to believe she had this kind of opportunity.

"Great," he smiled, "follow me."

He turned, and Taya travelled close behind. His stride was quick as he led her down several corridors, passing through the palace almost toward the back, finally arriving at an elevator.

"My main study is on the third floor," he explained gesturing to the elevator as they waited for it to descend. "Unless you're a 'stairs' person?" His eyes flashed with amusement as he glanced quickly down at her stilettos.

Taya followed his gaze and regarded him with curiosity. She blinked. "Um, no, at least, not today," she agreed.

She studied him as they waited, her interest piqued. He was wearing just a white dress shirt and black pants. His shirt collar was open and his sleeves were rolled to a three quarter length; he no longer used the sling. His attire was simple, yet he appeared regal and graceful. But he wore nothing to indicate his position. The fact that he had greeted her personally, offered to escort her to his study, and was now joking with her at the elevator left her utterly bemused.

As they ascended, she continued to consider him, anticipating her chance at being able to speak with him one on one. The elevator stopped, and Derek allowed her to precede him out into the hallway.

"It's this way," he said, indicating she turn right.

"Signore," she said, now falling in step slightly behind him, "if I may make an observation, your mannerisms are more casual in nature than I would think of them to be for a monarch," she paused, "with all due respect, Your Highness, you are not what I expected you to be."

They reached their destination then, and Derek turned to her, a smile on his face.

"That's good to hear," he replied simply. "Won't you have a seat?"

Like the rest of the palace, the monarch's personal study was a large space, adorned with marble, columns, large windows, and intricate wooden detailing. The marble tile was black, and it covered the floor as well as the fireplace off to the left. Soft, plush, grey rugs lay across the tile and Taya's shoes sunk into them as she walked toward his desk. The furniture was classically styled with large wing-back chairs, a chaise lounge off to the side, and beautiful mahogany accents. Natural light flooded into the room through the French-paned windows and the double doors which lead out onto a balcony.

She took a chair facing the large desk, also made from mahogany and marble, as he took his place opposite her.

"So, Ms. Mariano," he began, "welcome to the palace. I can only assume that the impending conference as well as you're being new to parliament has encouraged your stay here. I imagine you're wishing to learn and observe as much as you can so that you can represent your party well. You are with the *partito del popolo*, correct?"

Taya nodded in response. "Yes, signore, I represent the people."

"Congratulations on your recent election," Derek added. "The People's Party are not leaning favorable to the concept of entering the European Union," he stated, "how do you currently feel about this matter?"

"Are you trying to determine my vote before the conference, Your Highness?" Taya asked with her eyebrows raised.

Derek grinned. "Perhaps," he replied, "but, that's why you're here, isn't it? To determine for yourself whether or not you trust me, as your monarch? Or is your mind already made up?"

Taya blinked at his intuitiveness. She realized quickly Derek Landino was not to be underestimated.

"I feel very strongly with regard to certain issues, signore," she explained carefully, "entering the EU is a platform I am personally undecided on. I am, however, looking forward to hearing the proposals as a result of your negotiations at the conference."

Derek's piercing eyes met hers as he laughed lightly at her response. "Spoken like a true politician," he said. "Tell me, which platforms do you feel strongly about currently?"

Taya shifted, knowing if she were to be honest, her position would not be popular or potentially received well. Then again, she had always been a risk-taker and didn't shy away from her beliefs.

"Well," she began, taking a breath, "I believe a Constitutional Monarchy would suit the people of Calina better than our current form of government. Your ability to enact executive decisions and veto power, even without the overall consensus of parliament is dangerous, in my opinion."

Derek's expression at her comment was unreadable. She had just told the king he needed to relinquish power. He surmised that this could be an opinion circulating amongst the people, and it was enlightening for him to hear it now. He, of course, had no intentions of abusing his position, but how could the people know that? Especially considering the track record of previous rulers. In fact, he had only executed on his authority once, and that was to dismiss power-hungry parliament members with malicious intentions. But, perhaps, this act gave a wrong impression to those who may not have understood the reasons or history behind his decision at the time.

"A Constitutional Monarchy?" he repeated, "it's interesting. Do you not feel joining the European Union will satisfy hesitations or concerns with regard to the power of the monarch?"

"Perhaps some," Taya replied, unconvinced. "But, if we were to not join, it would make sense to reevaluate a new form of government. A constitutional monarchy would allow us to maintain our traditions, but also give the power back to the people."

"There has been no monarch serving this country for the past 30 years," Derek replied evenly, "things did not improve." He paused, tiring of the political dance, and chose a direct question next. "Was my dismissal of Marco DeGrassi concerning to you?"

Her dark green eyes flew open wide. Was he assuming she was a DeGrassi sympathizer? Her heart rate increased, knowing that he could discharge her if he chose to.

"Your Highness, no, I—" she began, but a sharp knock cut her off. The door swung open and Vincenzo Costa entered, followed by the prime minister, Luca Mattia, as well as Christine.

Derek gave Taya a curious look, but said nothing as he stood, rounding his desk to greet those that entered. After a quick bow from Mattia and Costa, Derek shook hands with the prime minister, then greeted Christine with an embrace. Guiding her back toward the desk, he helped her settle into a chair. Taya noticed that she no longer used a cane, but continued to walk with a slight limp.

"Taya Mariano, please meet my fiancée, Christine Dayne, and I'm sure you know the prime minister, Luca Mattia."

Taya rose from her chair, shaking hands in introduction with Christine and Mattia, in turn. She studied the American quickly, determining that she was very beautiful.

"Taya is a new member of parliament and she will be staying at the palace for a short while," Derek continued, then he turned to Taya. "It's been a pleasure meeting you, and I appreciate you taking the time to speak with me today. If you remember the way, take the same elevator back down to the main floor. I will ensure our head of staff, Signora Nucci is waiting for you. She will help you get settled into your quarters while you are staying here."

Knowing that her private dialogue with the monarch was over for now, Taya bowed to him.

"Thank you, Your Highness, the honor was mine." Then, turning to exit the study, feeling slightly uneasy with how their conversation ended, she left the room, allowing the wooden door to swing closed behind her.

Now out in the hall, however, she realized that she wasn't sure of the way back to elevator. Refusing to embarrass herself and re-enter the study to ask, she made the decision to go left.

Wandering for a few minutes, Taya realized soon she had chosen the wrong way. Retracing her steps, after having made another wrong turn, she found herself back at the study. Walking past it to head in the opposite direction, she stopped, surprised when she heard a piece of the conversation taking place on the other side of the door.

"I'm not afraid of Enzo DeGrassi, and neither should you be, Luca."

Taya inspected the door, realizing it had not closed properly behind her and now stood just ajar. Hearing the name "DeGrassi" once again, Taya couldn't pull away from listening just outside.

"The rumors are true, signore," Mattia was now saying, "he seeks revenge. He has resources and he's well connected," there was a heavy pause, "we just don't know who all he's enlisting. It's not clear who we can trust, and we need to be very careful with who we allow into the palace."

Inside the study, Derek watched as the prime minister made a quick glance at Christine. "I know who I can trust," he replied resolutely. "I will instruct Romano to gather intelligence on this matter. In the meantime, I think this conversation is best suited for another time."

Making haste to avoid being seen, Taya spun quickly away from the door and almost ran right into an attendant who was ostensibly standing behind her.

"My apologies, Signora!" Olivia cried, taking a step back to give Taya space.

Afraid the sudden noise would alert those inside the study to her presence, Taya nodded curtly at the attendant, offering her a quick smile as an apology, then turned and strode down the hall toward the elevator.

Her heart was beating in her throat, both at what she had just heard and almost being caught hearing it. She boarded the elevator feeling unnerved at the encounter with the attendant. She needed to be much more careful, she decided. Pushing the incident from her mind as she descended to the main floor, Taya concluded that it didn't matter if that girl saw her listening, she was after all, just a maid.

Christine stood as she watched Mattia take his leave from the study. She turned to Derek.

"This sounds threatening," she said, "I think you should take this seriously."

He placed his hands on her shoulders.

"You don't need to worry or be afraid either," he consoled. "Enzo is not a real threat, he just likes to hear himself talk. He's no different than his father," he paused, "or mine, for that matter."

Christine managed a small smile. Derek glanced in Costa's direction, as she stifled yet again, another yawn, hoping he couldn't see how exhausted she was.

Averaging about three hours of sleep a night, Christine felt beyond sleep deprived. Her night terrors persisted, and all she could think to do at this point was to keep setting alarms to wake herself up every hour so no one would discover her torments. So far, the alarms had sufficed. Each night her dreams began the same, but before she was able to wander past her bedroom door or begin screaming, she had been saved by the bell. She knew this wasn't a long term solution, but until she could discover what that was, she concluded that a lack of sleep was the best alternative.

Derek had dismissed Costa for the time being, and he now held his hand out to her to take. "Come with me," he told her with a smile, "I have something for you."

Unable to suppress a slight grin, Christine placed her hand in his and allowed him to lead her to the door.

As they walked down the corridor, passing through the center of the palace, then toward the south end, she could no longer contain her curiosity.

"Where are we going?" she asked, tugging slightly on his arm.

He gave her a mischievous smile. "You'll see," he replied, "it occurred to me that I don't spoil you enough, so..." his voice trailed off as they arrived at a large double wooden door.

Christine had never been to this area of the palace before, but she could guess by their location the large, rose garden, which had come to be one of her favorite spots, was just on the outside of these walls.

"Ready?" he asked smiling, placing his hand on one of the French door handles.

She couldn't help but feel excited, and as he opened the door and moved aside to let her enter the room, her eyes widened and her mouth opened in awe. She had stepped into the most beautifully designed and spacious art studio that she had ever seen.

She walked slowly into the room, attempting to take in every detail. It was still early morning, and the natural sunlight streamed into the room from walls of glass which overlooked the palace grounds. The atmosphere was one that felt light and airy, breathable, and comforting. Several easels were set up throughout the room. Palettes, paints of all colors, stacks of canvas in all sizes, and brushes were neatly organized in beautiful white cabinetry. There were hundreds of books adorning a built-in wall shelf, and even, Christine noticed, several of her own works and pieces were stationed throughout the room.

As she looked closer, she realized he had moved in all of her things from her studio flat in France, including unfinished projects and...

She reached down and picked it up from where it lay on a stool; her

35

favorite, paint splattered and worn artist's jacket.

Feeling like she had been reunited with a long-lost friend, she couldn't help but smile and hug the lab coat as she continued to gaze about the room. There was a double glass door that opened out onto a balcony, and as she opened it up and stepped outside, she instantly took in the sweet scent of roses. She had been correct in determining the room's location, and she looked below, taking in the scene of her favorite garden. She turned back to Derek, grinning from ear to ear.

"Do you like it?" he asked hopefully.

She approached him and let out a laugh as she embraced him, bringing her arms up around his neck. "This is amazing," she replied, unable to prevent tears stinging her eyes in gratitude. "I can't tell you what this means to me," she pulled back meeting his gaze.

"This is your home, Christine," he said gently, "you needed your own space," he paused, "and you need to do what you love." He reached for her face, stroking her cheek with his thumb. "Just because other things are happening in your life doesn't mean you should give up who you are."

Her heart swelled at his words, and a wonderful sense of relief washed over her knowing that he felt that way. She knew becoming his wife and taking on the responsibility of becoming royalty would be a full time job, and she had accepted that her passion and love for painting would have to take a back seat to other duties. But he was right, and she couldn't deny that she was first and foremost an artist, and she needed this in her life too.

With her arms still around his neck, she leaned forward and met his lips with hers. They shared a soft, tender kiss then he broke apart from her. She could tell he was searching her eyes, looking for a sign.

As he held her gaze, blood began to course through her body, filling it with desire. Her lips parted slightly and her breath caught in her throat just as his mouth recaptured hers, this time with fervor. He cupped both sides of her face with his hands, continuing to kiss her as his lips parted hers open, his tongue seeking to connect with her own. She gave a soft, breathless moan against his mouth which just increased his intensity.

He pushed against her, backing her up to the edge of a desk. Lifting her just slightly so she was able to sit on the desk, he moved in between her legs, closer to her. His hands glided up her thighs resting on either side of his waist, her skirt riding up along with them. His mouth left hers to trail kisses down her neck and throat, his hands now underneath her skirt at her hips as he pulled her in closer until her body was flush against his.

Christine knew he wasn't stopping and wouldn't unless she told him to. She weaved her fingers through his silky hair, relishing in how he felt against her, knowing that she needed him. But, could she do this now? Was it time? She had been so afraid of giving herself to him with the prospect of her night terrors intensifying further. But she couldn't deny how right this felt. And how good.

She was about to suggest they move to a more comfortable location when his phone began to buzz. There were very few people who knew Derek's number, and if it were ringing, it was assuredly important.

He looked up into her eyes and she gave him an expression of understanding. The corner of his mouth upturned in a sexy smirk.

"To be continued," he said softly, then kissed her nose before moving away from her.

Christine took a deep breath to help slow her rapid heart rate, irritated at the interruption, but realizing this came with the territory of being with him.

She watched him curiously as she straightened her clothing and stepped down off the edge of the desk. He had wandered to the other side of the studio, speaking in hushed tones, but mostly, he was just listening intently. His demeanor indicated the call had, indeed, been urgent.

After a few minutes, he hung up. The phone still remained in his palm as he gazed out the window, a grim expression now on his face.

She walked over to him, almost timidly, but she couldn't contain her interest. "Derek," she said quietly, "what's wrong?"

He didn't turn to face her, and only answered her after several moments.

"It's Nicola," he stated.

Chapter 5

It was evening and Nicola Landino had just passed through customs in the small, but pristine airport in Calina. He took in his surroundings as he set foot for the first time since he was a baby in his home country.

After calling Derek and explaining to him his situation, the monarch had agreed to arrange an opportunity for Nicola to leave New York. Knowing that was the safest option for him, Nicola had agreed, and within the hour, he had packed light and boarded one of Land Corporations private jets bound for Calina. *Of course*, Nicola thought, as he proceeded now to the baggage claim, *Derek couldn't have sent me to the Bahamas.* His older brother had had only one condition to secure his help: Nicola had to come home.

Waiting now for his one piece of luggage, he scanned the area. He had expected that attendants would have been waiting for him to assist, but there was no one. *Of course Derek would leave me hanging…*

Spying his bag, with a grimace on his face, he leaned over gracefully and effortlessly lifted the suitcase placing it by his side, now considering his next move.

He noticed many looking in his direction, which wasn't surprising to him. Dressed dapper in black pants, a dark grey dress shirt and a black, silk vest, he knew he stood out from the crowd. No doubt everyone around him could see he was someone of importance. The duffle bag he sported was Gucci, and the sterling cuff links adorning his wrists matched the sheen on his Aviator's.

Not that anyone knew who he was actually. Most citizens knew of Nicola's existence, seen as how he had been in line for the throne for a very short period of time, but no one had really been given the opportunity to know what he looked like before his brother declared he would take the position after all. He had also never been in Derek's company throughout his climb to celebrity status, and for the most part, he had stayed out of the tabloids. He was simply a person of interest standing in the middle of the baggage claim, and those around him continued to eye him with curiosity as he now proceeded to exit outside throwing a dashing grin back at several young women.

As he stepped out onto the sidewalk considering his transportation options, (*a cab? a bus? What was he supposed to do, walk to the palace?*), a sleek black Mercedes pulled right up in front of him and stopped. Nicola half smiled, appreciative that Derek had at least been gracious enough to send him a ride. The driver of the Mercedes exited and walked over to the back door, opening it for him.

"Signore Landino," the driver said stiffly, "if you please."

Nicola consented, tossing his bag into the back seat, then climbed into the car after. The driver closed his door, then took his place back behind the wheel, pulling away from the airport curb. As the Mercedes took off, almost immediately following, another car, this time a black limousine bearing flags, pulled up in front of the airport terminal.

Now out of his sight of vision, Nicola hadn't seen the limousine behind him.

"How far is it?" he asked the driver in the Mercedes lazily. Having not slept a wink, he was exhausted and all he wanted to do was crash. Hopefully Derek wouldn't be around when he arrived at the palace and he could avoid the third degree until tomorrow.

"Not far," the driver grunted.

Nicola rolled his eyes behind his sunglasses.

As they continued, he peered out the window, watching the outside traffic and signage. He furrowed his brow when he noticed they drove straight passed a sign labeled "Il Palazzo Calina." Nicola knew Calean, his mother having made him learn it when he was a kid.

"Hey mack," he called, "I think you missed the exit." The driver didn't respond. Nicola leaned forward, "Oh," he said more loudly, attempting to gain the driver's attention.

The driver continued to ignore him as he turned off onto another exit. Looking out the window, all Nicola could see were fields, and it was clear they were headed into a remote location.

"Fuck," he muttered under his breath, coming to the conclusion he had been abducted. His heart rate ticked up. It would seem unreasonable that he had been followed from New York. Not so soon anyway. He still had two days to meet their deadline. The only other reason someone would take interest in him then is because of Derek. Gregory had said he had many enemies here.

He considered his options; there were none. All he could do was wait until the car stopped.

"Look," he said, hoping to clue this "kidnapper" in to the fact that he and Derek despised one another, "if you think Derek will pay for my life, you're wrong."

No response.

The car took a turn, then another down a dirt road. Soon it slowed coming into a clearing. There were no buildings in sight or other cars driving by. Once the car stopped, Nicola immediately grabbed for the door handle, but his door swung open anyway, and the barrel of a nine millimeter pistol greeted him.

"Get out," a voice instructed him.

Nicola did as he was told and exited the vehicle. "What's going on?" he demanded, sizing up the man with the gun.

He was shorter than he was, maybe about 5'9, stocky, and wore a black suit. Nicola surmised he could take him physically, but the man clearly had the upper hand with a gun. He raised his hands on instinct, then leaning toward the man he asked in a confused tone, "do I owe you money?"

"Shut up, Landino," the man snarled.

Suddenly there were footsteps behind him, and Nicola spun around dropping his hands. Another man was walking toward them; he was clearly the one in charge. He was in his mid-30's, his black hair was slicked back, and he wore what appeared to be an expensive three piece pin-striped suit.

"Nicola Landino," the man said as he approached Nicola. His voice was thick with accent. "Welcome to Calina." He smirked at his own joke as he spread his arms wide. "I trust you know who I am?"

Nicola's eyebrows came together in a mocking gesture. "The Godfather," he replied, unimpressed, and his head began to throb from stress.

Maybe he should've just taken his chances in New York, and Nicola was coming to the quick deduction that calling Derek had been a mistake.

The other man didn't respond right away, and he paced in front of Nicola, a smug smile playing at his thin lips as he held his hands behind his back.

"I am Enzo DeGrassi," he stated.

If he was looking for a reaction, he would have been disappointed.

Nicola stared at him blankly, waiting for him to get to the point.

"Look," he said and sighed, "I'm exhausted. If you're looking to rob me, I have no money. If you want to use me for ransom, you're wasting your time. Other than that, I really don't see what use I am to you."

Enzo narrowed his eyes at the young man's candor, but a small smile appeared on his face that resembled a sneer.

"You got me all wrong, Nic," he said, his tone measured, "I'm not here to do any of those things."

Nicola glanced behind him at the stocky henchman. "The gun would suggest otherwise," he stated plainly.

Enzo held up a hand, the gold ring he wore on his pinky finger glinting in the sunset light. "All I want from you," he began, "is your help to make you king."

Nicola responded with an unconvinced expression.

"Let me explain," Enzo continued, "you may be unaware, but we share a common foe: your brother," he paused, watching Nicola raise his eyebrows, then continued, "we both want the same thing, you and I. We both want Derek Landino out of the way so you can become king."

Nicola crossed his arms. This was an absurd conversation. "Why would you want that?" He questioned.

"He killed my father," Enzo replied simply, then his tone turned angry, "and he is ruining this country. He's also dangerous, having already abused his power to dismiss, arrest and execute parliament members."

"Replacing one king with another won't exactly solve that problem," Nicola pointed out.

Enzo shook his head slowly. "You are correct, Landino," he agreed, "this is ultimately why His Highness needs to go. He will never listen to reason; to the voices of the actual people."

Nicola scoffed and shook his head, not buying what Enzo was trying to sell. "By 'people,' you mean to you," he stated, "Derek wouldn't do your bidding."

Enzo pursed his lips. "You catch on quickly, Nic," he replied, his upper lip curling slightly. "But you would naturally. After all, you don't care about ruling or responsibility. As long as you were secure in title and luxury, which you would have as king, you'd gladly give up the actual authority."

"How do you know anything about me?" Nicola demanded. "Do you understand that you are asking me to conspire against this country's monarch? My brother?"

The sun was setting low in the sky now and the air was turning chilly. Nicola's head pounded from the lack of sleep and this surreal dialogue unfolding in front of him. Of course he wanted to be king, but that was when Derek had renounced. He would never consider actually *overthrowing* his own brother... would he?

"Think about it Nic," Enzo was saying now, "I know you hate your brother. You didn't even care when he was at death's door. Maybe you were hoping he'd succumb to his injury?"

Nicola's eyes widened at Enzo's information.

"Oh yes," Enzo continued, "I know. I know why you're here now. You see, the organization you are indebted to in New York are friends of mine," his smile made him resemble the Cheshire Cat, "you will find that I am very well connected. It would be interesting if I made a call and they were to not only learn of your location, but I gave them the means to get to you." His threat held heavy in the air, and Nicola knew he would be blackmailed if he didn't comply. "Your part in this will be simple and easy, and you will be contacted at the appropriate times. As you may have guessed by now, I also have friends inside the palace walls."

For once, Nicola was rendered speechless. Did he even have a choice at this point?

Enzo persisted. "If you continue the path your brother has offered you and take your place as the prince of Calina, you will forever be under his thumb. Doing his bidding, obeying his authority. Hell, he'll probably give you an allowance, at least," and he gave a snicker. "Or," he emphasized, "you can work with me. Together, we will ensure he steps down, either willingly or by force. He will then turn the reigns over to you. That is when you pay me back for helping you become king." Enzo pulled out a small case from his jacket and removed a cigarette from it.

Nicola regarded Enzo with a raised eyebrow as he lit the cigarette and inhaled deeply.

"And by pay back, you mean place you in a position of high regard with the monarchy, free to influence the government to serve your own agenda." Nicola finished out Enzo's end game for him. "Either way, you have me playing the puppet."

Enzo shrugged in response, arranging his features in a non-committal way. "I'm not sure how that is of consequence to you," he replied, "you will be in a much better position if we work together than you are now, and your brother will get what he deserves. Tell me, Nic, how did it make you feel when you learned he only chose to be monarch after he found out you wanted it?"

Nicola winced internally. It had hurt him gravely that Derek was fine to abdicate the throne, that is, until Nicola had claimed the birthright as his own. And it was unsettling that Enzo knew this, clearly proving his connections ran deep.

Enzo took another puff on the cigarette before tossing it to the ground. He then stuck his hand out in a partnership offering and Nicola eyed it, countless thoughts running through his mind.

"Do we have an agreement," Enzo said and paused, "Your Highness?"

After her uneasy conversation and introduction that morning with the monarch, Taya had spent the rest of her day getting settled into her guest chambers at the palace. She was given quarters on the second floor, and she had been quite pleased with the accommodation. Irena Nucci, the head of staff, had helped her get situated, then offered her a tour of the palace and grounds, which Taya had enjoyed immensely.

Not only was she enamored with the palace, the history, and its architectural beauty, but she figured having one on one time with the king's head of domestic staff would be valuable time spent. After all, it was usually the staff members who had the information. But if Irena Nucci held any secrets, reservations, or hidden agendas against the king, she harbored it well. She was nothing except professional and respectful, especially when referring to His Highness. Taya determined Irena's loyalty ran deep. Be it due to his position or that she genuinely held him in high regard, she wasn't sure. Surmising that if she wanted to learn any real dirt, she needed to get into the good graces of staff members who were perhaps lower on the food chain.

Regardless of the lack of gossip, being new to her role, the tour was very informative and helpful to Taya as she was able to see where Parliament held session in the south wing on the first floor, which seemed to be where all government and business conferences took place. She was shown where she could go and not go, what she had access to during her stay and where she was not permitted. Obviously, any personal office space belonging to the monarch or the prime minister were off limits.

Under normal circumstances, the senior members of her own party, as well as her political team, would be with her, ensuring she was familiar and accustomed to parliament's functions within the palace. But with Derek's prolonged absence, his reign only in its infancy itself, and the urgency of the decision surrounding the European Union, the current situation was not normal, and Taya was glad to be given the chance for a prompt showing of the ropes.

As the day progressed, she had been given the opportunity to dine in the guest dining hall, but since she was the only guest staying at the palace currently, other than the prime minister, she had chosen to take dinner in her own quarters. Taya had hoped to have been offered a place at the monarch's table, as she was anxious to clear any air of misunderstanding from their last encounter, but she was told he was dining privately this evening, so she could only hope there would be another time.

Wired from the long day and it now nearing 10:00 p.m., Taya roamed the first floor. Her mind was buzzing with thoughts of her next move and what she hoped to uncover.

As she walked down a long corridor, she soon came upon two life-sized portraits. Glancing at them, she instantly knew they were of the former king, Luciano Landino, and the queen, Sofia. Although she had been just a baby when Luciano was overthrown and executed, the depression his reign caused haunted Caleans to this day.

Growing up through the aftermath of the revolution, she knew how it felt to watch people starve; friends, neighbors, family. Not only was the economy poor and unemployment high, the politics surrounding the revolution caused many families to divide. Some agreed with the revolutionists, but others still sympathized with the monarchy. Many chose sides, ultimately breaking up family units. Taya's family was one of those. Her father being more extreme, he saw the opportunity for a power grab. Her mother ended up leaving it all behind, including Taya and her older brother.

She couldn't suppress feelings of rage when she looked at Luciano's portrait. Regardless of others at fault then and still now, it all came back to him and his former reign. It struck her how much he and her current monarch resembled one another. What if Derek turned out the same? *The apple doesn't fall too far from the tree*, she reminded herself, and she vowed once again to herself she would do whatever was necessary to ensure her country was never put through such devastation again.

A deep seated sadness threatened to overwhelm her as she thought about how things for her and her family might have turned out differently if it weren't for Luciano's mistakes and greed.

She turned away from the portraits, continuing down the hall, pausing in front of a door which hung open. It was a small library of sorts, and the cozy atmosphere drew her into it, inviting her with its subdued lighting, beautiful glass lamps, and plush, ornate rugs. She immediately liked this space, and as she wandered to the shelves next to the large, dark marble fireplace, she wondered if anyone minded her borrowing a book to help her relax.

Her eyes scanned the titles on the upper shelves, and she glimpsed the painting that hung above the fireplace. She blinked, her full attention now on the artwork, and she stepped back so she could view it better.

Intrigued by the colors and textures, she was instantly entranced by the stir of emotion that swelled within her as she gazed at what she assumed was a work of abstraction.

"Do you like it?" a voice suddenly asked her from behind.

Taya turned quickly to see Christine standing at the door frame. She glanced from Christine to the painting and realized it was the future queen's work.

Having researched Christine heavily, Taya knew she was a very popular artist in France and no doubt would have continued on to be a world renowned success. She also knew Christine was the reason Derek abdicated at first, choosing her over his country. Then of course, there were several scandals surrounding the American painter, and she wasn't sure yet if the rumors and allegations were just sensational news or born from truths.

After all, if one had followed the head-lines, Christine had broken off her relationship with Derek when he was still the CEO of Land Corporation. Shortly after, there were rumors and photos that showed her messing around with his attorney, Timothy. She was then engaged to the French Supermodel, Sean Laurent, for a hot second, only to reunite with Derek after taking a bullet for him. After he was coronated king, that is.

Those who spoke against Christine in Calina called her a gold-digger, someone who had only used Derek to secure her own career advancement. It was suspect to say the least, and Taya, like most Caleans, did not trust the overall intentions of the pretty American and she couldn't help but harbor resentment.

"It's amazing," Taya replied truthfully, unable to deny that regardless of her suspicions, Christine was indeed very talented.

Christine smiled warmly at Taya as she walked further into the room.

"Do you understand what it represents?" she asked, curious.

Taya shook her head slowly. "No," she admitted, "although it inspires me to feel many things."

"What things?" Christine prompted.

Taya looked back at the painting, attempting to label the emotions passing through her. "I'm not really sure," she said slowly, "it just makes me 'feel,' if that makes sense."

Christine nodded, satisfied with the response. "Have you ever been in love?" she asked now.

Taya looked at Christine with interest. *What a random question*, she thought. "No," she answered honestly, "I don't have time for that."

"I felt that way once as well," Christine replied knowingly, "it wasn't until I fell in love and understood what it meant that I was able to create the painting you see now."

Taya narrowed her eyes. "You must have had quite the number of love affairs to create something that stirs such emotion," she suggested, then paused. "Many 'research specimens'?"

She raised her eyebrows wondering if Christine would take the bait. But if she were looking to rile the future queen, she would have been disappointed.

Christine only smiled, understanding the insinuations Taya presented as what they were: ignorance. "No," she said calmly, "that painting only represents one man to me. One love."

Taya was silent for a moment, considering her next query, but unfortunately she would be unable to ask anything more before they were interrupted. The maid she had almost collided with outside Derek's study had just rushed into the room.

"Signora," she said, breathless, as she addressed Christine, "His Majesty is asking for you," she glanced at Taya, her eyes widening slightly, then she looked back to Christine. "The um, *guest* that was to arrive this evening has been reported missing."

The maid emphasized the word "guest" and Taya surmised she was withholding information for her sake.

"Thank you, Olivia," Christine replied politely, then she looked at Taya, "excuse me, Taya, I must go. I hope we get to chat again soon."

"Of course, signora," Taya replied.

Christine smiled again. "Please call me Christine," she said, "I don't think I'll ever get used to all these formalities."

Taya nodded, then watched her turn to leave the room, following the attendant.

Alone once again, Taya wondered curiously who this "guest" was. And how were they missing? Her mind flooded with questions, she looked back at the painting.

"One love, huh?" She muttered under her breath. She considered her conversation with Christine. If she really did paint this out of inspiration from hers and Derek's love, maybe she was genuine after all. You couldn't believe everything you read anyway. And even pictures can lie. Perhaps, the people were wrong about her.

Needing to let her mind rest and think of something else, Taya snatched a book off the shelf, not too concerned with the subject, and turned to settle into a very comfortable velvet chaise in front of the fireplace.

She practically sank into the luxurious fabric as she opened the cover of the book and started to read. As the minutes ticked by, she stifled a yawn, the words on the page beginning to blur. She thought she should just go upstairs, but she felt so cozy. It wasn't long before the book fell from her hands to the floor as her eyelids dropped.

"Where the hell have you been?"

The stern voice just outside the door startled Taya awake. She squeezed her eyes tight, then opened them wide, sitting up straight on the chaise where she had fallen asleep. The book she was reading was at her feet, and she picked it up, rising from the chair to squint at the clock on the mantel: 1:15 a.m.

Intrigued as to what woke her up, Taya moved silently to the door and peered into the hall. The door was half shut, and not wishing to be seen, she inched it a bit more closed for better concealment. Now able to witness the scene in the vast hallway, she saw two men facing

47

each other in an argument. The man facing slightly in her direction, she did not recognize, but she knew instantly that the other, whose arms were folded across his broad chest, was Derek.

"What's it to you anyway where I was," the other man now responded, "I'm here now, aren't I?"

Taya's eyes opened wide with wonder. Did he really just speak like that to the monarch?

She studied the man more closely, fascinated by his demeanor. He was tall, had Derek's build, and was incredibly handsome. His features were refined and held within them a mischievousness; the way his dark eyes glinted, and even though he was getting bawled out by the king, he still smirked. Although he was dressed elegantly, Taya noticed his clothes appeared disheveled as though he had been in a fight, and he reached up to massage the back of his head, running his hand through his thick curls.

Taya wasn't sure if it was his gorgeous face and form or his rebellious nature that she found more attractive, but she suddenly realized she needed to close her mouth as she had been gaping, mesmerized by him. She shook her head, irritated with herself and focused now on their conversation.

"Your plane landed at 6:30, Nic," Derek was saying, keeping his voice even, "the limo was sent to pick you up, but you weren't there. I had no idea if you had even gotten on the plane in New York."

"Well, maybe you should have better connections, then," Nicola replied with an unconcerned tone.

Taya stared then blinked. Nic? Nicola Landino? She considered the two men again and now noticed the strong resemblance. Yes, she realized, this mystery "guest" was in fact, the prince. *And*, she thought as she witnessed the exchange of glares, *the monarch and his brother are not fond of each other.*

Nicola sighed. "Derek, I'm really tired, can you finish yelling at me tomorrow?" He rubbed his face with his hand.

"Not until I know where you've been for the past six hours," Derek replied. "You called me, needing my help. I brought you here, and you agreed to take your place. Yet, the first thing you do is blow off your responsibility," he narrowed his eyes, studying him, "and you look like hell. Did you get into a fight?"

"You're not my mother, Derek," Nicola said, shoving his shoulder into his brother's as he walked past him.

Derek turned to glare after him. "No," he said, maintaining his composure, "and wouldn't she be disappointed in you." Nicola spun around, prepared to argue, but Derek held up his hand. "Enough," he stated, his voice now holding an authority that somehow cut off Nicola's retort. "I am not your mother, but I am as of now your king, and you are a prince. You cannot go off making a mockery out of our position or the government. You are no longer in New York and you can no longer act as such," he placed his hands in his pockets casually and raised his eyebrows, "or do you wish to go back and deal with your problem on your own?"

Nicola cleared his throat and narrowed his eyes, annoyed at the constant parade of threats that seemed to be his calling today. If only he were able to confide in Derek what he had actually been through...

After he had finished so-called "business" with Enzo, he had been hit on the back of the head with the butt of that gun, knocking him out cold and left in the middle of nowhere. Clearly, Enzo was giving him a message of his authority.

He had woken four hours later in the same clearing, his bag left next to him, with a pounding headache, a dead cell phone, and no means of transportation. Hiking his way back to the freeway, he had finally been able to hitch a ride and dropped off at the gates of the palace, (the driver looking at him like he was a lunatic at this request). He was beyond exhausted and in need of both some aspirin and a stiff drink. The last thing he needed was this lecture. Deciding that continuing to argue with Derek was unwise if he wanted the former, he switched strategies.

He held up both his hands in surrender. "You're right, Derek," he said wearily, "my actions were foolish. It won't happen again."

Derek gave him a pensive, unconvinced look in response, but to Nicola's relief, he didn't ask any more questions to his whereabouts.

"I'll show you to your room," Derek replied rolling his eyes. He was very familiar with his younger brother's tactics to appease when he thought he'd end up getting his way, but Derek couldn't see how prolonging this argument was beneficial either. "We can discuss your responsibilities while you're here in the morning," he added choosing to let the matter go.

Nicola let out a slow breath he didn't realize he was holding, and although he was relieved Derek wasn't going to push the issue, Enzo's offer and warning were still like a dark cloud hanging over him. He picked up his bag from the hall and proceeded to follow Derek anxious to find out if any agreements had been made. Maybe Enzo's threat didn't even hold any water.

"Speaking of New York," he began, "did you, uh, take care of that problem for me?"

Derek stopped walking and looked Nicola in the eyes. "You mean so you can just run back and return to your previous escapades?" he asked, then shook his head. "You don't learn, do you? I took care of what needed to be taken care of to the extent that you're still alive and fulfilling your duty here," he said, "which was our agreement."

Nicola's heart sank. So, he didn't pay them off, in other words, and Nicola was not yet free from this. Which meant Enzo could act upon his threat if he so desired. He squeezed his eyes tight briefly in a moment of defeat, then turned to continue to follow after Derek down the hall.

Taya listened at the door until the men were out of earshot. She twisted her hands attempting to make sense out of what she had just overheard. Clearly, Nicola was trouble and also *in* trouble, which is why he was here now, and she wondered fleetingly what the "problem" was in New York that had been referred to. There was definitely bad blood between the two brothers, she realized heavily, the rulers of her country, which unsettled her greatly.

As disturbed as she felt regarding their apparent disrespect for one another, Taya also couldn't help but be impressed by Nicola's lack of fear when it came to Derek, or anything else for that matter, and he most undoubtedly had an issue with authority. She couldn't suppress a smile as his image floated into her mind. There was something dark, almost sinister about him. It made her heart race, and she recognized she had never felt this way before.

If Nicola was able to stand up to Derek in that way, he could have great influence if Derek turned out to be like Luciano. Maybe she had found an ally…maybe she had found something more.

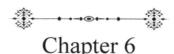

Chapter 6

E arly the next morning, a sharp knock woke Taya from a restless sleep. She had slept partly on the chaise, then retired to her room after witnessing the encounter between Derek and Nicola. But unable to get both, her questions and Nicola's face, out of her mind, she just tossed and turned most of the night.

She sat up and glanced at her phone on the stand next to her bed: 6:30 a.m. Groaning softly, she pulled a robe on over her cotton tank sleep dress and proceeded across the room to open the door. Attempting to tame down her wavy locks, she swung open the door, suppressing a yawn.

"Good morning, Signorina," a female attendant stated with a noticeably bright smile.

No one should be this cheerful this early in the morning, Taya thought as she gave a mild attempt to return the attendants smile.

The girl continued, "with apologies for the last minute invitation, His Highness would appreciate you joining him this morning for breakfast. It will be served in one hour."

Fully awake now by this news, Taya's eyes opened wide.

"Of course," she replied, interest and excitement brewing inside her, "I'd be delighted. Thank you." The attendant nodded pleasantly, then departed.

Taya closed the bedroom door and immediately strode over to the closet. She needed to make a good impression. Realizing this could be an opportunity to get into good graces with Derek, Taya also couldn't help but hope to meet the prince, and she wondered if his sudden appearance was in fact the cause for this impromptu breakfast meeting.

For some reason, she was unable to get him out of her mind. Her growing infatuation with this man annoyed as much as it intrigued her, as he was a distraction she didn't need.

She settled on choosing an off-white, knee-length dress. It was fitted and belted, with cap sleeves and a modest neckline. She wanted to appear confident and professional, and just perhaps a bit innocent. Laying the dress out across the bed, she then proceeded into the bathroom to shower and get ready for whatever opportunities the day was to bring.

Nicola stared into his coffee cup, half listening to the incredibly dull dialogue taking place around him. His one eyebrow was raised, and he rested his chin unceremoniously in his hand with his elbow propped on the table. Every so often he'd drum his fingers, clearly indicating to the rest of those at the table he was bored.

He was seated to Derek's left, and he caught his older brother's disapproving gaze. But Nicola really wasn't bothered. It was early, too early in his opinion. He didn't understand why he had to be dragged down to this breakfast.

The prime minister, Luca, was seated across from him at the intimate table in one of the smaller dining rooms. Once introductions had been made, Derek and Luca had fallen into what Nicola thought to be a cumbersome conversation surrounding some upcoming conference. He caught words like "European Union," and "parliament" among other political references, including the name of Enzo DeGrassi, that Nicola had absolutely no interest in right now, and Enzo being the last person he wanted to think about.

The only other person in attendance, and the only interesting thing in the room was Christine, who sat on Derek's right. In the back of his mind, Nicola had to give Derek credit; Christine was particularly stunning. But even he wasn't so brazen as to look at her twice. He knew what he could get away with as far as Derek was concerned, and what he could not.

Glancing to his left, he suddenly wondered why there was an empty chair and place setting. An oversight in planning did not seem possible with the efficiency of the palace staff, so he could only assume another would be joining their group this morning. Nicola suppressed a groan, knowing that soon he would most likely be forced into a dreary dialogue with a boring diplomat.

Weighing out in his mind exactly how much repercussion he was willing to endure, he began to form an excuse to leave when an attendant walked in announcing the arrival of their last guest. Nicola only caught the first name, "Taya," when he glanced up toward the door.

Then his eyes fell on her.

She smiled confidently as she entered the room. As radiant as her smile was, the first thing he noticed was her hair—long, blonde, wavy and thick. He had a thing for blondes. Her bangs fell just below her well defined eyebrows almost to her long, black lashes. His eyes moved down her slender figure, noting how her white dress clung to her hips and highlighted her hourglass silhouette.

Breathe, idiot, he reminded himself as her presence momentarily paralyzed him.

His gaze met hers, and her eyes widened just ever so slightly. He recognized the interest in her expression as he in turn, narrowed his eyes while a smirk formed on his lips. He had made an impression on her as well. Breakfast, he decided, as well as Calina in general, just got a whole hell of a lot more interesting. She blinked, looking quickly away from him as she made her way to the table.

Derek rose politely as she approached, and the rest around the table followed suit.

"Ms. Mariano," he greeted her, "I'm very glad you could join us this morning."

Nicola raised his eyebrows at the use of "Ms.," and as Taya gave a slight bow in Derek's direction, Nicola couldn't help but continue to take in her features. Her lips were so round and pink, and he shook his head slightly in an effort to regain his senses.

"Thank you, signore," she replied.

"As a member of our parliament, and since you are staying with us as a guest," Derek continued, "I thought it best for you to meet my brother, and the prince of Calina, Nicola."

Derek gestured to Nicola, who flashed a dazzling smile in her direction. Taya met his eyes again and hesitated just a beat before bowing again to the prince.

"It's a pleasure, signore," she said.

"The pleasure is mine," Nicola replied, his voice smooth like silk. He reached for her chair, the one next to him, and pulled it slightly away from the table. "Won't you have a seat?"

As they resumed their places, he kept stealing glances to admire her. Her eyes were a deep, forest green, and her fair complexion had a rosy glow, complementing the white color of her dress; she looked almost ethereal. He had never before been so taken by someone's presence.

"Nicola has consented to take his place here as the prince and fulfill his obligations in that role," Derek explained, looking pointedly at his brother.

"That's… great to hear," Taya replied with an even tone, covering a slight hesitation as she reflected back on the argument between Derek and Nicola last night. "I'm sure the people of Calina will be very happy to learn of the prince's restoration. It can only strengthen our monarchy and country."

As she spoke, Nicola caught her quick glances in his direction. Could it be that he had some effect on her as well?

Breakfast was being served then, and attendants placed a deliciously looking quiche in front of each of them along with fresh fruit and an assortment of baked goods. Coffee and tea were offered and poured.

Taya attempted to keep her attention to her meal, but seated next to Nicola, all she could think about was how good he smelled, somewhere along the lines of sandalwood, cedar, and a hint of citrus.

"That reminds me," Mattia was now saying as he turned to Derek, "when will be the announcement of Nicola's return? It should be sooner, rather than later. The people need to know he's here."

Derek nodded thoughtfully.

"Traditionally, there would be a ceremony and a reception," Mattia added.

Nicola's ears perked at that suggestion. He was always down for a good party.

"I think it would be best for Nicola to get settled first and learn some of his responsibilities before we plan that," Derek responded, then he looked at Nicola, "in fact, Nic, you need to be briefed on the details of the upcoming conference, and there are several meetings I wish you to attend with me today."

Nicola did not bother to hide his displeasure at this news. He really only had one day before his *friends* from New York realized he had left town, and it wouldn't be long before they knew where he was— either the media or Enzo would surely clue them in. Staying within the confines of the palace was his safest option until his debt was paid, and he didn't want to spend his last day of freedom working or in meetings.

"I actually had other ideas," he replied, and he let his gaze rest on

Taya again just briefly.

"I'm sure you did," Derek said, eying his brother knowingly, "but, please, share your thoughts."

"Well, considering it is my first day in Calina, I was hoping to actually see it," Nicola began with a light tone, "I can't exactly help you run the country if I don't know anything about it."

Derek shook his head. "I'm sorry, Nic," he said, "I'm too busy to take you sight-seeing."

"It's actually not a bad idea," Christine interjected. Both Derek and Nicola looked in her direction with their eye brows raised, but for different reasons. "Nicola should see Calina, Derek," she said, "and, it would be easier for him now versus after the public knows who he is. He won't be able to move freely within the country once he's a public figure."

"Exactly my thoughts," Nicola chimed in and smiled triumphantly. He knew he liked Christine.

Taya glanced between the two brothers, the struggle to win the upper hand was evident. She knew the monarch would not cater to a disagreement in front of her or the prime minister, but it was clear he was not pleased with the change in agenda. It would seem, with Christine's assistance, Nicola had won this round.

"Fine," Derek consented, "but, you cannot run around by yourself."

"You can't give me an entourage," Nicola countered, "that would defeat the purpose and just draw attention."

He suddenly looked at Taya, an idea too perfect to pass up formulating in his mind. If she had been just any other woman he had met, he could have just naturally asked her out. But she wasn't just any woman, she was a member of parliament. He needed a reason to spend time with her. "How about you, angel?" he questioned with an easy smile, "what are your plans for today?"

Taya's eyes flew open wide. *What?* She thought. A heat flew to her cheeks with being put on the spot, and glancing at Derek, he seemed to note her unease with having to answer the question without permission.

Feeling it best to relieve her from any awkwardness, he took control of the situation.

"Taya?" he said, "would it be terribly inconvenient to ask your assistance in escorting the prince today? You are a responsible member of our government and having been born and raised in Calina, no one would know more about the country or its history than you."

Derek wasn't sure he trusted Taya yet, but she actually was a viable and convenient solution at the moment. He had determined with certainty that she was very passionate about what was best for the country and the people of Calina. He also wasn't blind to the apparent attraction his brother had toward her. Who knows, maybe she could have a positive, productive influence on Nicola.

Knowing that she couldn't say no, and in the back of her mind, knowing that she didn't want to say no, Taya nodded.

"I would be happy to," she replied, swallowing a nervous lump that formed in her throat and feeling slightly shell-shocked at the turn of events.

She stared at Nicola for a moment unsure what to say or do next. There was a brief pause of silence, then he stood up abruptly.

"Great," he exclaimed, grabbing Taya by the hand and pulling her to her feet. "No time like the present." Sticking around to be drawn back into political conversation did not appeal to him.

"What about breakfast?" She protested, stumbling slightly as he tugged her to the door.

"I'm sure we can find a much more relaxed atmosphere," he replied nonchalantly, "somewhere in town perhaps?" Without a backwards glance or declaration of their departure, Nicola lead Taya out of the dining room and into the hallway.

Derek blinked at the unceremonious exit then shook his head slowly.

"Are you sure it was wise letting her go off with him like that?" Christine asked.

Derek turned to her, a half smirk on his lips. "Wasn't it you who backed his suggestion?" he said, narrowing his eyes slightly.

"Well, it was a good idea," she defended, "but, I didn't mean for him to take Taya with him. I thought you'd send Costa or one of the guards." She paused, staring at the door, "he seems like he's a bit…irresponsible?"

"That's a vast understatement," Derek replied with a sigh, "Nicola has a lot to learn if he is going to be accepted by the people of Calina. I just hope he wakes up before he does something damaging to our reputation." He smiled slightly as his eyebrows came together, "but I don't believe for an instant that Taya will allow Nicola to do anything that would harm the standings of the government with the people."

"It's not really the monarchy's reputation that I'm concerned about," Christine replied, remembering the look in Nicola's eyes when he saw Taya, and she was made well aware of his playboy tendencies. She took a small sip of her coffee, then met Derek's gaze. "If he's anything like you, he will pursue heavily what he wants."

"He's nothing like me," Derek replied quickly, "Nicola is much more impatient."

Christine took a deep breath in and furrowed her brow, grateful that Taya at least, seemed like a woman who could take care of herself.

Studying Christine now, Derek's face grew concerned. Even through the reading glasses she wore, he couldn't help but notice the dark circles under her eyes, and he had observed how fatigued she seemed over these past weeks. He had hoped that by now she would have felt more relaxed and at home in Calina, but it appeared she was still struggling to adapt. Clearly she wasn't sleeping well.

"Christine," he said, placing his hand on hers, and he glanced quickly at Mattia, who was addressing what he felt was an overcooked quiche with the staff. He did not wish to draw unnecessary attention to her state but felt the need to address it as well. His eyes went back to her, "was something keeping you from sleeping last night?"

The thought entered his mind that he shouldn't even need to ask his fiancée such a question. He should just know how she slept because she should be with him, not in a separate bedroom. But he pushed his frustrations to the side, focusing on her.

Even at the mention of sleep, Christine fought to stifle a yawn. *If only he knew,* she thought suppressing a grimace. She couldn't honestly remember the last time she had a full night's rest, and she knew she couldn't go on like this. She was already risking her health as well as developing insomnia. But this was not the time to discuss it.

"Oh," she said casually, knowing that he wouldn't buy a denial, "I've been mulling over a project lately, and I guess I'm losing sleep over it," she managed a smile, "sometimes the creative mind won't shut down."

He returned her smile and asked no more questions, but his eyes remained pensive realizing she wasn't being honest with him. Soon, he would have to find out, he decided. Even if she wasn't ready to share yet, this couldn't go on. He knew she was still keeping something from him.

Out in the hall, Nicola continued his stride, pulling Taya along with him. He was elated at not only the opportunity presented to get to know her, but also at being relieved of what he had originally thought to have been quite a dreary day.

She squirmed her hand free from his grip, causing him to halt and turn to look at her.

"Your Highness," she gasped, "please wait. I didn't bow before leaving the king's presence. And, do you even know where you're going?" His dark eyes glinted; they made her breathless. Standing face to face with him, she was able to drink in the details of his refined features and the way he upturned only one corner of his full lips.

He was dressed in a solid black polo paired with belted khaki trousers. Her gaze trailed from the sharp lines of his cheekbones to his right bicep noticing part of a tattoo peeking out from just below his sleeve. A curl from his chocolate colored hair fell on his forehead and his eyes were a shade darker, making them appear almost black.

"First of all," he began, "if we're going to spend the day together, you need to call me Nic. And second of all," he paused, glancing around, "no, as a matter of fact, I don't know where I'm going," he looked back at Taya, "do you have a car?"

She shook her head slightly. Crossing her arms in front of her, she half smiled, unable to be frustrated with him. "Yes," she answered, "if you'd slow down for half a second, I'll take you to it."

Nicola took a step away from her and waved his arm in gesture that she should pass in front of him. "Of course, lead the way, angel."

She raised an eyebrow at him, then turned on her heel and began to walk in the opposite direction. "It's this way, actually," she said, "and, with all due respect, do not call me that."

Nicola smiled as he fell in step beside her. "Why?" he asked, "it suits you."

Taya let out a laugh, then rolled her eyes in disbelief that she was having this sort of conversation with a member of the monarchy. "You don't know anything about me," she replied.

"Whatever you say, angel."

They had indeed found breakfast elsewhere. Per Nicola's

recommendation, Taya drove him into the capital, *Citta di* Calina, which was the largest settlement in Calina and home to approximately two-thirds of the micro state's residents.

The palace sat just on the outskirts of the city, and as they made the short drive into town, Nicola was able to glimpse the beautiful views of the vast mountains around them. Calina was nestled in a valley near Mount Blanc, which bordered both Italy and France, with Switzerland to the north. As such, the small area was a supposed cash cow for tourism and recreational activities, skiing in particular.

Sadly, given the economic state of the country as well as the prolonged corruption in leadership, these ventures had not been capitalized on properly in decades. Derek was working to change all that, and already signs of life were beginning to show not only in town, but in the country's bottom line.

During the drive in, Taya deliberately drove through areas laden with poverty, feeling the need to showcase the struggles a majority of their citizens were still going through. It would have been easy to just highlight the beautiful or prosperous neighborhoods, but those were few and far between and would not have painted an accurate description of the country. As she drove, she watched his face, noting the raising of his eyebrows and interested expression at what he saw.

She took him to a local, family-owned cafe for breakfast where they enjoyed a freshly brewed espresso along with croissants and jam. Throughout breakfast, she began to educate him on the statistics of the country and its surrounding geographical area.

She found herself enjoying his easy-going manner and was grateful she felt she could speak openly with him and be herself. His relaxed and even playful demeanor was refreshing, and not what she would have ever thought the prince to be like. In fact, he was the complete opposite of every politician she had ever encountered, and she didn't consider that to be a bad thing.

Once they had left the cafe, she continued providing him a tour of the capital, taking him to key places of interest including the Calina Art Museum, historical society, library, and stopping by several educational facilities. She pointed out the new shopping district as well as the construction site for a new upscale ski resort; results of Derek's initiatives, which was helping to provide many needed jobs.

As they toured, she regaled him with Calina's history, how it won its independence with the fall of Napoleon in 1815, making Calina an older micro state. The Landino family had been in power since, establishing the monarchy, parliament and their political parties.

Nicola followed along to the places she suggested, listened to her history lessons and didn't ask too many questions. The reality was he didn't care too much for the antiquity, and only found the economical state interesting. Although he was impressed with her array of knowledge, the subject matter for the most part was boring him to tears. This wasn't how he had envisioned his time with her.

It was now nearing noon, and they were standing in the middle of a vast cathedral staring up at the large stained glass rose window while Taya filled him in on the important works of art around them and main events that took place in the church.

Being that it was late morning on a weekday there was no mass in session, and the cathedral was practically empty. Their footsteps echoed on the marble tiled floor as they walked slowly down the main aisle.

Taya continued her tour-chat, and Nicola found himself almost tuning out her words. Instead, he became mesmerized looking at her lips as she spoke, which were full and dewy. He had to put an end to the dull direction their day was heading, and he yearned to draw out the fire he sensed in her. Perhaps a bold move was called for to turn the tide.

"Taya," he said suddenly, cutting her off mid-sentence.

She stopped, her eyes widened at the abrupt interruption. "Yes?" she asked.

He stepped closer to her, invading her personal space. She looked up into his eyes, which were narrowed mischievously.

"Shut up for a minute," he said bluntly.

His voice was low and deep. Shock appeared on her face at his words, and she opened her mouth to respond, which Nicola took full advantage of. Grasping her chin, he brought his lips down on hers. The taste of her mouth was soft and sweet; everything he knew it would be since he first saw her.

His kiss immediately made her breathless, and before she even knew it was happening she found herself swept up in the embrace. She could taste the longing on his lips and breathe in his beautiful smell. She felt her knees give, and as she began to kiss him back with enthusiasm, it dawned on her where they were and what they were doing. She pushed him away quickly and brought her hand to her mouth, a look of astonishment on her face.

"What are you doing?" She exclaimed.

He didn't look ashamed, only quite pleased with himself. His dark eyes twinkled. "Only what I had wanted to do since I first laid eyes on you, angel," he replied.

"We're in a church," she responded quietly, feeling stunned.

He grinned. She wasn't upset he kissed her, only at their location.

"Yes," he said softly, "you know, even if we are in a church, it's ok if you want me."

She was speechless as she locked her gaze with his. Even if he was correct in his assumptions of her desires, she would rather die than admit it to him. She didn't even know him.

"You wanted it too," he coaxed, his voice was husky and his smile teased her.

"No," she practically whispered, but her eyes gave away her true intentions.

"You shouldn't lie in church you know," he replied.

He winked at her, then turned away. Placing his hands in his pockets, he strolled back up the aisle toward the entrance.

"Where are you going?" She called after him.

"This is boring," he replied, not looking back. "I'm leaving."

Taya blinked at his audacity. She looked around making sure no one was within earshot, then stomping slightly after him, she began to follow him. "Your Highness," she hissed.

"I do not acknowledge that title," he replied in a playful tone.

Having reached the large double doors to the cathedral, he opened one and exited. Taya rushed to keep up with him, then followed him out and down the front stoop.

"Nic," she said sternly. Finally he turned and looked at her, his eyebrows raised. "You can't just go off on your own," she said, shaking her head in disbelief, "His Majesty basically entrusted me to ensure your safe and productive tour of Calina."

"Fine," he consented, "and you've done a fantastic job. I can't remember when I learned so much."

She knew he was mocking her, but she crossed her arms letting him continue.

"But I'm done now," he said. "I'd love it if you'd continue to join me, however I've decided that a change in pace is in order." He grabbed her hand and tugged her toward him. "What do you say, angel, care to have a little fun?"

Chapter 7

"What, what do you mean?" Taya stammered, forcing herself to meet his eyes and cursing the blush that was rising in her cheeks.

Nicola met her gaze with an intensity, but then he broke into a full smile and turned from her to his left, his eyes shifting as he nodded pointedly down the street.

The cathedral was situated in the heart of town, just blocks away from the city center. As she followed his gaze, she noticed bright tents set up, vendor stalls and a Ferris wheel. She could hear faint music coming from the town square. Her eyes widened with recognition.

"The Grape Harvest Festival?" she asked confused.

The Calina valley was no novice to wine making and the Grape Harvest Festival was an annual tradition in the country. She had personally not attended in quite some years, always having been too busy with her work, and she had completely forgotten that it was even happening this week.

Still holding on to her hand, Nicola began to walk in the direction of the festival, pulling her with him.

"Nic," she tried to plead, "I don't think this is what His Highness had in mind. Today is supposed be about you learning about the country. He won't like it if—" but Nicola cut her off.

"Come on, Taya," he reasoned, "Derek isn't going to be-head you for having a little fun. Grape Festival you say?" He raised his eyebrows and smiled, "that means there's wine. Besides," he continued, "this is very educational to me. Local culture is important."

She narrowed her eyes at him. "Are you always this spontaneous and manipulative?"

He considered the question, she could see his eyes gleaming.

"Usually," he replied. He paused realizing he was still holding onto her hand. Releasing her, he began walking again in the direction of the festival, and she immediately missed the contact with him. "You coming?" he asked.

Taya sighed, coming to the conclusion that Nicola Landino was just about the most infuriating individual that she had ever met. She wasn't sure if she trusted him yet, and he was the epitome of entitlement. But she also admired his fearlessness, recalling his ability to confront Derek, his candor with speaking his mind, and his confidence.

With his carefree, likable personality, along with his calculating nature, Taya suddenly realized that Nicola will make an outstanding politician. Sure, he was rough around the edges, but with some experience, he could prove to be a powerful asset. With certainty, Derek had also recognized his potential in this regard. It was key that Nicola was in the monarch's corner. But was he? She reflected again to the way they seemed to despise one another. Was their family feud substantial enough to prevent him from supporting the monarchy?

She began, once again, following Nicola, making her way down the cobblestone carefully in her heels. The center of the city leading up to the square where the festival was taking place was old-world and charming. Much of the street structure was original and very narrow with small houses, and some boarded-up shops nestled close together lined up and down the sidewalk. Although it was nearing autumn, it was a beautiful, partly sunny day with a few fluffy white clouds scattering the sky.

After a short and silent walk toward the festival, they arrived at the tents. The music was now clear, and Taya recognized the lively tune of a traditional Calean song. In the middle of the square, a crowd of people were dancing; some attempting to maintain the time-honored steps within the dance, others simply making up their own.

Dozens of stalls were lined up to form aisles, and within them contained several of the native wineries' current vintages, local artisan's craftwork, and tastes of the city's culinary delights. The fresh smell of baked goods and fried festival treats wafted toward them. Attendees were moving from tent to tent, children were running about, games were being played, and Taya noticed the annual grape stomping competition was well under way.

She turned to Nicola and took in his expression, which was one of excitement with his standard mischievous smile. His smile was infectious, and she couldn't refrain from smiling as well.

"Why don't you share with me the origins of the festival?" He suggested, "just so you feel better about being here." He winked at her, putting her immediately at ease with their new agenda.

Taya's expression turned pensive. "Well," she began, "grape harvest festivals are a very old tradition amongst people in the region. As with similar festivals in other countries, it's a way to celebrate the harvest naturally, but here in Calina, it's also a time for many of our citizens to make a living." Nicola raised his eye brows as Taya continued. "Unlike other thriving countries who only hold festivals now for entertainment, ours is necessary for many to sustain any kind of lifestyle," she paused, watching his brow furrow.

"Calina is, right now, a very poor country," she informed him gravely, "many here suffer, and this festival is, for some, their one shot to make it another year. Thankfully, tourism has picked up this year, so that will help many of these small mom-and-pop vendors."

Nicola looked closer at the merchants of the festival, taking in the weight of her words. Indeed, he noticed the tired faces, well-worn clothing, and almost desperate expressions they wore as patrons passed by their tents; it was sad. He had no idea.

"So," she said, noticing his interest, "what would you like to do first?" *Maybe coming here was a good idea after all*, she thought.

Nicola didn't respond, only placed his hands in his pockets and began to stroll casually down the first aisle of stalls, continuing to take in the scenery.

As they continued to pass through, Taya couldn't help but notice he drew attention. He smiled naturally, and he walked with a confidence that let his presence be known; as if he owned the place. Which, Taya realized, he sort of did.

Noticing that most of the people who looked in his direction were women, Taya instinctively moved closer to Nicola's side. She subconsciously lifted her chin a notch as she tried to ignore her annoyance at the amount of stares and nods of approval he was receiving. *We're not here together*, she scolded herself. Did she actually feel jealous? Although he did kiss her, she knew better than to take that seriously, and she tried to convince herself it meant nothing to her either.

Passing by a particularly beautifully decorated tent, Taya let her eyes wander inside to see a dazzling display of intricately designed silver jewelry. She moved closer, interested in inspecting the craftsmanship. She smiled kindly at the old woman behind the counter as she approached. Although she was elderly, the woman had a certain grace about her, and Taya noticed her hands were worn, her fingernails cut short—clearly showing the signs of age and experience.

She couldn't help but admire this woman who had made all the beautiful items now on display. Indeed, just behind the counter sat a small workbench, tools, and a lamp, where she was still clearly hard at work when there were no customers to attend to.

"Your jewelry is lovely," Taya complemented.

The craftswoman smiled.

"*Grazie, Signorina*. I have just the piece for you," she replied.

Before Taya could object, the woman took her by the wrist and wrapped around it a delicate silver bracelet. The links in the chain were small, flat, and woven together to form a beautiful patten. Taya couldn't help but realize how much time this item must have taken the woman to make. The bracelet chain was thin, but it wrapped around her wrist three times before connecting to the clasp. The effect of the simplicity of the design was one of elegance, and Taya immediately fell in love with the piece.

"It's stunning," she breathed, "how much would you like for it?"

"50 francs," the woman replied, but as Taya reached for her credit card, the woman's face fell. "*Mi dispiace*," she said, "I have a very small shop, and I only accept cash."

"Oh, that's too bad," Taya replied, feeling disappointed, "I don't have any on me today." She moved to release the clasp on the bracelet so she could hand it back.

"Will you take American?" Nicola asked.

Taya looked sharply at him not even realizing he had been standing beside her. Not waiting for an answer, he pulled a hundred dollar bill from his wallet and placed it on the counter. The woman stared at the bill for a moment.

"I'm sorry, signore, I can't exchange that here nor make change for you."

Nicola smiled. "You may keep it," he replied simply, "I believe the bracelet is underpriced given your level of expertise anyway."

Taya watched with slight amusement as she thought she saw a hint of blush in the old woman's cheeks at Nicola's complement. But, immediately Taya's smile fell; she could not allow him to pay for it.

"No," she said, turning to Nicola, "it's not your place to pay for this. It's fine." Feeling slightly embarrassed, she attempted to remove the clasp again.

Nicola's smile broadened, then he quickly changed his expression to one of regret as he looked back at the merchant. "I'm terribly sorry," he said, "it seems my companion doesn't like it after all."

Taya watched in horror as the woman's face changed to one of confusion then sadness. "No, that's not it at all," she said quickly, "I love it, it's amazing."

"Then why can't I buy it for you, angel?" he asked raising his eyebrows, a smirk forming on his lips.

She met his eyes for a moment, knowing that if she continued to argue with him, he'd make a scene. The woman's eyes lit up as she glanced from Taya to Nicola, and she gave Taya a knowing smile.

"He is quite the gentleman, *e molto bello*," she observed nodding in approval, further fueling Taya's feelings of awkwardness with the woman having the wrong impression of their acquaintance. Her gut reaction was to correct the woman's misguided assumption, but she couldn't foresee Nicola's response.

"Fine," she consented through slightly gritted teeth, deciding a hasty exit was best.

As soon as the transaction was complete, Taya grasped his arm, dragging him back into the aisle.

"What's the matter with you?" she accused. "I don't appreciate being embarrassed."

Nicola opened his eyes wide. "So much for gratitude," he stated, lifting a brow.

"You manipulated me to get your way," Taya hissed back, "I didn't ask you to buy me anything."

"You didn't need to ask me," Nicola emphasized, "I wanted to," he paused, "what's wrong with that?"

Taya rolled her eyes.

Not wishing to argue, Nicola reconsidered his position on the matter. Usually when he offered to buy a woman something, they gushed with appreciation, practically falling at his feet. But Taya was unlike any of the other women he was used to; she was strong, confident and independent. And he found himself having never been more intrigued.

"Look, I apologize if I crossed a line," he added, sincerity in his tone.

She folded her arms across her chest and attempted to continue to glare at him, but he smiled making her want to return it. She bit her lip to keep her expression intact. Knowing that her wall was breaking down, he changed the subject.

"You can decide what we do next," he suggested, "anything you want."

Taya raised her eyebrows, still chewing on her lip. Not wishing to relinquish the upper hand so quickly, she lifted her chin slightly.

"I'd like to have lunch," she said, "then, maybe I'll let you take me on the Ferris wheel."

He gave her a dazzling smile, loving her strong-willed attitude. "After you, angel," he said, stepping to the side.

As she began to pass him to head back to the food tents, she stopped mid-stride. Turning to face him, she grabbed his shoulder to reach forward and then placed a gentle kiss on his cheek.

"Thank you for the bracelet," she said softly.

He blinked, something inside him melting at her gesture. As she turned from him, he caught a whiff of her perfume. Anxious to see where the remainder of the day went, he quickly caught up with her casually placing his arm around her waist as they walked together.

Over the next two hours, Taya pulled Nicola from tent to tent insisting he try at least a sample from every food vendor. Proud to show off the country's unique and diverse array of dishes, they were soon feasting on paella, Fontina cheese fondue topped with thin shavings of white chocolate truffle, risotto, hazelnut cake, and danish pastries. She was pleased that each sample tasted earned a smile of approval from Nicola, and before long he was insisting that he couldn't eat another bite.

After lunch they wandered through the rest of the tents and activities, and although he had attempted his best argument, Taya had flat-out refused when he suggested grape stomping. Completely willing to remove his shoes, roll up the legs of his pants and hop into a vat, she stood her ground.

"Look at what I'm wearing," she exclaimed, refusing against his tug on her arm. She would never get grape juice stains out of her white dress.

He stopped pulling on her, and taking her up on her suggestion, he once again admired her curves.

"Perhaps you're right," he said, his gaze locking on hers, his eyes halting her breathing as a clear look of desire crossed his features.

"Let's go over here instead." He gestured to the middle of the square. Following his lead, she consented to joining the group of dancers.

She had to give him credit for trying to learn and keep up with some of the traditional steps, which consisted of many heel-toe taps, turns, clapping, and not much touching. He laughed at his clear mistakes, almost stepping on Taya's feet several times before he finally gave up. Grabbing her by the waist, with the same look of desire in his eyes, he pulled her flush against him, and clasping her hand tight in his, he brought his cheek next to hers.

"This is how I like to dance," he murmured close to her ear.

She felt her entire body warm at his soft breath in her ear, and she suddenly craved they were not in a crowd, but alone together.

She pulled back slightly to look him in the eyes, conflicting emotions passing through her and across her features. She didn't want to feel this strongly toward someone she only met that morning, but there was something about him that pulled her to him that she couldn't deny. He had begun to stir feelings within her even from the first moment she saw him last night. And as much as she rationalized she should resist how she felt, being honest with herself, she realized that she just didn't want to. But was this real to him as well?

When the dance had finished, Nicola released her, and she caught a look of reluctance on his face at the loss of contact, which caused her face to blush. He clearly felt the same attraction she did.

Breaking the silence, he mentioned they sample some of the local wines next. She nodded in agreement, and he grabbed her hand heading in the direction of the wine tents. Taya didn't object to his holding her hand and leading her through the crowd, in fact, it felt natural, and she found herself enjoying the feeling of her hand in his.

As they began to sample the wines, Taya noticed that he was very knowledgeable and appreciative of wine, with his preferences seeming to lean more toward the dry vintages. But there was nothing he wouldn't try as he explained his taste in wine greatly depended on his mood and what it was to be paired with.

She became entertained with watching him examine each glass with refinement, first checking the color, the aroma, and finally the taste. He seemed very impressed by most of the samples, stating that the wines from Calina rivaled any of the expensive imports he was used to in New York, and casually joked that Derek should export the commodity, further increasing capital for the country. Taya refrained from trying them all, not wishing to allow the alcohol to go her head. Nicola, however, had no problem taking each glass offered—not that it appeared to affect him one bit.

After they'd had their fill of wine, they headed to the Ferris wheel. Once they were airborne however, Taya found it made her stomach drop and her head spin, (although the wine may have had something to do with that.) Nevertheless, she found herself laughing, and each time they'd reach the top, she'd gaze out over the city, awed by the raw beauty once again that was her home. Sitting so close to him, she shivered each time his arm brushed against hers.

Nicola offered her his hand to help her down when the ride finally came to an end, which she accepted still feeling giddy from the spinning and being off the ground. She caught his eye as he grasped her hand, pulling her from the cab. She became lost momentarily in his dark orbs, the thought running through her mind that she couldn't imagine a more perfect day. Or more perfect company.

It was nearing evening now, and as the sun started to hang low to the west beyond the mountaintops, clouds began to move in slowly creating a now soft purple hue which was beginning to fill the late summer sky. As they wandered together back through the festival grounds, Taya removed her heels, deciding that her feet have had enough, preferring to walk barefoot on the cobblestone.

"You better be careful," Nicola observed, watching her swing her shoes in one hand as she walked, the silver bracelet on her wrist twinkling underneath the festival lights. "What if you step on something?"

Taya smirked. "My feet are killing me," she said with a laugh. "If I had known this was how we were going to spend the day, I would have most certainly worn something else."

"Well," he replied, "I'll take the blame for that," he paused, "or should I say full credit?"

Taya shook her head slightly, again in disbelief at his immodesty. "You're unbelievable," she responded, amused and annoyed at the same time.

"Didn't you have a good time?" he asked.

She thought a moment. Truth be told, she found herself in awe at just how much fun she did have. But she wasn't willing to let him act any more triumphant than he already was.

"It was a nice day," she said shrugging noncommittally.

69

Nicola laughed seeing through her ruse. "I guess I'll have to make our agenda clear next time so you can plan accordingly with your attire."

Taya stopped walking, and he turned to face her. "Next time?" She met his eyes and held her breath. Had he meant to say that? In response he took her hand in his.

"I want nothing more than there to be many 'next times,'" he replied softly, and for a rare moment, there didn't appear to be an ounce of humor or mischief in his eyes.

She admitted to herself that she wished the same, and the intensity of the moment caused her heart rate to increase rapidly. Recalling what his lips felt like against hers back in the cathedral, she suddenly yearned to relive it. But he didn't make a move, and she once again felt conflicted; she barely knew him. The more time she spent with him, the more her desire continued to grow, and it was going to slowly drive her insane.

Clearing her throat, she decided to change the subject and let the moment pass. For now.

"What would you like to do for dinner?" she asked.

Nicola gave a laugh and patted his toned abs through his shirt.

"I don't think I can handle anything else that's too heavy today," he paused, "although it was all delicious."

Taya was in agreement on both accounts—she felt almost too full from lunch to even eat dinner, then a thought occurred to her.

"I have an idea." And she smiled to herself, thinking it was her turn to act a bit spontaneously.

Chapter 8

Approximately thirty minutes later, Taya had set up a blanket she grabbed from her car along with a fresh baguette, several different kinds of cheeses and some prosciutto.

Deciding that a light picnic was a better option to a large meal, they left the festival and headed to one of the local markets just off the main street. She purchased the essentials along with a bottle of wine (letting him choose one of his favorites that he had tried earlier), then they headed back to her car just a few blocks away.

Driving a short distance just out of town, she pulled into a popular park. It appeared crowded, and she could only guess that many of the other festival-goers had had similar ideas to visit the serene place.

A narrow river ran through the middle of the park, and the mountains appeared in the distance. With the sun approaching the horizon, about to set, the ambiance was one of mythic beauty, the sun itself appearing to be a bright golden ball surrounded by clouds of deep pink, lavender and grey. During the summer months especially, the park was usually littered with picnic blankets and it was a favorite spot amongst both families and couples.

Taya now sat on the blanket with her legs folded up underneath her, their shoes set off to the side, as Nicola opened the wine with the corkscrew she had purchased. Pouring her a glass, he set down the bottle, then clinked hers with his own.

"Cheers," he said and smiled, "this was a great idea."

She returned his smile as she sipped the wine.

"I'm glad you approve," she replied.

Minutes passed while they ate in a comfortable silence, watching the river flow by, the water splashing on rocks that peeked up from the depths, the last rays of sunlight glittering across the surface. She glanced at him, becoming slightly mesmerized by how the slight breeze ruffled his hair.

"So," she said after finishing her last bite, breaking the tranquility, "what do you think of Calina?" She paused, "not that you had much of a tour or anything."

Nicola chuckled. "I'm sure I saw the best parts," he replied, and he leaned back on his hands letting his gaze linger on her golden hair and sweet smile.

She ignored his flirtatious attempt. "I'm serious," she impressed on him, "I imagine it's much different here than in New York?"

He nodded slowly, thinking of the contrast between the busyness and night-life versus this seemingly slow-paced, quaint environment. But not just that, he was used to living a life of luxury, and gaining a deeper understanding of what many Caleans were currently facing grounded him, causing something to change within him.

"Yes," he confirmed solemnly, but then he smiled, "but I can say, I don't think I've ever had as much fun in New York as I did today."

Taya studied him, suddenly wondering what it would feel like to run her fingers through his hair. She pursed her lips and pushed the thought from her mind. "Is that the only way you measure things?" She questioned, half-jokingly, "In terms of how much fun you have?"

He frowned and answered instinctively. "Of course not," he said quickly. But the question made him pause. Did she think him shallow? She waited for him to continue, but in a rare moment, he wasn't sure what to say. He didn't like feeling as if he needed to defend himself, but as he continued to think about her question, he realized that maybe he did. He had never taken anything seriously in his life, nor had he ever aspired toward a career or any kind of responsibility or obligation. He considered Taya; the woman sitting next to him, and he admired her for her ambition, intelligence, and achievements along with her beauty. What could she possibly think of him?

His eyebrows came together in a brief scowl as he suddenly felt, for the first time in his life, that he wasn't good enough.

As if his doubts were confirmed, she then asked, "so what did you do in New York?"

Again, he hesitated.

Nothing, he answered to himself, for once being completely honest with his indignity at his own lack of accomplishments. Maybe he should have been listening to Derek all this time…

Misreading his expression, Taya feared she made him angry.

"Are you ok?" she asked, furrowing her brow. She had not yet seen such a look of discontentment on his face.

"Sure," he replied, albeit stoically. "How long are you staying at the palace?" he asked her, ignoring her question and changing the subject.

"Just a couple more days," she answered, "until after the EU conference." Curious to his current thoughts on the topic that had their country at political odds, she asked, "what do you think about Calina joining the European Union?" She took another sip of wine and tried to make her voice sound unconcerned as if his answer didn't matter.

"I'm not sure yet," he answered truthfully. Before now, he hadn't really cared, but he knew Derek was pushing for it. And maybe, it was time he cared. "Derek thinks it would be good for the country."

He sat up straight, resting his arms on his knees, fully aware that he didn't yet know enough about the topic to form an opinion. He eyed her now intently, realizing a strong desire to suddenly match her knowledge and passion around the main issues in Calina. He was the prince, after all.

"So you support him?" Taya asked.

Nicola averted his gaze and stared straight ahead, watching the clouds cover the darkening sky.

"He's my brother," he stated.

It didn't escape Taya that he didn't directly answer the question, and it was still very unclear whether Nicola was loyal to Derek.

He turned the question to her. "Do you think the country should join?"

"Calina has always had its independence," Taya replied, "I don't want to lose our culture and uniqueness, nor do I like the idea of accepting outside influence over our policies and decisions."

"It sounds like you've made up your mind," Nicola observed.

Taya shrugged.

"On the flip side, joining the EU will also mean the monarchy has less authority over some things as well, which I am in favor of," she paused, thinking. "Many of us are torn, but I will remain objective until I hear the king's argument at the conference."

He laughed lightly. "Derek will get his way," he replied, "he can be very persuasive."

"I've heard," she said quietly, and Nicola picked up on a note of dissatisfaction.

"You don't approve of him?" he asked, eyeing her keenly.

Taya met his eyes, unafraid of being honest with him. "I fear his power," she said, "I'm very familiar with what corruption can do to someone, to families and to a country," she paused, "no one should be given the kind of authority he has. The decisions should be made by the people."

"Then why have a conference?" Nicola asked. "If Derek was the kind of leader who was going to make the choice, what would be the purpose of bringing everyone together to vote?"

Taya narrowed her eyes. "The conference is just a political show, so it looks like he cares what we think. Regardless of what the people want, he can still make the decision on his own."

Nicola remained quiet for a moment. "Derek isn't corrupt," he finally said almost with a tone of defeat, "and I believe he would respect the majority."

"You seem very certain," she replied with an air of disbelief.

He broke into a grin at her, feeling that the heaviness of the conversation was enough for one evening, and there were other objectives on his mind he yet wished to explore.

"Don't worry, angel," he said, "everything will work out." His grin turned into a smolder as he locked his gaze with hers. "You know," he added, leaning in toward her, "as much as you accuse me of just wanting to have fun, I could say the same about you for being too serious." He reached up and gently brushed a stray strand of her hair away from her face.

He couldn't remember ever feeling so captivated by someone. Usually when he was with a woman, it was all about the chase for him, the conquest, but being with Taya felt different somehow. He wanted her with a passion, but he cared more about how she felt toward him than he did about getting his way. He yearned to know if she felt the same connection he was experiencing.

Taya's lips parted as he neared her, her breath catching in her throat.

"Maybe we're perfect for each other," he murmured.

He trailed his fingertips along the side of her cheek, his face now only an inch from hers. She wanted him to kiss her, but at the same time, she knew if he did, she wouldn't be able to control herself. She trembled slightly as he closed the remaining distance.

A loud clap of thunder sounded just as his lips touched hers. The clouds that had been moving in all evening opened up, and as the rain began to downpour on them, Taya shrieked and scrambled to her feet.

Caught up in their conversation and being with him, she had been completely oblivious to the change in weather, as well as the park, which had been steadily getting emptier. Nicola laughed out loud as she quickly grabbed up the wine glasses and their shoes. He scooped up the rest of their belongings, folding everything within the blanket, and together they ran barefoot back to where she had parked.

By the time they reached the car, they were both soaked to the skin. Throwing the blanket, remnants of the picnic, and their shoes in the backseat, they quickly climbed in, slamming the doors against the pounding weather. Taya sat behind the wheel, now shaking from being drenched and cold, as she tried to wring out her hair.

She heard him laughing still next to her in the passenger seat, but he suddenly stopped. She glanced at him and noticed he was staring at her with intensity. Wondering at first what he was looking at, she quickly recalled she was wearing white. Sure enough, as she looked down at herself, it was evident the now saturated fabric of her dress was not only sticking to her, but see-through. Meeting his eyes, she saw a raw, hungry gleam in them.

He let his eyes travel over her figure, the white material now revealing a peach hue where it stuck to her body. Her thin, lace bra betrayed her curves, leaving little to the imagination. He broke his stare, turning to look through the windshield, a hard look set on his face as though he was contemplating some inner turmoil. *Damnit*, he knew he needed to stop this before someone got hurt. He never expected to experience such powerful feelings. Feelings that were becoming impossible to resist.

Cursing under his breath, he turned back to her, quickly grabbing her by the arm and pulling her into him. The tension that had been mounting between them all day was at its peak, and Nicola could no longer bear it. Wrapping his hand behind her neck, he seized her mouth with his, devouring her lips and giving in to his carnal need.

"Oh God, Taya," he breathed into her like she was life itself.

Just like the rain outside, the touch of his lips on hers opened the floodgates of passion she had been harboring, but until now, refusing to act upon. His kiss was unyielding, and unable to breathe or think, she let out a soft moan against him. It briefly occurred to her that this was reckless, but she cast the doubt aside, the exhilarating thrill of how good he felt against her momentarily overriding her common sense. His fingers, which were tangled in her wet hair, held her firmly to him, while his other hand moved freely, kneading her breast slowly, then wrapped around her waist in an effort to pull her closer.

She was willingly following his lead, and it was evident she wanted him as much as he wanted her, which made him not only more aroused, but it triggered his voice of reason, registering to him this involvement was dangerous.

With as much effort as he could muster, he gently broke their kiss and his hold on her. He met her eyes knowing there was too much hanging over his head to be able to follow through on any kind of emotional commitment. The reality came crashing down on him hard; he was already infatuated with her. Taya could not just be a casual fling to him, and therefore, he couldn't have her, regardless of how he felt.

She looked at him questionably, not understanding why he suddenly stopped. He couldn't explain his situation to her, it wasn't safe. The less she knew, the better. Unsure what to do, he said the first thing that came to his mind.

"We should get back to the palace," his voice was apologetic, and he looked away from her. "I'm sure everyone is wondering where we are."

She stared at him in response. Feeling utterly rejected and embarrassed, she turned to face forward and started the engine of the car.

"Ok," she replied sharply, "sure."

She wasn't sure what had just happened, all she knew was that she was suddenly freezing, wet, and on the verge of tears.

Why did he change his mind? Was he just toying with her? Throughout the day, she had felt such an immense pull toward him; a chemistry unlike anything she had ever known. Surely he had felt the same? But maybe he didn't, she concluded. Maybe he was this way with every woman.

No longer in his embrace, she shivered from the damp cold that now reached her bare arms and soaking clothes. She reached over to turn the heat up in the car. Although the warm air now flowed through the car as she began to drive, it did nothing to comfort her breaking heart.

The rain was still coming down when they arrived back at the palace. As they entered into the main hall, Irena and an attendant were there to greet them. Nicola was relieved to see that Derek was not present.

76

Once she had bowed to acknowledge his presence, Irena regarded them with a disapproving glance, taking in the state of their condition.

"I'll inform His Highness you have returned, signore Nicola," she stated. She turned to the attendant to give instructions, but Nicola spoke first.

"Ok, you do that," he replied, making it clear he was the one giving direction. "Let him know that I will speak with him in the morning. I'm going to bed after I escort Ms. Mariano back to her quarters."

Irena nodded curtly, displeased with his control, but she had no choice but to follow orders. "Of course, Signore," she said curtly.

Taya remained stiff and silent, hugging her freezing arms as Nicola placed his arm around her shoulders and led her down the hall and up one flight of stairs to her room. She wanted desperately to ask him the questions running through her mind, but she walked with him in silence, feeling too hurt to speak. As they approached her door, she found her voice and the courage to say what was on her mind.

"Do you not feel what I feel?" she asked, finding it difficult to look him in the eyes. She finally raised her face to him. "Is it just me?"

He shook his head slowly.

"No," he replied quietly, "it's not just you."

"Then why are you suddenly pulling away from me?" she asked. She placed a hand gently on his chest, his shirt still damp from the rain. She felt his muscles tense underneath her touch.

Nicola tried to think of a reasonable explanation to give her. Out of all the times he had been able to talk his way out of difficult situations, why couldn't he now?

"We just met today," he tried, but he knew it sounded forced, "and a relationship between us might be considered a conflict of interest considering our positions," which wasn't exactly untrue.

Taya raised an eyebrow at him in response. Not only did his tone not sell what he was saying, but the personality and behavior he had shown her all day indicated that the fact they had only met that day wasn't a problem for him. With her hand still resting against his chest, she pushed him away from her.

"You think I'd believe that?" She rasped, her brows coming together in fury. "I'm pretty sure you could handle an involvement with anyone if you chose to. If you don't want this, then fine, but don't insult me by lying to me," she paused, not only feeling hurt now, but hostile. "You're weak and a coward." She added, hoping to sting him.

He narrowed his eyes at her words, knowing that he had wounded her pride, and this was her retaliation. He turned from her, a storm brewing in his eyes, and started down the hall. *Just walk away*, he told himself, *it's for the best*.

But he stopped.

Clenching his fists, he looked back at her, frustration welling up in him. She stood there still, beautiful and broken. Her large green eyes were wide, the perfect combination of pain and desire on her face. He was already feeling a dangerous array of emotions, ones that he wasn't at all familiar with and didn't know how to control. The question was, did he wish to maintain control over the passion coursing through him? *Fuck.* Striding back toward her, he realized she was right; he was weak, just not in the way she accused.

Coming face to face with her, he placed his left palm firm up against the door next to her head. He leaned in close to her, his nose stopping an inch from hers.

"Don't make me angry, angel," he cautioned, his voice was hoarse and almost strained. As he spoke, he brought his other hand up to her throat, wrapping his fingers around the back of her neck. Her skin was so soft, so delicate. His fingers tensed, squeezing just slightly.

As she stared into the dark pools of his eyes, her breathing halted. He could feel the vibrations of her wildly pounding heart through his fingertips.

"Are you afraid?" he asked in a whisper.

"No," she replied, and her voice was thick with lust. In fact, she had never before felt more turned on, his touch and scent wreaking havoc on her insides, his dominance sending pleasurable shivers down her body.

His thumb moved up her jawline to find and caress her lips. Letting his hand then trail down her bare arm, he bent his head and nuzzled into her neck. His mouth made contact, gliding along her skin, his tongue massaging a hot trail all along to the base of her throat.

She moaned softly and grabbed his shoulders for stability, then gripped the front of his shirt, feeling like she could melt through the door.

He stopped, standing upright and reached behind her for the door handle, opening it to her room. She stepped back from him into the room, while he followed, then shut the door firmly behind him.

He regarded her standing before him, letting his mind wander to all the things he wanted to do to her. He tilted his head to one side.

"Take off your dress," he said quietly.

Willing to comply, Taya held her breath as she reached behind her back for the zipper to her dress, which was now partially dry. Slowly gliding the zipper down, she removed her arms from the sleeves, allowing the dress to fall to the floor. In turn, Nicola grabbed his shirt collar, pulling it over his head and tossing it to the side.

Taya's eyes opened wide as she took in his physique. They roamed over his sculpted abs, chest and shoulders, finally resting on his tattoo, which she was surprised to see covered not only his upper left arm, but the design sprawled out over his shoulder and upper left chest as well. It was done all in black ink, and attempting to make out the details in the dim lighting, she could see it was an angel's wing. A fleeting thought occurred to her to ask him what it meant to him, but he was already embracing her, wasting no more time to pull her body against his.

The feel of his bare skin was smooth and seared against her own, and his breath was hot near her ear as his arms circled around her back, effortlessly releasing the clasp on her bra.

He brought his hand gently to her cheek and brushed her hair back away from her face. Finally, his lips found hers in an urgent kiss that lit her entire body on fire. His tongue entered her mouth with vigor, and she felt him push against her as he propelled forward causing her to collapse on the bed behind them.

Falling next to her, he buried his head once again in her neck, devouring her soft skin as he also worked to free them both from the rest of their clothing confines. Her hands moved through his hair, and after untangling her fingers from his curls, she let them roam freely over his hard, chiseled body, touching and exploring every single part of him.

He moved in between her thighs, positioning himself on top of her.

"Are you sure this is what you want?" he asked, the question more for himself, giving himself one last chance to stop, but knowing that he would not give in to the hesitation unless she said she didn't want it. Getting lost in her deep green eyes, he silenced the voices in the back of his mind telling him he would only end up hurting her.

She nodded in answer to his question, reaching up to pull on his neck toward her, breathless from the anticipation of what her body needed from him.

"Say it," he said, not taking her nod as an answer.

"I want you, Nic," she whispered, a hint of desperation in her tone, her insides already melting.

Hearing his name from her lips in the moment drove him wild. He lowered himself, easing into her. As he entered her completely, she moaned out loud, feeling his impressive manhood stretching her in all the right places.

"Oh, Taya," he breathed, his voice raspy as he relished in how her hot flesh felt around him. He paused for a moment before he began to move, pulling back, then digging into her further.

Their limbs soon tangled together and their bodies rocked rhythmically as though they were already familiar with one another. His hands moved over her peaks, caressing her breasts, as each stroke created the friction she craved. He bent his head down to capture one of her erect nipples in his mouth, and she arched her back, sighing his name in response.

"How are you so perfect," he murmured, cupping her breast and claiming her sweet mouth again as he continued to fulfill every need she had.

Before long, her gasps and moans indicated to him she was close, and he grabbed onto her hips, thrusting hard into her, sending her over the edge of intense pleasure. He didn't dare close his eyes, eager to drink in every expression on her face.

He continued his pace, letting her ride out the waves until she had taken in every last ounce of the sensation. Then, knowing he was nearing his end, he picked up speed until at last, he climaxed with a fierce satisfaction.

She expected him to pull from her, but he didn't. Instead he wrapped his arms tight around her back and rolled her over on top of him, allowing her to straddle him. As he grasped the back of her head and pulled her down to him in a passionate kiss, she realized he wasn't near done. Rocking her hips now into him, she concluded she wasn't either. And she didn't think she ever would be.

Hours later and finally sated, Nicola sat in an armchair facing Taya's bed. She lay sleeping on her stomach, her arms hugging her pillow. The rain clouds had subsided throughout the night and now a soft moonlight streamed into the room from the large bay windows which highlighted her golden hair, a messy array of tangles, and her dark pink, pouty lips.

He folded his hands in front of him and sighed softly. He knew he had been selfish and careless tonight. It wasn't fair to have taken her down this road. It would have been so much easier if he had just rejected her in the hall. It would have hurt her, but now it would be worse. But he had been incapable of resisting, unable to stop his own feelings. It was the worst time in his life to actually fall for someone, but he had.

He had fallen hard.

Allowing his thoughts to stray where he refused to let them go for the past several hours, he now considered the position he was in and what he had no choice but to do.

When Enzo DeGrassi approached him yesterday with his proposition, he had inadvertently assigned Nicola a death sentence. Regardless of his choice to aid DeGrassi in his efforts to overthrow Derek, it would not end well for him.

Nicola knew with confidence that any attempt to dethrone his brother would be foiled, leaving the conspirators apprehended and most likely executed. There was the off chance that Enzo would succeed, but understanding Derek, Nicola did not like his odds. On the flip side, if he had refused to help Enzo, he was positive Enzo would make good on his promise to ensure the organization he was indebted to in New York knew how to get to him. Enzo didn't need to tell any hitman where he was, it was only a matter of time before the whole world not only knew who he was, the prince of Calina, but also where he was. But Nicola feared Enzo's endless resources and contacts would help and allow his seekers the ability to infiltrate their security.

For the thousandth time, Nicola considered what Enzo had said to him: *I have friends within the palace walls*. Not only did he have no future, Taya wasn't safe with him. He felt certain Enzo had spies that were watching. If anyone saw what she meant to him, it could put her in a position where she could potentially be used as leverage against him. Enzo had already proven he would blackmail.

Although Nicola had already made his choice known to Enzo, neither road led him to a place of peace or freedom to pursue a relationship. He didn't know if any path laid before him could lead to his survival, but he did know he needed to keep her safe, whatever the cost. The only option he had was now to break both their hearts.

He briefly wondered if Derek could and would still help him. If he could somehow pay off the organization, maybe he had a chance. Perhaps an apology would be a start…

He gazed at her face again; she truly looked like an angel in the moonlight. He had never before cared about any woman he was with. Any relationship he would have gladly walked away from. Now that he had within his grasp the first person that had meant something to him, and he would be forced to push her away.

As if sensing him, her eyes opened.

"Nic?" She raised herself up on her arms, and began to scan her surroundings. Her immediate thought when she woke alone was that he had gone. But, glancing to her right, she saw him seated in the armchair, apparently watching her. She relaxed visibly, relieved he had not left her. "What are you doing?" she asked.

He smiled, then stood, walking back to the bed and sliding in next to her. He wrapped his arm around her, and she nestled herself in the crook of his shoulder.

"I was letting you rest," he said softly.

She ran her fingertips along the outline of the ink splayed across chest and arm. "Tell me about your tattoo," she said sleepily, and she gave a small yawn against him.

He considered her request, and his brows furrowed together.

"My mother died tragically when I was 16," he began, choosing to relive a painful time, "I kinda spiraled and was in a dark place for a while after that." He paused, remembering the day he decided on the design. "When I climbed out of my grief, I got the tattoo as a symbol to remind myself that even in the darkest of times there is always hope and light to lift you out."

She was quiet, and he thought she had fallen back to sleep.

"That's beautiful," she murmured however. She turned her face up to look at him. "Are you saying that you see hope and light in me?"

He kissed her forehead. "Like I said," he replied, "it suits you, angel." She smiled and nuzzled back into his shoulder. "Now, go to sleep," he instructed, "unless you want me to take you again."

She smiled and yawned again, clearly on the edge of drifting off. "Tomorrow…" she said, her voice barely audible.

He waited, holding her for about another ten minutes, until he knew she was sound asleep. Sliding his arm out from underneath her, he stood and gathered his belongings to dress. He reached down and kissed her gently one last time on the cheek, knowing that after tomorrow, she'd hate him. The thought tore his heart in two. But it had to be this way.

"You have information," it wasn't a question. Enzo DeGrassi leaned back in the leather chair behind the desk in his luxurious home. He laid his cell on the shiny desk top and placed it on speaker, then folded his hands in front of him touching his two index fingers together in a "steeple" as he waited for a response from the caller.

"Yes," the female voice replied through the phone. The voice was hushed, and Enzo knew the call was coming from inside the palace. "They are aware of your threats," the voice continued, "they don't know what you're planning, but that you're planning something. But you should know the king doesn't seem to take you seriously...." The voice trailed off as though afraid to speak.

Enzo considered this information, it slightly enraging him, and he stood suddenly, rounding his desk. "What about the American?" he asked, "haven't you gotten any information on her yet?"

"There's been nothing so far," the voice insisted, "nothing that we can use."

"You're not looking hard enough," Enzo replied, the frustration now showing through his tone. "I can't just keep playing up the fact that she's American, it'll get old very quickly."

"Why is she so important anyway?" The caller asked. "Who cares what anyone thinks of her. It's the king we should be trying to find information on."

Enzo sighed. *Such incompetence*, he thought with agitation.

"It's clear to anyone who's paying attention that Landino has one weakness," he replied simply and didn't care to elaborate further on the matter. There was a pause and he changed subjects. "Tomorrow is the reception leading up to the parliament conference. I've already taken measures to ensure more than half the parliament members will vote against the monarch's wishes to join the EU. I need you to confirm this will be the case." His instructions were straight to the point.

"How can I do that?" The caller sounded exasperated. "Do you understand the risks I'm taking to get the information that I'm able

83

and then relay it back to you? Romano is being asked to look into your threats, Signore DeGrassi, he is an excellent intelligence advisor. If I were caught…" there was a clear tone of fear in the caller's voice. "You said you were going to find me some help. I can't do what you ask alone," the voice continued in desperation, "I'm close to His Highness, but, you said you could employ someone even closer."

"And I have done so," Enzo said, growing impatient to the caller's concerns. "They will contact you tomorrow during the reception. Also, the reception is a social event," he persisted, "they will all be drinking. All you have to do is play your cards right. Between the both of you, you should be able to secure me the information I require. And I promise you, the reward will be worth the risk."

"What is rigging the vote going to accomplish?" The voice suddenly asked. "Just so the king won't get his way?"

"Don't worry about my agenda," he snapped, annoyed at all the questions. "If you want to be paid, just do what you're told," he paused, "and find something on the American."

Without waiting for a further response, Enzo ended the call. He sighed as he stared blankly at the phone sitting on the desk, doubt setting within him on this person he had enlisted to gather intel from inside the palace. Thank God he had secured someone else in his effort, he thought. As for this other one… they may be more of a liability, and when the time is right, disposed of.

Chapter 9

It was too early yet for the sun. Taya opened her eyes in the stilled darkness of the room. Immediately she knew she was alone. She rolled over onto her back and glanced to her left. No, he wasn't there. She let out a slow sigh in an effort to keep disappointment from consuming her. Should she be surprised? Did the fact that he left mean this was just a one-night stand? Her heart told her no, yesterday was real.

She sat up slowly as images of the previous day leading into the night replayed themselves like a movie in her brain. *What now though?* she wondered. Just thinking of Nicola; how he looked at her, the things he had said to her, the way he held her—it brought a smile to her lips and a race in her heartbeat. Was it too much to hope he still felt the same? She thought of his admission of his feelings to her. But now that he was gone and left her alone, she felt torn and couldn't stop the doubts from creeping in.

She threw the covers off and pulled herself out of bed, grabbing her robe that was flung over the chair, and switching on a side lamp. As she cinched the belt around her waist, she became irritated with herself and a slight frown crossed her face. *This is ridiculous,* she decided. She had spent one day with him after all, last night was just lust. Not to mention, she should be focusing all of her efforts on gathering information to bring back to her party, not falling for the prince… The sudden realization made her sit back down on the bed slowly.

Had she? Fallen for him?

Taya didn't like the sudden surge of emotion coursing through her, nor did she care for the fear it caused. Fear that he might not return her feelings. A sense of urgency now washed over her; she had to find him.

Derek barely looked up from his lap top when his study door swung open unexpectedly.

"Oh, it's you," he commented upon seeing his younger brother enter as he shifted his piercing eyes back to his work.

Nicola didn't respond to the lack of greeting and took a seat in front of the desk. He made eye contact with Costa, who stood, seemingly on guard behind Derek's left.

He waited to speak until Derek decided to acknowledge his presence, which he did after some moments, finally averting his attention to Nicola.

"It's 5:30 a.m.," he observed, "this must be important."

"It is," Nicola replied, his tone serious. "I'm here to begin holding up my end of our bargain," he paused, "and to apologize to you."

Derek's expression remained unreadable. "That's a first," he said as he raised an eye brow. He scrutinized Nicola, picking up on the rare sincerity in his voice and expression. "What exactly are you apologizing for?" Derek's curiosity was peaked at just which infraction his brother had decided to take ownership of.

Nicola stood and ran a hand through his hair. Swallowing his pride in this way had never been easy for him. But, he had made a lot of mistakes, and it was time to grow up and try to move forward.

"I realize now that you were right."

"Another first," Derek interjected, "this must be my lucky day."

Nicola made a face at his brother's sarcasm. "I should've listened to you," he continued, finally his words drawing a slight reaction. "All those times you tried to make me understand to take responsibility, do something with my life," he slumped back into the chair, defeated. "I was a mess after mom died, you know that. The way she died... it was so sudden, and you were the only one left who cared. I didn't listen to you and I'm sorry." There was a heavy silence, and Derek realized that Nicola had something else to say. "I shouldn't have blamed you for taking what was rightfully yours," he admitted quietly, "I would not have succeeded."

Derek took in the weight of what Nicola was saying, knowing his brother, he understood this speech took a lot of effort.

"I appreciate your gesture," he replied, "I'm curious as to what helped you come to this enlightenment."

Nicola knew he would ask, but he wasn't ready to share. Even as he thought of how to answer, Taya's face formed in his mind. He pictured her yesterday, sitting on the picnic blanket, the way she had looked at him when she questioned his ability to take his life seriously.

She hadn't even known the impact she had on him at the time. It was her words to him that made him want to become something more than he was. However much time he had, he knew he needed to make the most of it. Even if he couldn't be with her, at least he could become the kind of man she would have respected.

He averted his gaze to the window, realizing she must be awake by now, wondering why he left, wondering what last night meant to him. It gutted him to know she was most likely an emotional mess right now, and he'd give anything if he could run to her right now.

"It's complicated," was all he answered, then turned back to meet his brother's gaze. "Look, Derek, I know I'm late to grow up, but hey," he smiled, the dimple appearing in his left cheek, "better late than never, right?"

Derek considered his brother. "All right," he said slowly. He was willing to give Nicola a chance; let him earn his place. But it would not be handed to him.

He stood from his desk and walked over to a cabinet, removing a large file folder. Striding back to the desk, he dropped the file in front of Nicola, the weight of the amount of paper evident by the resounding "thud" it made when it landed.

"That," he said, pointing at the stack of paper, "is a hard copy of the negotiations with the EU." He looked Nicola in the eye. "You want a shot? Then I expect you to understand the details by tomorrow so you can attend the conference." He paused to see if Nicola would object or offer an excuse, but his brother remained attentive. "You'll also need to familiarize yourself with the members of parliament before this evening's reception. I believe you're already familiar with one." Nicola clenched his jaw at the implication, and Derek's expression was knowing as he met his brother's eye. "Once you've settled into your own study, you will be given a laptop with access to the information you need."

Nicola nodded and scooped up the stack of paper. He rose to depart, then stopped.

"Derek, I know you've never had a reason to take me seriously before, but I'll do whatever it is I need to do now to fulfill my duty."

He hesitated, debating if he wanted to ask the question he desperately needed the answer to.

"Why can't you just pay off my debt in New York? I will work off every dime," he paused, "and no, it's not so I can just go back to the states."

If Derek would let him off the hook this last time, he had a chance at a future. Enzo would have nothing to hold over him and he wouldn't have to hurt Taya.

Derek stood and looked his brother in the eye, honestly feeling sorry for him. He had deliberately neglected giving Nicola this news, but it seemed he now had no choice.

"I tried, Nic," he replied. Nicola's eyes opened wide. "I even offered them interest. They don't care. You embarrassed them..." Derek trailed off, stalling after seeing his brother's expression turn gaunt. "I wouldn't leave the security of Calina or the guards that protect our monarchy if I were you. There's a price on your head."

Before Nicola could respond to this devastating news which in turn complicated things even more for him, there was a sharp knock on the door. Derek's expression and gaze, one mixed with intensity and remorse, didn't divert from his brother's face as he called out.

"Come in."

With that, the door swung open, revealing the prime minister and a woman in her late-30's that Nicola didn't recognize. He stepped to the side so the party could enter and approach the desk.

"Nicola, this is Rosana Gallo, the monarchy's public relations advisor," Derek introduced the woman once they had bowed their respects and had taken seats.

Mattia looked at Nicola, who still stood next to the desk.

"I'm surprised to see you up bright and early, signore," he said, his voice slightly patronizing.

Nicola knew the prime minister didn't think much of him, and it solidified to him he had much to prove.

"Looks like you're the one who's late," he replied evenly, refusing to be upstaged. His pride had taken enough of a beating for one day. He tucked the file he held firmly under his arm, then moved across the room to the chaise.

Expecting Nicola to depart, Derek's gaze followed his brother's movements as he settled in to begin looking through the file, clearly making everyone aware he wasn't leaving. Derek's eyes narrowed in slight amusement, then he turned his attention to Mattia.

"Well, Luca, you called this meeting. What can I do for you?"

Mattia glanced at Rosana.

The public relations advisor had an impeccable reputation, and she had been in the employ of the monarchy for several years, but now in front of Derek, she appeared timid and lacking confidence. Her hair was a lighter shade of brown, pulled up into a high, sleek ponytail. Her features were rather pointed and petite, and her glasses seemed a bit large for her face.

"Rosana wished for your audience, signore," he explained, "she felt you needed to be aware of the effect certain publicity is having on the people of Calina," he paused, "and the image of the monarchy."

Derek raised his eyebrows in mild interest as he turned his gaze to Rosana, anticipating she did not have good news to share.

"Your Highness," she began, then cleared her throat by means of hesitating, "it's surrounding Signora Dayne. The peoples' opinions of her are very unfavorable." Her brows came together in an apologetic way, clearly indicating she didn't wish to be the one giving him this information. "Not only do they disapprove of an American becoming queen, they don't trust her intentions nor have faith in her abilities to lead the people."

It was no secret to anyone just how devoted Derek was to Christine. He had once before made the decision to abdicate in order to stay with her in the States, and certain citizens took that action as them being "passed over" for her, or that he cared more for her than he did for his country.

Derek had hoped that these rumors and mounting tension surrounding Christine would have died down by now, especially now that she was here with him making public appearances. But unfortunately, it had persisted.

His gut reaction to Rosana's news was to make it clear that he didn't give a fuck, and in his former life, he may have been afforded that luxury. But in his new political environment, his actions and decisions needed to be more diplomatic, especially if he didn't want the outcome to be at Christine's expense.

"Signore," Mattia now interjected, "how the people view the monarchy is crucial to the stability of our country. Think about the history, the scandals, the uncertainty. Adding in the major changes you are looking to make by joining the EU as well," he gave a heavy sigh, unwilling but needing to say what was on his mind, "do you feel your marriage to Christine is in the best interests of the country? If they are already turning on her, it is only a matter of time before they turn against you as well. Is that worth it to you?"

Derek didn't respond immediately, his infamous unreadable expression in place.

"I like Christine," Nicola suddenly offered from where he lounged on the chaise, continuing to pour over the pages in front of him.

The three at the desk turned to look in Nicola's direction, and Derek couldn't suppress a slight smirk at his brother's gall. He turned back to Mattia and Rosana.

"Yes," he answered firmly, "Christine will be a successful queen and leader. I have no doubt. Regardless, I love her, and I will settle for nothing less. You are well aware of this, Luca." He met their eyes, "she's been on our soil for a little over a month," he continued, "hardly time for her to have made any kind of impression based on her actions or statements. The fact that this bad press has continued to plague her leads me to believe that it is being fueled by some unknown and disloyal source."

He drummed his fingers on the desk. "I think it would be in our best interests to find out if that is the case and if so, where is it coming from," he looked pointedly at Mattia now, "before jumping to any conclusions."

Mattia cast his eyes to the ground briefly as Derek continued, "I will maintain a unified and supportive image to my fiancée, and I will expect the same loyalty from those in my employ." He spoke with a finality that put to rest any potential doubts to how he felt about the matter. He stood suddenly as a means of indicating the end of the discussion.

"Of course, signore," Mattia said, now standing as well and giving a slight bow. "You are perhaps correct in thinking there is malicious intent at play. If that is so, my guess would be DeGrassi."

"All the more reason for us to not pay this noise any mind," Derek added, "Romano is still investigating, but I doubt he'll find anything to link DeGrassi to causing a smear campaign against Christine. I, for one, will not cater to the hype." He addressed Rosana, "I'll be looking for some options from you, Rosana. As head of public relations, it's your job to figure out a positive way to combat this issue."

"My team has already begun working on a strategy, Your Highness," Rosana said, "you will continue to be informed of progress and steps taken."

Derek nodded and she bowed her head before turning to depart, Mattia following her out.

Nicola was glad he stuck around to hear this, and it further solidified his impression that Enzo DeGrassi's influence had a very long arm.

"DeGrassi sounds like bad news," he commented, looking to gain any additional information.

Derek looked in Nicola's direction. "He's a nuisance," he replied. "A thorn in my side. His family has been trying to seize power in Calina since day one. He'd do anything to make the monarchy look bad, and he doesn't care who he steps on or destroys."

"Why don't you just have him arrested if you know he's plotting against you," Nicola asked.

"I have no evidence," Derek replied, "no facts."

"Do you need evidence if you're king?" Nicola's question was made in jest, but Derek glanced at him sharply and raised an eye brow.

"Not technically. But, I'm not our father, and I will exhaust efforts to obtain justice in the manner it should be obtained," he said sternly. "Don't you have your own office you can go to?"

Nicola smirked, then shrugged, gathering up the file to make his way to the door.

"Nic," Derek called after him feeling the need to address their interrupted conversation, "about earlier, regarding New York—" but Nicola cut him off.

"It's ok, Derek," he said, "I appreciate all you've done to help me. And I will pay you back," he lifted the file indicating the work to be done, "I guess I need to get used to looking over my shoulder from now on."

Nicola then turned and walked out the door, leaving Derek with Costa still standing behind the desk.

"I want your best man on it," he murmured to the guard, watching his brother depart.

———————

By midday, lunch had been arranged at one of the outdoor terraces in the rose garden. Hoping she might find Nicola there, Taya made her way through the vast hall toward the back of the palace. As she stepped out into the garden, the delicate sweet scent of roses permeated her senses.

She scanned the bistro tables with their umbrellas littered throughout the garden, but there was no sign of Nicola. She took a place at a nearby table, annoyed at the nagging sensation of her chest tightening with anxiety. *Of course he's not avoiding you,* she attempted to convince herself, *he's just busy.* The reception to welcome the parliament members to the palace was this evening after all. An attendant placed tea at her table.

"Mind if I join you?"

Lost in her thoughts, Taya hadn't noticed Christine approaching her.

"Of course, Sig—" she started, then stopped herself recalling her wish to be addressed informally, "Um, Christine." Taya returned her smile as Christine took the chair opposite her.

"I was glad to see you here," she commented, "at least I don't have to eat alone today."

Taya took a sip from her tea as she regarded Christine with interest. "I'm sure His Highness is extremely busy preparing for the reception this evening," she offered, choosing her words to hopefully open the door for information. Christine only nodded as she poured tea into her own cup. "I assume the prince is seeing to arrangements as well," Taya prompted, keeping her tone casual.

Christine looked up from her tea and caught Taya's eyes, seeing the carefully veiled interest within them.

"I haven't seen Nicola," she replied honestly.

She had joined Derek for breakfast in his study around 6:30, but his brother was not there, and Derek had not mentioned him. She meant to ask him about Taya and Nicola's outing the day prior, but Derek had seemed preoccupied, and the subject didn't appear to be important. Now, with Taya in front of her, she couldn't help her curiosity. Especially with the way she kept darting her eyes to look for someone.

"I hope showing him the country wasn't too taxing on you yesterday," she said, wondering if Taya might open up to her. Not only was she intrigued by what transpired between them, Christine couldn't help but miss having someone to talk to. She liked Taya, and thought perhaps, in a normal setting, maybe they could have been friends.

Taya took a bite of the chicken salad placed in front of her before responding.

"Not at all," she replied brightly with a smile, masking any fear or doubt she held concerning her feelings for Nicola. She then briefly gave Christine a seemingly professional account of their whereabouts, and although she mentioned taking him to the festival, there were deliberate omissions.

Even as she spoke, she glanced down at the bracelet wrapped around her wrist, the silver suddenly feeling cold against her skin. The recollection of his manner yesterday now paired with the mixed signals of his absence today caused her facade to slip ever so slightly and she frowned, biting her lip.

Christine recognized the uncertain, fearful look that briefly crossed Taya's face. It was the same expression she would get when she thought of Derek after they had first met. It now dawned on Christine that Taya was deeply infatuated with Nicola, and she pursed her lips with an expression of empathy. But did Taya know what she was getting herself in to? Christine felt an obligation to find out. She didn't want to see Taya get hurt.

"I hope you didn't take anything Nicola might have said to heart," she said.

"What do you mean?" Taya asked slowly in response.

Christine now hesitated. She wanted Taya to be cautioned, but not alarmed. After all, she didn't even know what, if anything, Nicola did.

"He just has a bit of a reputation, that's all," she explained, "he's been known to... not take things seriously." She chose her words carefully, trying to think of a dignified way to tell Taya Nicola was a womanizer. "I guess I just hoped you wouldn't become too offended if he said anything to you that was distasteful."

Unbeknownst to Christine, Taya was doing a very good job of not letting on she momentarily couldn't breathe. What exactly was his "reputation"? She slowly exhaled and sipped her tea in an effort to hide her growing apprehension with Christine's comments launching a million questions now in her mind that she wanted to ask, but knew she couldn't. Was everything he said and did just an act then? Did he say the same things to every woman he was with? She needed to speak to Nicola, desperately needing affirmation from him that he hadn't played her for a fool.

Taya looked back at Christine and smiled. It was clear the future queen was trying to look out for her, and Taya couldn't help but wonder why. After all, she was nothing to Christine—why would she care?

For the first time that morning, Taya pushed aside her focus on her own feelings and looked at Christine, noticing the dark circles under her eyes. *She seems exhausted*, she thought, startled, feeling a stab of sympathy for the American as she realized the pressure and strain she must be under. Taya could only assume it was due to the harsh, and perhaps, unjust, publicity she was currently facing. But she admired Christine's ability to not let the weight of the stress she's bearing affect her outwardly.

"You don't have to worry," Taya replied, retaining her smile, knowing that, even if she wanted to, she couldn't confide in Christine how she was feeling. At least, not yet. "He was a perfect gentleman."

Christine's eyebrows came together and she frowned slightly, not buying a word of Taya's last remark, the lie only solidifying to her that something happened between the two of them.

"That's good to hear," she said, knowing it would be futile to pry. She made to rise from her seat. "Thank you for allowing me to have lunch with you. I'm sure I'll see you in a few hours at the reception?"

Taya also stood and made a slight bow. Each time she encountered Christine, her respect for her grew; she was graceful, charming and honorable. A brief thought occurred to her that she was, in fact, nothing like the tabloids made her out to be.

"I'm looking forward to it," she told Christine, who then smiled and departed.

Taya watched her return back into the palace, the slight limp when she walked serving as a constant reminder to anyone what she had been through. Taya took a deep breath processing what Christine told her about Nicola. At least, she thought, he couldn't hide from her forever. He had to make an appearance at the reception.

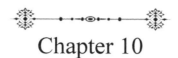

Chapter 10

T hat evening, Taya left her room and headed down the hall toward the second floor ballroom with a determination to find Nicola. Although the reception was just a formality and more of a social event, she still needed to be thinking straight and represent her party with the utmost professionalism. Until she was able to settle her mind (and heart) about Nicola, however, she could concentrate on nothing else.

She chose a simple but elegant jumpsuit to wear with a halter-style top and a scarf tie at the waist. The wide-leg style of the suit allowed the soft material to sway with her movements, and it was a dark green color which set off her eyes. Her hair was down in loose waves, and the cascading blond strands partially hid her provocative bare back. As she now entered the reception, she held her head high in confidence, her eyes scanning the small crowd beginning to gather.

The Calean palace did not boast outlandish grandeur, however, this smaller ballroom where the event was to take place was perhaps the most extravagant room in the palace. From its beautifully designed hardwood parquet floor to the hand-painted intricate details of the plaster molding throughout the ceiling, it was more consistent with the flair of the 200 year old architecture of its time. The wooden paneling and trim were of a darker shade and stretched up the sides of the 20 foot walls to the cathedral ceiling. The chandeliers were gold which matched the sconces placed on either sides of the large doors and windows, the style ornate and just a touch gaudy. Luxurious mauve velvet drapes framed each of the French styled window panes, several of which opened up onto balconies looking out over the back of the palace. The room held a sense of splendor and pride, seeped in history. It was only fitting that parliament met here for social occasions or times of celebration, as the monarchy itself was established and agreed upon by Caleans in this very same room.

There were ten parliament members, five each representing the two major political parties in Calina. Most of the members held longevity within the government, the years of holding their positions spanning decades and before them, their fathers held the same seats. But there were a select few, Taya included, who were newly elected, the opportunities to hold a seat stemming from Derek's own dismissal of corrupt members once he took the throne.

Taya was one of only two women who served her country in this way and she was the youngest. As such, she took her duty to serve the people seriously. For professional reasons, as well as deeply seated personal ones, she desired to prove herself.

Aside from the members themselves, certain guests of parliament were also permitted to attend tonight's social function, but even so, the affair would be exclusive and intimate. Top shelf liquor and fine wine would pour freely, and everyone was dressed to impress as members tried to network their way into uncovering the agendas of their rivals. Taya had been cautioned by the senior members of her party to be on her guard, but tonight, she couldn't help but try and push an agenda of her own. One that had nothing to do with politics.

As she entered further, her heart skipped a beat as she finally spotted Nicola next to Derek on the other side of the room. Several men from the King's Guard were stationed nearby, and guests had formed around the monarch and the prince, attempting to greet and rub elbows. Of course Derek would be introducing Nicola to the members as they appeared, and if Taya wanted to gain his attention, she would have no choice but to try and join the "receiving line."

She maneuvered her way through the room, dodging groups of people and the palace staff who were passing through holding trays of wine, champagne, and delicacies. Taya noticed Irena Nucci, efficient as always, giving directions and seeing to details, as well as the attendant she practically collided with outside Derek's office. The young, blonde maid was smiling cheerfully as she worked diligently, seeing to the needs of the guests. The girl's manner made Taya stop for a moment, and it occurred to her, watching her interact with an older, well-established parliament member, that her behavior was a bit *too* friendly. But Taya reasoned, quickly dismissing the scene with a shake of her head, this was a social event and stranger things had happened. God only knew how many times she had been hit on by drunk, older men of power.

Taya reset her sights on Nicola, blatantly ignoring several people who smiled at her by means of greeting or to begin a conversation. As she got closer to him her stomach flipped, nerves threatening to overwhelm her. Considering what they had shared mere hours ago, why did she feel so scared?

His image halted her breathing; he wore an all black tailored suit, emphasizing the broadness of his shoulders, and the tall, lean form of his body. He was always dapper, and tonight was no exception for Nicola, his presence commanded attention assisted by the royal blue sash under his jacket which clearly indicated his position and authority.

She watched as he shook hands and smiled his charming smile, but his manner gave her pause as well. This was not the Nicola she knew from yesterday. She half expected to find a bored expression on his face or some kind of smirk, maybe even complaining he had to be present at all. Instead he was attentively listening to a senior member, narrowing his eyes in interest, asking questions in turn, then graciously turning to the next guest vying for his time; in short, he was acting like a politician. Taya wasn't sure if she was more alarmed or impressed, and as much as his behavior seemed foreign to her, she had also predicted from the start that he had this natural political talent within him.

His dark eyes met hers as she approached him, and she watched his face carefully as his gaze briefly surveyed down the length of her body. Although he hid his reaction to seeing her well, she recognized that look of hunger, and the knot held within her chest loosened just slightly; he still found her desirable at least. But he did not smile nor move to embrace her, and he did not seem "happy." She stopped in front of him, waiting to see if he might speak first. When he didn't, she had no choice but to bow her head to him.

"Your Highness," she greeted stoically. It was clear he did not wish to acknowledge their acquaintance publicly.

"It's nice to see you, Ms. Mariano," he replied professionally.

She lifted her eyes back to his, his game now beginning to annoy her. At the very least, Taya felt, he owed her an explanation—and she was resolved to get it. She placed a hand lightly on his arm.

"Do you mind if we speak, signore?"

The smile on her face didn't reach her eyes, and immediately Nicola knew he could not deny her request. He nodded once, and as she turned her heel to leave their small group, he followed, glancing around discreetly to see who might be watching them.

Not seeing anyone take particular interest in their departure, he allowed her to lead him to the edge of the room, out of earshot from the other guests. And why would anyone care if he left briefly to discuss business with a parliament member, he assured himself, it was only natural. He just needed to ensure that was what anyone who saw them together assumed as well. He knew he could hide his feelings for her outwardly for only a short time, otherwise, anyone looking at them would know how much he cared for her.

She stopped and turned to face him. He couldn't help but see the hopeful look in her eyes. Knowing he was about to hurt her destroyed him, even if it was for her own safety that no one guessed what she meant to him. He breathed in her perfume, wanting nothing more than to pin her against the wall and claim her with passion. However, he needed to bury those instincts, as well as surfacing images from last night, deep down. Instead, he drew from his vast experience he had with rejecting women and raised an eyebrow at her, regarding her with an uninterested expression.

"You wanted to speak with me, Taya?" he asked, not an ounce of emotion in his voice.

"I thought I would have heard from you today," she replied, trying to hold his eyes, but his gaze looked out over her, scanning the room. Secretly, he was searching for anyone watching them interact, but his wandering eye only reinforced to Taya that he did not wish to be with her.

"I was busy," he said nonchalantly with a shrug, his eyes refocusing on her now, "I thought you, of all people, would understand my position and the importance of this event."

She cast her eyes downward, his tone was sharp and his callous dismissal stung. There was no warmth in his expression; he was clearly regretting their involvement, deciding afterward that he felt nothing for her. She tried to wrap her brain quickly around his rejection.

"Of, of course," she stammered quietly.

He could tell she was losing her nerve. Damnit, he hadn't expected this reaction from her. Taya was strong and independent, and he had anticipated that she would just tell him to go to hell. But this...

She couldn't walk away from him distraught, with tears in her eyes. Everyone would know they were involved. Her unexpected reaction made him feel even worse, and he knew he had to make her angry. At least if she despised him, she could move on quickly. Hating what he was about to do, he reached for her chin, giving it a tweak, and she lifted her face back up to him, her eyes glassy.

"Hey," he said, a wicked grin playing across his lips, "why the sad face? Last night was a riot, wasn't it?"

She blinked, the tears threatening her eyes were gone, replaced instead by rage welling up within them.

"So I was just a laugh for you?" She hissed, her voice practically shaking, "a good time?" Her eyes now bore into his. "You didn't mean anything you said to me?"

His response was to wink at her. "Come on," he coaxed, "tell me you didn't enjoy yourself." His cockiness stunned her into a brief silence. *Time to end this*, he thought sadly. He leaned closer to her and lowered his voice. "Don't worry," he leered at her, "I'd recommend your tour to anyone who comes to visit."

Taya's expression turned to outrage and horror at his implication, and Nicola saw it coming. Maybe it was because he had seen the same look many times before, but due to his experience with being slapped, his reflexes were sharp, and he caught her wrist hard before her palm made contact with his cheek. His eyes darted, once again looking to see if they were drawing attention. He narrowed his gaze upon her as he held on to her arm, the squeezing pressure almost painful to her.

"Careful, angel," he said now, his expression dead serious, "I'm pretty sure assaulting the monarchy could get you arrested."

She wrenched her wrist from his grasp.

"Funny how you use your title when it conveniences you," she spat at him.

She gave him one last hateful glare, then turned away, walking back into the crowd. He watched her go then closed his eyes briefly.

"I'm so sorry," he whispered to himself after her. But at least she would be safe. He grabbed a glass of whiskey off a tray passing in front of him, and downing the entire drink, he strolled over to rejoin Derek.

Once again meandering her way across the room, attempting to put as much physical distance as she could between herself and Nicola, Taya now made a bee-line for the open balcony. She felt as though she were suffocating; she just needed some fresh air so she could calm down. *Goddamn him!* she screamed internally.

As she reached the balcony, an attendant handed her a wine glass, which she gladly accepted, the sweet taste helping to placate her rising blood pressure. She sipped the wine again, then breathed in the cool, night air, her emotions caught somewhere between sobbing and raging. No, she couldn't break down here. How could she have misread someone so completely? Was he just that good at playing the game? Deciding that yes, she had been very stupid, she took a larger gulp of her wine and pushed Nicola from her thoughts for the time being. Having one's heart ripped out was not an excuse to not fulfill one's duty, and Taya now focused her mind on the event and its purpose.

She needed to be making connections, and as the newest member of parliament, she should be making her presence and objectives known. As she turned away from the balcony's edge to reenter the reception, she saw a man striding toward her.

He was younger than most of the guests here, his straight black hair was neat and short, the longer strands on top brushed back. His eyes were a golden brown and crinkled at the corners when he smiled as he approached. He was boyishly handsome, a slight dimple in his strong chin, and she furrowed her brow, trying to place his face. Was he in parliament?

"You're Taya Mariano, correct?" He smiled warmly and outstretched his hand to her.

She shook his hand firmly, it finally dawning on her who he was.

"Yes, and you're Bryan LaPointe," she replied, returning his smile professionally.

Bryan, she recalled, was a newer member like she was, and she had heard his name far more than she had seen his face. He supported the opposing party and he maintained a strong reputation. Seeming to have come out of virtually nowhere when running for political office, Bryan had climbed the ranks quite rapidly, and many whispered about just where his financial backing came from given that he claimed no ties to any of the prominent Calean families. But his good looks, sincere speeches, and law background won over the people within his district, and he was voted into his seat by a landslide victory.

He nodded, affirming her guess, continuing to smile at her.

"You should mingle," he observed, "an event like this has a lot to offer, especially considering the gravity of the conference tomorrow."

"I am mingling. I'm talking to you, aren't I?" Taya took another sip from her glass, her eyes not leaving his face.

He gave a laugh and raised his glass in a mock toast. "How did I get so lucky?"

She lifted her eye brows. "It's lucky to speak to me?"

He shrugged slightly. "Well, aside from being the most beautiful woman here, it seems you're also well connected. You were speaking to prince Nicola in confidence, were you not?"

Taya narrowed her eyes, seeing his flattery as a ruse to butter her up—he thought she was important because he saw her talking to Nicola.

"Believe me," she began coldly, "speaking with that—," but she caught herself. She closed her mouth quickly, scolding herself for almost vocalizing her distaste for Nicola to another member of parliament. Regardless of her personal feelings, he was still the prince. "His Highness," she corrected, "does not make me well connected. I was merely hoping to gain some insights into what the king was planning to present tomorrow so that I could better prepare some questions or arguments if necessary."

Bryan gave another nod in understanding. "I see," he replied, the light from the room catching a golden speck in his eye, "and I'm assuming you learned nothing new?"

"Why would you assume that?" she asked curious.

"Well, you appeared quite," he paused, "dissatisfied, before I walked up."

Color began to rise in Taya's cheeks, and she placed a look of indifference on her face. The last thing she needed was for anyone to think that Nicola had gotten the better of her, in *any* way.

"Perhaps I was slightly disappointed," she admitted, "but, I guess we'll all just hear what the king has to say tomorrow." She now offered Bryan a wide smile, which he returned.

"I'm looking forward to it," he replied, taking a step closer to her, "maybe afterward we can compare notes."

Taya's eyes widened at his comment. Being from opposing parties, there would be no benefit to collaborate after tomorrow's conference. Was he asking her out? Unsure of his intentions, Taya gave him a noncommittal answer.

"Oh, um sure," she hesitated, "maybe?"

Bryan chuckled at her response. "Sounds like a date to me," and his eyes seemed to twinkle. "Come on, let's rejoin the others, shall we?"

Taya nodded slowly, regarding him with cautioned interest, and allowed Bryan to lead her back into the ballroom. She needed to make contact with her senior colleagues anyway, and Bryan was a popular member right now. It wouldn't hurt to be seen with him here tonight.

As he guided her over to a small group near a table, he lightly placed his hand on the small of her back, where she immediately tensed when his fingertips brushed her bare skin. He promptly removed his hand, and as certain as she was it was just a friendly gesture, she was nowhere near prepared to entertain any thoughts other than professional ones.

On the outside, she kept her demeanor cool and collected, inside however, she was unraveling at a rapid pace, practically crumbling. Perhaps tonight, when she was alone back in her room, she could untangle all the emotions she needed to hold in right now. Perhaps tonight, her mask could come down, and she would let out all the tears, coming face to face for the first time with a broken heart.

She thought of going back to her cold room after the event was over, knowing that just being there would bring back memories from the previous night.

Although she continued to masterfully plaster a smile on her face as she interacted with other guests, it hurt just to breathe. She just had to get through this evening, then she could return home tomorrow and do her best to move on. How long would it take, she wondered, how long before she felt normal again?

"Derek, who is that?" Nicola's voice was low and laced with a slight edge of malice.

Derek turned to his brother and raised an eyebrow, then followed his gaze across the room to observe Taya Mariano smiling and laughing with Bryan LaPointe. He looked back at Nicola, eyeing him.

"I assume you mean the man with Ms. Mariano? That is Bryan LaPointe, a newer parliament member with the *Partito Lealista*."

"The Loyalists?" Nicola responded. "So, he would favor the monarchy?"

"Traditionally." Derek replied. "The Loyalists tend to side with platforms that support the wishes of the monarchy and are responding positively to joining the EU."

"Wouldn't it be unusual for him to be taking such an interest in Taya considering their opposing views?" Nicola raised his whiskey glass to his lips, appearing to be only curious with no ulterior motives to his questions, but Derek saw through it.

"Not necessarily," he replied watching Nicola's expression closely. "If he were trying to gain insights into her vote, he may approach her, *or*," he paused with emphasis as Nicola met his eye, "he may just think she's attractive." He looked back toward Bryan and Taya, unable to keep the smirk off his face. "They look good together, don't you think?"

Nicola didn't reply, but his jaw clenched.

"Anyway, why do you care?" Derek asked knowingly.

"I don't," Nicola replied quickly, his fingers gripping the glass in his hand tightly. He then turned and walked away from Derek toward the nearest drink tray.

He had no right for it to bother him upon seeing Taya with another man.

But it did. It bothered him a great deal.

The reception had ended, and it was nearing midnight as Derek was wrapping up in his study to retire for the night. Long had he discarded his jacket and royal sash to a chair. Choosing to work the rest of the night in semi-comfort, he now had the crisp, white sleeves of his shirt rolled up and collar open. His expression was set pensively, yet signs of weariness showed on his chiseled features as he left the study, locking the door behind him. It had been a long day, and tomorrow would be longer still.

He made his way down the hall, stopping at the turn-off toward the west wing when a light caught his eye coming from Nicola's study. *Was Nic actually still working?* he thought, and his curiosity overpowered his tiredness.

Nicola's study door was ajar, and Derek rapped on it once with his knuckle before pushing the door open and entering. Not seeing his brother at his desk, his eyes scanned the room, and he spotted him seated in a chair over by the wet bar, a drink in his hand.

The room was quiet and Nicola remained still as Derek approached. He sighed and took a seat across from him. Nicola did not acknowledge that Derek was there, and Derek recognized the dazed and sullen expression. Derek had only ever been afflicted by a broken heart once, and he did not envy his brother's current state.

"She means a great deal to you, doesn't she," he said with empathy.

Nicola snapped his gaze to Derek, his eyes were bloodshot with intoxication. "Who?"

Derek leaned back in his chair. "Play games if you like," he said. "I saw the way you looked at her. You were with her all day yesterday—come to think about it, no one knows of your whereabouts last night, yet you come to meet me bright and early this morning with an apology?" He raised his eyebrows with a knowing look on his face. "I also saw the way you reacted to seeing her interact with another man." Derek paused then continued, "not to mention the way she looked at you this evening. Like she hated your guts." He leaned forward resting his forearms on his knees and laced his fingers together. "What exactly happened between the two of you?"

Through the sea of alcohol, Nicola attempted to process Derek's queries. A slight panic rose within him; Derek was uniquely astute, but, if he could piece together how he felt about Taya, was it obvious to anyone? Of course, no one but Derek knew he was drowning his sorrows right now.

"It's none of your business," was all he responded with, taking another drink from his glass.

"Well, it's kind of my business," Derek replied calmly, "this sort of 'drama' is not permitted nor welcome within the government."

"This will not impact the monarchy," Nicola said dryly. He pushed her away to make sure of that. Whatever DeGrassi was playing at, his schemes that were certain to eventually impact the monarchy would not be at Taya's expense.

He rose and took the few steps over to the bar, stumbling on the last. "Why don't you join me? I hate to drink alone."

His words were somewhat slurred, and Derek surmised he had been drinking for some time. It took quite a lot to inebriate his brother to this degree.

Nicola turned back to him, "oh, right," he added, bottle in hand, "you're still a dry one, aren't you?"

Derek didn't respond right away, only regarded Nicola intensely. He had no inclination of discussing his choices to abstain from alcohol, and he didn't like where he foresaw the direction of this conversation going.

"You should go to bed, Nic," he said.

Nicola just laughed. "You know, you're just letting him win by making your choices based on what he was and what he did." Nicola swayed slightly where he stood by the bar, spilling the whiskey a bit as he poured it into his glass. Derek remained silent, refusing to take the bait. Nicola continued, "it's been 16 years since mom died," and a sadness now filled his voice. He looked back at Derek, "you know there was nothing you could have done right?"

Derek raked a hand through his hair and sighed. Yes, 16 years since his mother had died, and he had not thought about that night in almost that entire time.

When Derek was 15, his mother had remarried in New York, his step-father turning out to be just as ruthless as his real one. Only instead of taking his need for control out on a small country, Dean only had him and his mother. Nicola was 11 at the time, and Derek did whatever he could to protect him from their step-father's drunken wrath, which included practically throwing him out of the house.

He made sure his younger brother always had somewhere to go or someone else to be with. From an early age, Nicola learned to rely on his trust fund to go places and buy friends—a habit that stayed with him most of his life. Spoiled and entitled, but at least he had been safe.

After five years of suffering and begging his mother to leave, things escalated when Dean came home one evening particularly drunk and began to lay into her. Nicola had been out partying with friends, and now at 20, Derek had decided he and his mother had endured enough. If he knew then how that night was going to end, he would have never confronted his step-father regardless of how brutal he was. If he had made different choices, maybe his mother would still be alive.

"You weren't there," Derek replied, the years of mastering the ability to maintain a straight face regardless of the emotional turmoil he was facing was paying off for him now. "I made sure you weren't there."

"What do you mean, you made sure?" Nicola questioned. "I went to a party the night mom died."

Derek grimaced. "A party I secured your invitation to."

A confused look crossed Nicola's face. "I don't understand," he said quietly, "tell me what happened."

Derek took in a slow breath. Maybe it was time. Maybe he could share some of it.

"That night…" he began but paused. He didn't want to share his most painful memory; he had never intended for her to get hurt. "I knew it was only a matter of time before I stood up to him," he tried again, "I should've done it sooner, or maybe not at all, but I knew if I were going to face him, it had to be done when you wouldn't be around. I just wish I had taken steps to protect mom too…" his voice cracked, and Nicola's brow furrowed, his mouth slightly parted as he listened. "Dean and I fought," Derek continued, "I really thought I was going to put him in his place, that I could make him leave. But he landed a blow and I lost my balance," his eyes diverted, recalling how he fell when his step-father knocked him down. It was only for a moment, but it was enough to make his mother attack Dean. To protect her son.

"Mom was there, she tried to intervene. She got in the way, and he backhanded her shoving her into the fireplace. She fell and hit her head…" Derek stopped for a moment, his mind on replay of the images of that night; the bloody gash in her head, the exact moment he saw his mother die. "I rushed to her, but she was already gone. Dean seemed to be in shock, but he didn't look sorry."

A look of renewed hatred crossed Nicola's face for his step-father.

"I called the police after that," Derek said, "they came and took statements of course. Dean was finally out of our lives soon after that. He didn't even go to her funeral." His tone was wistful as he finished.

Nicola's expression turned somber. All these years, he had only been able to guess what happened that night. When he had returned home, Derek had given him the news that their mother passed away after hitting her head on the fireplace.

"I wasn't there," Nicola acknowledged, "But, I know you, and I know you would have done anything in your power to save her."

The gravity of the conversation caused him to sober up a bit. Derek had never spoken before about their mother's death, and it gave Nicola a small sense of closure.

"I still don't understand how that bastard got away with it," he murmured, retaking his seat across from Derek. "The cops called it an accident, but Dean was never suspected of causing her death. He was never even questioned."

Derek stayed quiet, his expression unreadable, and he had deliberately omitted certain facts about what happened after their mother died. Although it was true, there was never legal justice for her death or the abuse they endured, he still found a way to get Dean out of their lives for good.

"Although," Nicola continued, "I didn't understand why he left after she died. He was still technically our step-father. Mom was shrewd with the family's money, but she had to have left him something. Why would he have just skipped town? I always thought he had to have felt guilty…"

He trailed off as a realization dawned on him; his step-father was not the type of person to have a conscience. He would have stayed for the money, so leaving would not have been voluntary.

Even at just 20 years old back then, Derek had already established not only wealth, but a solid reputation in their community and city. His connections ran deep, as did his supporters and investors. If he had wanted Dean to go to jail for causing their mother's death, he could have seen to it that it happened. The fact that the incident was labeled an accident and their step-father seemingly up and left one day led Nicola to only one conclusion.

He looked Derek in the eye, and a shadow seemed to pass over his brother's face. "What did you do to him?"

Derek frowned. "I don't know what you're talking about," he replied evenly. But Nicola read it knowingly within his eyes.

Derek reached over to Nicola, removing the glass from his hand. "But you're right. He is why I don't drink, and never will. And, you're done tonight, Nic, go to bed," he repeated. He then rose from his chair, poured the rest of the whiskey down the sink drain and left Nicola alone in his study.

Nicola watched Derek leave, understanding the lengths his older brother had gone to, and would go to, to protect his family.

Derek bolted upright in bed. It seemed he had just barely fallen into a restless sleep. He listened intently and heard nothing. It was dark and still; the dead of night. But, something had woken him. He grabbed his watch from the nightstand while running a hand over his tired features: 1:10 a.m.

Suddenly, he heard it again: an ear piercing scream coming from down the hall. Instinctively, horror washed over him.

Oh my God, he realized, *Christine!*

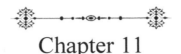

Chapter 11

Without thinking twice, Derek dashed from his bed, neglecting to throw a robe on over his bare shoulders. He swung open his bedroom door in an effort to get to Christine as quickly as possible, his mind frantically trying to find a reasonable explanation as to why she might be screaming as though she were being assaulted.

How could anyone get inside the palace? he raged. Was the palace under some kind of attack and if so, where were the guards?

As if on cue, in his haste to enter the hall, Derek practically collided with Costa who had ostensibly also been alerted to the distress coming from Christine's room. To ensure security, the monarch's personal guard, as well as Christine's attendant, shared quarters within the same wing, and Olivia now emerged from her room as well, a shocked and scared look on her face.

"Signore, wait, it's not safe!" Costa exclaimed as he grabbed Derek's arm in an effort to gain ground and reach the threat first. But Derek was not to be deterred and pulled free from Costa's grasp as he sprinted down the hall toward Christine's room, the other two right on his heels. As he reached her door, a softer cry came from inside, sounding almost as though she were weeping.

Without hesitation, Derek shoved open her door expecting to find some unknown assailant, and he was prepared to defend. However when his eyes darted around the room, what he found instead made him stop in his tracks: there was no one. Only Christine, standing in the middle of her bedroom, hugging her arms and sobbing. She didn't look up when Derek entered, and Costa and Olivia now stood behind him, also staring at her with the same confused expressions on their faces. Derek stepped into the room approaching her cautiously.

"Christine?" His voice was soft, a concerned look crossing his features. But, Christine didn't show any signs of being alerted to his presence or that three people had just burst into her room. *She's sleepwalking*, Derek realized, and he heard a faint beeping coming from her cell on the nightstand. *An alarm?*

Suddenly, many pieces began to fall into place in his mind. He considered her constant fatigue as of late, her distance from him, her continued unhappiness; she was being tormented by the events of their recent past, and suffering from night terrors. *Did this happen every night?* He wondered. Why had she kept this from him?

He wasn't sure if the right thing to do was to wake her or not, but he couldn't allow her to continue in her current state. He reached out to her, gently grabbing her shoulders.

"Christine," he repeated, more loudly. She reacted upon feeling his touch, and she cried out, struggling and straining against his hands in an effort to break free from him. He tightened his grasp, afraid if he let go of her, she'd hurtle herself into something. "Christine, stop!" he said forcefully, and he was shocked at the amount of strength she was exerting against him.

"No! Please!" She shrieked, clearly still caught in the traumatizing images she thought were real as she fought against him.

"Wake up, Christine, open your eyes," he commanded, grabbing hold of both her wrists, "look at me." He shook her in his efforts to make her come to, and as her body went slack, he caught her before she fell to the floor.

Her energy now spent, her eyes suddenly flew open. A sheen of sweat formed along her forehead and she shivered. She gazed at him for a second, unfocused, but as she began to realize where she was, a terrified look crossed her face.

All he could do was stare at her for several seconds, wondering why she chose to go through this by herself. She must have felt his disappointment, and a few real tears began to slide down her cheek. He cradled her body, supporting her, and as she found her legs underneath her, he released her.

She backed away from him, uncertain how to explain, instead diverting her eyes to the floor. She hadn't heard her alarm go off tonight, she must have grown too accustomed to it. She sighed, knowing this had to end at some point, she just wished he hadn't found out this way.

She moved over to the nightstand, her legs still trembling and turned off her phone, then she turned back to face him, wondering why he wasn't interrogating her yet. And damn that expression of his that made it impossible to tell what was going through his mind!

"Are you ok?" he finally said, "are you hurt?"

She shook her head, then glancing past him, she realized Costa and Olivia were also in the room.

"I'm sorry, Derek," was all she could say. Her voice was strained, and she felt torn between shame and pride. She did what she thought was best for her—she hadn't been ready to share this with anyone. Did she really owe anyone an explanation right now?

As if also remembering they had an audience, Derek turned to face Costa and Olivia.

"Please return to your rooms," he said, "I will ensure everything is all right."

Olivia immediately bowed and retreated hastily, Costa however looked uncertain. He hesitated just a moment, glanced at Christine, then back to Derek.

"As you wish, signore," he stated, then bowed his head before departing.

Once they were alone, Derek approached Christine.

"You've been suffering for some time," he stated, not bothering with questions he already knew the answer to. She nodded again. "Christine, why didn't you tell me?"

"I was scared," she whispered, finally looking into his eyes, pleading through them for him to understand. His response was only to embrace her, wrapping his arms around her shoulders and bringing her tight against him.

She nuzzled against his chest, listening to the sound of his heartbeat, the steady rhythm soothing her own. She took in a deep breath, feeling comforted by the warmth of his smooth, bare skin and powerful, defined form. Even in this moment of uncertainty and in the dead of night, wearing nothing except a pair of flannel pajama pants, she couldn't deny how alluring he was. Or how much she needed him. He held her for a moment, then pulled back from her slightly.

"Christine, you can tell me anything," he began, brushing back a few strands of her hair with his fingertips. "If anyone could understand why you're going through this, it would be me," he took a breath and looked into her hazel eyes, "I can't help but feel this is my fault. You have to let me be there for you."

She furrowed her brow, she couldn't let him blame himself. "What happened wasn't your fault, Derek," she replied quietly, "the people to blame are dead or behind bars. I never for one second blamed you or resented you. I just haven't been able to personally get beyond the trauma," she raised her chin a bit in defiance, "but I will." And her promise was more to herself than to him.

"Then you have to trust me," he said, "we're both harboring guilt that we need to let go of, and I can't until I know you trust me. Keeping this from me..." he trailed off feeling pained at knowing after everything, she was still afraid of him.

"It's not that," she insisted, shaking her head, "you don't understand." She grabbed his hand and squeezed it, as if the touch could convey to him what she was feeling.

"Since the shooting I developed post-traumatic stress disorder," she explained, "the anxiety was bad, and I would have nightmares, but when I agreed to marry you..." she hesitated and met his eyes timidly, "it escalated. The dreams became more real. I began sleepwalking and crying out. I thought I was going insane, and it felt like the closer I got to you, the more crazy I would become." She could no longer hold his gaze, and her eyes fell to the floor. "And I didn't want everyone to know I was crazy. Or weak."

Derek was quiet for a moment as he digested what she was telling him. He suddenly narrowed his eyes and ran a hand through his hair. Why did she not see what was obvious?

"Christine," and she looked back up at him, "we're not close," he stated. Her mouth opened slightly at his response. "We're engaged, and I love you, but you've been pushing me away for the past two months." She was ready to respond, but he refused to let her. "Didn't it occur to you that since we found each other again, the reason these night terrors have gotten worse isn't because we're becoming closer, but because you're shutting me out?"

Her eyes widened at his thought process. No, she hadn't thought of it that way, but it made sense to her now hearing it out loud.

As she stayed quiet, he could tell she was thinking of a way to object to his reasoning. Impatient at the thought of her just being stubborn, he decided enough was enough. He wasn't going to let her rationalize her distance any longer. He sighed and bent forward, effortlessly lifting her off her feet.

"What are you doing?" She exclaimed, having no choice except to cling onto his shoulders as he began to stride toward her door, carrying her in his arms out into the hallway. "Where are you taking me?"

"Where you belong," he stated matter-of-fact.

He carried her down the hall and into his room, then once inside, set her back down on her feet. "This is where you'll be staying from now on," he told her as he shut the door. He then approached her and placed his hands gently on her arms, drawing her closer. His tone dropped, "and I don't want to hear a word about appearances."

Christine could only stare at him wide-eyed, feeling quite literally swept off her feet. She glanced around the room; she had not yet seen the master palace suite. Like everything else in the palace, it was large and ornate, and she quickly surmised her whole apartment back in North Carolina would easily fit inside this one room.

There was a grand marble fireplace, a sitting area and separate rooms for the bath and vanity. The decor matched the old world traditional styles as was prominent throughout the palace with its wide use of marble, mahogany, velvet and silk. Christine concluded that although, of course, the room was beautiful, it also lacked character or personalization. She shrugged.

"I suppose this will have to do," she offered him a smile, "for now anyway."

"You can do anything you want with it," he said, "it's yours now."

"Well, it's ours," she corrected him. Her face grew serious, "what if I still continue to have nightmares?"

He looked at her with tenderness. "Then I'll be here to help you through it," he replied, "I want to be there for you, and I will ensure you feel safe."

He brushed her soft hair back with his fingers, letting them graze the side of her cheek. Cupping her jaw, he brought her lips up to meet his, his mouth lingered lightly on hers at first, then seized her with passion robbing her of her breath. His hands pulled her body flush against his, and he griped the satin material of the camisole she wore. He broke the kiss and looked into her eyes.

"Christine," he whispered, "I need you." He hesitated for an objection, but when he saw only desire in her eyes, he bent his head to nuzzle into her neck.

Her body was practically crushed against his, and she could feel his want in the tenseness of his muscles and rapid pounding of his heartbeat. Breaking free from his vice-grip, she turned from him to walk towards the bed in the center of the vast room. No sooner had she left his embrace, however, he reclaimed his hold on her from behind, his strong arms circling around her waist pulling her back into him. He nipped her ear with his teeth. She reached up with one hand around his neck and looked over her shoulder at him, giving him a demure smile.

"You seem eager," she said softly.

He narrowed his eyes slightly, a half smirk playing on his lips. "You know how long I've waited." His voice was low and coarse as he grasped the bottom of her camisole, pulling it off over her head.

His hands smoothed down her hair, brushing it back off her shoulders, before trailing them down to caress her breasts. She leaned back into him and let out a moan at his touch. He bent and picked her up again as he had before and carried her the few feet to the bed. He laid her down, then promptly removed her shorts and panties. Standing up straight, he looked down on her, admiring every inch of her beauty.

Her eyes met his, and she saw an intense heat burning in his gaze. He made her feel loved and wanted, and she knew she needed this from him right now. Freeing himself from his pajama pants, he joined her, positioning himself over her. Her thighs cradled his waist, and her breathing labored in anticipation. It had been so long since she had been with him—she knew this time would feel like the first. He lowered his head first, bringing his mouth to capture hers in a tender kiss.

"I love you so much," he whispered, "you're everything to me."

She weaved her fingers through his hair.

"I love you too—ah," and her words to him caught in her throat as he entered her then. The initial thrust was powerful but sweet, catching her momentarily off guard, but quickly her mind went to that place of pure ecstasy only he could take her. He stilled, then began to move slowly as her body responded and remembered him again.

"God, I've missed you," she whispered.

The pleasure began to build, and Christine felt like she was thrown backwards in time, to a time when all that mattered was the fact that they loved each other, and it meant they could get through anything together.

Her thoughts became numb, and she gave herself, mind, heart and soul over to the soft commands of his body and what it needed from her. She knew she would rest later tonight; Derek would make sure of it.

———————

"How could this happen?" Nicola hissed at Derek, as the two walked side by side in haste, with the prime minister following close behind. The three were surrounded by guards as they made their way from the conference hall toward Derek's study.

The conference had ended. After an eight hour meeting where each party had shared their opposing views, followed by another three hours of heated debate, the parliament members had agreed to then vote; which resulted in a tie. Five of the members had voted to join the European Union, while the other five had not. The outcome had caused an immediate uproar amongst the members, and regardless of how the prime minister had attempted to control or calm down the outbursts and arguments, it had been in vain. Mainly because many members did not vote according to what seemed natural for their parties' views.

Derek had felt confident going in that at least seven members would vote in favor of joining, and with Taya's vote, (which he had not been counting on), it should have been a shoe-in. But three additional members had made surprising decisions. It was impossible to tell if they had been corrupted or had made their choices based on their own pure beliefs.

It wasn't long before some of the members had begun to show aggression, their shouting quickly turned to shoving. Meanwhile, others had attempted to break up any physical outbreak, and they were thrown back into onlookers. Derek had watched the scene unfold with a tense jaw until deciding to call in the guard to handle the situation, coming to the sad conclusion the members themselves would not be able to gain back control.

Once the guard came in however, the hostility had focused on him with accusations thrown his way for even putting the country in this position. He, Nicola, and the prime minister had been immediately surrounded by Costa, Nicola's personal guard, Stefan Martino, as well as others, and then ushered from the hall while the guard was left to deal with the aggressors.

Derek gave a heavy sigh.

"I don't know," he now answered his brother slowly. The truth was, he had been not only shocked at the outcome of the tie vote, but deeply dismayed by the inability of some members to maintain any kind of composure: their actions going beyond disappointment. Although he knew tension was mounting among the people surrounding this issue, this was a clear indication of just how much. Everyone seemed at breaking point.

They had reached his study, and the three men entered followed by Costa and Martino.

"Please go find Christine," he instructed Costa, "if she's not in her room, escort her to it. I don't want her anywhere near the vicinity of that clusterfuck down there."

Costa nodded his head then bowed. "Yes, signore," he said, then departed.

Derek turned to Nicola. "I'm sure Taya is fine," he said under his breath.

Nicola clenched his jaw. It was true, he had been horrified to see Taya thrown into the fray amongst the pushing and shouting, and he had felt helpless at not being able to protect her. She had not been engaging in the rough housing, but had been collateral damage, and at one point he saw her inadvertently shoved to the ground as she attempted to get between others. He had also seen Bryan LaPointe help her to her feet, then shield her from the group as though he were her savior. Nicola wasn't sure yet which part of the whole ordeal made him more angry.

The prime minister raised both his hands.

"That," he emphasized, "did not go well at all."

Derek lifted a brow at him. "Really Luca? Are you sure?" He couldn't contain the sarcasm in his voice.

"You've created a powder keg, signore. This is but just a small explosion," Mattia replied.

Derek gave the prime minister a sharp look. "*I've* created?" He inquired in a low voice. "You think that in a matter of mere months, I've somehow run this country into the ground to the point that joining the European Union is the only shot for any kind of sustainability?"

Nicola could tell his brother was at the peaks of anger, although his face didn't show it, and he was for once glad not to be on the receiving end.

Mattia however, shifted his eyes uncomfortably. "Signore, I only meant—," Mattia tried, but Derek cut him off.

"You only meant to comment on what we're dealing with now," he finished for him, "and obviously you don't realize that what we're dealing with now is a direct result of the serious lack of leadership and

115

accountability this country has had over the past 30 years!" His voice was now tensing, giving way to a rising forcefulness in his tone. "Don't blame me for doing now what no one else had the backbone to do previously. What *needs* to be done."

Derek rarely raised his voice to put someone in their place, it was never needed from him, and it was clear to Mattia where he stood.

"You are correct, of course, signore," the prime minister admitted with a sigh, "but, if the people and parliament can't come to an agreement over this matter, one that they feel good about, then I'm afraid it could become a stepping stone toward another revolution."

"That's ridiculous," Nicola now interjected. He took a seat near the desk, grateful to pivot the conversation in a forward direction. "I really don't understand what the problem is here. Joining the EU is a good business decision, one that will benefit the entire country, stabilizing our economy. Why are the members reacting this way? Don't they realize this will be a massive step toward relief from poverty for the vast majority of our people?"

Derek looked at Nicola with interest, impressed with his economical understanding in such a short period of time.

"Because there are powerful people who are at risk of losing a lot of wealth if we join the EU," He stated calmly, joining his brother by the desk. "Those people are backing many within our government who have been sitting pretty now for many generations, reaping the benefits of those less fortunate. So, they do not always speak on behalf of the people who elected them. Instead, they have their own pockets padded, and will easily be swayed by those who are pulling strings behind the scenes."

"Enzo," Nicola added.

Derek nodded. "One of the bigger players, yes."

"But you have executive power," Nicola said, "just override the vote and make the decision."

Mattia's eyes widened, and Derek shook his head.

"That's what someone like DeGrassi *wants* me to do," he replied. "Don't you see? You saw what an outrage those members had toward each other over a tie vote. If I enacted executive power and made the decision for them, the people would rise up against the monarchy. He's itching for a reason to showcase that I would abuse my position."

"But surely the people would see that joining the EU is not only in their best interest, but it actually also reduces the power of the monarchy!" Nicola exclaimed. "How could they fault you for doing what's right for them?"

"They wouldn't even understand that, Signore," Mattia said sadly, "all they would see is your father again."

"And DeGrassi would make sure that's what they saw," Derek finished.

"But—," Nicola began,

"It's out of the question, Nic," Derek stated sternly, cutting him off, "forcing the people is a one-way ticket to revolution."

"So, now what then?" Nicola asked.

"The vote will have to be re-done," Derek said, "only this time," he paused, "we will let the people decide. The vote will be open to the people of Calina, not just the parliament members."

Mattia furrowed his brow. "That has never been done before," he commented. "It is parliament, who represent the people, who decide, with your final approval. Not the people themselves. This is not a democracy."

"No," Derek replied evenly, "it's a monarchy, and therefore, I will determine what the next best course of action is to be."

His tone made it clear that additional arguments to his decision would not be wise, and this entire conversation had used up all of his patience. He looked at Nicola.

"There are extenuating circumstances at play here. I don't trust that this last vote was carried through with the most honorable intentions. It will be your responsibility to oversee and tally the final vote. Ensure that it is conducted with complete integrity."

The conversation was interrupted by a sharp knock. Derek looked toward the door to see Costa re-enter followed by Rosana Gallo. Her expression was grim. She raised her head a notch and took a deep breath as she approached him.

"Signore," she said and bowed, then handed him a local tabloid which translated to English: *Future Queen of Calina, Deranged and Unstable.* Derek blinked at the headline, disbelief crossing his face.

The article went on to describe Christine's PTSD in detail casting further doubt on her ability to lead, claiming that she is uncontrollable, and it even mentioned she attacked the king during an "episode." Derek's heart sank and rage rose up within him. The article was outlandish and exaggerated greatly, but it poured gasoline on an already delicate situation surrounding the people's views of Christine.

"How did this happen?" He questioned angrily, "who is responsible for this?" He looked at Costa; he had been there last night, he had seen Christine, and Olivia too. But, did anyone else know? It was certainly possible, and her screams last night could have woken up others, he just hadn't realized it being so focused on helping Christine. He looked at Mattia.

"I need to see Romano immediately," he stated.

His enemies were rising up against him, and they were fighting from the inside. Someone from inside the palace leaked this information on Christine. He looked at the faces currently surrounding him; who was here that he couldn't trust?

"A tie!" Enzo was outraged. "How could it have been a tie?" His voice thundered through the phone.

"Clearly, you didn't pay up enough," the lazy male voice on the other end responded. "Actually, you're lucky you got a tie out of the vote," the voice continued, "did you really think you could buy it?" The flippant attitude of the caller did nothing to calm Enzo down.

"What happened?" He seethed through gritted teeth.

"The guard was brought in," the caller reported, "a couple members were detained for assault, but I doubt any charges will be made. The monarchy won't want the way parliament conducted themselves public news. They're all just a bunch of hot heads who are too used to getting their way." The caller emphasized his last point, and it didn't escape Enzo that he was also being lumped into that group.

"Is Landino going to enact executive power and override the vote?" Enzo asked impatiently.

The caller laughed. "Of course not!" he exclaimed. "He'd be stupid to do that. And Landino is not stupid. I'm sure he'll hold another vote."

"We'll just have to make sure this next vote goes the way I need it to go," Enzo said thoughtfully. "I will need your help this time. The plan will need to be full proof."

"You know I will aid you given what you promised me," the caller replied, his tone cold. He then changed the subject. "I don't need to ask you if you were responsible for releasing that damaging information on Christine Dayne to the press," he continued, "why are you so intent on making the people hate her?"

Enzo smiled slowly.

"Landino killed my father," he stated, "he needs to suffer, and I enjoy toying with him. This will hit him where it hurts him the most. She won't be able to handle the pressure and will eventually leave him. He will be destroyed."

He leaned back in his leather chair and lit a cigarette, taking a long drag, enjoying the vision playing out in his mind, then gave a sinister smile. "The way parliament reacted to the tie vote is very interesting," he said softly, "as I expected, the matter of Calina joining the EU is turning into the perfect opportunity to turn them against the monarch, all the while exploiting his unnecessary absolute power. Once the members see him for who and what he is, they will demand his crown. Landino will have nothing left after that. He will pay dearly for murdering my father."

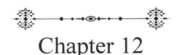

Chapter 12

2 Months Later

I t was early morning and Taya turned off the alarm on her phone, glancing briefly at any text messages.

"I'll be by to pick you up for breakfast at 7," one message read. It was from Bryan, and Taya couldn't suppress a small smile.

Since she had met him at the conference, she had since spent quite a lot of time with him. He was intelligent, considerate, and handsome, and she enjoyed being in his company. The public had also noticed the two of them spending time together: witnessing them in town, dining in various restaurants, and attending social functions.

Being from opposing parties, there was a great deal of interest in their alleged relationship, and there were many rumors and whispers going around about how they appeared to be the perfect Romeo and Juliet.

Except, Taya did not have romantic feelings toward Bryan. To her, he was a friend, someone who had common interests, and a confidant. And try as she might, she couldn't develop anything for him beyond that. She knew his sentiments for her were different, however, and he had made it clear he wanted more. At the end of the last evening they shared, she let him kiss her, briefly thinking that maybe, over time she could grow an intimate interest in him. But the kiss left her disappointed and frustrated. She felt nothing. Deciding that it was wrong to lead him on, she told him it probably wasn't a good idea to see him again. He had backed off then, stating that he would rather just be friends then not be with her at all, so Taya had agreed to continue to see him in a platonic manner.

Any woman in her right senses would be flattered and smitten with Bryan, which only told her there must be something wrong with her. Unwilling to admit it to herself, Taya knew in the back of her mind she compared Bryan to Nicola; it was impossible not to.

Even though their time together was brief, the prince had secured his place within her; a deep seated need that could not be fulfilled by any other, and now that she knew what it felt like, she could settle for nothing less. She hated this, and she strived to lock him away, refusing to let his dark eyes or sexy smile invade her thoughts. Even as she reflected on being with him now, she could smell his wooded cologne.

She rose from her bed to begin getting ready. Bryan would be here in an hour. Today, they were to attend a public appearance made by the monarch and their future queen.

There was to be an unveiling at the hospital in the capital; a beautiful new mural that Christine had designed and painted herself. To give such a large piece of her work to the city made a statement— that Christine was committed to Calina and its people. Her paintings were considered valuable and highly sought after, especially given that any new works by her would be few and far between, and would no doubt belong to the people of Calina.

Regardless of her efforts to secure love and respect from the people, however, Christine continued to receive constant ridicule from the press. It saddened Taya to think what Christine had to endure almost every day, and she felt passionately that the slander against her was unwarranted. She wondered just how much Christine was capable of coping with. So far, she had yet to see her crack, and it was surprising as much as it was inspiring in Taya's eyes.

Showered and dressed, Taya now poured water into a kettle and placed it on the stove in the kitchen. She lived just outside the capital, in a detached estate with a terrace, a view of the mountains and a pool. She enjoyed her solace, away from prying eyes.

Much of her early childhood had been spent struggling through the notorious limelight her father always seemed to be in, and once she was old enough, she left to get away from that sort of drama. She went to school and college abroad, and afterwards spent some years outside of Calina, having only returned after graduate school. Once she had reestablished herself in her home country, she chose to live alone, refusing to acknowledge what was left of her broken family. Her mother had left when she was just a child, and she preferred not to associate herself with her father nor her brother. She had no one, no family that she spoke of, and when her father died recently, she was glad.

She turned on the small television in the breakfast nook off the kitchen while she waited for the kettle to heat. Switching to the morning news, she bit her lip upon seeing Nicola's face flood the screen. Her heart skipped a beat remembering his passion, the hot intensity of his touch, and his scent. She shook her head to clear the imagery and turned back to the tea.

He was constantly in the news these days. He made more appearances than the king did, and he presented himself well. It hadn't taken Nicola long at all to find his way into the hearts of Caleans; every speech he made was impassioned but sincere, every negotiation flawless. She watched him on the screen now, giving a smooth interview, intrigued by the easy way he spoke and laughed with the host.

He was rapidly becoming Europe's most eligible bachelor, and everyone was talking about him; every woman, it seemed, wanted him. But Taya had never seen him with a girl on his arm. Every appearance he made, he made it alone. This was rather contradictory to what Taya had assumed she would see from him in the public eye.

After the way he had broken her heart and with Christine's warnings of his playboy tendencies, Taya had done her own research on him. Indeed, she had found quite a bit of evidence of his frivolity in New York that supported the image Christine painted of him. Taya had been saddened and disappointed by what she had learned, but seeing him now... he was not acting like that same man from New York, and she couldn't help but wonder what made him change.

The fact that he now refused dates or escorts of any kind, of course, only made him more desirable and sought after, but Taya found herself wishing for nothing more than to despise him. However, even with how he had treated her, she just couldn't bring herself to hate him. Maybe it was because deep down she clung to the belief that she hadn't been wrong about him; that he really did care for her. After all, she had read correctly in him that he would go on to become a great leader, an advocate for the people and the country. And he was doing just that.

She was cleaning up the kitchen when there was a knock on the side door. Knowing it was Bryan, she called out to him.

"It's open."

"*Ciao*, good morning," he greeted her brightly as he let himself in.

She turned from the sink, giving him a smile. "*Buongiorno*," she replied. He looked charming, dressed in a pair of khakis, a white dress shirt and a fitted, navy sweater. Appropriate of his clean-cut and preppy image.

"You ready?" he asked.

She nodded, "yes, I just need to go grab my bag and jacket."

She left him in the kitchen as she walked back into her bedroom to get her things.

"Taya," Bryan called after her, "I was going to wait, but there's something I need to ask you."

She paused in her room, his voice sounded hesitant. Picking up her purse from the dresser, her eyes fell on the silver bracelet Nicola bought her at the festival. She touched the chain links gently, remembering that day with him. Regardless of everything, it was her favorite piece of jewelry. She quickly wrapped it around her wrist connecting the clasp, attempting to discard the memories with it as she walked back toward Bryan.

"What is it?" she asked curiously.

He pursed his lips slightly and gave her an uncertain look. He looked quite adorable, she realized.

"Well, as you know, this Saturday is the official reception presenting Nicola as the prince of Calina," he said taking a breath, "I was hoping you might allow me to escort you to the event."

"Bryan, I—," she began, furrowing her brow, but he lifted his hands cutting her off.

"I know you said you didn't want to change things within our relationship, and I respect that," he placed his hands lightly on her shoulders, locking his eyes with hers, "but, I can't imagine taking anyone else except you." He smiled at her a bit shyly. "I would love it if you were at my side, Taya. Please."

She searched his gaze, he looked hopeful. She couldn't deny it felt nice that he wanted to be with her that much. She really had not intended on going to the reception, afraid of facing Nicola, but it was a major government event. Having Bryan there would make attending less stressful for her, and she always had a nice time with him. Maybe this didn't need to be complicated. Perhaps she could simply make an appearance, enjoy Bryan's company, and not have to even speak to the prince at all.

"Ok," she consented, nodding, "why not."

His face broke into a wide grin, and it felt good to make him happy. "Thank you," he said, then with his hands still on her shoulders, he pulled her into an embrace against him.

She let her arms wrap around his torso in return, allowing herself to enjoy his warmth for just a moment. She pulled back promptly however, not wishing to give him the wrong idea and cleared her throat.

"Um, we should get going, don't you think?" she asked, throwing on her jacket. He nodded, following her out the door.

Later that morning, Taya stood with Bryan amidst a crowd in the after math of the unveiling of the new mural outside the hospital. The artwork itself lived up to expectations of a piece inclusive of beauty, wonderment, and as always with Christine's art, a stir of emotion. As she looked around, Taya could tell the crowd shared an overall appreciation and was impressed with the piece, however, although the applause was there, it was lukewarm at best, laced with an undertone of reluctance.

Christine and Derek both stood side by side with the hospital director in front of the mural, and Taya couldn't help but notice the director even had a distant and rather cold manner toward Christine. In fact, the director almost acted as though she wasn't there at all, choosing to only interact with Derek as he bowed then shook hands with the monarch.

When the presentation was made, however, everyone was a bit surprised that Derek turned the podium over to Christine, bringing her front and center, determined that she not be ignored. She had seemed a bit unsure at first, but when she began to speak, Taya could tell her words came from the heart.

She spoke of her struggles as an artist in the States; how it wasn't until she came to Europe that she found acceptance for her work and a sense of belonging. How this, more than anything, made her feel as though she had found her home, and now, here in Calina, she craved to give that sentiment back to the people. Her speech was moving and sincere, and she spoke every word of it in Calean.

When she had finished, there was a brief silence before a louder, more receptive applause erupted from the crowd. Taya smiled and clapped along proudly, feeling happy for Christine that she had obtained a small victory here with the people.

The moment was short-lived however, when grumblings and murmurs began rising, finally resulting in an attendee actually shouting:

"Gold-digger! Go back to America!"

Taya turned toward the noise, trying to see who exactly was causing the disruption. As she scanned the crowd, her eyes zeroed in on a recognizable face: the young blond attendant from the palace. She squinted in confusion, then dismissed her appearance, she was a palace employee after all. Taya diverted her gaze to a group of four middle aged men near the back of the crowd, the clear culprits of the ruckus.

She glanced up at Christine, trying to gauge her reaction to the outburst, and most had also turned to stare at just how the future queen would respond. But Christine didn't bat an eye, only smiled, as though the incident didn't even happen. She then thanked everyone for attending and invited them to come up and take a closer look at the mural. There was another round of applause and the crowd began to disburse, Christine and Derek now surrounded by guards as they retreated back into the building.

Unable to keep her rising anger and frustration at bay, Taya turned away from Bryan to the direction of the group of men.

"Where do you think you're going?" Bryan said grabbing Taya's arm, stopping her.

"To give him a piece of my mind," Taya replied, "that was completely disrespectful and uncalled for." She attempted to tug her arm free, but he tightened his grasp.

"I agree with you," Bryan said calmly, "but confronting them is just asking for trouble."

"But they can't just treat the monarchy that way," Taya said aghast.

"Your passion is one of the things I admire most about you," Bryan replied, a grin spreading across his face, then he grew more serious. "But she is technically not part of our monarchy yet. And anyway, she handled the situation perfectly."

"I just don't see how all those rumors about her could be true," Taya replied, relaxing now and no longer struggling to free her arm.

Sensing her ease, Bryan slid his hand down from her upper arm to grasp her hand.

"It would be only natural for her to have some kind of mental instability after being shot," he said gently.

"Yes, but even if that's so, she's not crazy," Taya countered, "and it's wrong that she's being judged like that—her hardship put on display."

Bryan sighed. "That is the life of a public figure," he said, "and if she truly desires to be our queen, she'll have to take the heat. If she can't...," he paused, "well, then maybe she doesn't belong here."

Taya met his warm, brown eyes, suddenly aware that he was holding her hand. She was a bit surprised to hear Bryan be anything except supportive of the monarchy in any way, but what he said made sense. Of course, Bryan always made sense; he was an incredible politician.

She allowed him to continue to hold onto her hand, wishing desperately to feel some deeper attraction toward him, and the unwelcome image of Nicola's face flooded her mind once more.

"Do you think it's strange that prince Nicola didn't make an appearance today?" she asked casually, scanning the crowd, refusing to meet Bryan's gaze.

He eyed her curiously. "I don't think so," he replied slowly, "he has his own engagements I'm sure." He was quiet for a moment, watching her closely. "Taya," he said gaining her attention, "you'll have to forgive my curiosity because of how you know I feel about you, but," he hesitated, "was there something between you and Nicola?"

She let out a nervous laugh. "What would make you think that?" she said, trying to look him in the eye.

"When I saw you *talking* to him at the reception," he said, drawing out the word "talking" to indicate he noticed more than just chit chat, "well, your conversation appeared to be...you seemed really upset." He struggled to find the right words.

She finally locked her eyes with his.

"I already told you," she stated flatly, "he disappointed me in the lack of information I was looking for. There is nothing between us," and her tone was matter-of-fact. *Not anymore, anyway*, she added in her mind.

A sheepish grin crossed his face. "I'm sorry, Taya, I have no right to ask you that," he said, "it's just that, a relationship between a member of the monarchy and a member of parliament would have serious consequences as a conflict of interest."

His tone was a bit airy, and Taya agreed that no, he didn't have the right to discuss this with her at all. But her heart skipped a beat, she definitely didn't need her job at risk nor any stupid rumors flying about.

"There is nothing for you, or anyone working within the Calean government to be concerned with here," she repeated, making it clear. And although it hurt her to say it, she knew the words she spoke were true.

Her direct response seemed to pacify Bryan, and as they left the hospital together, she couldn't help but notice he gripped her hand a bit more tightly, a satisfied smile on his face.

"You have not paid me, Signore DeGrassi."

Enzo had accepted the incoming call with a groan. He had not summoned this contact and now, he was not appreciative of her cool, crisp tone.

"Our agreement was that the money would be wired to you by the end of the month," he replied irritably, "it was you who said you needed time to get information."

"Yes, but I got you information on Christine Dayne," the voice insisted. "Good information that was risky to come by." There was a loaded pause, then the voice continued in a hurried and pained voice. "My mother is ill," she stated, "what you offered me won't be enough to cover her expenses. I need double what you owe me."

Enzo practically dropped the phone at the absurdity of the request, and he was quickly losing his temper.

"Who do you think you are?" he roared. "What I offered you is more than enough, especially for the kind of information you bring me." A disgusted look crossed his face. "It's out of the question."

"Pay me what I want, or I'm prepared to go to His Highness," the voice remained stubborn, and Enzo noted how confident she suddenly seemed.

"You'll go to jail," Enzo sneered, his teeth now bared. "In doing so, you'd reveal that it was you who leaked that the future queen is insane."

"She's not insane," she said now empathetically, "and anyway, I'd rather go to jail than be executed for treason. Maybe His Highness will go easy on me if I bring him evidence to lock away the notorious Enzo DeGrassi." Enzo practically snarled over the phone. "You have two days," the voice continued, "or I tell the king everything I know." She gave a small laugh, "you know in my position, I can request an audience with him any time I choose."

Before he could retort, the caller clicked off. Livid now, his face turned red at the audacity of this nobody. Who was she to blackmail him! Clearly, she had no idea who she was dealing with. Scrolling through his contacts, he punched up another call.

"Enzo," a male voice answered, "to what do I owe the pleasure to this time."

Ignoring the mocking tone, Enzo raged, "you need to take care of your *partner*." He continued to seethe. "The bitch is blackmailing me for more money."

The voice on the other end chuckled. "And you didn't see that coming?" he asked.

"Shut up," Enzo snapped, "I didn't think she'd have the guts…" he trailed off thoughtfully, almost admiring her gumption now. "But regardless, you know there's only one way to deal with a blackmailer."

There was a heavy pause as the man considered what he was being asked to do. "That wasn't part of our agreement, Enzo," he said now, his voice dead serious.

"She's a threat to both of us!" Enzo argued. "She's sympathetic to the American, and at any time she could go to Landino." He waited for an objection, but there was none. "If I go down, you will go down with me," he finished, a finality in his tone making it clear he wouldn't think twice about turning in accomplices.

"Fine," the voice agreed, but with an edge of resentment.

"Do it soon," Enzo urged, "she's only giving me two days to pay her."

The other man sighed. "Then it'll have to be at the reception event this Saturday," he said, "there'll be a crowd and lots of commotion. I'm sure I could get her alone to do the job, then when her body is found, the suspect list will be endless." He paused, "it's a shame, I was looking forward to enjoying myself at that party."

"That's perfect," Enzo agreed, his dark eyes gleaming.

"By the way," the voice said, changing the subject, "I might have an idea to secure the EU vote."

Enzo's eyes widened at this information. "Really," he replied, intrigued, "how?"

"I just have a hunch right now," the man said, "but, I'll know more after the reception. When I call to inform you that the other task is done, I'll be able to share for certain if my suspicions are correct."

"I will expect good news," Enzo said darkly, "on both accounts."

Chapter 13

Christine lifted her gaze to her reflection in the mirror where she sat at the vanity in her room. Her eyes held a look of determination and focus as she considered her next public appearance, tonight, at Nicola's formal reception here at the palace.

She took a deep breath, reflecting on the mural unveiling at the hospital. She had been nervous, heavily anticipating the reaction, then elated at the actual response. She loved feeling like she had the ability to give the people of Calina a piece of her, something unique they would not find in anyone else. Even the couple of unforeseen hiccups during the event: the hospital director's standoffish attitude toward her, and of course the rude shouts from the crowd, had not quelled the deep sense of satisfaction her work had given her nor the way she had handled herself.

Since she had begun to repair her bond with Derek, she had been sleeping more consistently. She now felt safe, and although the nightmares still invaded her sub conscience certain nights, it was no longer every night. The vividness of the dreams were also fading, and even Courtney's taunting facial features were becoming difficult to recall. As promised, Derek had been right there with her each time she woke up in distress, which as he had predicted, helped her to begin to overcome her fears.

However, the emotional roller coaster she was on due to the constant public pressure left her more times than not feeling exhausted still. And it felt as though she had overcome one traumatizing hurdle only to face the next. Her gaze moved from her large, hazel eyes in the mirror, where the fatigue lines surrounding them were cleverly hidden with make-up, down to her hands which lay in her lap. She turned them over, inspecting her palms, and smirked slightly at seeing paint stains among her less than perfect, short nails. *These are not the hands of a queen,* she thought as mixed emotions flooded through her, doubting once again if she was strong enough to hold this position. Derek needed a powerful, confident woman by his side. Could she really do this?

"Signorina, I have your dress for this evening."

Her thoughts were interrupted as Olivia entered the dressing room of her suite carrying a beautiful burgundy gown.

The dress was made of silk, with velvet trim. The a-line skirt was floor length and the neckline plummeted in a wide v shape. A sheer cape flowed from the tops of the shoulders of the long, delicate lace sleeves down the back to the floor.

"It's lovely," she said breathlessly, fingering the luxurious fabric.

"It's going to look amazing on you!" Olivia exclaimed, and Christine smiled at her apparent giddiness.

In a small way, Olivia reminded Christine of her best friend back in the states, April. The attendant was always upbeat and full of life. She also seemed to have a keen fashion sense, like April, which Christine appreciated and missed from her friend, as she no longer had that "expert" opinion when it came to getting dressed up.

Thinking about April now, Christine realized what she missed most was just having a friend. Olivia could not technically fill that space, she was her personal attendant, but she spent so much time with her, she became the closest thing Christine had to a friend. And Olivia seemed to genuinely enjoy spending time by Christine's side as well.

Olivia assisted Christine with the gown, then helped her into matching heels. She chatted in a lively way, and Christine listened and laughed at her anecdotes about some of the other staff members, her family, and a date she went on last week. As Christine stood now in front of the vanity mirror, checking the completed look one last time, Olivia addressed her.

"Signora," Olivia began, her tone turning a bit more serious.

"Olivia, please," Christine said, turning away from the mirror, "I've asked you to call me 'Christine.'"

Olivia smiled a bit shyly and nodded. "I just wanted to tell you how happy I am to see that you're better." Her expression was a bit uncertain, and she wondered if Christine would get upset with her for acknowledging her trauma. But Christine gave her an appreciative smile, realizing that Olivia's comment came from a place of sincerity.

"I'm proud to know that you've risen above what people have said about you," Olivia continued, "and I would be honored if you were our queen. What you've overcome is surely a sign of your strength."

If Christine had thought it wouldn't cross any boundaries, she would have hugged Olivia, but she wasn't sure how the attendant would react. Instead, she smiled at her graciously, as tears of gratitude stung her eyes, making them appear very bright.

"Thank you, Olivia," she said softly, "that means so much to me."

She thought she saw tears sparkling in the girl's eyes as well, but before either of them could say more, Christine heard the bedroom door open. Knowing it was Derek, she gave Olivia one last smile, then turned from her and walked through the vanity and dressing room to the main bedroom chamber. As she emerged, his eyes widened.

"You look stunning," he murmured, his gaze taking in the graceful way she moved in the gown. Christine felt a heat rise to her cheeks, and she marveled at the way he still made her blush, even after all this time.

Olivia appeared from the dressing room next, and Derek's smile faltered slightly when he saw her. She bowed in front of him.

"Hello Olivia," he greeted her.

"Your Highness," she replied, then turned to Christine, "Signora, if you will excuse me, do you require anything else at this time?"

Christine shook her head. "No, thank you, Olivia, I will see you shortly." The attendant lowered her head a final time, then departed from the bedroom.

Derek's gaze followed Olivia as she walked out of the room, then he turned back to Christine, noticing her eyes seemed a bit misty. Was she upset?

"Are you all right?" he asked, concern crossing his features.

Christine gave a short laugh. "Yes, of course," she replied, but he didn't look convinced. She continued, "it's just... it's been a while since anyone but you has said anything kind to me."

He took her hand in his and gave her a reassuring smile. "We will overcome this," he promised, and he drew her into an embrace. "What you're enduring won't last."

Christine noted that his tone made it sound as though he knew something she didn't. She pulled back slightly to look into his eyes.

"We're pressed for time right now," he said before she could ask any questions, "but there is something I need to talk with you about."

She furrowed her brow. "Is everything ok at least?" she asked.

He nodded slowly. "It will be."

Later that evening, Nicola suppressed a yawn as he attempted to focus on the girl in front of him. Her hand was held tight in his, his other around her waist. She was saying something that he only caught bits and pieces of.

He was well into his fifth (*or was it the eighth?*) dancing partner for the evening, and he was beyond bored. It was expected, of course, that he be sociable during his own reception, and it would have been considered rude for him to turn down any request for his attention. But tonight the requests didn't seem to stop, and the faces of every woman he encountered seem to muddle together.

Internally he grimaced at the irony of his situation, realizing that only four months ago, he would have been in his element, wanting nothing more than to be sought after by so many. But now...

It amazed him how much had changed in such a short time, and all because of one person. His gaze wandered past the brunette in his arms as his eyes scanned for the woman he desperately desired attention from. The one woman who had chosen to avoid him the entire evening.

The ceremony leading up to the reception passed by in a blur for Nicola, and he was still reeling from the fact that it had been made public, to the world no less, that he was taking his place as the prince of Calina. Though he had already begun making himself a prominent political figure in Europe, formally taking a royal position definitely took his visibility up a notch. There was no hiding his location now, and subconsciously, he was already looking over his shoulder. Even in the palace, which was logically the safest place for him, he felt tense, and countless times, he found himself checking the doors of the ballroom, watching to see who might be coming and going.

During one such occasion, he had witnessed Taya enter, on the arm of none other than Bryan LaPointe. He had been expecting it, but the expectation did nothing to prepare him for how he had felt upon seeing them together. He had been made aware of the rumors suggesting their relationship, soon after the conference no less. Although he had been the one to push her away, he couldn't help but feel hurt at her apparent ability to latch on to someone else so quickly.

Personally, he had felt rather empty inside since she had almost slapped him in the face (not that he blamed her), and it didn't take him long to realize that he no longer felt any joy in the things he used to find much joy in—partying and women mainly. Instead, he found himself on a mission to finally begin down a path of achievement, fueled by his desire to prove himself worthy. He knew Taya was his reason for both: this new found passion, as well as his recent preference to give up his night-life. However, he had no business having feelings for her nor in using her as his inspiration to make more of his life. So, he buried those reasons deep down.

Putting aside his personal motivations, he tried to sell his drive for success on his political agenda. Regardless of what ultimately happened with the monarchy, (obviously he knew of DeGrassi's wishes to plot against it), he now had favor with both the government and the people, and he felt secure he could end up in a good place, provided he could stay well out of reach from the organization from New York. Whether or not DeGrassi succeeded, Nicola figured he may as well spend his time placing himself in a favorable position versus risk being overthrown and outcast. Politics at its finest.

His eyes scanned the crowd again, and his partner continued to chat away to him, not realizing that he wasn't listening. He had gotten good at acting interested when his mind was somewhere else. Currently, his mind had settled once again on Taya as he caught another glimpse of her, dancing not too far away with Bryan.

She looked particularly beautiful this evening, wearing a simple, but elegant, off-shoulder black gown. Her thick, golden hair was piled on top of her head revealing the graceful curve of her neck, and the flowing material of her dress swayed with her as she danced in Bryan's arms, the high slit in the skirt every so often revealing a flash of her thigh.

A surge of jealous emotion shot through him, and the need to approach her suddenly became overwhelming. He knew he should ignore the force that was pushing him back toward Taya, but it was becoming just too unbearable.

"Nicola?"

His partner drew his attention back, he hadn't realized that his thoughts had momentarily paralyzed him, and he had stopped dancing.

"Excuse me, won't you, Teresa?" he said absently, releasing her from his grasp, not even looking at her, but still at Taya.

A look of disappointment crossed her face. "It's Tessa," she

133

corrected him before bowing her head. "Your Highness," she added, her voice clearly indicating her dismay at his rejection. Then she turned away to leave promptly.

Nicola watched her go and immediately felt guilty for his lack of chivalry, but he was too distracted to care too much that he had just made a bad impression. He knew he would not be able to think straight until he spoke to Taya.

Now that Tessa was gone, he searched again for Taya. She was no longer dancing, but sipping from a glass of champagne and laughing with Bryan. He wasn't sure what he was hoping to accomplish by confronting her, all he knew was he would go crazy unless he did, and he wasn't able to stop his emotions from driving his actions. At the very least, he had to find out, once and for all, if she really was in love with someone else.

He strode over to where she and Bryan stood as he placed a pleasant, presentable expression on his face. As soon as Taya realized he was walking toward her, her eyes widened as they locked with his. She looked almost fearful, as though she were a deer caught in headlights, but she quickly composed herself. It was clear to Nicola that she had wanted to avoid him. As much as he understood those intentions, the thought saddened him as well.

"Bryan, Taya," Nicola greeted them both, making eye contact with Bryan, then letting his gaze linger on Taya a moment.

"Your highness," Bryan replied with a friendly smile, while he and Taya gave a slight bow. She attempted to hold a disinterested expression, but Nicola could tell she was struggling to maintain her mask.

"I hope I'm not intruding," he began, looking at Bryan now, "but, I was wondering if I might borrow your partner for a dance?" His eyes moved to Taya again. "As a parliament member, I was looking for your insights into a matter, Taya." His excuse was necessary, even if he was well aware she could see through it. He needed the illusion that his ask was strictly professional as well as not give her the opportunity to say no.

Taya's eyes opened wide at Nicola's request as she tried to wrap her brain around his motives. What game was he trying to play now? She didn't for one second believe he actually wanted her opinion on a political matter. She glanced at Bryan, who's smile had faltered. It was clear he wasn't pleased to hand her over to Nicola. But what choice did either of them have?

"Of course, signore," she replied stiffly, and he took her hand, leading her away from Bryan.

As the orchestra continued playing, Nicola placed his hand firmly around her waist, leading her gently along with the music.

"You look beautiful," he told her in a low voice, his dark gaze locked with hers. Her eyes remained fixed as she stared back at him, refusing to respond.

Holding her hand in his as they danced, he glimpsed the silver bracelet around her wrist. She still wore it? Maybe she didn't hate him after all?

"Are you giving me the cold shoulder, angel?" he asked, raising his eyebrows.

She gave him a look of disgust at his audacity. "Were you expecting something different, signore?" she asked cooly, breaking her silence, "I believe the last time we spoke you had made it perfectly clear I meant nothing to you."

Nicola furrowed his brow, his hand subconsciously holding hers more tightly. His desperation was rising, needing to tell her why he said those things to her.

"Taya, I...," but he trailed off, unable to speak the words he wanted to say.

She took his hesitation as cowardice and sighed. "Well, Your Highness," she emphasized his title with mockery, "what was this matter you wished to speak to me about?" When he didn't reply she continued, "although, I have to say, I don't see why someone like you would need my opinion on anything. In fact, I must congratulate you on establishing your most impressive political reputation." She paused, and the haughty tone left her voice. "You're all I see or hear about everywhere I go." Her comment was quiet as she lowered her eyes from him.

He could see the hurt; she wasn't over him, he realized. Then why was she with Bryan?

"Funny," he finally replied, "it seems all I ever hear about are your numerous dates with Bryan LaPointe."

His tone was sharp, and Taya looked up at him, narrowing her eyes. He couldn't possibly care that she was seen about with Bryan, or even that some suspected a relationship between them. Why would he? She decided to call it out, hoping to anger him.

"Jealous?" she asked, the confidence coming back into her voice.

She expected him to scoff or deny her claim, but instead he pulled her closer to him, pressing gently on her back. He needed to feel her once more, his limbs practically aching from wanting to hold her. His breath was near her ear, and she could breathe in that wonderful cedar and citrus scent of his.

"Oh, I'm very jealous, angel," he murmured.

Her throat went dry at his admission and the closeness of his body to hers. His fingertips trailed lightly from her back to her neck, sending pleasurable shivers up her spine. Images of that first night flashed back to her, and she couldn't prevent her body from wanting him, the chemistry between them simply undeniable. Why was he doing this to her?

A sense of confusion coursed through her, and as easy as it would be, she couldn't allow herself to become swept up by him again. Clearly, this was just one of his games.

Recalling Bryan's questions about their involvement, Taya began to panic, and not wishing to draw attention to them, she removed her hand from his and pushed against his chest slightly. Her eyes met his, and she could see the storm of desire brewing within his dark, near black orbs.

"Thank you, signore," she stated, then bowed her head to him, giving the impression of showing the utmost respect.

Inside however, she wanted to either throw herself at him or throttle him. She just wasn't sure which emotion was stronger right now, and she didn't trust herself to be near him for fear of acting on either one. She then quickly turned from him and walked into the crowd, her gaze now searching for Bryan; she needed to be where she knew it was safe.

Nicola watched her leave, he couldn't blame her. What had he expected? But she had felt so perfect in his arms... and he realized he could no longer live with her false impression of him.

He decided to give her some time to cool off, but there was more he needed to say, more he needed to do, and the urgency rising within him continued to dictate his behavior. As foolish as he kept telling himself it was, he was numb to his logical mind which was trying to convince him to just leave her alone. Instead, like stalking prey, he began to follow her from a distance.

Making his way through the throngs of people, stopping every so often to shake a hand or accept congratulatory remarks, he tried to keep one eye on Taya. Although he lost her at one point while he was engaged with one of the prominent parliament members, he finally spotted her again as she was exiting through an open door leading out into the gardens. Following her to the door, he had almost caught up with her when he felt a hand on his shoulder stopping him. Turning, he met the raised eyebrows of his personal guard, Stefan Martino.

"Signore," he stated.

Martino had served the Calina monarchy almost his entire life. He was loyal to his core, nearing 50, but he kept fit and trained daily. Nicola had heard rumors in regard to his impressive marksmanship; his ability to consistently reach out and touch his target at 800 meters with his 308 Blaser made him respected by any of his peers throughout Europe.

"I'm only stepping out into the garden for a moment, Stefan," Nicola explained. The guard nodded and opened the door for him, and Nicola knew he was planning on following him.

"Actually," he hesitated, "I need to have a conversation in private. I need you to wait here for me." Martino stared blankly at Nicola for a moment, clearly indicating his disapproval of this decision. "I'll only be 20 minutes." He added. Stefan nodded curtly, and Nicola passed through the door, knowing that if he wasn't back in 20 minutes, the guard would come find him.

He couldn't be too irritated, he decided, Martino was only doing his job. And since there was a price on his head, the guard had been given strict instructions. But Nicola couldn't help but also feel like a prisoner in his own home. His eyes squinted in the darkness outside, he needed to find where Taya went quickly.

It was dark as she entered, only soft moonlight shining in, and she decided to keep it that way, refraining from turning on any lights. She couldn't take the risk of anyone finding out who she was meeting with or why.

She had been working the crowd in the ballroom, when she caught his eyes, clearly giving her the signal that he wanted to meet. This location had been predetermined, and she could only hope that he was looking to meet with her to give her the money she had demanded from Enzo.

Since her last conversation with Enzo, she had not heard from her "associate" at all, but she had felt that tonight, considering the amount of people in attendance, he would definitely make contact. Her heart raced as she waited for him. She made sure he had seen her leave the ballroom, and he was alone, there was no reason he would not have followed her.

She had been on edge for days, highly anticipating Enzo's payment. She desperately needed the money to help her mother, which was the whole reason she ever agreed to work with Enzo in the first place. Of course, now that she was so close to securing the financial well-being of her family and finally able to pay off the medical expenses, she no longer wished to be under Enzo's thumb.

Ready to accept the consequences of her actions, which would include imprisonment, after she received this last payment, she was going to go to the king anyway and confess. She just had to get through this night, and she smiled slightly at the thought that she might be the one to actually put an end to Enzo DeGrassi.

Her thoughts were interrupted as she heard footfall behind her. She turned to face him, even in the dim lighting, she could make out his dark, handsome features. She twisted her hands nervously; she just wanted this to be over with.

"Do you have it?" she asked meekly.

He smiled, although the upturn of his lips didn't really reach his eyes. He approached her casually.

"Enzo has authorized the payment," he said lazily as he studied her small frame, her blond hair was up, off of her slender neck.

Her eyes darted around, expecting him to pull a package from his jacket. She stood, rooted to the floor as he neared her, and she lifted her chin a touch in an attempt to appear confident. But, he made no effort to hand her anything, and as he grew closer, it was then that she noticed he was wearing gloves. She looked into his eyes, the dark, sinister intention shining back at her, and fear unlike anything she had ever experienced shocked her body.

She gasped, understanding too late, and darted to her left in an effort to get around him, but he was between her and the door and already within reach. In a flash, he caught her arm, dragging her to him and clamping a hand over her mouth so she couldn't scream. Her eyes were wide in terror, and he didn't say a word as he pushed her roughly to the floor, now seizing her by the throat. She flailed her arms and dug her nails into his gloved hands, trying to pry them loose as she choked for air. But she was no match for his strength as he squeezed the life from her. She heard a grinding, crunching sound as he crushed her throat. It was over in a matter of minutes, and as her world went dark and cold, Olivia wondered who would take care of her mother now.

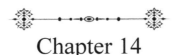

Chapter 14

Needing fresh air after her encounter with Nicola, Taya wandered away from the crowd and into the quiet, serene garden located just outside the ballroom terrace. The moon hung high in the clear night sky, and as she moved down the path further into the garden, the soothing sound of night cicadas soon began to overpower the faint music and chatter coming from the reception.

The air was a bit cool, and Taya hugged her arms as she strolled through a row of rose bushes, the perfume from the fragrant buds helping to relax her nerves. She took several deep breathes, thinking she'd just stay out here for a moment longer before heading back in to find Bryan. Then, she'd ask him if they could leave. She didn't want to chance running into Nicola again. It was too painful to her heart.

"Taya?"

She spun around at the sound of his voice behind her, and she stared at him in disbelief that he had followed her; the exact person she didn't wish to see. His hair looked as though he had run his hands through it several times, but the disheveled effect was alluring on him. She shook her head, refusing to recall how it felt to touch him.

"What do you want, Nic?" she asked quietly, the tone of her voice practically begging him to stop torturing her.

"I need to be honest with you," he said.

She gave a short laugh at his answer. "Honest?" She hissed, "I don't even think you know *how* to be honest!" He placed his hands in his pockets, letting her continue. "You've done nothing except lie to me since I met you," she accused, her words coming quicker in her eagerness to confront his actions. "I was just some game to you. Something to amuse yourself with." She took a breath as tears pricked her eyes. "That's how you've always treated everyone, isn't it? In New York? I read about you…" she trailed off as he diverted his gaze to the ground. "What I don't understand is why you're different now." He looked back up to meet her eyes. "This 'image' you've created for yourself here, in Calina," her tone genuinely curious now, "it's like you've decided to become a different person."

He walked toward her, closing the distance between them.

"It's true," he affirmed, "what you read, who I was. I'm not proud of it. But no, I'm not like that anymore." He placed his hands gently on her shoulders. "There was only one time I lied to you, angel," he said softly, "and that was at the parliament reception when I told you that night meant nothing to me."

Her eyes searched his, looking for his mischievous glint or mockery, but she only saw earnestness within them. "Why should I believe anything you say now?" Her voice was quiet and uncertain.

"The truth is," he continued, deciding to bare his heart, "although I tried hard not to, that night I fell in love with you." Her eyes widened at his confession, and he reached up to brush his thumb across her cheek. He gave a half laugh. "You made it impossible for me not to fall for you, as much as I knew I shouldn't." He paused, staring into her eyes, "I'm still in love with you."

She furrowed her brow, looking at him with bewilderment. "I don't understand," she practically whispered, her voice catching in her throat.

Overrun with emotion, the tears that were stinging her eyes now fell. How was he saying this to her? How could he be in love with her when he broke her heart? In an instant, she realized he was able to hurt her so badly because she loved him too.

"You are the reason I gave up who I was, angel," he said now, needing her to understand the impact she'd had on him. "That day, in the park, I knew I wanted to become a better man. For you." He brushed her bangs away from her eyes and rested his forehead gently on hers. "I had to tell you how I truly feel," he murmured.

He brought his lips within an inch of hers wondering if she would pull away. But her desire for him which had been building since the dance won over her doubts and questions and she closed the gap, responding to him eagerly. Her mouth parted to give his tongue access as his hand tangled in her hair, releasing several strands from their pins. His other arm wrapped around her waist, crushing her hard against him, and she felt that his passion may just end up swallowing her whole.

"Nic," she moaned, her eyes closed, as she took a much needed breath of air.

His name on her lips reminded him of a question that had been burning in his mind. He pulled back from her slightly. "Are you in love with him?" he asked.

Taya brought her eyebrows together as she looked at him, confused at first at who he was talking about. "Bryan?" she said, then smiled. "No. Nic, there's nothing between me and Bryan."

He cupped both sides of her face with his hands, bringing her close again. "I can't tell you how happy I am to hear that," he said softly, the relief clearly visible on his face.

She leaned into his touch, her heart racing and bursting with emotion at learning how he felt about her. But if he loved her, why did he push her away? She knew there was still something he wasn't telling her. She looked up into his eyes.

"Why did you say those things to me?" she asked quietly, "you mocked my feelings, you were distant and cold." She shut her eyes briefly, swallowing a sob that was rising in her throat at the memory of how he had dismissed her so cruelly.

A look of remorse crossed his face and he pulled her head to rest against his chest in an embrace.

"I am so sorry I hurt you," he whispered in her hair. "It was the only way to keep you safe."

She raised her head to look him in the eyes. "What do you mean, 'safe?'"

Nicola paused. He still couldn't reveal to her his reasons. "My position is complicated right now," he finally said. "It's dangerous for you to be with me. I've made mistakes, Taya, I can't let you pay for them." She opened her mouth to ask more questions, but he stopped her. "I wish I could tell you more, but I can't now. I shouldn't have told you this much, but I just couldn't let you go on believing that I don't care about you. When the truth is, I care about you more than I've ever cared about anyone, or anything."

She could hear the sincerity in his voice, she could also hear the pain. She didn't understand what could possibly be hanging over him, but whatever it was, there was no doubt he deemed it serious and threatening.

There was so much more he wanted to say to her, so much more time he wanted to spend holding her, but time was short and he refused to put her at any more risk than she already was. His hands moved to her waist bringing her even closer to him.

"I want to finish the dance with you," he whispered. The music coming from the ballroom was faint out in the garden, but he didn't care. They didn't need music anyway.

"But I—," she began, hesitating, clearly still wanting answers, but he placed a finger to her lips as he began to sway her gently.

"We have a moment," he said lowly, "just a moment. Please let me hold you." He felt her relax in his arms.

"Ok," she said quietly, then she allowed herself to melt into him, resting her head down against his chest, while her arms circled around his shoulders.

The soft music continued far off and she became so wrapped up in their dance, she almost completely forgot where they were. If only they could freeze time, she could live in this one moment forever. For just a minute, she allowed herself to indulge in the fantasy of living happily ever after with him.

But a second later, she was jarred back into reality when a sudden piercing scream coming from inside the palace made them both jerk their heads in the direction of the reception. They broke apart from one another and Taya looked at him fearfully.

"What's going on?" she asked quickly.

Nicola shook his head. "I don't know," he looked back at her, "but you stay here a moment. Don't follow me right back inside. No one should see us together."

She nodded, but a sadness crossed her face. "But then, what about us?"

Commotion began to rise within the ballroom and the music had stopped. Something was seriously wrong. He reached for her face again, caressing her cheek.

"I'll find a way out of this mess," he promised.

His eyes told her he needed to go now, and she nodded again, not even knowing when she would hear from him next. He turned from her and continued up the path leading back to the palace in the opposite direction.

No sooner had Nicola left then she heard hurried footsteps approaching her from behind. She whirled around, nearly in a panic when she saw Bryan jogging toward her.

"Taya," he called, "I've been looking for you everywhere. What are you doing out here? Don't you know what's going on?"

His voice sounded frantic, and her eyes flew open wide. Had he seen her with Nicola? But Bryan didn't say anything about the prince, his features lined with worry at not knowing her whereabouts. Clearly, he was concerned for her safety. But why?

"I've been here in the garden," she explained, her brow furrowed in confusion, "I just needed some air. Bryan, what's happening? Did I hear someone scream?"

He reached around her pulling her into a tight embrace. "I was so worried when I couldn't find you," he breathed. Then he pulled back from her, studying her, noticing the loose strands of her once perfectly smooth twist. He narrowed his eyes, keenly observing her "roughed up" appearance. "Are you ok?" he asked.

She nodded quickly, attempting to fix her hair. "Oh this? It's been a long night," she said, "these pins were giving me a headache."

He blinked at her, squinting an eye at her explanation, but then shook his head, dismissing the questions about her hair with impatience.

"Taya," he began, "yes, you heard a scream. A palace employee was found. She was strangled to death, in a study just off from the ballroom."

Horror twisted her features.

"What?" She exclaimed, "someone killed her?"

Bryan nodded solemnly. "We need to go back inside," he said, placing his arm around her shoulders, "the guard has already begun to gather possible witnesses. I'm sure they'll want statements."

Taya took a step to follow him, but then realized she stepped on something. Looking down, she bent to pick up a cloth glove from the ground. Puzzled, she handed it to Bryan.

"You dropped your glove," she stated, but he shook his head.

"No, I don't have gloves," he replied then chuckled, "no one wears gloves anymore. Someone else must have dropped it." He tightened his grip on her shoulder, disregarding the item, "come one, we've got to get inside."

Taya gripped the glove in her fist, but as she allowed Bryan to lead her back into the ballroom, she glanced back at where she had stood moments ago with Nicola. Had he dropped it perhaps? Gloves were part of formal, royal attire.

After she and Bryan had made their way back into the ballroom, they had waited for what seemed like forever to give their statements in regards to their whereabouts and their relationship with the deceased palace employee. Which, for Bryan, was none at all, but

Taya realized that she had recognized the girl. She learned that her name had been Olivia, and she was, in fact, Christine's assigned personal attendant.

As she was questioned, the head of the king's guard, Antonio Esposito, could tell that Taya knew Olivia, as she had been unable to keep the shock from her face when seeing her photo. Taya had then admitted to bumping into Olivia outside the monarch's study door, as well as observed her serving a parliament member in a rather friendly manner the evening prior to the vote, and then finally in the crowd at the hospital. Romano, the head of intelligence, had seemed rather interested in what Taya had to say, however, Taya couldn't fathom how any of the random times she had seen Olivia was relevant to who had killed her and why.

As they were answering questions, Taya overheard one of the investigators informing Esposito that Olivia had been strangled by an unknown assailant wearing a pair of cloth gloves, which was consistent with the bruising on her neck.

"I will instruct the coroner to collect any possible fibers underneath her fingernails as well," the investigator reported, "we will collect samples as evidence in case we recover the gloves. We should be able to match them up," he shrugged, "it'll be the closest thing we have to a murder weapon."

Taya had shoved the glove she found in the garden into her clutch, and although she dismissed the thought that the glove in her purse and the gloves used to kill Olivia were related, she couldn't help but notice her purse suddenly felt like it weighed a ton. She chose to keep the glove she found a secret, the back of her mind still wondering if it had been Nicola who dropped it.

Once they were told they could leave and she and Bryan were making their way out, Taya had noticed Christine. She was pale, and her eyes were red from crying; she was clearly very distraught upon learning that her personal attendant had been murdered.

The last thing Taya saw as she was hastily ushered out of the palace by Bryan, was Nicola. Among the organized chaos of the guard facilitating the interviewing and securing a crime scene, he stood calm and silent off to the side. His face was stoic, but as he caught her eyes, his expression brewed with an intensity. She could sense he wanted to call out to her, but he remained quiet, instead following her with his gaze until he no longer could.

It was well into the night by the time Bryan was driving Taya home from the reception. She leaned back against the headrest as she gazed out the window, her mind too full of thoughts to speak, her head heavy from fatigue. The constant hum of the car wheels on the smooth pavement was calming, and she let the sound as well as the darkness of the night quiet her otherwise emotional state. Too much had happened, and she wasn't sure if she was in a mind frame of shock or disbelief from the evening's events.

She felt a sudden lurch in her stomach as she thought of Nicola, they had shared such a magical moment in the garden, and it made her feel somewhat giddy, but almost immediately following was a pang of irritation. In the wake of the gruesome death of Christine's personal attendant, feeling "happy" about anything felt wrong. Although, she wasn't sure what she felt happy about either. His confession of his love to her amongst the roses was astonishing and left her light-headed while a ridiculous sense of hope threatened to overwhelm her that they might actually work it out; they could be together. But reality brought her back. Regardless of how he said he felt, there was still something he was hiding from her, something that caused him enough alarm to break the little trust they had begun to establish. Then, there was still the glove…

She let out a small, disheartened sigh as Bryan pulled up the driveway to her house. Without a word, he exited the car, then moved to her side to open her door. As they walked together up the sidewalk, they remained silent, and he only spoke once they had reached her front porch.

"So, you lied to me." His voice was quiet, and his tone was sad, but he spoke with confidence nonetheless.

Taya met his eyes with confusion. "What?" she asked, "when did I lie to you?"

Bryan ran a hand through his hair. "I saw you with him," he explained, "when I was trying to find you. In the garden. You told me there was nothing between you."

Taya's eyes flew open wide, and a look of guilt instinctively crossed her face. But almost as quickly as the concern appeared, it subsided, her pride taking over. She had no commitment, had made no promises to Bryan. Was her encounter with Nicola inappropriate?

Perhaps. She never intended to display that for anyone; it just happened. However, as she looked into his face with empathy, she couldn't help but feel remorse for hurting him.

"I never meant to deceive you, Bryan," she began, "my...relationship with Nicola has been complicated, to say the least. I've been nothing but upfront and honest with you about my feelings for you, and I don't believe I owe you an explanation."

"Is he the reason you refuse to look at me differently?" Bryan asked, his tone slightly defiant. "Are you in love with him?"

Her heart began to race at his question. She wasn't prepared to explore these emotions now regardless of what was obvious. Her denial kept her momentarily sane.

"How I feel about him doesn't affect how I feel about you," she stated. "You know where I stand here, and that's not going to change," she paused and looked down, no longer able to hold his gaze. "I'm sorry," she added quietly.

He nodded in defeat, showing his understanding. "You were right, Taya, we shouldn't see each other anymore," he said, his tone low. "I'm unable to move past how I feel about you, and putting certain expectations on you isn't fair."

Tears pricked at the backs of Taya's eyes, knowing that she was losing a friend. "I understand," she whispered.

He began to walk away from the porch, but he stopped and turned to look back at her.

"Just so you know," he said as re-met his gaze, "I don't know the prince very well yet, but I don't trust him. I'm not sure I believe he's good for our country. I'd think twice about getting involved if I were you. He's not worth risking your career over."

He then turned and walked back to his car, not giving Taya the chance to respond. She watched him leave feeling slightly breathless. Again hearing Bryan speak in an unsupportive way against the monarchy was out of his character, and she couldn't help but wonder if she should she feel threatened. Would Bryan say something? She unlocked her front door and entered her home slowly, her brain processing everything from Bryan's words just now to the loss of their friendship, and back to Nicola.

Maybe it was because of his warning to her, or maybe it was because of the murder that just took place, but Taya couldn't stop a sudden anxiety laced with fear wash over her. She laid her clutch down upon the counter in the kitchen, eyeing it, considering again its contents. She pushed the disturbing idea from her mind—it just couldn't be...

The sense of unease stayed with her as she removed her gown and got ready for bed, and for the first time, she didn't feel safe in her home. For the first time, she regretted that she lived alone.

She double checked the door locks, then returned to her room. As she climbed into bed, she closed her eyes, allowing the images of the evening to replay themselves. Sheer emotional exhaustion began to take over her body, and she dozed lightly and restlessly, knowing in the back of her mind, something bad was yet going to happen.

Christine's head was pounding as it neared 1:00 a.m. Still working through the aftermath of the murder of her attendant, she now waited with Derek, Nicola, Antonio Esposito and Romano as they continued to investigate and make inquiries. Although the prime minister had been questioned and allowed to retire, members of the guard were still present as well as Costa and Martino.

There were no obvious suspects, there was no surveillance in the particular room she was killed, and there was very little evidence found. She had been strangled quickly, the gloves the killer wore ensuring that no fingerprints would be left behind.

Christine had moved past her state of shock and was now facing an overwhelming sense of despair. Olivia wasn't just her attendant, she had been her friend. The one person she felt like she was getting close to in this country.

She was riddled with fatigue as she waited in a lounge across the hall from the study where Olivia had been discovered. Nicola was also with her, but he hadn't said a word in the past twenty minutes or so, his normal smirk or jovial demeanor replaced with a sense of gravity and also, what appeared to be impatience. He was currently pacing, but every so often, he'd take a seat, restlessly tap his fingers, only to sigh, then stand a moment later and resume pacing. It was clear he anxious to be relieved. But why, Christine couldn't fathom.

She raised her head from where it was resting in her hand on the arm of the chair when Derek, Esposito and Romano reentered the room. She stood as they approached her, and she met Derek's eyes, for once his expression showing emotion and a look of uncertainty.

"What is it?" she asked, "have they found who did this or why?"

Derek ran his hand over his jaw and the back of his neck. Christine narrowed her eyes as he appeared to be hesitating.

"We know why," he said quietly. She waited for him to continue. "Christine, Olivia was being paid to leak information on you. She was the connection between you and the press."

Christine brought her hand to her mouth, a sense of disbelief flooding through her. "No," she protested, "she wouldn't..."

Refusing to believe Olivia had betrayed her, she recalled their conversation just prior to the reception; how Olivia had seemed so sincere, so kind...

"How do you know?" she asked, a deep seated sadness now settling into the pit of her stomach.

"The guards present the day of your unveiling at the hospital confronted the men who taunted you from the crowd," Romano informed her, "when questioned, the men stated they were paid off by a girl matching Olivia's description to do what they did. We were able to confirm through several witnesses that Olivia was, in fact, there that day. Taya Mariano also confirmed it just this evening. Even prior to Taya's confirmation however, I had already begun making inquiries into her bank accounts.

"We found several untraceable wires of large sums of money going into her account over the past few months," he continued. "She's been getting close to you so she could sell the information to a source, who's clearly working very hard at making sure your image here in Calina is tainted."

"She was also there that night," Derek added gently, "in your room."

He didn't elaborate on the details of the night he referred to; the one where he found her in the middle of a night terror, but she knew immediately he was right. Olivia had, in fact, exposed her for profit.

"Olivia's been doing this to me," Christine whispered, more to herself, her brow furrowed. She looked at Derek, "this is what you wanted to tell me earlier," she said, not needing to ask, but knowing. At the time, she could tell something heavy was weighing on his mind.

He nodded. "I was going to tell you in the morning," he said, "I know how close you were with her, and I wanted you to be able to process what was happening before she was just arrested. By the time the information was confirmed, there just wasn't an opportunity before the reception."

"But, that doesn't explain why someone wanted her dead," she stated, "she was obviously delivering valuable information. This 'source' was benefiting from her, right?"

Romano and Esposito exchanged glances.

"Well, we have two theories," Esposito said, "it's possible she decided the amount of money she was receiving wasn't enough. If she had begun to blackmail who she was working for, this may have been how they decided to deal with her. *Or*," he emphasized, "strangulation is psychologically a crime of passion, leading us to believe that whoever killed her did so out of anger or hatred. Perhaps hatred over what she had been doing." Esposito locked his gaze with Christine's. "It's like you said, Christine, we have to ask ourselves who would have wanted her dead…"

Christine blinked, not understanding at first what Esposito was telling her. As his words sunk in, however, she put the two together. The one person who had been suffering due to Olivia's actions was Christine, herself. She had the obvious motive. Since Derek had not been able to talk to her, he could not confirm she didn't have prior knowledge of Olivia's betrayal. Plus, when he had entered the bedroom earlier, she appeared to have been crying or upset, right after having a conversation with the attendant. Had he told Esposito this? She glanced at Derek, then met the eyes of the guard.

"You think *I* killed Olivia?"

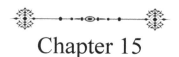

Chapter 15

Christine stared at Esposito in disbelief. *This can't be happening,* she thought, *how could any of them think I'm capable of murder?*

Her eyes immediately went back to Derek, searching his face, fearful of seeing anything in his expression that reflected he considered her a killer. But he met her gaze with reassurance, although pensive, she instantly knew he was on her side, and she gave him a weak smile in relief.

"Did you have any knowledge of Olivia's treason?" Esposito now asked Christine. "You obviously spent a lot of time with her. Something she said, perhaps? Or maybe you found evidence?"

Christine shook her head, eyeing Esposito with bewilderment at his blunt questions to her. "Wouldn't I have said something if I had known?" She shot back defiantly.

He lifted an eyebrow. "Would you have?" he asked. "Or, would you have maybe been enraged enough to take matters into your own hands? After all, you've been at the center of our tabloids since you got here because of her. Our people don't trust you, they don't want you here," he paused, "they think you're crazy."

Not willing to give Esposito the reaction he was seeking, Christine glanced at Derek before responding. She could tell he was on the verge of losing his temper, and as he opened his mouth to address the manner in which Esposito was speaking to her, she placed her hand on his chest to stop his words.

"I wonder," she began, straightening her shoulders, "if you would be speaking to me this way if I was already your queen." Esposito's eyes widened slightly, taken aback by the statement. "It's clear you know nothing about me," she continued, "and thanks to Olivia and whoever she was working for, you, like many, have a very false impression of me, even believing that I'm capable of murder. Because you think me unstable, or even insane? Would you be jumping to these conclusions if you had not read those things about me?" She turned to

Romano, "you just said she's been working hard to ensure my image here is tainted. Then why are you basing your questions on something you know is falsified? Shouldn't you be conducting your investigation according to evidence and fact, not bias?"

Romano glanced down at the floor, as Esposito cleared his throat by means of hesitation. "We... have to explore any possibility," he said with less conviction in his voice now. She raised her eye brows at him. "Signora," he added.

"I had no prior knowledge of her betrayal, and I did not kill her. You will find nothing that says I did," she stated plainly. "Now, if you will excuse me, I'm going to bed."

If Derek had thought it was impossible to love Christine any more than he already did, he was wrong. He watched her turn and walk out the room, leaving the men behind her speechless. He hadn't needed to come to her rescue. She stood on her own and said everything that needed to be said. He half-smiled in spite of the situation, incapable of stopping the pride swelling within him. He turned to Esposito, his gaze turning cold.

"You heard her, we're done here," he said, "I suggest you get some rest so you can begin early on finding out who really did this."

Esposito bowed his head, and Derek turned to leave, but Nicola hurried after him and caught his arm.

"Derek," he said as his brother looked back at him, "you know she was working for DeGrassi, right?"

Derek narrowed his eyes, then glanced at Romano, who exchanged a knowing look.

Of course Derek knew, just like everyone knew, who the mastermind was, but proving it was an entirely different matter. As much as Romano had dug trying to trace anything back to DeGrassi, including the wire payments to Olivia, there was nothing.

"And if I could prove it and arrest him, I would see it done," Derek replied. "But, even if DeGrassi ordered Olivia to be killed, he didn't do it himself."

"We've checked all surveillance footage," Romano interjected, "we've interviewed all the witnesses, and we've looked into his whereabouts this evening. DeGrassi never set foot on palace grounds tonight."

"It's best to focus on finding the actual killer," Derek added, "for now. Finding them may open a door that leads back to DeGrassi."

Nicola's expression remained thoughtful as he watched Derek turn and leave the room. Romano and Esposito had begun to discuss things amongst themselves, and since Derek had left, Costa left as well, leaving only his own personal guard, Martino, with him. He glanced at Martino and gave a loud yawn.

"Damn, it's been a long day," he stated, clearly indicating his desire to leave. "I'm going to bed, no need for you to hang around." He looked at the guard pointedly, and Martino responded by bowing.

"Of course, Signore."

Nicola left the lounge, heading in the direction of his room. Martino followed until he arrived at his own room. When the guard had entered and closed his door however, Nicola continued past his bedroom and headed down the hall toward the elevator. Once inside, he punched the button taking him down to the car garage.

Derek entered his room eager to check on Christine. He found her sitting on the bed; she appeared to have been waiting for him. She had changed out of her gown, and now, with her hair down and wearing a simple chemise, she held a slightly dazed expression. As he neared her, he could see sadness as well in her eyes. She didn't acknowledge him until he sat gently next to her. He waited for her to speak first, only taking her hand in his to show his support.

Now, away from others who might judge her, safe in the solitude behind their closed doors, she allowed her unrestrained reactions to take over and let her composure break down. She turned to him and buried her head in his chest as the tears began to roll down her cheeks. He remained quiet, letting her cry, knowing she needed to deplete her emotions.

"I'm a pawn in his game, aren't I?" she asked, raising her head to look at him. Her eyes were bloodshot and glistening, although the look on her face held resolve. He brushed a tear from her cheek gently, in awe of her raw beauty which was only magnified by the flush in her face from crying.

Derek didn't need to ask her what she meant. He was surprised however that she had caught on so quickly, as he had tried to shield her from the dark, political schemes that had been plaguing the country. He nodded slowly, knowing she was strong enough to withstand the facts.

"DeGrassi," he affirmed. "We can't prove it, but I do believe he bribed Olivia to work for him as a spy. It makes sense in his twisted mind that to target you would make me vulnerable." He looked into her eyes and brushed a strand of her hair behind her ear, then lifted her face to his. "It's no secret it would destroy me if I lost you again, Christine," he said softly.

She knitted her brow. "Is that his plan? To make me leave you?"

Derek gave her a pensive look. "I think that's part of what he's trying to do," he replied slowly, "to avenge his father would be to hit me where it hurt the most." He watched her face carefully. "I can't express to you how disappointed I am in Esposito. His assumptions were out of line and disrespectful," he paused, attempting to gauge her reaction, which was nothing, and she would not meet his gaze. "Christine," she raised her eyes to him, "I need to know where your head is. Don't let DeGrassi win."

Derek couldn't deny that he feared Christine might consider leaving after tonight's events. She was under constant strain from the press, and being accused of murdering her attendant was most certainly the final indignity. Thanks to DeGrassi, she never had a fair chance at winning over the people, but even through everything, she had yet to give up.

"I'd be lying if I said I haven't wondered what it'd be like to go back to an ordinary life," she said quietly after a few moments, "I'm just not sure I belong her, that I'm supposed to be doing this."

Her words stung, but he attempted to push aside his own disappointment, this was about her, not him.

"You didn't see yourself just now, speaking to Esposito, putting him in his place," he mused, looking at her with admiration. "You belong here, Christine, you just haven't been given the opportunity you deserve to feel like this is your rightful place," he paused, "but it is." She just sighed in response, and he could see the sadness, the fatigue in her eyes. "Maybe," he said slowly, "you should get away."

She looked at him with surprise. "You want me to go?"

He shook his head and pulled her against him, kissing her hair. "No, of course not," he replied, "I mean, get away, take a break," he raised her face up to look at him. "Then, come back."

She studied him, considering his suggestion. It would be nice to visit her family, she thought. But distance from Derek would be tough, especially with political tensions running so high right now. And what if her night terrors came back? She'd be alone.

"I can't leave," she objected, "the EU vote is just over a week away. It's such an important time for the country, and I should be here."

He placed his hands gently on her shoulders. "Everything will be all right," he reasoned, "Nicola is overseeing the vote, and I have no doubt that it will succeed. I have it on good authority that over 75% of the people will vote for joining the union. They are beginning to understand that they are only starving because DeGrassi has too much influence over the economical state of our country. By joining the EU, much of his power is taken away. There should be no reason it shouldn't go smoothly."

She stood up from the bed and began pacing. "But you have suspicions that DeGrassi influenced parliament members during the last vote, right? Don't you expect him to make some kind of move to sway the outcome of this one? He has so much at stake, and he's reckless..." she trailed off and shivered. Now with Olivia dead, it was clear just how dangerous and desperate DeGrassi was. He would clearly go to any lengths necessary to take Derek down.

He took her hand and pulled her back down onto the bed beside him. "You need this, Christine," he said soothingly, "let me worry about Calina for now."

He pulled her back into him and stroked her hair. She gave a small nod, consenting, and he let out a slow breath he didn't realize he was holding. He knew he was taking a risk by letting her leave, but her leaving this way was better than being driven away for good due to the pressure and false allegations. He could only hope that even if she did go home to the States, she would still return to him.

Derek was not one to cater to fear, but the thought of how close DeGrassi was coming to driving Christine away scared him. His jaw tightened. She was right, of course, DeGrassi had much to lose with Calina joining the EU, and Derek was sure he was planning something, but so far he had come up empty as to what.

Opening the vote to the general public of Calina was highly unorthodox for their government, but he felt the extremes were necessary to ensure that DeGrassi could not rig the outcome in his favor. This time, the people's voices would be heard.

The low roar of a car outside startled Taya awake. She sat up in bed quickly, squinting in the darkness of her bedroom. Peering at the nightstand clock, she saw it was a little before 2 AM. She groaned as she realized she had barely just fallen asleep.

With her head cloudy, she stood and walked over to the bedroom window, pulling the curtain back to look outside. She could see the driveway, and because she lived far enough away from both neighbors and main roads, the sound of a car could only mean that someone was here. It occurred to her that maybe Bryan had come back, but her eyes flew open wide, her tired brain fog clearing completely, when she saw a sleek, red LaFerrari pulling up to a stop on her approach. She knew the ridiculously rare automobile belonged to Derek, but it certainly didn't make sense that the monarch would drive out to her house in the middle of the night.

She watched from her window as the door to the car opened, and Nicola stepped out. Her heart missed a beat as about a dozen different emotions flew through her body at once.

Withdrawing from the window, she forced a shaky breath. She began walking out the bedroom door, anticipating a knock, which she heard a moment later. As she passed the kitchen counter, she glanced again at the purse she had left there with the glove inside. Was he here for that? Had he realized it was missing and she must've been the one to pick it up? She swallowed a suddenly dry throat, wondering if opening the door was potentially a dangerous thing to do. Was Olivia's killer on the other side?

She moved to twist the knob, hesitating, and he knocked again making her jump slightly. Shaking her head, feeling neurotic, she opened the door to see him standing there. She breathed in, prepared to ask him what he was doing here, but before she could even register what was happening, he moved toward her, grabbing her face with both hands and crashing his lips against hers.

He stole her breath from her lungs as his mouth devoured hers, his tongue sliding along her lips, seeking to taste her fully. She opened her mouth slightly, obliging to give him access. She became lost in how right he felt against her, and she bit gently on his bottom lip, her desires for him swelling within her.

Stepping forward, he pushed her further into the kitchen until she was backed into the counter. She braced one hand behind her on the countertop as his mouth now moved down her throat. Heat pooled in her stomach and was spreading throughout her limbs. She couldn't resist running one hand through his thick hair, pressing him closer to her. As she did so, a deep groan left his lips, revealing his intense yearning for her.

She was only wearing a simple, oversized t-shirt to sleep in, and his hand now left her face, traveling down the length of her body finding its way under her shirt and across her bare hip. He grabbed her firm rear, pushing her into him, and she let out a soft moan.

Encouraged, his hand softly grazed her skin farther up her shirt, his fingertips searing her flesh as they made their way across her abdomen to her sensitive breast. He moved slowly, almost teasing her, barely allowing the slightest brush of his touch across her nipple. Her body reacted to him on its own, shivers of pleasure coursing through her, and he was driving her insane with need.

"I want you so bad, Taya," his voice was strained and low, sounding almost painful, his breath hot against her neck.

Her head rolled back as she held tight onto him. Pressed against the counter top, her eyelids fluttered just open when she glimpsed her clutch, right next to where they were standing. Her breathing hitched, the sight of the purse knocking some sense into her, remembering what the glove could possibly mean. She couldn't allow this to continue, not without knowing if she was in love with a murderer.

"Nic, wait," she gasped, pressing against his hard chest with her hands.

He ceased his onslaught of affection abruptly and groaned, his head still buried in her neck. He stood up straight and took a step back away from her, his expression clearly showcasing his displeasure at being told to stop.

"What are you even doing here right now?" she asked.

"I had to see you," he replied with a reserved desperation.

She looked into his eyes, searching for any malicious or ulterior intentions; she saw only desire.

"After tonight," he continued, "what had happened... I couldn't help but need to see you again. I had to make sure you were all right."

She hugged her arms, more so to prevent herself from flying back into his embrace. But there were questions she had to have answers to.

"Does the guard know anything yet?" she asked. "Who did it, or why?" She watched his expression closely, looking for any sign of guilt.

He shook his head. "Who? No, they have no idea," he gave a short laugh, "they went so far as to accuse Christine though," and a grimace crossed his face showing his disgust at the thought.

Taya's eyes opened wide. "Why on earth would they think Christine did it?"

"She's an easy target," Nicola shrugged, "they don't like her. And," he paused, "it was discovered that it was Olivia who had been leaking information on Christine to the press."

"What? Olivia?" Taya questioned, "why would she do that though?"

"She was being bribed," Nicola stated. "Olivia was taking bribes by someone to gather information on Christine, probably Derek too, and deliver any damning news to the press."

Taya shivered and unconsciously gripped her arms more tightly. She could only think of one person that would be so bold to enlist palace employees to spy on the monarch: Enzo. Apparently he would stop at nothing to collect anything he could to use in his favor to make the monarchy look bad, further creating distrust and tension among the people.

If Olivia was secretly working for Enzo, she had no doubt he had her killed. Especially if he thought she could point the finger back at him. But, it still didn't answer the question of who had done the deed. Again, she glanced at her purse, then at Nicola.

If Enzo could bribe Olivia, were others buyable as well? After all, if Derek were overthrown by the people or parliament, wouldn't his brother take his place? And if that person taking Derek's place was already in Enzo's pocket...

She looked at Nicola with a pleading in her eyes and a desperation to believe he was the man she had come to know, not someone who would sell out for power or position. She briefly recalled Nicola's demeanor toward his brother when he had first arrived in Calina. Neither of them knew she had witnessed their exchange, and at the time, Taya remembered thinking that they did not respect one another. Was Nicola's dislike for his brother enough to make him agree to treason? If Nicola was working for Enzo, there was no question in Taya's mind that he had killed Olivia.

She thought back to earlier in the evening; by the time she had left him on the dance floor and made her way outside, it had been about 15 minutes or so before he approached her in the garden. There had been enough time for him to kill Olivia.

"She had to have been working for Enzo," she said quietly.

Nicola nodded to her conclusion, having already voiced this suspicion to Derek. He studied her expression carefully, almost seeing the wheels in her head turning. He could tell she was contemplating something heavy, yet all he wanted to do was kiss her again. He watched as she gathered her mass of hair in both her hands behind her head as though she were pulling it up into a pony tail. But, she had no hair tie, so she let it fall down again around her shoulders. At that moment, in his mind, he had never seen anything more sexy. She chewed on her lip before speaking again, and he had to shake his head to snap out of the trance she held him in.

"What?" he asked, realizing she had said something.

"Whoever killed her must also be working for Enzo," she repeated, continuing her train of thought out loud. "In order to enlist someone to conspire with him, he would need someone in his corner who had much to gain if he were successful in removing Derek from the monarchy."

She looked at him and swallowed a lump in her throat, but the sensation of choking was abundant. She had never been more afraid of an answer than she was at this moment, but she had to know.

"Is it you, Nic?" she whispered, locking her eyes with his. "Did you kill her?"

Chapter 16

Nicola's face went blank at her question. "How— how could you think that, Taya?"

He looked at her in disbelief. Did she really believe him capable of what she had just accused him of? He turned from her in frustration, running a hand through his hair. He knew he had a mixed past, and he had done things he was not proud of. He had also been deceptive, even if he had felt it was in her best interest, but it was clear she was still trying to figure out exactly who he was.

He owed her an explanation.

His mind flew back briefly to the first day he landed in Calina. He had been basically abducted, driven by some crony to see DeGrassi, who had made him a startling proposition: to conspire against Derek, placing Nicola on the throne, but only to serve as a yes-man for Enzo.

"And by pay back, you mean place you in a position of high regard with the monarchy, free to influence the government to serve your own agenda." Nicola finished out Enzo's end game for him. "Either way, you have me playing the puppet."

Enzo shrugged in response, arranging his features in a non-committal way. "I'm not sure how that is of consequence to you," he replied, "you will be in a much better position if we work together than you are now, and your brother will get what he deserves. Tell me, Nic, how did it make you feel when you learned he only chose to be monarch after he found out you wanted it?"

Nicola winced internally. It had hurt him gravely that Derek was fine to abdicate the throne, that is, until Nicola had claimed the birthright as his own. And it was unsettling that Enzo knew this, clearly proving his connections ran deep.

Enzo took another puff on the cigarette before tossing it to the ground. He then stuck his hand out in a partnership offering and Nicola eyed it, countless thoughts running through his mind.

"Do we have an agreement," Enzo said and paused, "Your

Highness?"

Derek may have pissed Nicola off, and they definitely had their share of differences, but Nicola was loyal to Derek, knowing deep down that his older brother was the one person who had always had his back.

"You know nothing," he emphasized, a look of disgust flooding his features as he locked eyes with Enzo, challenging him silently. "I would never betray my brother. Regardless of what was being presented. You and your 'offer' can go to hell." Enzo's face turned to stone.

"We'll see," he stated. Then, he nodded at the gunman standing behind Nicola, who approached the price from behind. Before he could react, Nicola felt an immense pain erupt in his skull, then saw black.

His eyes focused on Taya's face, bringing him back into the present moment. Yes, DeGrassi had made him quite the proposal, but Nicola had rejected it, even it if meant constantly looking over his shoulder in fear for his life. Even if it meant giving up the only woman he had ever loved to keep her safe.

The organization he was indebted to had a ruthless reputation, and they always followed through on their promises. Nicola had thought that with Derek's security and resources, he could pacify them, pay them off, and be free of his mistakes. But the organization had refused to be paid back. And since Nicola had declined to side with DeGrassi, he knew he would use any resources and contacts at his disposal to aid their manhunt. Nicola could only hide behind the palace security for so long; it was only a matter of time before someone messed up and he was exposed. He did not underestimate DeGrassi's connections and ability to access inside information.

"After everything between us," he said, his eye brows coming together with conviction, "do you honestly believe I could be a murderer?"

Taya could tell he was processing her suspicions of him, and the raw, shocked expression on his face at her accusation made Taya regret her question; he was no killer. But he was keeping something from her.

"Then what are you hiding?" she asked in desperation, "you said it wasn't safe for us to be together, that you've made mistakes. If you're

161

not involved in some conspiracy, then what?"

Nicola sighed and hung his head slightly. It was his fault he was in this place, his own doing. He had hoped not to reveal to Taya his shameful past.

"I crossed the wrong people in New York, and it came to be that I owed them a lot of money that I couldn't pay," he explained, unable to meet her eyes, "when I realized they were going to come after me, I came to Calina for refuge." He finally looked into her face, anticipating with a heavy heart the disappointment he knew he was about to feel from her. "Even after my brother agreed to help me, they would not settle this monetarily. Their goal is to kill me," he stated, "and they will use anyone to get to me." He waited for her reaction, but she stayed quiet, her eyes wide. "I'm so sorry, angel," he said quietly, "I should have never revealed to you how I felt about you knowing it could put you in harm's way." He paused, coming to terms with telling her everything now. "There's more," he added, and her eyes narrowed slightly. "DeGrassi knows. He knows who's after me, and he's helping them."

Taya's heart fell into her stomach listening to Nicola's explanation. She knew Enzo had spies everywhere. If anyone saw them together, it could be dangerous for both of them. It made sense to her now; his rejection of her, his mixed signals.

She could tell he was in fear of her judgement of him, but she had already made peace with who he used to be, and despite it all, she had fallen in love with him and everything that he is. She studied the remorse within his features, understanding the position he was in.

Unable to control her actions, she moved close to him and wrapped her arms around his torso. She ignored her ability to think rationally, allowing her heart to believe that somehow this could work between them. Even though, deep down she knew it would be impossible for them to be together. Her eyes burned with tears as he she tried to memorize how it felt to be in his arms.

"I love you, Nic," she whispered against his chest.

His arms encircled her and crushed her to him. He had known. Even if she had never said it until now, he had known all along.

In spite of everything, he felt an enormous relief flood his heart. Hearing her say the words out loud and knowing she accepted him, even with his past. His hands lifted her face to look at him. "I love you too, angel," he said as he used his thumb to brush away a stray tear that had begun to roll down her cheek. "No matter what happens, I don't think I could ever stop loving you, and I want nothing more than to be with you." He kissed her gently on the forehead, then released her from his embrace, knowing that his time was up.

He was taking a great risk coming to see her in the first place, but he had been incapable of resisting, even if he knew it would only be for just a few brief, sweet moments with her.

"I need to get back before anyone sees me here or realizes I'm gone," he said regrettably, and he took a step back toward the door, as she now held her own arms, immediately missing his warmth and comfort. "Unfortunately, I didn't have much choice with my transportation tonight. It was either the LaFerrari or a limo," a smirk formed on his lips. "Considering I'm trying to not draw attention to myself, I'm not sure I made the right choice."

She nodded and couldn't help but agree that he couldn't stay any longer, as much as it pained her to see him go.

"Won't the king be mad that you took his car?" She teased, and he smiled, grateful for the humor in spite of the situation.

"Hopefully," he said, "Annoying my brother is one of my favorite hobbies." She shook her head at him as he turned to leave. He paused as he reached her door and looked back at her. "Regardless of what I've done in the past, Taya, I would never side with someone like DeGrassi. I would never sell out my family. Or my country." He lifted a shoulder in a shrug, "I am a Landino, after all. Just the name 'DeGrassi' is a bane to my existence."

She swallowed a sudden lump forming in her throat. "I know," she replied, all her doubts about Nicola now put to bed.

He gave her a saddened smile, his gaze lingering on hers. Striding quickly back to her, he grabbed her by the arms pulling her toward him. He stared into her eyes longingly, the tension building as the moment lengthened. Lowering his head, he placed his lips once again on hers in a slow, sweet kiss that held promise. Drawing back from the kiss, he placed one more on her forehead, then turned away from her to the door, closing it behind him as he left.

Ensuring the door was locked after he had gone, Taya made her way back to her bedroom, her heart continuing to ache, but also pounding furiously. She recalled the last time she felt so broken; the night following the parliament conference when his harsh rejection shattered her into pieces. Now, she yearned for him knowing his love was true, but understanding there was no way they could be together. The pain was just as excruciating.

She no longer worried about Nicola's intentions, and she believed he had never made any agreements with Enzo.

If only she could say the same.

She sighed heavily and climbed back into bed considering her position and options. Maybe she should have told him everything… after all, he had been honest with her about his past. But he might never forgive her, and his final words lingered in her mind: *"I am a Landino, after all…"*

No matter now though, the man she loved was in danger, and she was desperate to help him, desperate to find a way to be with him. Nicola had yet to learn of her own connections.

Perhaps he was above making deals with the devil, but she was not.

In a remote area on the outskirts of the city, near the French border, a sleek, black Mercedes waited. Inside, in the back, Enzo lit a cigarette and glanced at his watch impatiently. His dark features twisted in annoyance; it was after 2:00 a.m., and his "associate" was late.

Suddenly, a set of bright headlights pulled up and parked next to the Mercedes. Enzo set his jaw as he heard a car door slam shut, and a moment later the door opposite him opened. A man entered and took the seat next to him. Enzo inhaled before saying anything, taking his time to address the man.

"You're late, LaPointe," he finally acknowledged.

Bryan didn't reply to the statement, and he grimaced as he fought the urge to re-open the car door for fresh air. He despised Enzo and the fact that he was meeting with him. If he stopped to think about it, he'd find himself regretting ever agreeing to work with the scum, but he couldn't think about it—he was in much too deep now.

"You may have heard, but the job is done," he stated plainly, again refusing to think about what his actions tonight actually meant.

Enzo exhaled, filling the car with more smoke. "I have heard," he confirmed, "and no one suspects you?"

Bryan gave a bitter smile. "No," he said, sure that no one would ever look to him as Olivia's killer. Even if he had left evidence.

Regardless of his better judgement, he had been incapable of resisting trying to throw suspicion on Nicola. His common sense was

164

clouded by anger when he saw Taya with him. He dropped the glove himself, knowing that Taya would see it and put two and two together, assuming it was Nicola who dropped it. He had hoped she would have mentioned the glove to the guard, further casting doubt on Nicola, but she had kept the glove to herself. Perhaps it was better that way. Nicola wouldn't necessarily become his scapegoat, but at least the guard didn't have the glove which could potentially lead back to him.

"I'm assuming you have more news for me?" Enzo said evenly, raising an eyebrow at Bryan, "you said this 'hunch' of yours could help with the outcome needed for the vote."

Bryan hesitated. When he first suspected there was a relationship between Taya and Nicola, he had no qualms about handing the information over to Enzo. But now... he had come to really care for Taya, and he didn't trust Enzo not to put her in danger. Not after tonight's job that he had instructed Bryan to carry out.

However, Taya didn't return his feelings, he reminded himself, growing angry again. Why did it matter what happened to her? Still, he paused.

"Nicola, as we know, is responsible for delivering the outcome of the vote," he said finally with a sigh. "Using him, you can rig the vote in your favor."

Enzo eyed him disapprovingly. "Nicola has already rejected my proposal," he replied dismissively.

"You clearly didn't have the proper leverage," Bryan stated plainly.

"Continue," Enzo prompted, leaning back against the headrest.

"He's in love with Taya Mariano," Bryan revealed.

At that, Enzo raised his eyebrows and lowered his cigarette. "Oh?" he asked with interest, sitting forward in his seat.

Bryan nodded. "We could use her to get him to do whatever we needed, but," he added, "she can't get hurt, Enzo. I won't hurt her."

Enzo chuckled and gave a sick smile. "Seems Signorina Mariano is quite popular," he replied, then spoke with malice to his voice. "The only reason you sit where you do within the government is because of me, LaPointe." Bryan didn't reply, and Enzo could see him clench his jaw. "It was my financial backing that won you that election," he continued, "you were nobody before the DeGrassi's found you." Enzo matched Bryan's glare, a slight snarl curling upon his lips. *So ungrateful*, he thought as he sized Bryan up beside him, knowing that he, too was expendable. "You will do as I say," he said with finality, his expression daring Bryan to argue.

Unfortunately, Bryan knew he was deep in Enzo's pocket; there was no backing out. He only nodded curtly, his anger refusing to let him reply.

"Besides," Enzo continued, "Taya might be a willing participant. There may be no reason for anyone else to get hurt."

Bryan furrowed his brow. Taya was not the kind to throw in lots with someone like Enzo. She cared about her country and its people. To hear Enzo speak of her this way gave him courage to find his voice again.

"Taya will never work with you of her own accord," he retorted.

Enzo's smiled widened. "You don't know Taya the way I do," he said calmly, "and now that I know of her feelings for the prince, I think I might have quite a valuable bargaining chip..." he trailed off, a confident grin on his face.

Bryan briefly shut his eyes, closing them to the stinging of the smoke that was quickly filling the car. He gave Enzo an annoyed expression.

"Even if you do somehow coerce Nicola to engineer the vote using Taya, the people will be so outraged at the result, they'll demand the king do something about it. As of now, it's a no-brainer for us to join the union. I don't see how you think you can win this."

Enzo looked unconcerned and fixed Bryan with a keen eye.

"It's Landino who can't win," he replied, "once the vote reveals that Calina will not join the union, you're right, of course, the people will be outraged, on the verge of revolution. They will suspect corruption, because, after all, it was the king's idea to hold the public vote," he paused, a slow smile crossing his face. "As you said they'll demand he do something, which he may, and exact executive power overturning the vote, which will prompt a further outrage and parliament will have to act. He will have no choice but to step down," he chuckled to himself.

"Whether he lets the vote outcome stand, further spiraling our economy straight into my pockets, or overturns it himself, showing what a dictator he is, parliament will insist he hand over the crown."

Bryan shook his head. As much as he'd like to see Landino's downfall, he held doubts.

"You're forgetting," he said, "if Nicola delivers an outcome that doesn't match what the computers show, it'll be clear he lied, and the true voting result will be revealed. There's no way the country is not joining the union."

Enzo sighed impatiently. "If it's revealed Nicola lied, all the more better," he stated, "don't you get it? Whether we join the union or not doesn't matter in the slightest. Joining will not hurt me much, I have other resources at my disposal. And the monetary loss will be worth it to take down that tyrant who murdered my father.

When the people find out its beloved prince lied it will only lead to his arrest. Landino's own brother on trial for treason would be a scandal that the people of Calina would not tolerate."

Bryan processed Enzo's plan, realizing he was right, he had set up the perfect coup. As long as Enzo secured the vote, there was no way Derek could walk out of this as the monarch of Calina.

Unfortunately, he knew the only way Taya would ever help Enzo would be against her will. But if he was going to come out of this on top with Enzo, he couldn't dwell on the knowledge he just put her in danger.

Enzo couldn't keep the devious smile off his face as he sat behind his desk in his office two days later. He once again picked up the tabloid and scanned the headline, translating to read: "Future Queen Leaves Calina."

The article went on to insinuate that the American "fled" Calina only a day after her personal assistant was found brutally murdered. As usual, the tone of the story painted Christine in an unfavorable light, suggesting that either she, herself had something to do with the murder, or that she was so mentally unstable, she simply was not able to cope with the situation. The article did not say if Christine would return, leaving it up to the reader to decide.

He set the tabloid back down on his desk next to an expensive looking brown, leather briefcase with ornate detailing, which lay open.

All of this was working out better than Enzo expected, and the timing could not have been better with the vote so soon. Christine, herself being accused of murdering her own attendant was a pleasant outcome he had not been counting on, and he knew Derek was now distracted with Christine's absence; he would not be expecting a coup.

Of course the monarchy had released a statement immediately

following the publication of this article, stating simply that Christine had gone abroad to travel to the states to visit family, and that she would, in fact, return. But in Enzo's mind, the damage was already done. Christine was gone.

Soon, all his endeavors would pay off. Bryan's information had been invaluable to ensuring that his scheme fell into place. All he had to do now was wait.

As he was preparing to make a call, his intercom buzzed, his secretary delivering the announcement of the arrival of a visitor without an appointment.

"Who is it?" he asked sharply, his features twisting together in irritation.

"A Signorina Maria Albano," the secretary replied curtly.

A slow smile spread across Enzo's lips. "Ah yes," he said pleasantly now, drawing out the words, "I have been expecting her."

He leaned back in his chair, the amused expression still playing on his lips as he waited to receive this guest. He was surprised it had taken her this long to come and see him, and he was almost becoming impatient, the thought occurring to him just yesterday that Bryan's information to him had been misinterpreted. But now that she was here... he could move forward with his plan.

There was a knock and he called, "come in."

A moment later the door to his office swung open and Enzo's eyes narrowed, recognizing all too well the woman who stood in his doorway. Despite her attempt to conceal her identity, he could never mistake the familiarity of her face; he had known it his whole life.

"I think we can dispense with the facade, 'Maria,'" Enzo commented, emphasizing the fictitious name.

The woman removed her hat and glasses as she strode into the office, revealing Enzo's real visitor: Taya Mariano.

Her disguise was necessary, as was the fake name she gave. She knew Enzo would recognize the name, it being the same she had used before when "dealing" with the less than honorable businessman. But she couldn't endanger her reputation by being seen nor heard of in Enzo's company.

It had taken her two days to muster the courage to face him, her desire to free Nicola from his influence building to the point she could stand it no longer. The danger he was in grew each day that passed, and she couldn't bear to continue to think of his life at risk.

Enzo did not rise from his desk and watched as Taya took a seat in front of him.

"So," he continued, his dark eyes glinting maliciously, "it's certainly a surprise seeing you here. After all, you've barely graced me with your presence in over 10 years. What could I possibly do for you?" (As if he didn't know already.) He tapped the side of the briefcase then promptly snapped the lid closed.

Taya hated his arrogance. He was playing with her, and she could tell he knew she wanted something from him. She fixed him with a cool, but hard look in her eyes. One could not show timidness in front of Enzo.

"I know you are aiding an organization that wishes to see prince Nicola dead," she stated bluntly. She felt no need to beat around the bush. She despised this man, and the sooner she was free of his company the better. "I want you to stop. Or better yet, convince them to settle their disagreement monetarily."

Enzo folded his hands, taking his sweet time to reply, and placed a look of contemplation on his face as though he were considering her request.

"I'm not sure what you mean," he replied, choosing not to show his hand to her.

Taya rolled her eyes. "God, you are just like father," she spat out, crossing her arms. "As if no one knows you're the one orchestrating the corruption. I know you tried to buy parliament members, and I know you had that palace worker killed." She glared at him. "But you couldn't buy Nicola, could you? And that pissed you off, so now you're resolved to help hand him over to those after him."

Enzo eyed his sister, who refused to acknowledge any relation to him. She was so ashamed of her true "DeGrassi" name that she had changed it legally. She even left the country to attend school, returning as a completely new person. Her loyalty to the monarchy, the Landino family, who was responsible for the death of their own father was sickening to him.

"I'm assuming you can prove any of the statements you just made?" he asked with an eyebrow raised. When she couldn't reply, he continued. "Even if I had the sort of power you claim I do with regards to your new boyfriend, my answer would be no," he said, enjoying the harsh look that crossed her face. *God, it was so easy to rile her.* "Why should I do something like that for you?" he asked, "you have offered

169

me nothing for this alleged 'favor.'"

"What do you want, Enzo?" she asked, trying to stay on point instead of his preference to speak cryptically.

"Your 'interest' in the well-being of the prince intrigues me," he began, "it's clear you have a certain influence over him—you obviously mean a lot to one another." He laced his fingers together as he watched Taya's expression closely, which did not disappoint as her eyes went wide.

"I have no influence—" she tried, but Enzo cut her off.

"Now, now, Taya, let's not pretend any longer," he said, "Nicola is responsible for delivering the outcome of the vote to join the EU. Of course, as you know, it would be in my best interests if that outcome were to not join."

"Of course it would be in *your* best interests," she sneered, "but not what is best for the people of this country. And it will be the people who decide. Not Nicola."

Enzo stood and rounded the desk, propping himself on the edge. He leaned over causally, pushing the briefcase out of his way and grabbing a cigarette to light it.

"But Nicola delivers the results," he said suggestively. "I'm sure you could help him understand, regardless of how the people vote, that delivering an outcome to not join is what this country needs," he paused, taking an extended drag, "especially if you were offering him his freedom in return."

Taya stood up abruptly causing Enzo to lower his cigarette and raise his eyebrows.

"Do you really think I would aid you in conspiracy?" she asked incredulously.

Whatever she had expected Enzo to ask her for in return for Nicola's liberation, this was not it. She had been prepared to pay or even do him a small favor from her government position, but this was too much.

"You're not going to rig this vote, Enzo," she stated clearly, "it wouldn't matter what anyone offered Nicola, not even for his own life, he wouldn't commit treason against his brother."

"You speak very plainly, Taya," he said evenly, emphasizing her name, "maybe you're making assumptions, because I'm sure we're strictly speaking hypothetically." It didn't matter to him that Taya knew of his desire to manipulate the vote. She had no proof and divulging the possible scheme would mean revealing her true identity; which, he knew she would never do.

She glared at him for a moment, then sighed and walked toward the door.

"Of course, Enzo," she replied, "hypothetically." She then donned her hat and glasses and exited his office, shutting the door with more force than was necessary.

A slow smile crept up on Enzo's face as she left. He had foreseen her unwillingness to be cooperative, although he had hoped she would have agreed to play along. Now, he would have to get a bit more creative to convince Nicola to deliver the vote outcome he needed.

Maybe he wouldn't do it to save his own life, but Enzo now knew Nicola would to save hers.

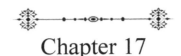

Chapter 17

"We're here, signora."

Christine blinked, and her head snapped up, bringing her out of the daze she had been in since she had arrived at the airport in New York. She had traveled from Calina to North Carolina to Tennessee and finally to New York in just a few short days. She was weary and drained, and her visit with her family had been less than jovial.

She only had her father and her sister, the former being the ever-protective parent (she had been shot after all), and her sister's, Emilia, apparent jealously seemed to know no bounds. Christine had hoped that her family would accept her new lifestyle as long as she was happy. But her father kept hinting that she should just leave Derek, give it all up, and stated quite plainly that her previous career as an art program director had suited her just fine. Meanwhile, her sister wasn't even capable of pretending to be happy for Christine and never missed an opportunity to ridicule both her relationship as well as her future position within the Calina monarchy.

She wasn't sure how she would feel being back in the States; if she would feel as though she were coming home, or if it now felt foreign here. What would it be like if she came back for good? Did she need to return to Calina? Was her father right in thinking that really wasn't the life she should be leading?

Now back in Manhattan, it was late afternoon and the sun was beginning to dip lower in the sky. She wasn't sure if she would've had the time to come to this place before she was scheduled to be at April and Gregory's for dinner, but at the time, she felt this little side trip was necessary. Her door to the flag-bearing limousine opened and Vincenzo Costa, who had been ordered to accompany her to the States, exited the car first to help her climb out. He presented his hand for her to take, but she paused, gripping the bouquet of flowers closer to her chest. Her eyes peered out the door, past Costa, to the cemetery gate. Her features hardened as she thought about where she was and why she was here. She sought closure. Closure from her past, the series of events that led up to her torturous heart-break, hers and Derek's traumatic injuries, and ultimately the death of the woman who lay buried beyond the gates of this cemetery: Courtney Metcalf.

She placed her hand in Costa's, one heeled foot stepped out from the car onto the paved ground.

Would visiting Courtney's grave give her what she was looking for?

"No," she said out loud, releasing Costas grasp and settling back into her seat. The guard looked inside the car at her quizzically. "Please take me to April and Greg's," she told him.

He nodded curtly, then shut her door. A moment later, the opposite side door opened, and the guard seated himself across her. Christine noticed him eyeing her curiously as the limousine pulled away from the cemetery. She met his gaze and raised her eyebrows as though giving him permission to say what was on his mind.

Throughout her entire time so far in Calina and including this trip to the States with him, Christine still had no idea where she stood personally with this guard, and he had not spoken any more than was required of him to do his duty. Although his presence had been appreciated; he kept her safe and the paparazzi at bay, he definitely left something to be desired from the perspective of "company."

"Why didn't you go in?" He inquired stoically.

Christine found his newfound interest a little strange. He didn't seem to care what she did or did not do any other time. But the question was actually refreshing to her. Not just the prospect of having conversation, but the ability to voice her reasons felt like validation.

"It's not that I was afraid," she explained as she lifted her chin a notch. "I thought that if I visited her grave, brought her flowers, or voiced that I was sorry she died, it would lessen my guilt over what happened. Maybe then I would be able to put it all behind me and never think about it, or her, again."

"So why didn't you?" the guard asked again.

"I decided that I don't feel guilty," Christine replied simply. "I didn't kill her. And," she paused, "I'm not sorry that she's dead." Her gaze shifted to the window as she watched the scenery go by in a blur.

"So is it all behind you now?" he asked.

"She will haunt me no more," she stated quietly.

When Costa didn't respond, she turned to look in his direction again. She considered him, and how she had felt so insecure around him. She was tired of always wondering what was going through his mind.

"You don't like me, do you?" she asked him bluntly.

"How would you like me to answer that, Signora?" he replied with his own question.

She practically snorted. *Well, there's my answer*, she thought. "How about honestly," she said however.

"The king holds you in high regard, therefore it is my duty to serve and protect you," Costa answered.

Christine rolled her eyes. "That's not what I asked you, Vincenzo," she pushed, then continued, "you believe what the tabloids have said about me, don't you? You think I'm some gold-digger? That I care nothing for Derek, Calina, or its people?"

Costa took a moment to respond. "I don't actually," he said.

Christine furrowed her brow, briefly feeling offended.

"I don't believe those things about you," he continued, clarifying. "But, I do think you need to stop letting what other people say about you define who you are. Let your actions and decisions speak for themselves," he paused, "soon, no one will dare question your loyalty."

Christine brushed a strand of her hair behind her ear as his words resonated with her. She had no idea Costa felt that way.

"Thank you," she murmured quietly.

"I will say this though," he added, and she met his eye, "the tabloids have hinted that you do not wish to return to Calina. If you've ever even once thought that or considered not returning, then no, I don't like you at all."

Christine stared at Costa for a moment, and as she processed his statement a slow smile formed on her lips.

"Now *that* is honest," she replied, and her smile was genuine, like the man sitting across from her. She agreed with the guard, having already decided that her place was by Derek's side, as his was by hers. "You know what, Vincenzo?" she asked, and he looked at her with eyebrows raised, "I think you and I are going to be friends."

———————

April Blackburn clenched her phone in her fist tightly after hanging up from her last call. *Was Greg crazy?* She thought. She walked slowly through the spacious kitchen, ensuring dinner was well underway for their guests this evening. Pausing by the marble countertop, she drummed her nails nervously. *How could he do this to her?* she continued her internal rant. *Couldn't he see this would make things worse for Christine?*

She and Gregory McKenzie lived just outside of New York City in the suburbs of Scarsdale, an affluent area with easy access to the city, where Gregory spent much of his time. When April had met Gregory, almost two years ago, he was still working as Derek's right-hand man at Land Corporation, one of the most successful corporations in the world. They had clicked instantly, and when Gregory took over as CEO, after Derek resigned, he asked her to move to New York to live with him. With his constant need to travel, leaving April more often than not pining for him, she was more than willing to pack up her life as she knew it and relocate what she knew to be "home."

They were not married, and April had no desire to get married. She had worried at first, when moving in with him, that he would expect a more traditional arrangement. But he had been just fine with their relationship as is, and April couldn't be happier. After all, she was deeply committed to Gregory, and he to her. She had no need for anything else; to her, weddings were a hassle and, in the end, it was simply a piece of paper. She didn't need that to know they belonged together.

Gregory had one brother, Timothy, a highly successful attorney who also resided in the suburbs of New York City. As such, April saw quite a bit of Timothy, and he and Gregory were pretty close. So, it wasn't out of the ordinary when Timothy had called, asking if she needed him to bring anything to dinner tonight.

April had not realized that Gregory had invited Timothy to dinner, and under normal circumstances, this would have been totally ok and normal. However, April was expecting to receive the company of her best friend, Christine, for dinner tonight, who was in town for a short visit. Christine had history with Timothy. Although it had been brief and almost non-existent history, the drama surrounding it had made national news at the time.

Furthermore, when Timothy had called April, he had also shared the news he was bringing along with him a companion for the evening, the woman he was currently involved with, Cynthia Masterson. Or as most knew her, the ex-Mrs. Derek Landino.

175

April had not seen Christine in months, so when her friend called and asked if she could stay for a couple of days, she was more than ecstatic. She, of course, had been following the news feeds and tabloids where Christine was concerned, and she had been disturbed by all the bad press coming out of Calina, with the most recent news of Christine's own personal attendant being murdered. Christine had come to the states to visit her family and friends, and get away from the spotlight, not be thrown into a dramatic situation involving her fiancé's ex-wife and an additional reminder of a past scandal.

April had explained to Timothy that she and Greg were expecting to have dinner with Christine tonight, and he must have the dates mixed up. But Timothy had assured her that he knew of Christine's arrival and that Greg had invited them too. Timothy had not seemed one bit bothered by the fact Christine would be here this evening, but April was deeply concerned.

Needing to confront Gregory for his apparent lack of judgement, April hastened out of the kitchen, her heels clicking on the tile as she practically stomped up the stairs toward the master bedroom suite, located on the east side of the large, Georgian mansion. She found him there, adjusting his tie as he stood in front of the adjacent bathroom mirror. Her phone was still in her hand as she shot daggers at his reflection. His gaze drifted to her scowling at him through the mirror.

"Hey baby," he said easily with a knowing grin. It was obvious she had spoken to his brother, and he knew where her thoughts had gone. But it was all very clear to him.

She crossed her arms and his grin widened. He couldn't help it; he found her adorable when she was angry. Of course, he found her adorable any way she came; made-up like now, wearing an elegant, sleeveless, dark-blue knee-length dress, or first thing in the morning when she rolled out of bed in a t-shirt and shorts with her hair sticking up in different directions. He turned away from the mirror to face her.

"How could you do this, Greg?" She accused, gesturing with her phone, "you knew Christine was coming tonight, how could you invite your brother as well? And Cynthia too!" Her face was turning slightly red. "You call him back right now and tell him not to come," she demanded.

"April," he replied in a reassuring tone, placing his hands gently on her bare shoulders, "I would never do anything to hurt Christine."

"She's been through so much," April stated, not understanding why he didn't get it, "don't you think forcing her to have dinner with Timothy and Cynthia would be just a tad bit uncomfortable for her?" She was unable to keep the heavy sarcasm from her voice.

His eyes met hers.

"Trust me," he said evenly, "I believe this evening is just what Christine needs." He turned from her, walking toward the bed to retrieve his jacket laying across it. "Not to mention Derek," he added lowly.

April caught the comment. She knew Gregory was forever loyal to his former boss, but how could putting Christine in such an awkward situation help Derek?

Approximately an hour later, Christine, followed closely by Costa, walked along the pathway toward Gregory McKenzie's front door. Costa had been adamant to wait in the car, but that seemed ridiculous to Christine, so she insisted he come inside and have dinner. The gated, Georgian-style home was set far back from the road, providing plenty of privacy from public eyes.

Nearing the front porch, Costa pointed to the bouquet still in Christine's hands.

"You're going to give them the flowers you were going to put on a grave?" he asked.

Christine gave him a sharp look, then noticed he was grinning. She gave a small laugh, and at that moment, she realized Derek was right all along; the guard *did* have a personality.

"Well, better than throwing them out I guess," she replied as she rang the bell, "at least they'll go to someone special."

She smiled brightly thinking about seeing April in just a few short moments, excitement flooding through her. She arrived only 15 minutes late, and she was glad she had made the choice not to spend more time than she did at the cemetery. A few seconds ticked by until the door flew open.

April answered the door herself, anxiously anticipating Christine's arrival. Upon seeing her friend, she shrieked before throwing her arms around Christine's neck.

"I thought you'd never get here!" She exclaimed, and Christine smiled, always finding April's energy infectious.

"We're only a few minutes late," Christine choked out as April released her, "and you smashed your flowers."

April laughed and took the bouquet from Christine's hands. "Oh, you didn't have to bring me anything," April said as she sniffed one of the buds, "but, they're beautiful."

Christine exchanged a look with Costa as they crossed the threshold into the grand foyer. "Well, truth be told," she admitted, knowing that April wouldn't care, "I intended to put those flowers on Courtney's grave. But I decided you deserved them more."

April paused and turned to look at Christine, her face serious for a moment, then she broke into a huge grin. "Ha!" she chuckled, "you're right. I do." She then gestured through a doorway. "Go on in, everyone else is already here. I'll just take these into the kitchen really quick and join you in a minute."

As April left in the opposite direction, Christine walked down the hall their hostess indicated, unable to keep from wondering who "everyone else" was. She had thought it would just be her, April, and Gregory. Costa followed her as she entered a sitting room where several people who were talking suddenly stopped to look in her direction.

She blinked back her surprise upon seeing Timothy McKenzie and a blond woman whom she had never met but recognized as Cynthia Masterson, Derek's ex-wife. Costa must have sensed the immediate tension because Christine felt him stiffen beside her.

"Christine," Gregory said as he approached her quickly, guiding her further into the room, "it's great to see you," he hugged her briefly, "you remember my brother, Timothy of course, and this is Cynthia."

As always, Gregory's demeanor was casual and pleasant, promptly diminishing any tone of apprehension. Christine nodded in Timothy and Cynthia's direction.

"It's good to see you again, Timothy," she said politely, and he smiled.

She considered how seeing Timothy again made her feel. He looked exactly the same, tall and broad, sandy brown hair and dark brown eyes; undeniably attractive. She supposed she should feel a bit awkward or even ashamed considering their last encounter had not ended well.

During a time of peak vulnerability for her, she fell into his charms for a brief moment only to realize all to quickly how wrong an involvement with him felt. She knew she had not used her best judgement, but he had also taken advantage of the situation. Long afterward, she learned from Gregory that Derek ended up firing Timothy from Land Corporation because of that night, as well as punching him in the face. Thinking about it all now seemed a bit humorous to her, and it was water well under the bridge.

Although her greeting with Timothy seemed sincere, she couldn't say the same when she offered a hello to Cynthia; her smile was tight-lipped and didn't quite reach her eyes. Just like any picture Christine had seen of her, Cynthia was beautiful, blonde, and leggy, and Christine couldn't help but feel a bit underwhelmed with her own appearance. Leaving her reading glasses in her luggage, she chose to wear a simple pair of tailored, black slacks and an off-shoulder plum colored blouse. Of course, next to Cynthia's dark fuchsia, short cocktail dress, Christine felt rather unimpressive.

"This is Vincenzo," Christine introduced Costa as she brushed a strand of hair behind her ear, a nervous habit of hers. "Greg, I believe you've met Derek's personal guard? He's been traveling with me, and I invited him to dinner. I hope that's all right."

"Of course," Gregory assured her as the men shook hands.

"A personal guard?" Cynthia replied, "how *royal*."

Christine eyed Cynthia suspiciously unsure how to take her comment. Was she mocking her? She didn't want to be quick to judge Cynthia just because of the stereotypical narrative of the "ex-wife," so she didn't respond.

April walked back in at that moment announcing dinner was ready, and as they all made their way toward the dining room, she grabbed Christine by the elbow pulling her to the side.

"I'm sorry I didn't tell you about Timothy and Cynthia being here," she said in a hushed voice, "I didn't know they were coming until late. I hope this isn't uncomfortable for you."

Christine brushed aside April's concern with a wave of her hand. "Of course not," she replied, "we're all adults, aren't we?"

April gave a relieved smile. "And Cynthia's really sweet, you'll see," she added.

Christine gave pause, it dawning on her that April must know Cynthia pretty well. It was a bit surreal to her, but realizing that April's life had moved on in great strides without her, including the making of new, close friends, was something Christine had not considered and made her a bit sad. She glanced at Vincenzo as he gave her a reassuring nod.

The knot in April's stomach loosened slightly as Christine responded to her apology with words that helped put her mind at rest. *Maybe this will turn out ok after all*, she thought. Maybe Christine wasn't as fragile as she thought. She followed behind her guests as they took their seats in the dining room, which she had laid out beautifully. She knew she didn't need to "put on airs" for anyone, especially Christine and Gregory's brother, but she wanted tonight to be fun for Christine, it had been so long since they had seen each other.

She glanced over at Gregory as he took his place, an easy smile on his face. He had said this evening, which included Timothy and Cynthia, is just what Christine needs. She knew her other half had a knack for being insightful, but what exactly was he trying to accomplish?

The attendants she had asked to work this evening entered with an array of dishes April herself had prepared. Of course they could afford cooks, but April more often than not preferred to cook herself, finding the activity relaxing and enjoyable. She had become so enthused with preparing food that she had started taking culinary classes to learn more.

Although April spent much time attending events with Gregory, she also led her own life. In addition to taking classes, she continued to teach various topics of art including art history and humanities. Instead of working for colleges and universities however, she chose to partner with non-profit organizations. She didn't make much money, but she also didn't need to, and her charitable work left an impression on the community. Not only was this good for Gregory's reputation, but she knew she needed a sense of purpose other than just his arm candy.

"Everything looks amazing, April," Christine commented, showing appreciation for the mouthwatering looking feast, and as the table unanimously agreed and gushed, April couldn't help a slight blush pink her cheeks.

As they dined, April kept a sharp ear and eye for any sense of unease or edginess, but the evening was passing by quite amicably. Even Vincenzo Costa seemed to be enjoying himself. Although it did seem as though Cynthia was choosing to ignore Christine for the most part, and even if April had noticed the couple of side-eye looks, Christine, herself did not seem aware of it.

"Christine, how long are you staying in New York?" Timothy now asked as an attendant was coming around with a delicious looking chocolate mousse for dessert.

"Just a couple of days," she answered, "I'm staying here. April and I have a lot to catch up on." She met April's eye with a wink. "Then I'll be heading home."

"And where is home? North Carolina or Tennessee?"

The question came from Cynthia. It was the first direct comment she had made toward Christine all evening. The room seemed to pause with a heavy silence. April looked at Christine with wide eyes as she saw her friend blink slowly, the look on her face making it clear she was pondering whether or not she wanted to address the question.

"Home," she stated finally and clearly, "is Calina." She made eye contact with Cynthia. "Home for me, is with Derek."

Cynthia refused to look away. "Does he know that? I've heard you've come back to the States to stay."

"Cynthia," Timothy interjected with a tone of surprise, but she didn't acknowledge him. April subconsciously held her breath, internally cursing Gregory.

Christine studied Cynthia for a moment before replying. She had hoped that this would not turn confrontational, but it seemed that the glances she kept receiving from Derek's ex-wife were intended to make her feel awkward after all, even though she had tried to ignore them.

It passed through Christine's mind that Cynthia might be jealous, but that didn't seem quite right. Although Cynthia and Derek's divorce had been messy, and at the time, it was Derek who wanted out, it was clear they had both moved on. As Christine had watched Timothy and Cynthia interact this evening, it was obvious they were in love. No, Christine could only conclude that Cynthia's attitude was stemming from a place of respect for Derek. Which, even though there was, to a small extent, some understanding there, Christine felt that constantly having to defend herself to every Tom, Dick, and Harry she met was getting old.

"I'm not sure what you're trying to accomplish with that question, Cynthia," she replied evenly.

"Derek is a very dear friend of mine," Cynthia said, clearly unafraid of saying what was on her mind, "I care about his well-being and success, and from what I hear, it seems as though you're not committed to supporting him."

Costa remained quiet, but tense, as his eyes followed the verbal exchange between the two. His gaze now rested on Christine as he watched her give a slight laugh to Cynthia's comment. She glanced in his direction.

"It seems no matter *where* I go I have to answer to someone's ignorance," she said, a hint of amusement in her voice, then she turned back to Cynthia, her smile gone. "First, Derek's well-being is my concern, not yours," she stated flatly, "and although I don't feel that I owe you any kind of explanation, I will humor you since I do feel that your care for Derek is genuine given your history," she paused, "I'm sure you don't mean to be impertinent." Cynthia's eyes widened and her mouth opened slightly, but Christine continued before she could respond. "If I did not support him," she said, her tone calm and measured, "I would not have left my successful art career in France to move to a strange country. I would not have risked my own life taking a bullet for him, and I certainly would not be sitting here explaining myself, because you, like so many others, have chosen to believe the slanderous nonsense coming out of the tabloids."

She paused, waiting to see if Cynthia had anything else to say, when silence followed, she added, "I am returning to Calina in two days, after which, the vote to join the EU will take place. I will be there to stand by and support my fiancé, regardless of the outcome."

Again, silence followed, the room was tense, and only Gregory smiled at the dialogue unfolding. Every set of eyes were now on Cynthia, waiting for her reply. Or apology.

"I was only speaking from a place of concern," she finally said, but her tone had dropped a notch, the confidence had left. "I'm actually really glad to hear you feel that way, Christine," she took a breath, "I'm sorry if I offended you."

"Accepted," Christine replied graciously. She had no qualms about feeling the need to draw this out, and to her, the matter was settled.

In fact, she felt completely at ease, not just with Cynthia, but with her response and decisions. Maybe it took this specific interaction for her to put to rest any doubts in her own mind, but saying the words out loud to Cynthia allowed her the chance to finally voice all the arguments she'd been holding in. And it felt right.

She glanced at Costa again, who gave her a smirk, and she saw pride within his eyes as well. Yes, she was looking forward to spending the next couple days catching up with her old friend, but, in all honesty, she couldn't wait to get back home.

It had been several days since Taya had gone to see her brother, Enzo. She had failed miserably in bargaining with him to aid her. She hadn't been too surprised, even if they had, (to no one's knowledge), helped each other in the past.

Mostly her dealings with Enzo included her paying him in some way to keep his mouth shut about who she really was. They had been small favors, and she had surrendered any claim to any asset under the DeGrassi name left by her parents. Enzo had all of it. Just so she could be free from ties to that name. She knew she would never have any chance of representing the people of Calina with that name.

Even though keeping her true heritage, as well as her past dealings with Enzo, a secret was crucial to her political standing, she feared now that she might have no choice but to lay the cards on the table. After days of trying to come up with any option that would ensure Nicola's safety, she could only come up with one viable solution. She would have to go to the monarch and tell him everything she knew.

The career that she had built and worked for her entire life was suddenly crashing down around her, and although it pained her to see it, the anguish she felt over potentially losing Nicola was far worse. It amazed her how in such a short period of time her priorities and everything she cared for had changed. She had never loved anyone or anything so strongly before as she did him, not even her own ambition. And if her job needed to be sacrificed, then so be it. At least, if she was removed from parliament, there would no longer be any conflict of interest with a relationship between them.

She would admit to Derek she had petitioned on behalf of his brother for his life to Enzo. She would admit that she thought she could because she was, in fact, Enzo's sister, and they had made deals in the past. And she would admit that she desired to help Nicola because she loved him. Derek already knew Nicola was being hunted by the organization from New York, but did he know Enzo was helping them? Maybe that information would be useful, as well as the knowledge that Enzo would be attempting to rig the outcome of the EU vote in his favor.

With the vote being held tomorrow, timing was of the essence. She didn't specifically know Enzo's plans, but if she were to warn Derek, maybe extra measures could be taken. As a trusted member of the government, maybe her personal testimony of what Enzo said to her would be enough to at least bring him in for questioning. Maybe it could lead to his arrest.

Sitting at her office desk, she had already keyed in the request to her party asking for an audience with the monarch, stating the matter in which she needed to speak to him was of the utmost urgency and was related to the vote tomorrow. She had not been able to sleep nor eat knowing this was the path she now needed to take. Her head was pounding, yet she looked at her untouched lunch, now cold, on her desk with disgust.

She tapped her nail on the keyboard for a moment, realizing the message she was about to send would lead to the destruction of her career. She pressed send. She only hoped she would be able to see him in time.

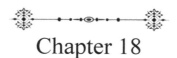

Chapter 18

It was drizzling rain, dark and chilly, the night sky appearing almost ominous beyond the mountain tops. Bryan sat behind the wheel of his car, still heavily contemplating the task he was just given by his "employer." He watched as the raindrops splattered against his windshield, then glanced at the expensive, brown leather briefcase in the passenger seat next to him; the one Enzo left as payment. It was the largest payment he had ever received. It wasn't enough.

Not for this.

Bryan had gotten good at not thinking too deeply about what many of his actions actually meant. Strangling Olivia had been simple and easy, for example, and the thoughts of morality didn't bother him. Would he have preferred to not engage in the extreme activity of killing? Yes, of course. But also, he knew there were certain prices that had to be paid. There was a bigger goal, a greater good, and she had been in the way of that. This latest assignment he struggled with, however, and for the first time, he wondered what would happen if he just walked away.

He had been working for Enzo off the record for the past six months or so, having previously been a loyal servant to Enzo's father, Marco. Bryan had preferred Marco. He had respected Marco, growing up idolizing him as some kind of "hero."

Like most families in Calina, Bryan came from a background laden with poverty. His mother had fallen ill when he was eight, and his father left the country to "find work," but never returned. When his mother passed away, Bryan was bound for the streets with his sister, Collette.

But he didn't think about Collette...

This was during the time of the assassination of Luciano Landino and with the country in the midst of a revolution, Marco was campaigning heavily for power. As a boy, Bryan found hope in Marco, anything to better his situation, and not only did he gravitate to the larger-than-life political figure, who, according to rumors, conquered the evil king, he sought him out, begging the politician for work. Marco took pity on the ambitious, eight year old boy, recognizing the potential of a loyal servant, desperate to do anything asked.

At the time, it had been easy for Bryan to turn a blind eye to the unlawful nature of the tasks he was asked to do, mostly breaking and entering to start, because being able to eat had been a priority. He had grown up blurring the lines of right and wrong, and Bryan had been doing Marco's bidding ever since. The pay-offs became greater as he got older, and it was through these assignments Bryan earned his living, eventually putting himself through law school, which had been Marco's suggestion, as if he knew having another attorney in his pocket would benefit him.

Bryan had never met Enzo, nor any of the DeGrassi family, after all he was just an under the radar employee. It wasn't until Marco was killed and Enzo took over his father's businesses that Enzo discovered Bryan on his father's payroll.

Since Enzo, himself, could never petition for a government position, Bryan seemed a convenient choice to place in parliament. After all, they both hated the Landino family, and they both sought revenge against Derek for Marco's death; it made sense for Bryan to continue his loyalty to the DeGrassi's. Especially since Enzo was offering him a government position and power within the country in return.

Bryan soon realized however, that Enzo was not Marco. Marco had visions and organized uprisings to stand up for what he felt was needed in Calina, even if his actions were fueled by motivations to usher in a new era where he, himself sat on the throne. Enzo preferred to operate behind the scenes, making shady deals, and enlisting spies and accomplices. Although the goals were the same between father and son, the methods were extremely different.

Marco would have never asked Bryan to do what Enzo just did, for example, and he gave the briefcase a hateful glare. If Marco had wanted this vote to go a certain way, he would've simply asked the parliament members to see it done. But Enzo didn't have that kind of influence over parliament the way Marco had, so he had to resort to things like blackmail, kidnapping, and murder.

It was late, and placing his car in drive, Bryan began toward home.

Again, it was best not to think too deeply about what needed to be done, and he placed his hand on the briefcase, shoving it off the seat onto the floor. The vote was tomorrow. By then, it would all be over.

Derek peered out the window for what felt like the hundredth time. The weather was turning bad, the rain getting stronger, and the wind was picking up. *Could the storm be delaying them?* he wondered, although he knew that was foolish. *Was she even coming back at all?* That was more foolish.

Christine was due home any minute, and although he had been given updates throughout her trip, as well as notified of her plane landing, he would not feel at ease until she was physically standing here in front of him. Regardless of what she said, a small part of him still questioned her intentions to return, and the longer she stayed in the U.S., the more concerned he had grown. He needed her assurance, her commitment, once and for all.

And he knew specifically what it was that he needed to hear from her.

Christine had, up until this point, refused to set a wedding date, and since she had moved here, he had been afraid to push her. After everything they had been through, it seemed only natural to him that she needed time to adjust. Especially after discovering all of the mental hardship she was bearing. But he had been doing some thinking of his own while she was away, and he could wait no longer.

He let out a slow sigh. If she was serious about marrying him, staying here in Calina with him, becoming the queen, then it was time she set the date. It didn't have to be for next week, but just so it was set. That would be enough. He would ask her tonight. If she refused again… well, he was unwilling to consider that at this point.

His thoughts were interrupted as the main door opened. He had been pacing the foyer, but stopped, his hands placed in his pockets as he watched Costa walk into the palace, then hold the door for Christine.

She picked up her stride as her gaze met Derek's, a broad smile spreading across her face. As she approached him, she threw her arms around his neck while he encircled her body in a tight embrace, her fragrance enveloping his senses.

"I missed you," he murmured as he held her against him, and it was true, he had been slowly losing his mind the past week.

Over the top of her head, he saw Costa walk past him, giving a slight nod, then continue walking down the hall, making his exit. An attendant followed him with Christine's luggage.

"I missed you too," she said as she released him, still smiling.

He took a step back to look at her. She was practically beaming. He narrowed his eyes a bit trying to remember the last time he had seen her look that happy.

"What is it?" he asked, genuinely curious.

He expected her to feel tired after the flight, naturally. He expected her to be drained, maybe anxious about returning to the stress of the "palace life." He had not been expecting this level of contentment.

"I'm really glad to be home," she stated, "the whole way here, I just couldn't wait to see you. To be here with you."

Derek's eyes met hers, he felt her emotions then as his own heart swelled. He didn't understand the stinging he felt pricking at the backs of his eyes, (it was most likely some dust), but he blinked a few times, and all he could think to do was grab her around the waist, and let his fingertips trail down the side of her beautiful face taking her lips with his. She ran her hands through his raven hair as he kissed her, his arms tightening around her and lifting her a few inches from the ground.

She was happy, and she called this "home."

He set her back on her feet as he pulled back from her slightly.

"I love you, Derek," she said, looking into his eyes. "I enjoyed visiting places I used to call my home, seeing my family and friends. But I realized I don't belong there anymore," she paused, "I belong here. With you. If you'll have me."

"You are the love of my life, Christine," he said, "you are my only queen." She smiled in response.

He cleared this throat slightly. "About that," he started, feeling now was as good a time as any to bring this up, "have you given any thought recently to when you wanted to make that official?"

She bit her bottom lip, her grin turning playful. She had known the date of their marriage had been on his mind, something he was eager to finalize. And it was time.

"I was thinking June. Do you like June?" she replied softly.

He closed his eyes briefly, letting her words wash over him, feeling whole and complete. He leaned in toward her, resting his forehead against hers. "June is perfect," he said. He then took her hand and began to lead her down the hall.

"I'm glad I made it back in time for the vote tomorrow," she said, and she tugged on his hand, making him stop to look at her, "regardless of what happens, I will be there with you when it's announced."

A brief look of concern crossed his features. "There's no reason tomorrow should not go smoothly," he said, "but, in case it doesn't, I don't want you anywhere near the meeting room where the result will be delivered."

"But I want to be there," Christine insisted.

He took her elbow and began to guide her down the hall once again.

"For any other event I wouldn't have it any other way than for you to be present," he replied, "but not for this. If the people do end up voting against joining the union…" he gave a heavy sigh, "it will turn ugly. I can't have you in a place where you'd be at physical risk."

Christine knew it was futile to continue to argue, and they walked in silence until they reached the master suite they shared. Entering the room, she saw her suitcase had been brought up.

Feeling too tired to unpack tonight, she ignored the suitcase for now and headed toward the bed, taking a seat. She remained quiet for a moment, still pondering the importance of tomorrow's event. She considered the threats and the risks involved, debating if she wanted to share with Derek her concerns.

"I know Nicola is your brother, Derek," she began deciding it was best to say what was on her mind, "but given everything with his past, are you sure you trust him to hold the responsibility of delivering the outcome?"

"Yes," he said without hesitation, making his way toward her on the bed, "we've had our differences, but I believe Nicola has changed, realized his mistakes, and has grown from them. I decided he should deliver the outcome because he is, in fact, the only person I trust to do so.

"The citizens will cast their vote into a machine, which counts everything, leaving very little room for error. All the parliament members need to do is bring their own district results to Nicola. He will then be responsible for ensuring the final count is correct, revealing the result. He will be the only one who has that information."

"I guess that's what puts me on edge," she said folding her arms, "what if he makes a mistake, or…lies?"

"It's in his best interest to deliver an honest result," Derek replied, "he has no motive to lie. Unfortunately, we are not sophisticated with a public voting process," he further explained, "our country has never done this before. We are not a democracy. We have district voting machines because that's how parliament is elected, but we have no means of this level of voting. That is why the district results will be delivered to Nicola."

Christine nodded. "I'm just nervous, I suppose," she said, "I know Nicola will do what's right of course."

Derek shrugged. "If there is any question, the result can always be checked against the information that was delivered to him by parliament."

She nodded again, thinking that made sense and it seemed like the way it was set up, it was the best option.

She knew her doubts stemmed from all the rumors surrounding DeGrassi; his attempts to buy parliament in the past, his suspected involvement with Olivia's murder, and his need to maintain his death grip on too many businesses impacting the country's economy. Not to mention his extreme motives of revenge toward Derek. Everyone would be uneasy until after the conclusion of this vote, and she couldn't help but "expect" something to go wrong.

"Taya Mariano is coming here to see me tomorrow morning," he informed her now as he wandered toward the closet, removing his shirt.

"Why?" she asked.

Derek shook his head slowly. "I'm not sure yet," he said, "she requested to see me as early as possible, claiming she had something urgent to tell me with regard to the vote."

Christine's eyes opened wide. "What could she possibly have to say?" She wondered out loud. "As a parliament member, won't she be responsible for ensuring her own district numbers are accounted for?"

"Yes," he replied, "she will need to oversee the poll in her district, then deliver the results to Nicola here once they close."

"Do you think she might have information on anything DeGrassi has planned?" she asked quietly, knowing that's where Derek's mind had gone as well, further creating a feeling of unrest in her chest.

"I don't know how she could," he said, "but if she does, I'd be most interested to hear about it."

Taya had received the call last night that the monarch would consent to see her this morning. The polls opened at 10:00 a.m., and she hoped her information would prompt extra measures to be taken. As it was, with Nicola overseeing the delivery of the final outcome, she couldn't see what Enzo could possibly be planning.

Enzo had already tried to enlist Nicola, so she felt confident her brother could not corrupt him that way. There was the chance Enzo had been able to buy parliament members, as he had in the past, and have them deliver faulty information, but with the voting machines in each district, such a plan would be practically impossible. Even if a parliament member wanted to deliver false information, the computer would show the truth. Still, if warning Derek could help thwart any attempt of tampering with the vote, as well as help put Enzo behind bars, she intended to do so.

By 7:00 a.m. she was out the door, headed for her car. Her appointment at the palace was scheduled for eight. Driving through town, as she always did, she stopped at the local coffee shop. It was a small, family owned business, in the heart of the city center. She frequented the little shop, knowing the family who owned it as well as the struggles they faced to stay afloat.

Parking her Peugeot 208 GT along the little narrow side street, she made her way along the cobblestone sidewalk past a couple of closed up stores until she reached the shop.

The bell dinged as she entered, smiling, expecting to see Marguerite, the middle-aged woman who owned the shop and always opened in the morning, her husband taking over the afternoon shift. But instead, there was a young man behind the counter.

"*Buongiorno*, how can I help you?" he asked as Taya approached.

He was polite, but Taya noticed he didn't smile, spoke quickly, and seemed agitated, as though she had interrupted him doing something important. She sniffed the air, picking up on a faint smell of burnt bread. *Maybe that's why he seems upset?* She thought. *He burnt the baked goods?*

"I didn't realize Marguerite had hired someone new," Taya replied, working to keep the smile on her face, "is she not here?"

The young man stared at her for a minute as though he wasn't sure how to answer.

"Yeah, I'm new," he said, "she uh… had to step out for a minute. Did you want to order something?"

Taya felt this new worker of Marguerite's needed a few lessons in customer service, but he wasn't her employee, so she dismissed his abrupt manner. Not to mention, she was surprised that the shop owner could even afford to hire someone, so Taya felt certain he wasn't experienced or even paid well.

"Just a coffee to go please," she said kindly, "with just a little cream."

He nodded curtly and turned away from her to pour the drink. After a moment, he returned to the front counter, a cup in his hand.

"Here you go," he said simply as he set the drink down in front of her.

She handed him the couple francs for the coffee, then took her cup. "*Grazie*," she said.

He did not smile nor say anything else, and as she was the only customer at the moment, he turned away from her and headed into the back. Raising her eyebrows, Taya shook her head slightly then left the counter to walk back out to her car.

She sipped the coffee and made a face as she left the shop. *Not only did he burn the bread, he burnt the coffee too*, she realized. She rolled her eyes thinking she'd have to talk to Marguerite about what happened. She wouldn't get him in trouble, she was sure he needed the job. But no harm in letting his employer know so she can advise him to do better. She took another drink as she reached her car, tolerating the bitter taste that stayed on her tongue.

As she climbed into the car, her phone buzzed notifying her of a new message. She continued to sip the burnt coffee, needing the caffeine while she checked a few messages and a quick email. She put down her phone and started the car, placing the coffee in the cup holder.

As she set down the coffee, a sense of dizziness washed over her. She blinked rapidly, attempting to clear her head, but it wasn't any use. Leaning her head in her hand, her elbow propped up on the steering wheel, she suddenly felt a massive heaviness take over her mind. *What is happening to me?* She thought, unable to keep her eyes open. The fog creeping in completely overtook her then, and she slumped to the side over the console losing consciousness.

"Thank you so much for your support," the coffee owner gushed as she grasped Bryan's hand with both of hers in a firm shake, "your business will help pay our rent for the next month."

Bryan smiled at Marguerite where he was keeping her busy across the street from the shop. He had approached her just ten minutes prior asking her to speak privately as he wanted to offer her an opportunity to provide his office coffee and baked goods every Friday.

He knew Taya's schedule and routine by heart. She always left her house at seven, and she always stopped at the little coffee shop in town to grab her morning coffee. In the past, he had joined her frequently for breakfast.

As he allowed Marguerite to shake his hand, he peered over her head, watching Taya leave the shop, sipping the coffee in her hand. His eyes followed her as she approached her car, climbing in.

"Excuse me a minute, please Marguerite?" he asked as he freed his hand from her grasp.

Pulling out his phone, he opened his email to a message waiting in drafts addressed to Taya. Just a typical government news update he thought she might be interested in, but he knew she'd check it. He pressed send. *That should be enough time*, he thought. "Sorry about that," he said as he now put his phone back in his pocket.

He watched as Taya's car lights turned on, but it never pulled away. His smile grew. "It's my pleasure to assist," he now told Marguerite, "and it's my responsibility to help out our local businesses," he nodded toward the shop, "why don't I walk you back."

"Yes, I need to get back," the shop owner replied, "Sal is new." She laughed, "young. But his family needs the money so he had to find a job."

Bryan nodded in understanding as he crossed the street with Marguerite. He knew exactly how hard up Sal was for cash.

As they entered the shop, the counter was vacant, but an odor lingering in the air was evidence that something had burned. A look of horror crossed Marguerite's face.

"Oh no!" She exclaimed, leaving Bryan by the counter as she rushed into the back.

A moment later he heard her scolding the young man, then instructing him to watch for customers as she took care of his mess.

"Rough day?" Bryan asked leaning against the counter as Sal emerged and approached the register. Sal shrugged. Bryan raised his eye brows expectantly.

"I did what you asked," Sal told Bryan as a look of uncertainty crossed his face. It was clear he wasn't comfortable putting something in anyone's coffee. "You said this was just a prank right?"

Bryan chuckled. "Of course," he replied easily, waving a dismissive hand, "she's my ex. It'll just make her sick for about a day, that's all." Sal nodded slowly. A sheepish grin appeared on the young man's face as Bryan slid 100 francs across the counter to him. "Thanks for helping me get even with her," he said with a wink. Sal stuffed the note in his pocket as Bryan then turned and walked out of the shop.

Arriving at Taya's car, he peered into the front driver's seat, finding her still unconscious. He knew he only had about thirty minutes or so. The sedative wasn't that strong. He went around to the passenger side door. Opening it, he reached for her under the arms, dragging her body across the console and into the passenger's seat. He buckled her seatbelt then returned to the driver's side. Climbing in, he put the car in drive. He glanced at her, her head lolling to the side toward the window.

"I'm sorry, honey," he said quietly as he stared out the windshield now, "I wish you hadn't fallen in love with the wrong man."

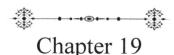

Chapter 19

The first thing Taya felt was an immense amount of pain splitting her brain in two. Her eyelids opened slowly, feeling as though they were being weighed down. As she forced them open she next became aware she couldn't move.

Seated upright in what felt like a hard chair, she realized her arms were restrained behind her back. Fear overtaking her body, she jerked, testing her lack of freedom. Upon instinct, she opened her mouth to scream, it was then she discovered a scarf tied tightly covering her mouth.

What happened to me? She thought frantically, her brain working overtime through the heaviness to remember or understand her situation. *Where am I?*

The last thing she remembered was the coffee shop, and then… had she fallen asleep in her car? She had a meeting with Derek, did she go? Trying to piece together how she ended up like this made her already aching head pound even more. She closed her eyes, and breathed deeply through her nose attempting to settle her rising panic. She needed to calm down and think clearly. One thing she did know, she needed to get out of wherever she was fast.

She re-opened her eyes to take in her surroundings. She was tied to a wooden table chair in what appeared to be a small house that had definitely seen better days. The air was stale and hung heavy with the distinct smell of must. The floor was made from wooden planks, old and dirty. She could see a small dated, dingy kitchen, and although there was a window, the dust-covered shades were drawn, making it difficult for her to determine the time of day.

If she was still in Calina, which she assumed she was, she deduced she was being held in one of the vacant homes on the outskirts of the city where many citizens had been evicted. But she could only guess.

Her eyes searched for a clock, but there was nothing working in the home, and no lights were on. She strained to listen for traffic or any noise that would give her any clues to her location, but again, there was nothing, and she also concluded that she was alone; for the time being.

Coming up practically empty as to where she was, Taya tried to think of why she was possibly here. Who would have done this to her? She could only come up with one answer, and it made her blood run cold.

Enzo now knew of her relationship with Nicola. He must have informed the organization after him, and they kidnapped her to trade. If Nicola found out they were holding her, he would most certainly turn himself over; they would kill him.

Knowing she needed to free herself before someone returned, Taya tried moving her wrists and feet. They were bound tightly together with duct tape, she realized, and unless she had a way to cut through it, there was no loosening her binds.

Her eyes scanned again around the small house, desperately seeking something that could help. Crestfallen, she found nothing, until her eyes landed on the table off to her right. An expensive, brown leather briefcase with ornate details sat on top of it. She eyed it curiously.

She had seen it before. Where?

Her heart leapt in her throat as she now understood who her captor was, and it wasn't the organization after Nicola.

By 10:00 a.m., Nicola had checked in with all districts within Calina ensuring things were operating smoothly prior to the polls opening. He had received validation from each member of parliament, except one: Taya.

Unable to reach her, both at her office and through her cell, he had finally selected someone else within the party to cover her district results. This was unlike her, he knew, and her absence worried him. A frown crossed his features, one that had graced his face more often than not recently, unless he was in front of a camera.

Taya was always the reason for this discontentment; the inability to see her, be with her, and protect her. She consumed his thoughts and desires, and now, it seemed as though she might be missing.

He attempted to diminish the rising unrest in his chest at being unable to contact her, trying to reason that she was just busy. Although he knew he was selling himself false truths, as today was too important for her to simply not take his call. No, something felt... wrong. He picked up his phone to try her again when a knock on his study door made him pause.

"Nic," Derek said as he entered the study and approached the desk where Nicola was seated. "Everything going smoothly?"

Nicola hesitated before nodding. After all, the lack of Taya's presence didn't necessarily mean something was awry. Yet.

"So far," he replied evenly.

Derek remained quiet for a moment. "Have you been able to reach Taya this morning?" he asked suddenly.

Nicola raised his eyebrows. "No, I haven't," he admitted, "I had to assign someone else to monitor the poll in her district. Why?" He suspected there was a reason Derek had asked about her specifically.

"She was supposed to meet me at eight this morning," he said, placing his hands in his pockets, "a meeting she requested. She didn't show."

This was news to Nicola. "A meeting?" he asked, "what for?"

"I don't know," Derek replied, "her request only stated it was urgent and it was regarding the vote."

Nicola could tell there was more Derek wanted to say, but for some reason, he wasn't saying what was on his mind. It was unlike his brother to "fish" for information.

"The office tried to reach her several times this morning," Derek continued, "there has not been any answer, and none of her colleagues have neither seen nor heard from her."

With each word, Nicola's heart beat faster, and he took a breath to calm his rising panic. *Where the hell was she?*

"Have you sent someone to her house?" he asked attempting to keep his voice steady.

Derek nodded. "Her car is there," he stated, "but, no answer."

Nicola now raked a hand through his hair. "Something had to have happened to her," he said urgently, standing abruptly, "she couldn't have just, disappeared."

Derek's face remained calm, impassive, as he regarded Nicola's reaction carefully.

"No," he agreed, "she couldn't. Are you aware of any potential association between Taya and DeGrassi?" he asked knowing Nicola would not want to hear what was said next, but Derek had to entertain all possibilities.

197

Nicola looked at him, confusion written on his face. "DeGrassi?" he asked, "no. Taya wouldn't associate with him." His answer was resolute. He knew Taya; he loved her. There would be no way she would ever be caught dead in the presence of that slime. "Why would you say that?"

"What would she possibly need to tell me about the vote that's so urgent?" Derek replied, posing a question back. "For her to not show up and then to suddenly vanish is a bit odd, don't you think?"

Nicola threw up a hand. "Wait," he said, "are you actually saying you think *Taya* is the insider working for DeGrassi? You think she wanted to meet this morning to tell you she was going to conspire with him to rig the vote?"

Derek shrugged. "It entered my mind," he stated.

Derek knew how his brother felt about the pretty and assertive parliament member, but what did either of them really know about her? Unfortunately, Derek had learned that in Calina, few could be trusted, and he had to consider every angle.

"And what?" Nicola shot back, his voice rising, "did she kill Olivia too then?" Derek's lack of expression remained intact. "If she were conspiring, why would she want to meet with you to confess?"

"Guilty conscience," Derek suggested, "but then she realized that her actions would cause her arrest, so she fled."

Nicola shook his head. "No," he said resolutely, "that's absurd. You don't know Taya the way I do. There's no way she could be working for him. She's loyal." His tone made it clear he was barely controlling his anger at the insinuation.

Derek gave a heavy sigh. "There's more," he said. "As you may have guessed, since Olivia's murder, I've had Romano station some associates to watch some of DeGrassi's activities. His office is one of those designations. We were informed that a woman matching Taya's description entered his building several days ago. It appeared as though she were attempting to hide her identity. Actually, we didn't even consider it was Taya until she didn't show up this morning. Then the pieces kind of fell together."

Nicola dismissed the notion. This was crazy.

"That's impossible," he stated immediately, "it could not have been her."

"You are blinded by your emotions," Derek said, the comment only adding to Nicola's increasing temper.

"Yeah?" Nicola practically sneered, "how did it make you feel when Esposito accused Christine of killing her attendant?"

"Do you recall Taya mentioning anything to you about needing to speak to me or why?" Derek asked, refusing to take his brother's bait and ignoring the question; he didn't have time for childish arguing.

"No," Nicola seethed, "I haven't spoken to her. I've been avoiding her so no one would…" he trailed off as a sudden, daunting realization came over him.

The look on Nicola's face told Derek what he was thinking. He placed both hands on the back of the chair and leaned forward.

"Does anyone else know of your relationship with her?" he asked quietly.

Nicola wracked his brain trying to remember if anyone could have seen them together. At the festival perhaps? But that was before… in the garden at the reception? It was a possibility. Although his gut was to answer no, the truth was, she was missing. And there was a reason for that.

"Someone must know," he replied, the understanding crashing down on him that what he had feared most was coming to fruition. Taya had been taken as a means to get to him.

No longer interested in this conversation with Derek, Nicola grabbed his jacket off his chair.

"Where exactly are you going?" Derek asked as his brother strode toward the door.

"To find her," Nicola stated.

"Nic, stop, you don't even know what you're doing." Nicola turned around, his expression set in a determined glare. "You cannot leave," Derek continued, "you are responsible for delivering the outcome of this vote."

"I don't give a damn about the vote!" Nicola exclaimed, "not when Taya is—,"

"Is what?" Derek interjected, "potentially missing because she ran away of her own accord? The guard has been to her house and her office. They are making inquiries as to her whereabouts. If someone did, in fact, abduct her, it's best you let them do their job to try and find her."

"Are they even trying to find her though?" Nicola asked sharply, "or have you just decided that she fled for committing treason, and it's not worth their time."

"I won't lie to you, Nic," Derek replied evenly, "It looks suspicious to me, but even if that were that case, it's all the more reason I'd want her found. So yes, they are looking for her."

"You're wrong about her," Nicola said with confidence, "she's in trouble, Derek." And as he spoke, a desperation filled his voice, the sincerity of his belief in Taya impossible to mistake.

"I will keep you informed on anything the guard finds," Derek said, empathizing with his brother's pain in spite of his own doubts. "If you hear from her as well, you need to tell me."

Nicola nodded almost absently to what Derek was saying, shock overtaking his body at the thought of Taya being taken by someone. *Was she hurt? Where is she? Does the organization have her or some accomplice working for Enzo?* These were the only thoughts registering in his mind, and he didn't notice as Derek placed a hand on his shoulder in comfort before turning and walking out of the study.

Time had passed, and Taya wasn't sure how long she had been held in that little dirty house against her will.

She had struggled to no avail, tried to move the chair she was strapped to, but didn't get very far, and attempted to loosen the scarf tied around her mouth. Her efforts had been in vain, her energy was spent, and her still-pounding head began to nod a bit as her eyes closed, dozing off lightly.

She jerked upright as a sudden noise startled her awake. The lighting in the room seemed darker. How long was she out for? Had it been hours? A day even? Her throat was terribly dry, and her back and neck ached painfully. But her discomforts were forgotten upon realizing what woke her; someone had returned. She heard the creaking sound of a door closing then footsteps, echoing off the worn, wooden floor, as they moved down the front hall.

Rage filled her as her captor approached, and if nothing else, she was determined to give the asshole a piece of her mind. She began to struggle violently, using her shoulder to unsuccessfully dig at the scarf. Becoming frustrated, she starting rocking the chair she was tied to, so much so, it tipped to the side and crashed down to the floor. Her head jostled hitting the ground, but the fall finally loosened the scarf tied around her mouth as it slipped just enough so she could speak.

She yelped in pain as she hit the floor, and she heard the footsteps now entering the kitchen area behind her. From her position, she was unable to see who had entered the room, but her adrenaline momentarily overtook her common sense; the need to confront him becoming unbearably overwhelming.

"Enzo!" she cried out in fury, "you son of a bitch! How could you do this to me? Are you crazy? I'm your sister for God's sake!"

The footsteps stopped at her words, and Taya wondered why he wasn't responding. He then resumed toward her, and she felt the chair being lifted from behind. He tipped her upright again, and she flinched, closing her eyes tightly when the four legs came down hard on the floor. She opened her eyes as he rounded in front of her and came into her line of view. Her mouth opened in shock.

"Bryan? What—," her words caught in her throat as she stared at him: her friend.

A second's worth of hope flooded through her that he was here to rescue her, but the hard look in his eyes diminished the thought quickly. He was, in fact, her kidnapper.

"Why are you doing this?" she practically whispered. "I don't understand..."

Unsmiling and unkind, he didn't even look like the same person to her, and her head spun to think of how well he had masked his true self.

He bent down until he was face to face with her. His eyes were narrowed as they bore into hers, his lips and jaw set. He reached out a hand toward her face, and she regarded him with caution, attempting to hide the fear in her eyes. He threaded his fingers through her hair gently, then suddenly grasped a handful hard, yanking her head back. She grunted at the pain.

"You're a *DeGrassi*?" He hissed in her face.

She remained quiet, only glaring at him with hatred, although dread filled her as she realized the huge mistake she made thinking it was Enzo who had taken her. But it was Enzo's briefcase on the table; she had seen it in his office. He must have bribed Bryan, because of course, and she should have considered, Enzo wouldn't do his own dirty work.

The pieces began to fall into place now: Bryan was the one working for Enzo, he had killed Olivia, and he dropped the glove himself to cast suspicion onto Nicola.

His grip tightened in her hair, and she felt like he might snap her neck clean off.

"You are Marco's daughter," the rage evident in his tone, although dangerously quiet, "and you support the Landino's? You're even in *love* with one!"

She couldn't help but wonder where his passion was coming from or how he had ended up throwing in lots with her radical family, but this man was clearly her enemy because of it.

"You played me the entire time!" she exclaimed, straining against his hold on her, but refusing to show intimidation, "I thought you were my friend!" He let go of her as a smirk appeared on his face. "How can you do this?" she added quietly, her voice filling with not only disbelief, but despair at this unexpected revelation of his character.

He stood up straight and walked casually a few feet from her.

Although Bryan LaPointe was physically standing in front of her with a cold and calculating look on his face, a piece of her couldn't accept he was a villain. As friends and confidents, they had shared so much, and her heart broke to think it was all a lie. He had sold it all so well.

"I befriended you because I suspected you were getting close with the prince," he stated. "Turns out I was right, and it paid off for us."

"'Us,' you mean you and Enzo," she replied.

"I mean anyone who backs the rightful rulers of Calina, the DeGrassi's," he spat out, "I mean anyone who fights to bring down the tyrant Landino family."

She couldn't help but stare at his extreme words. Although she herself, along with many Caleans were cautious surrounding Derek's reign, fearful of the ultimate power the monarch held, most had to admit that his actions had proven thus far he was not the oppressor his father was.

Thinking back, it was clear to her now why she had not been able to formulate any feelings for Bryan beyond friendship. His true self, one who was capable of murder and kidnapping, was hiding just below his seemingly good-natured and just surface. And she could never love someone with such a black heart.

"You won't succeed with whatever it is you're planning," she stated coldly, "most Caleans now realize that the king is willing to give up power by joining the EU if it means a better life for them. His has not abused his position, he is not like Luciano, and the monarchy is earning the trust of the people."

"He ordered Marco's execution!" Bryan shouted, and his sudden raise of voice made her wince. "That's not power abuse in your eyes? You're a sell-out," he sneered, "and the people will soon understand they were mistaken." His tone was confident as he spoke.

She attempted to not let the confusion she felt at his words show on her face, but he saw the slight furrow of her brow. He gave her a glare then turned from her, walking into the small kitchen.

She sighed, her heart sinking as she pondered her predicament. She had to try and find out his plans. The more she knew, the better at least.

"How did I get here?" She called after him, unsure if he would even answer. If he chose to just ignore her, that wouldn't get her anywhere. But he gave a small laugh at her question.

"I bribed that coffee worker to put a sedative in your drink," he replied easily, "when you passed out in your car, I just drove you here."

A slight hope filled her. If she was still in Calina somewhere, maybe someone would notice her car... As if reading her thoughts, he shook his head.

"Your car is back at your house," he added, "you see, I left a rental there this morning after you had gone. I called a ride into town to get you, then I drove your car back after you were safe and sound here. No one knows where you are, sweetheart," he paused, "although, I'm sure they're looking for you. But that's ok, I only need to keep you here for a short time anyway."

"What do you mean?" she asked, frustrated that she felt like she wasn't learning anything important.

He glanced at his watch. "It's six p.m.," he stated, "the polls will close in two hours, then the parliament members will deliver their district results to Nicola. I only need to keep you here until after the vote." His eyes met hers, but they now held a shade of regret.

"I don't understand," she said quietly, although her instincts were kicking in, and she couldn't help a shiver of fear wash over her.

"We will need to say 'good-bye' after that, Taya," he replied.

He walked out of her line of vision for a moment, then returned with her purse in his hands. He pulled out her phone. "I need to get back to my own district before I'm missed too much," he told her, "so, let's call your boyfriend."

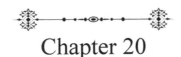

Chapter 20

The buzzing of his phone brought Nicola out of his thoughts as he paced in his study. The phone sat on the desk next to his laptop, left out and ready in case Taya called back after his countless attempts to reach her.

He had received several calls throughout the day, mostly through his office line, informing him of constant voting updates. This call however, was coming through on his personal cell.

He strode over to the desk, his heart rate increasing rapidly upon seeing the caller: Taya. Grabbing up the cell, he pressed the answer button.

"Oh my God, Taya, where are you?" he said immediately, his voice laden with worry.

"Nic," she sounded frantic, "don't do any—," but she was cut off, her voice muffled.

"Taya?" he questioned as he heard a scuffle.

He knew what was coming, as anger now overpowered his feelings of anxiety. "Don't hurt her," he gritted out, knowing it was no longer Taya who was listening.

"Right, right," a low, male voice whispered back, allowing a slight chuckle.

Nicola wanted to ask a myriad of questions, demanding to know where she was, if she was ok, who he was speaking to, and what he wanted. But he knew they were pointless questions that would go unanswered and just waste time. Instead, he clenched his jaw, waited, and tried to make out any background noise on the other end.

"Let's make this quick," the man rasped, "I will promise not to harm Taya if you do a small favor for me. Regardless of the actual voting outcome today, you need to deliver the result of not joining the EU."

Shock appeared on Nicola's face. So, it was DeGrassi behind this? Not the organization from New York? But was it Enzo, himself on the phone? It was impossible to tell.

"This is insane," Nicola protested, keeping his tone level, "it won't matter what I deliver to the monarchy and parliament. The true results can always be tracked back to the actual ballots."

"He who holds the vote, controls the vote," the man responded simply.

"I will be arrested for knowingly delivering a false result," Nicola shot back.

The man gave a heavy sigh. "It seems you need some persuasion," he said. There was a rustling sound as if the phone had been set down. "Say 'hello,' Taya," Nicola heard him say now, the phone clearly having been placed on speaker. There was a loud smack, and Taya suddenly cried out.

"What are you doing—," he heard her say in fear, but her voice trailed off into a choking sound; she was being strangled.

Hearing her gasping and gagging over the phone was excruciating, and Nicola was being forced to listen to it.

"Stop!" he yelled into the phone, and his voice cracked, "I'll do it, just stop hurting her!"

He heard her heave as though taking in air, and although instant relief flooded through him, it was minuscule compared to the pure helplessness he felt at not being able to protect her. He could tell the caller picked the phone back up.

"Smart choice," the man whispered, and Taya was now coughing in the background.

"You bastard," Nicola said, his fury evident in his tone.

The man ignored the comment. "We'll know if you don't do what you're told," he said, "an hour after the result is delivered, I will call you back again from her phone."

"Then what?" Nicola asked, but the line went dead. "Fuck!" he exclaimed as he slammed the phone down on the desk.

He crashed into the desk chair and placed his head in his hands, his nerves were raw and at breaking point. There was no way he could risk Taya being harmed; any more than she already had been, and the thought made him sick. He had no choice, he would have to deliver the vote as instructed. He understood of course, it didn't guarantee Taya's safety, but what alternatives did he have? If he didn't do as he was told, he felt fairly certain she would be killed.

The aftermath of his actions would no doubt be devastating to the monarchy. The situation was already precarious at best, the monarchy had been hanging on by a thread for months, and he couldn't help but reflect on how parliament reacted with a tie outcome. How would they react to a result of not joining? Heads would roll, and it would be Derek's and his own necks on the line.

He considered for a moment telling Derek about the phone call and demand for Taya's safe return. But based on their conversation this morning, would Derek even believe she was in danger? Regardless if he believed it or not, Nicola knew Derek would never allow the voting result to be falsely represented, and Nicola just couldn't take the chance of not complying. So no, informing his brother was out of the question.

For now, anyway.

The polls had closed, and Nicola had been notified that parliament members were beginning to arrive. He would greet each in turn, collect their results, then deliver the final outcome once everyone had assembled.

It was 20 minutes past eight, and as he made his way toward the meeting room, he could think of nothing except how the caller said he would call again an hour after Nicola had fulfilled his end of the deal. Meaning in about two hours, he'd know Taya's fate.

Or was she already…?

No. He refused to think that way. If he did, he knew he would break down. It was foolish, but he had to hold onto hope that she'd be ok; that his actions could save her.

Nicola had flat-out refused to join in DeGrassi's schemes for power, scoffed at the idea of seizing it for himself, and even brushed off the threat of the organization coming after his head. Regardless of it all, he was still to be Enzo's pawn, held captive to do his bidding because of the love he had developed for Taya. Of course, at the time he told Enzo to go pound sand, he did not even know Taya, and the last thing he ever expected his enemies to be able to use against him was *love*.

The irony was almost too much to bear.

Soon, the monarchy would be turned completely upside-down, and everything his brother had worked for would be destroyed. Maybe if he had just agreed to side with Enzo in the first place, at least Taya wouldn't be in mortal danger.

He had reached the meeting room on the ground floor, spying the first parliament member to arrive, Frances Bruno, or "Frankie," as most called him. Frankie was in his 70's and Calina's longest-term government official. He was well-liked, respected, and trusted, having always made choices which benefited the people and Calina over himself.

Upon arrival in Calina months ago, Derek had spent much time weeding out corrupt politicians, and although some he continued to question, Frankie, he had determined quite quickly, was "one of the good ones."

"*Ciao*, Frankie," Nicola said smoothly, swallowing back down his increasing distress and placing a calm expression on his face.

"Signore Nicola," Frankie greeted back, grasping Nicola's outstretched hand in a firm shake while bowing his head slightly. The esteemed politician smiled as he offered Nicola a flat, manilla envelope.

"That's it?" Nicola asked surprised.

Frankie gave a small laugh. "Were you expecting me to chain a briefcase to your wrist?"

Nicola furrowed his brow and smiled at the thought in spite of his situation. "Perhaps," he said, "maybe we'll do that next time. Just to make it more interesting."

"I enjoy your sense of humor, signore," Frankie replied with another incline of his head, then he gave a satisfied sigh. "I feel that today will be a historical and happy day for our people," he stated.

Nicola couldn't suppress a grimace as Frankie turned to look out over the meeting room, not catching the prince's expression.

Historical? Most definitely, Nicola thought.

"I don't mind confiding in you, signore," Frankie continued, turning back to face him.

Putting his skills at hiding inner turmoil to the test, Nicola shook his head, a smile now back on his lips. "Of course, Frankie, the monarchy has always valued your advice and opinion," he said.

"I will admit," Frankie began, "like many, I had reservations at first upon learning that Derek Landino was coming back to become our monarch," he paused, leaning against and adjusting the cane he used, "oh, I didn't buy into the hype that he would be Luciano all over again, but given his reputation as an ambitious entrepreneur was enough to make me have doubts if he would put the people first."

Nicola began to feel nauseated listening to Frankie, he could foresee where this conversation was going. Unable to bring himself to give false encouragement, he kept quiet and allowed the parliament member to continue.

"As you know," Frankie said, "I've been fighting for the wellbeing of our people for a long time. Joining the European Union was a bold move, and I will say I wasn't sold on giving in to certain influences. But I've realized that our monarchy is giving up more by joining, power I mean, and the stability is something we've needed here for decades," he gave another sigh, this time, heavy and sad. "No previous leader was willing to do what he's trying to do. As long as we join, our people have a chance."

Nicola's heart sank even lower as he listened to Frankie, for in just a short while, he would be delivering very disappointing news. Knowing he had to reply, he gave a political answer.

"All I can say, Frankie, is I genuinely hope today is successful."

Frankie gave a sincere smile. "I feel confident it will be, signore," he replied. "I am an old man, too old, and soon my home will finally be secure," he gave an emotional pause, "I've fought for this for a long time."

Nicola cleared his throat slightly, the air feeling stuffy. It disturbed him greatly to know that Frankie would soon feel his trust in the monarchy had been misplaced, and he was having a difficult time just keeping it together right now.

"I see additional members are arriving," he said, gesturing with the envelope, "excuse me, Frankie, I'm sure we'll chat again later."

He left the experienced politician and made his way around the room as more members arrived, collecting each district's results. The designee from Taya's district was permitted to deliver their envelope, but not permitted to stay, as the final outcome would be given to only the monarch, prime minister and parliament.

Not wanting to give any impression that anything was wrong, he attempted to chat briefly with each member, many sharing similar sentiments to that of Frankie, expressing optimism around joining the EU, and that the outcome of the vote would be in favor of it. By the time he had collected most of the envelopes, he felt on the verge of becoming physically ill.

"Signore Nicola," came a voice behind him, and Nicola turned to see Bryan LaPointe approaching him.

He raised his eyebrows slightly, placing a professional expression on his face. He knew now there were only feelings of friendship between Taya and Bryan, but he still wasn't a fan. Bryan held out an envelope to him as he bowed his head.

"*Grazie*, Bryan," Nicola replied, taking the results from him.

"I had attempted to reach Taya today," Bryan now stated, "but I haven't been successful. It's starting to concern me, because as you might have noticed, I care about her a lot. Did you happen to see her arrive yet, signore?"

Bryan's words felt like a gut-punch, the sound of Taya's name causing him to tense, and visions of her restrained in some desolate place flashed through his mind. Of course the other members would become aware of her absence, (it bothering him that Bryan had noticed first), and he hadn't thought of how to explain it. For now, it may be best to not address it.

"I haven't seen her," was all he told Bryan, but he couldn't hold back a sense of despair overtaking him, which must have shown on his face.

"Are you all right, signore?" Bryan asked, his voice laced with worry. "You seem upset."

Nicola recovered his expression and regarded Bryan with a keen eye.

"I'm fine," he said tightly, forcing a smile that did not reach his eyes, "if you'll excuse me."

Bryan offered a slight bow, and as Nicola turned to walk away, he didn't catch the satisfied smirk curling Bryan's lips.

All the results now in his hands, Nicola left the conference room quickly and began to make his way back to his study. After closing and locking the door, he threw the envelopes down on his desk, staring at them for a moment, wondering if he should even bother opening them. *It would just be a waste of time*, he concluded. It was of no consequence what was in those envelopes, at least, not right now. And honestly, he didn't need to spend time reading what he already knew. What everyone already knew.

Sitting in front of his laptop, he ran a hand over his face and jaw, opening the official document that he would sign off on. It was true what he had said on the phone, it didn't matter what he put on this document, the real information was sitting on his desk in the form of ten individual district envelopes. This document would only cause chaos, upheaval, distrust towards the monarchy, not to mention his own arrest. But he couldn't dwell on that, his only goal was to see Taya safe.

He finished the document, typing in the information, and printed it. Signing it, he added his seal and placed it in another separate envelope. Last, he grabbed the unopened district envelopes off his desk and a lighter from his drawer.

Heading over to the fireplace, he ignited the paper, placing them behind the grate and watched the results burn. He knew it would be found, but at least, it would buy him some time. He still had to meet the son of a bitch who has Taya, and he couldn't leave if he was immediately arrested after the meeting.

There was a knock on his door, and he rose from the fireplace. Upon opening the door, he saw Martino waiting for him.

"Signore," his guard greeted him.

Nicola just nodded, knowing he was here to escort him to the meeting. He strode over to his desk, picked up the "official" result, then followed Martino out of the office. As they walked the halls toward the conference room, Nicola couldn't help but feel like he was marching to his own execution.

———————

Derek checked his watch and shut his laptop. It was time. He stood up from his desk just as his office door opened. Expecting to see Costa enter, he was surprised to see Christine instead, although Costa had followed her in. She was dressed smartly, wearing a sand-colored pencil skirt, matching jacket, and a cream blouse.

He knew why she was here, and his eyes met hers, narrowing slightly as he tilted his head to one side. In response she folded her arms across her chest. He almost laughed out loud at her ability to communicate with him without saying a word, and he lifted his hands in mock surrender.

"Ok," he consented, "you can come to the meeting."

He took a breath, still not liking the idea of her potentially being in any kind of harm's way, but he supposed he had to get used to it at some point. Besides, guards would be present, and he knew Christine could handle anything verbally thrown her way.

"Well, that's nice of you, Derek," she replied, "but you know, I wasn't asking your permission."

"Is that so?" he asked, slight amusement in his tone. He glanced at Costa who was attempting to hide a smirk. "You heard the lady," he told the guard with a shrug, "let's go." He grabbed her hand, and as he led her out of the office, he leaned in near her ear. "You look beautiful, and I love you," he said lowly.

She squeezed his hand and smiled. "I love you, too."

The meeting room was small and where many intimate discussions and decisions were made among the monarchy and parliament. Tucked away on the first floor toward the back of the palace, the room contained a large, hardwood oval table ornate with intricate details. There were ten handsome leather chairs around the table, with four additional chairs at the head, the middle two slightly larger and instead of leather, they were covered with a dark blue velvet.

One entire long wall was floor to ceiling window panes dressed with swooping, rich blue drapes. A plush, blue rug sat underneath the table on the polished, parquet floor. There was a refreshment bar on the back wall, and on either side of the double-door entrance stood the Calean flag.

Derek had heard that his father preferred to sit higher in these meetings, on a podium set away from the table. But he had the podium removed, the idea of a "throne" ridiculous to him. He was used to interacting in a leadership role as a CEO or board member, not as a traditional monarch, and he didn't see any reason why that should change because of a title. Normally, the chair on his left sat empty, but not today, and he couldn't help but feel a sense of completion.

The other members were there when he and Christine entered the room. Costa followed closely behind, then took his usual spot behind Derek in the background. Additional guards, including Martino, were stationed throughout the perimeter.

Although seated, the others in the room including the prime minister and Nicola, rose when Derek entered and remained standing until he took his place with Christine next to him. Nicola took his seat next to Christine, with the prime minister on Derek's right.

There was a large level of tension in the room, the decision to be revealed weighing heavily in air. Derek could feel it as he attempted eye contact with each person seated around him, finding some throwing questionable glances at Christine. He had developed a sense for being able to read a room, and this one caused him a slight unease, which he did not show.

"Let's get started," he stated once everyone had settled into their place. "First, some may be wondering why Christine is here today considering she is not yet officially part of our monarchy, and the answer is simple; she is your future queen, so please get used to her presence because she will be here from this day forward." He caught some eyes shifting uncomfortably knowing they had been called out.

"Next, I am aware of Taya's absence," he continued as his eyes drifted toward the empty chair at the table, "regardless, you all should know that her district results were still captured and included." He paused, waiting to see if anyone questioned either of his statements. Silence ensued, and again, he felt the strain in the atmosphere.

He looked over at Nicola, prepared to address him, but his brother's expression caught him off guard. There was no sense of emotion on his face nor in his eyes, and although Nicola met Derek's gaze with the perfect poker face, that was the problem; Nicola didn't have a poker face.

Adrenaline now shot through his body, realizing exactly what was about to happen next.

It can't be, he thought as his mind attempted to grasp the severity of the very near future. *This is how this is going to go down then?*

He glanced at Christine, then back to his brother. "Now to move on to why we're here," he stated keeping his tone even. "Nicola, please give the prime minister the voting results."

Nicola paused a beat, then handed his sealed envelope to Christine, who then passed it across Derek to the prime minister. Mattia promptly opened the envelope, breaking Nicola's seal, withdrawing the official document. His eyes flew open wide.

Internally, Derek was bracing himself, outwardly however, he regarded Mattia with the most confident expression he could muster.

Here we go, was Derek's last thought before Mattia recovered his surprise at seeing the results.

He cleared his throat, sharing the outcome with the room.

"The people have voted," Mattia stated, "and Calina will not join the European Union."

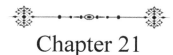

Chapter 21

There were several seconds of shocked silence following the prime minister's words, then as expected, at once, an abrupt outcry erupted amongst the parliament members.

"That can't be!" an enraged member shouted, as many rose from their seats, the sound of sliding chairs across the hardwood deafening as many began to voice doubt adding to the rising angst.

"It is unacceptable!" another member put it as he slammed his palm on the table, again to the general consensus, fanning the flame which fueled further arguing.

"Please, have a seat," Mattia tried, but no one was listening, and few even heard him try to speak.

As before, members began to quarrel and tempers flared. Fingers began pointing in Nicola's direction, who remained quiet thus far, as opposing members from the parties blamed one another.

"I have it on good authority how my district would have voted," an older member stated strongly, raising his voice even louder in order to be heard. "There is no way the majority of the people wished to not join! Either the prince made a mistake or he's lying." His comment hushed the room as members focused their whole attention and accusing stares at Nicola.

"There is no mistake," Nicola replied sternly, remaining seated, his voice cutting through the silence like a razor.

This was going sideways quickly, Derek realized, and it was only a matter of minutes until he would need to take action. He didn't wish for the guard to intervene again if it were at all possible, but he knew, as everyone knew around him, that this was not the correct outcome.

He attempted to read his brother once again, but Nicola's expression remained vacant. He was definitely hiding something. But although Derek could not foresee how calling him out publicly would cause the room to react, he had to surmise it would do nothing good. He needed to remain impartial for now, stall any formal allegations, or even possible arrest, until he knew why Nicola did what he did.

"Enough," he stated while rising. "That is a very serious accusation you just made." His eyes locked with the older member. "Let us not have a repeat of how this group handled themselves the last time we met about this matter."

As all eyes turned to the monarch he retook his place, an indication that the others do so as well. There were some continued grumblings and remarks as the members took their seats.

"I realize this is not the outcome we were all expecting or hoping for," Derek continued, "and I am just as shocked as you all are."

"Your Highness," it was Frankie who now spoke, "with all due respect for the monarchy, you can imagine how absurd this result is when you, yourself campaigned so heavily to see us join. We've seen those who were formally against the idea turn, and the vast majority of not only parliament, but the citizens as well, have voiced opinions that joining is in our best interests. We must wonder why now, how the outcome is what it is."

"I agree," Bryan added, seizing the opportunity to plant seeds which would lead the others to rise up against the monarch. "Personally, I can't help but consider who benefits the most by not joining. Although there are some serious businessmen who are reaping the rewards of our current economical structure, it is actually the monarchy itself who has the most to lose by joining." Several members murmured agreement, giving each other suspicious glances. "And it was the monarchy who decided on a public vote."

Bryan's comments changed the air, and Derek felt the shift. It was no longer Nicola they suspected of engineering the vote, it was himself. It always came down to the question of how much power the people were comfortable letting the monarch have.

"Are you actually insinuating that I petitioned for the country to join the European Union with the intention of setting up a public vote only to manipulate the outcome so we don't join?" Derek asked incredulously. "I approached the EU in the first place. If I didn't want the country to join, why would I even bother?"

"To gain the trust of the people perhaps?" another member, Isabela Fontaine, (and the only other woman in parliament besides Taya), answered as she shrugged nonchalantly.

"I think that is a ridiculous notion," Mattia declared, "the monarchy is not at fault for how the people ultimately decided."

"*If* that's how the people decided," Isabela now said, running with

214

the cues being given amongst the consensus of the members. "It seems," she continued, "we are all very much in agreement that the county should, in fact, join the EU. Whether this outcome was a mistake, or," she paused dramatically, "something else…, it's clear there is only one result that parliament will accept." She stopped to ensure all the attention was on her as she made her next demand. "Therefore, I ask that the monarch enact executive power and override the public vote."

Derek raised his eyebrows at the government official knowing this was a test, and he noticed the nodding agreements of the members around him. The silence that followed was deafening as they all waited his reaction to Isabela's request. He had feared being placed in this situation, knowing it was a catch 22, and he could almost hear the accusations of "power abuse." He glanced at Christine, whose face was expressionless, but she gave him a very slight shake of her head.

"We must respect the outcome given by the people," he stated, "there will be no override." His comment sparked an immediate reaction.

"Outrageous!" the older member cried.

Among the shocked faces and agreements, it was Isabela who stood. "As the monarch of Calina, you refuse to do what is right for the people," she now stated strongly, and she cleared her throat placing her palms on the table.

"Prime Minister and members of parliament, since taking the throne, our king has continuously made contradictory decisions, choosing to use his authority when it benefited him. He made the decision to remove Marco DeGrassi swiftly, among others, but now, when the decision benefits the people, he refuses to act." She paused, letting the words sink in around her. She looked at Derek now. "Your decisions have been radical, and not only have you refused to honor Calean culture in various ways, you've continued to flaunt that American in front of the people, insisting she be our queen."

Derek now narrowed his eyes dangerously, his look daring Isabela to continue. Her gaze shifted under his, but she swallowed and continued, although when she spoke again, her voice held less conviction. She was straight-up challenging their monarch, and if parliament didn't support her, she would most certainly be removed from her seat.

"Our people continue to starve, and knowing this is the answer, you won't do what is right. These actions can be considered unlawful," she said, taking a breath, "and you should not be our king. Therefore, I move to begin proceedings to dethrone Derek Landino." She spoke the final words quickly as though she would lose her nerve otherwise.

Eyes shifted as her words rang ominously to those in the room, the severity of her statement escalating the matter to another level. Derek clenched his jaw, his piercing gaze never leaving Isabela's challenging one.

"Who will support my motion?" she asked forcing a steady tone.

"I will," the older member spoke up, and another member also rose their hand in agreement.

"As will I."

"And me." The last vote of support coming from Bryan which caused many looks of pure shock in his direction.

This was getting out of hand, and as Nicola looked from his brother to Isabela, he knew he couldn't let other members jump on this bandwagon. This meeting was taking a dangerous turn Nicola hadn't fully expected, and it was time to confess. He couldn't let Derek take the fall. He had fulfilled his end of the deal; he delivered the outcome as he was instructed. Allowing Derek to become de-throned was not part of the agreement. He could only hope someone would still go after Taya after his imminent arrest.

"Listen—," he began, but he caught Derek's eye, who shook his head, his expression telling him quite plainly to "shut up."

The remaining members looked indecisive on voting Derek out, and the sudden turn of events felt mind-blowing to Christine. She looked at his face, set pensively as usual, but she could tell he was on the verge of acting. Someone had to say something, she realized, only two more members needed to agree to this and formal proceedings would begin.

She saw a slight shift in his expression, as if he had made a decision in his mind, was it…defeat? Her eyes opened wide as she realized now what he was about to do. He was going to consent to using executive power to override the vote. That was the wrong decision, she knew, and it wouldn't stop parliament from overthrowing him. The pressure was clouding his judgement, and she had never before seen Derek make such a miscalculated move. She couldn't let him make it now.

She stood.

"You need to sit down, Isabela," she stated flatly, her tone immediately diminishing the parliament member's air of superiority. "Now."

Isabela raised her eyebrows at Christine. "You have no authority," she said.

"Maybe not yet," Christine replied calmly, "I was only trying to prevent you from making a fool out of yourself."

Isabela gave a laugh. "I don't think *I'm* the one who's making a fool out of myself right now."

Christine pretended to think for a moment. "You're right, this isn't a rash decision here, is it?" and she shot daggers at Bryan and the other two parliament members currently backing Isabela. "After all, your king has not moved this country forward economically more in the past few months than it has in decades. There have not been more jobs created, nor has there been a drastic decrease in crime and corruption." Her tone was mocking, of course, and highlighting Derek's quick accomplishments for the betterment of the people caused a look of uncertainty now in Isabela. Christine continued, "so, instead of taking a step back and launching an investigation to uncover what happened with the vote, let's just decide to remove him."

Isabela glanced quickly at those around her, noticing they now refused to look in her direction. She took a breath and sat slowly back down.

"Signora Christine is right," Mattia added quickly, "This is premature. As Prime Minister, I will not allow this vote to happen at this time. There needs to be an investigation before anything is decided. If the result delivered by prince Nicola is not accepted, then steps will be taken to validate the information first."

Christine re-took her seat as she glanced at Derek. His expression showed appreciation, and he took her hand, squeezing it slightly. She knew he was back in control. It was the first time she had seen him lose his nerve, and she mused that he was human after all.

She couldn't stop a swell of pride within her that she was able to contribute in this way, and she shuddered to think what would have happened if she had just consented to Derek's original wishes and not come at all.

"And then what?" Isabela questioned directly, "Either the prince is lying or the vote was manipulated. If it is discovered that the people did in fact vote to not join the European Union, it will become clear this vote was rigged."

"Then that will need to be proven," Derek interjected as all eyes now turned to their monarch. Although Mattia gave a nod in approval in a show of support, Isabela lifted her chin a notch defiantly, clearly indicating her dissent.

"We will reconvene following an investigation of the information relayed by Nicola pertaining to the vote." Mattia stated, and his tone had a finality to it indicating that there was nothing more to discuss at the moment. "Everyone is excused, and the conclusion of today's meeting is that the results are currently 'indeterminate.'"

At the prime minister's words of dismissal, Derek stood still holding Christine's hand, before being escorted from the room by Costa, followed closely by Nicola and Martino. Upon nearing his study, Derek pulled Christine toward him.

"Are you alright?" he asked, concerned for the way she was treated.

She gave a slight smirk. "It would take more than that to get under my skin," she replied.

He nodded. "Thank you," he told her quietly, gratitude filling his voice. She gave him a smile in return. "Go to my office with Costa and stay there until I come back," he told her, "the wish for my removal was made very clear by some, and I'm not taking any chances with your safety."

Understanding too well the gravity of what just transpired during the meeting, she did not offer any objection.

Derek then turned and followed Nicola and Martino towards the prince's study. "Wait outside," he instructed Martino as they reached Nicola's door.

Martino bowed his head slightly. "The prime minister has notified Esposito and Romano of the imminent investigation," he relayed, "they will be here shortly."

Derek nodded then followed Nicola into the study. He closed the door behind him. "Where is it?" he asked immediately as Nicola strode over to this desk.

"They're not here," Nicola replied, making a show of looking over his desk. He met Derek's eyes. "The results from each district. They're gone."

Derek raised an eyebrow, on the verge of losing his patience. He had had enough. He crossed the room quickly as he approached his brother, his expression darkening. He grabbed Nicola's shirt collar and pushed him away from the desk pinning him up against the shelf behind him. His blue eyes now bore into his brother's near black ones.

"Do you know what you've done?" he seethed. "I know you're lying. I trusted you! Do you realize you just gave them cause to plan my assassination?" Nicola didn't respond but matched his glare. "One of us is going down," Derek continued, "you've left me with no alternative but to authorize your arrest."

Nicola grabbed Derek's wrist and wrenched from his grasp, shoving him back.

"They're going to kill her!" he finally gritted out. "I had no choice."

"What?" Derek demanded, although he knew exactly what Nicola was saying. "Explain," he stated, "and do it quickly."

Nicola glanced at his phone. He needed Taya's kidnapper to call back before they came to begin their investigation. He didn't know if Derek would let him leave, but he liked his odds more with his brother alone than backed by Romano and Esposito.

"DeGrassi has Taya," he told Derek, "I was told she would die unless I delivered the outcome to not join the EU."

"Why didn't you say anything?" Derek exclaimed, his anger rolling off him in waves.

"You wouldn't have believed it!" Nicola shot at him. "You wouldn't have let me try and save her."

"You mean I wouldn't have let you set up the perfect opportunity for parliament to overthrow me?" Derek retorted, "no, I would not have."

Nicola shook his head. "She was being strangled over the phone," he said in desperation, "what was I supposed to do?"

Derek groaned. "This could be just a set up," he said through a clenched jaw, "you don't know she's not a part of this!"

Before Nicola could argue further, a buzzing came from his phone on the desk. He grabbed the phone answering it promptly as Derek listened.

"Hello…I did what you wanted…I want to speak to her… How do I know she's unharmed?" Nicola ran a hand through his hair in clear frustration, then grabbed a pen and paper from the desk, scribbling out an address. "20 minutes," he confirmed then ended the call, meeting his brother's gaze.

"I have to go get her," he stated.

"Out of the question," Derek replied, "don't you understand? I have no choice but to tell them you lied. You will be arrested in about ten minutes!"

"What if it were Christine?" Nicola tried, as a last ditch effort to get his brother on his side.

Derek stared at him for a moment, his jaw set. "Go," he said, a hint of defeat to his tone, "try and get her back safe, then," he paused, locking eyes with his brother, "you bring her back here."

Not wasting time, Nicola bolted past Derek and hurried out the door, where Martino was still stationed.

"Follow him," Derek told the guard, who bowed, then left trailing Nicola.

Derek watched Martino leave just as Romano and Esposito made their way toward him. He narrowed his eyes.

DeGrassi was behind this, he knew, he just didn't know if Taya was really involved too. He let out a slow breath, coming to terms with just how close he had been to being voted out. If it hadn't been for Christine, he most certainly wouldn't be here right now. Nicola's betrayal had thrown him completely off-guard. DeGrassi had almost won. Almost.

Bryan hung up with Nicola after giving him an address. He had to make the call from Taya's phone while he drove back to where he was holding her, so there had been no way he was able to let her speak. Which was almost sad, if he stopped to think about it; she would never speak to the prince again.

He frowned as he neared the little, run-down house. Knowing what was coming next filled him with a dread he was not familiar with.

Taya was not meant to live. He had been paid to kill her, by her own brother. Only, Bryan did not wish to kill Taya, and regardless of everything, he held within him a soft spot for her.

He sighed as he exited the car; he needed to be quick about it. His plan was to leave her body for Nicola to find at the address he had relayed over the phone.

He entered the house, walking through to the kitchen where she was still tied to the chair. As he approached her, he saw the look of contempt on her face for him. He leaned against the corner of the table, and for the first time since he had kidnapped her, he took in her appearance and condition. He felt a pang of guilt; he supposed he should have at least given her something to eat or some water. *But no*

220

matter, she would be out of misery soon anyway, he thought as he tried to push the guilt aside. However, as he gazed at her, he pursed his lips in a rare moment of sympathy.

"What did you do?" she asked in a weak voice. "What happened at the conference?" Taya assumed he wouldn't tell her anything, but she heard Bryan tell Nicola to deliver a false outcome. Did that mean the country didn't join the EU? Was Derek even still the monarch at this point?

A grimace crossed Bryan's face. They had been so close to removing Landino from the throne. If any of those parliament members had had a backbone, they would have succeeded. Imagine Isabela backing down to that American just because she pushed back on her a little bit! Enzo would be furious when he found out.

He stood up straight from where he had been perched on the edge of the table and his thoughts went back to Taya. *Damn Enzo.* He stepped toward her.

"You needn't worry about such things," he said soothingly to her.

His words caused her stomach to knot, but she continued to glare at him as he reached out to touch her cheek gently where a purple bruise had formed; the result of his back-hand from earlier. She yanked her head back away from his touch, but he grasped her chin holding her in place.

"I'm so sorry I had to hurt you," he murmured, and he tilted her head to the side to inspect further bruising on her neck. "If only he had complied, I wouldn't have had to resort to such measures."

"You make me sick," she sneered at him.

He frowned releasing her, but ignored her comment and moved away toward one of the two small bedrooms.

He needed to stop thinking about her, what she had come to mean to him. He pulled a gun from a drawer and dropped it on the bed next where the briefcase lay. He eyed the money, knowing what was supposed to happen next. He picked back up the gun, gripping it tightly, feeling torn. Could there possibly be another way? Not to mention the thought of defying Enzo appealed to him greatly. Why should he do what Enzo wanted anyway?

No, he wouldn't do this the way Enzo wanted, and a thought occurred to him as he continued to stare at the money DeGrassi had given him. Taya was a DeGrassi. But no one knew that except for him. Perhaps he could use that to his advantage.

As an alternate plan formed in his mind, he realized maybe she didn't need to die. After all, they only needed her not to talk, whether she was dead or labeled as a "DeGrassi," either way, anything she had to say wouldn't matter. As a DeGrassi, her word would not be trusted nor credible. If he could make it so she was in a place where she could not point the finger back to him or Enzo, at least he wouldn't have to kill her.

However, if he didn't do as instructed, Enzo might come after him. Considering the money again, (it was more than enough to start over,) he picked up the briefcase and walked back to where she was seated.

"It's time to go," he told her. He removed a knife from his pocket and cut through the tape binding her to the chair as well as her feet together. He left her wrists bound behind her back.

"Where are we going?" she asked hurriedly, a thought occurring to her to kick him now that her legs were free. But she surmised she wouldn't get far as she eyed the gun in his hand.

"To see your boyfriend," he muttered. He hoisted her up onto her feet. "Believe it or not, Taya," he said, "I don't wish to kill you. If you behave, you may get out of this alive."

She swallowed, her throat unbearably dry. She didn't trust a word he said, but she also didn't have any options right now. If he took her to a new location, an opportunity to escape may present itself.

He walked her out the front door and toward the car parked in the drive. Her legs felt heavy and her entire body was weak. It occurred to her that she may not be able to run even if there was a chance, and overpowering Bryan was completely out of the question. It was dark, well into the evening, and as she took in her surroundings, she realized she had been pretty accurate with her location, although she didn't know this neighborhood specifically.

He threw the briefcase in the back, then opened the passenger door, indicating with the gun that she get in. She considered it for a moment, then complied and he secured her seatbelt for her. He took his place behind the driver's seat and started the car, backing out of the drive.

He drove in silence, and she didn't ask any questions knowing she wouldn't get any answers. All she could do was bide her time, but her heart was beating frantically, crazy with anticipation of what would happen to her.

He had said he was taking her to Nicola, but that didn't make any sense to her, and most likely he was giving her a false sense of security so she wouldn't struggle. But panic was setting in, and Taya was determined to stay on her guard. Maybe when they stopped and he let her out of the car, she should try to run for it. If only she didn't feel so weary and faint.

Her hopes for survival sank lower when she saw him pull into the lot of a vacant warehouse. She knew this building, it had belonged to the DeGrassi's at one time, a thriving business which used to provide many jobs. But it was now empty, the DeGrassi's having chosen to outsource for cheaper labor long ago, putting many Caleans out of work. The building was left to decay amongst others on the outskirts of town. She could only deduce he was bringing her to such a desolate place to kill her.

He exited the car after looking through the windshield, appearing to search for someone. Opening her door, he unclipped her belt, then grabbed her by the upper arm and pulled her to her feet. He was holding the gun, but then placed it in his suit jacket, ensuring she knew he still had it handy.

"Listen to me," he told her quickly as he now removed the knife again from his pocket, which she eyed fearfully, "I'm going to try and help you, but you need to play along."

She gave him a quizzical yet disbelieving look as he cut through the tape on her wrists. Adrenaline kicking in, she immediately made a move to run, but he was quick and caught her arm tightly. She winced at the pain.

"Stay put," he hissed, "or this won't end well for you. Don't leave me with any other choice." His words were threatening, and too scared to move, she massaged her wrists, now free from the tape. It was then that she noticed her bracelet was missing.

Realizing the clasp must have broken somewhere along through this whole ordeal, and although it was dark, Taya instinctively looked at the ground for it. Distracted, she didn't see Bryan looking over the top of her head at someone approaching them.

"Taya, I don't understand why you asked me to bring you here?" He questioned loudly.

She jerked her head up to look at Bryan confused, then her own eyes followed his gaze to a man approaching them from the other side of deserted lot. She squinted to make out the figure in the dark: Nicola. With Martino close behind him.

She was stunned into shock at his presence, relief flooding through her, unbelieving that Bryan had actually taken her to him.

When his eyes fell on Taya, alive and whole, Nicola picked up his pace, now jogging in her direction.

Nic!" she broke out of her momentary paralysis, her voice cracking as she cried out. Bryan hadn't been lying, he really was trying to help her.

She didn't care any longer if he ended up shooting her in the back, she only cared about getting to Nicola, and she ran the last few steps toward him flinging herself into his embrace. He returned her affection eagerly, pulling back to cup her face in his hands. She winced slightly as his fingertips brushed across the bruise on her cheek.

"God, I was sure I was never going to see you again," he breathed, and he placed a kiss on her forehead, taking in her injuries and her haggard appearance, a look of sadness crossing his face. But he gave her a reassuring smile before turning his gaze to Bryan who had now caught up to them.

"What are you doing here, LaPointe?" Nicola asked, his tone laced with accusation. It didn't make sense to him that Bryan was with her. He couldn't possibly be involved, could he? Or had Bryan rescued her? The thought turned his stomach.

Taya's thoughts were running rapid, unsure how to even begin to explain what Bryan had done. He had told her to "play along," but she didn't understand what he meant by that. She realized also that he had chosen not to kill her. The fact made her hesitate, which gave him the chance to speak first.

"Taya called me, signore," he told Nicola, "as soon as the meeting was over. She asked that I pick her up and bring her here. She didn't tell me why."

Taya's mouth fell open at what Bryan had just said. She shook her head, trying to find her voice outside her distress.

"That doesn't make any sense," Nicola dismissed, "Taya was abducted. What do you mean you picked her up? Where?" His arm was wrapped around her shoulders, and he brought her closer to him. His need to protect her evident.

"Wait," Taya objected, trying to get the words out, "that's not what—," but Bryan spoke over her, refusing to let her get a word in.

"I picked her up at a home belonging to Enzo DeGrassi," he said, giving Taya a suspicious look, "Hang on. Did you say that you thought she had been abducted?"

Nicola nodded, and he now looked down at Taya, her eyes were wide and fearful. Her mouth was slightly parted, as though she wanted to say something, but unable to form the words.

Bryan nodded as though understanding. "I get it now," he said, looking at Nicola, "you thought her life was in danger. That's why you delivered the outcome the way you did." He narrowed his eyes, then gave Taya a regretful look. "I'm sorry Taya, but, I need to tell the prince what I know." Horror now flashed across her face, then he cleared his throat and looked back at Nicola. "Your Highness, Taya Mariano is in fact, Enzo DeGrassi's sister—,"

"No, stop!" Taya attempted to cry out over him, but Bryan continued.

"—if your personal understanding was that she had been abducted, then I believe you have been deceived by her. I can't say whether Enzo himself is involved, I can only tell you what I know and where she was."

Nicola staggered a step upon hearing Bryan's words. No. Dread filled him as Derek's accusations echoed in his mind. It couldn't be true, she wasn't involved! He met her eyes as he pulled back away from her.

"You're not...," he practically whispered, the words catching in his throat, "you can't be, his *sister*. Are you?"

Her eyes filled with tears, disbelief crashing over her that Bryan had just outed her. Her mind began to frantically digest what was happening, and although anger flew through her, she still felt faint. She had been drugged, restrained, strangled, and threatened at gun point. It was too much. Now, Nicola knew the truth that she was a DeGrassi, and in that one second, she knew that everything he felt for her had changed. Her heart shattered.

Her lack of denial coupled with the look of desperation on her face told him it was true. She was a DeGrassi. Which means she had to have been the woman seen going into his office several days ago. She had set him up? All this time, she was working with Enzo? He recalled her demeanor when she had accused *him* of working for Enzo... her meeting with Derek that she never showed up for... Derek had been right. Had she actually killed Olivia too? The woman he loved, whom he thought he knew, had committed treason against the monarchy. Against him.

"Stefan," Nicola said, his tone and expression now lifeless, "take Ms. Mariano-*DeGrassi* into custody." Martino stepped forward and took Taya's arm.

"No!" She exclaimed, calling upon her last bit of strength to speak, "I wasn't with Enzo or at his home! It all wasn't a lie, Nic, please believe me." Her tone was pleading, but Martino's hold on her only tightened.

Refusing to look at her, Nicola hung his head until Martino had marched her back to his car, placing her within it.

"You'll need to make a statement," he told Bryan, who nodded, a grievous look placed on his face.

"I'm sorry, signore," he offered with a feigned sincerity that Nicola didn't pick up on. He turned away from Bryan and followed Martino back toward his own car.

Bryan watched as they left, then let out a breath he didn't realize he was holding. He had ensured Taya was arrested for treason, but at least she was alive. True, if she is found guilty, she could very well be executed. But at least he didn't have to do it.

He walked back to his car and climbed into the driver's seat. He grabbed the briefcase from the back and placed it in the seat next to him.

Taya was out of the way, but he didn't do the job Enzo paid him for. Maybe now would be a good time to walk away from it all. Enzo could go to hell for all he cared, and he had plenty to start fresh; create a new life.

Chapter 22

"We found ash in the fireplace," Esposito reported entering Derek's study. "It could suggest that the prince burned the actual results."

"Why would you assume Nicola burned them?" Derek asked, seated behind his desk, his voice calm.

"They were found in his office fireplace," Esposito replied, "clearly he was destroying the evidence that proves he lied about the voting result."

"You've been jumping to a lot of conclusions recently, Antonio," Derek said, and he glanced at Romano, "anyone could have burned those results. If that's what happened. Those ashes could be anything."

"Who else would have the motive to, Signore? It doesn't make any sense," Esposito expressed.

"Doesn't it?" Christine asked now. She stepped forward, closer to Esposito, her arms crossed. She understood the Head of the King's Guard had a job to do, and Esposito did it well, but she couldn't help but dislike the man. She certainly wasn't going to hold back telling him what she thought.

"I realize you weren't at the meeting, Antonio, but anyone here can attest to the eagerness several members of parliament showed to remove Derek as monarch. It could be that one or more parliament members delivered false results themselves, and Nicola was just reporting what was given to him."

"Signora Christine is not wrong," Mattia put in, then sighed, "I guess we'll never know what was in those envelopes. But at least we can trace the results back to the machines themselves."

Derek glanced at his phone, they had been at this for 45 minutes since Nicola had left to go after Taya. He had not heard any word on this "rescue mission," and it was getting difficult to stall. As of yet, he had not shared with Romano nor Esposito Nicola's belief that Taya was taken hostage to rig the vote. He wanted the facts first.

"Getting the information from all of the voting machines will take some time," Esposito said, clearly annoyed, "and we know that prince Nicola is the only person who would know what was in those envelopes." He raised his eyebrows suggestively, looking at Derek who met his gaze directly. "Which, I'm still unsure as to why he's not here to answer for this?"

"Martino is with Nicola," was all Derek offered as a reply.

"Your Highness," Costa now addressed Derek stepping forward, "I've just been notified that prince Nicola has returned."

"And Taya?" Derek asked.

At the mention of Taya's name, Esposito and Romano exchanged glances, unaware of how she could possibly be involved. Costa shook his head.

"Martino has her. In custody."

"Custody?" Esposito exclaimed, "what is going on here?"

Derek gave him a somber look. "Let's wait until Nicola arrives," he stated.

Although he had been suspicious of Taya, Derek had really hoped she was innocent as Nicola had believed. He furrowed his brow. Even if Taya had helped set him up, she hadn't acted alone. And if it was Enzo plotting with her, why hadn't he been arrested as well? It angered him to think that yet again, someone else was going to take the fall while Enzo himself slipped through the cracks.

The office door swung open, and Nicola entered as all heads turned in his direction. His eyes looked tired, his face was gaunt, as though he was a man who had lost everything. He approached Derek at the desk, not acknowledging the presence of the others.

"She is his sister," he informed Derek, his tone defeated. "Taya Mariano is Marco DeGrassi's daughter."

For several seconds the room was quiet. The inability to digest this news hanging heavy in the air.

"*Apetta un minuto*," it was Esposito who broke the silence, "I'm assuming that somehow the prince has learned that it is Taya Mariano who is the insider working for Enzo DeGrassi? And she is a DeGrassi herself? Although this news is critical to the death of the palace attendant, I don't understand what that has to do with prince Nicola delivering the voting outcome the way he did. Considering that is what we are investigating right now." He turned to Nicola, "Your Highness, what was the result of the vote in the envelopes delivered to you tonight?"

"I don't know," Nicola replied stoically.

Esposito blinked at him. "You don't know?" he repeated. "How could you not know? Didn't you look at the results, signore?"

Nicola hung his head, he had never felt so defeated before, so empty. His brain was operating on auto-pilot as he thought how to answer Esposito's questions, but the inquiry surrounding him was barely getting through to his comprehension. He could only think of Taya. He raised his head and looked at his brother for any kind of cue to follow. He saw Derek return a look of encouragement, and he took that to mean to be honest. He didn't have the energy to lie anyway.

Taking a breath, he took the chair in front of the desk. He then proceeded to recount for those in the room the phone call he had received shortly after the polls had opened threatening Taya in exchange for the outcome of the vote. He explained that he never opened the envelopes because it didn't matter considering what he was being forced to deliver. He then shared the details of the second phone call. How he left the palace in an attempt to rescue Taya, only to uncover that she had already been "rescued," by Bryan LaPointe. But Bryan, catching on to her scheme spilled the beans about who and where she really was.

The only thing he left out was burning the envelopes, which again, taking his cues from Derek, had given him a look which told him to not divulge the fact.

"So you did not knowingly deliver a false outcome?" Esposito questioned. Nicola shrugged.

"How could I have?" he said. "I don't technically know the outcome, do I?"

Romano looked at Nicola.

"What did Signorina Mariano have to say for herself?" He queried, but Esposito gave a short laugh at the question.

"What would it matter what she said?" he stated, "she's a DeGrassi. Anything she had to say without validation could not be trusted." The comment made Nicola feel numb.

Romano nodded, agreeing then rubbed his eyes and gave a tired sigh. "I think we can wrap up for this evening," he declared, then addressed the prime minister. "Signore, you need to prepare to make the public announcement of the voting result."

"Yes, of course," Mattia assented, then looked at Derek with an expression of apprehension as he let out a slow breath. "This will be very disappointing for a lot of people," he stated.

"It's only until we know for sure," Derek replied, "their minds will be put to rest soon enough. I feel confident the truth will be what we all assume it will be."

"I just hope we can get it delivered before anything drastic happens," Mattia added, "the sooner we confirm to the people what they expect, the safer you stay, signore. And it will definitely help satisfy everyone to have the true culprit for all of this mess on trial."

Thinking of Taya in a holding cell, Nicola's throat went dry at the prime minister's words. The concept of her on trial seemed unfathomable to him.

"Signorina Mariano is being held downtown," Romano said, "and we will interrogate her first thing in the morning. Additionally, we will also get to work on recovering the actual result from the voting machines tomorrow. As far as the prince is concerned, it's clear to me he was set up. Not to mention, signore Nicola had nothing to gain by delivering the outcome the way he had *other* than ensuring Taya's safety.

I would also like to look into the phone records of the cell phone used as well as get a collaborating statement from signore LaPointe."

Nicola was barely registering what Romano was saying, and an immense amount of remorse threatened to overwhelm him. His head was swimming with confusion, but through it all, he was unable to accept Taya's guilt. How could he come to terms with her taking full blame just so the monarchy might recover?

Esposito nodded along with Romano's direction. "It's safe to say, Your Highness," he said, turning toward Nicola, "that until this matter is cleared, you will not leave palace grounds?"

"Whatever you say," Nicola replied flatly.

Esposito lowered his head in a show of respect, then promptly left the office, followed by Romano and finally Mattia.

Nicola slumped back into the chair once they had gone leaving only Derek, Christine and Costa.

"This isn't right," he murmured.

"I'm sorry, Nic," Derek replied, "this isn't the development I was hoping to hear."

Nicola didn't look up, but narrowed his eyes. "What's going to happen to her?" he asked, his voice quiet.

"It really depends on the evidence," Derek answered, "did she say anything in her defense?"

"She claimed she was really kidnapped, but…" Nicola trailed off, thinking back to the look on her face; a look of guilt, "but, she *is* Enzo's sister. She was seen meeting with him days ago, clearly to plan this out. Enzo would not have known what she meant to me unless she told him." He ran a hand through his hair, and his entire body ached from sheer, emotional fatigue.

He sighed heavily, his mind reeling from the turn of events that took place in this one day. From realizing Taya was missing to discovering her life might be in danger, lying to his own government, facing possible arrest, the potential overthrow of his family, and finally, learning the horrid truth about the only woman he had ever dared to love.

"What about parliament?" he asked Derek now.

There was still a matter of addressing their sentiments voiced about Derek's reign after the voting results were announced. Derek furrowed his brow.

"I have no doubt the true result will come to light," he said, "but, I won't sugar coat this. The trust and respect I've worked tirelessly to repair for the monarchy of Calina has all but been destroyed. Regardless of if we join the EU or not, the scandal surrounding not only how the vote was delivered, but the reasons why it all happened will overshadow any good that we tried to achieve for the people." He paused, "there is no guarantee parliament or the people will not revolt. However, they may sympathize with how you were manipulated into doing what you did."

Nicola looked at Derek sharply, realizing what he hadn't even considered up to this point.

There was no hiding his relationship with Taya now. If they had any hope of repairing the standing of the monarchy, and to prove neither he nor Derek delivered the vote with malicious intent, the story would have to come to light. Of course it would become world-wide news. And Taya's true identity and his involvement with her right along with it.

"So, what, she becomes the scapegoat?" he spat out. "She takes the blame for all of this enabling us to keep our legacy, and Enzo just walks away? Everyone knows he's the one really behind this! What about him?"

"Well, I'm hoping Taya will be cooperative and give us some kind of evidence against DeGrassi," Derek said, "being a DeGrassi herself, she may not be willing to turn against her brother. But it may be her only saving grace."

Nicola shook his head slowly, knitting his brow, a deep frown on his face. "I just can't believe it," he said, "I can't help but feel we made a mistake."

"She fooled all of us," Derek replied, "she was very convincing as a loyal, government official."

Nicola stood, he couldn't hear anymore. He only wanted to crash, hoping that tomorrow when he woke up this would all just be a bad nightmare. He knew it was a ridiculous notion, but at the moment, he couldn't wrap his mind around who Taya really turned out to be, nor what she did. At the same time, all his instincts were telling him to run to her and protect her.

He didn't speak but gave Derek one last look of defeat before turning to make his leave.

"There will be extra security, just so you're aware," Derek said after him.

Nicola nodded, but didn't turn back around. "If there's a revolution tonight, don't wake me," he said warily, "just let me burn."

Late that evening, Enzo watched on the news as the prime minister delivered a voting result of "indeterminate." His jaw was clenched so tight it was painful.

He had been pacing for hours, along with the rest of the continent, waiting to learn the result, and now, hearing it from a live broadcast to the people of Calina instead of from Bryan was infuriating. Not only that, but, there had been no announcement of parliament's insistence on Landino's removal from the monarchy. Something had not gone according to his plan, he knew, and where in God's name was LaPointe!

There was a buzzing from his phone, and Enzo inhaled on his cigarette before making his way across the dimly-lit living room to where he left his cell on the glass coffee table. The message was from one of his many informants; those that he paid handsomely for tidbits of insider information. All the message said was: "Taya Mariano being held under suspicion of conspiracy against the monarchy." He had been expecting news on Taya's fate, what he had not been expecting was that she was still alive. And in custody?

Outraged, Enzo now knew what had happened: Bryan had failed him. Enzo had questioned Bryan's ability to follow through where Taya was concerned, he knew the fool had gone soft over his good-for-nothing sister. But Bryan had never not delivered before, he hated the Landino's almost as much as Enzo did, so he had quieted his doubt. It seemed however, he had been vastly mistaken in putting his faith in Bryan.

It was obvious now that instead of killing her, Bryan had set Taya up to take the fall for orchestrating the kidnapping and coercing the prince to lie. But if Taya took the blame, parliament would never overthrow Landino.

Enzo slammed his phone back down on the table. *Damn that double-crossing bastard!* He yelled in his mind. He had been so close to getting rid of that tyrant who killed his father, now he'd have to think of something else. But first, he needed to take care of his "employee."

Enzo curled his lip, practically snarling to himself in contempt at his own misjudgment. He strode to the wet bar and poured some scotch into a glass. He snuffed out the remains of his cigarette, and drink in hand returned to the coffee table in the middle of the living room. Grabbing the phone, he sank into the expensive leather sofa and searched for a contact while sipping the scotch.

The line rang three times before it was answered.

"I hope you're calling with something decent to tell us," a gruff voice answered, not bothering to even say "hello." "I can't remember the last time you gave us good news or information."

"I need you to do a job," Enzo said, leaning back into the sofa and crossing his ankle over his knee.

The voice scoffed. "A job, huh," and there was a chuckle, "well, that's funny, Enzo, because we haven't been able to finish the last one yet, have we."

"Don't blame me for your incompetence," Enzo snapped.

"We turned down a pretty penny from Landino because you said you'd pay us double," the voice continued, "so far, you've only paid us a quarter of the original amount."

"Last I checked, Nicola Landino is still alive," Enzo sneered back, "when the job is finished. That's when I pay."

"You've provided very little in terms of leads, Enzo," the voice replied calmly and gravely, "we would've never taken this contract knowing the power we were up against. But you made us believe Landino would not be in his position for long, and that with your help and intel, the job would be simple. So I risked having Landino as an enemy," the voice paused, "I'm regretting that decision, Enzo."

Enzo downed the rest of the scotch in his glass. Frustrated, he set the glass down on the table hard.

"I think you need to remember who provides many of your resources. How much I have invested in your operation," he seethed, then leaned back again into the sofa. "There's been a minor setback to my plan," he continued easily, "and my inept accomplice needs to be taken care of. He's the one who fucked up. Landino will still be gone, one way or another, and then it's open-season on his brother."

The voice sighed. "We're losing faith, Enzo…"

"Well, that would be your stupidity," Enzo stated, unfazed. "If you'd like to call off our 'arrangements,' I'm sure I can run some figures for you to buy me out, but I have a feeling you can't afford it. I guarantee I will find a way to take Landino down. He may have been provided with an excuse over this voting scandal, but it's left the monarchy on very thin ice. It won't take much to break it."

The line was quiet for several seconds, and Enzo's heart began to race—had he hung up?

"What's the target?" the voice finally asked with a tone of reluctance.

Enzo let out a breath of relief. He needed this loose end tied up. "Bryan LaPointe."

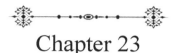

Chapter 23

The first break of dawn made its way into Nicola's dark room. He squinted as the sun dared to show its face, trying in vain to shine some light into his being. He didn't deserve light, and he found himself in a familiar place; a frame of mind he hadn't known since well after his mother had died.

A knock on his door brought him out of his dark thoughts, and he ignored it, hoping whoever it was would go away. But the knock came again. Irritated, he scowled at the door, thinking it must be too early to have anyone disturb him, but then he considered with this time of year, the sunrise would be a little past 7:00 a.m.

He returned his gaze to the window, he had clearly lost track of time, drowning in his guilt, thoughts of Taya, what should have been between them, and what the ultimate consequences of her actions could yet be.

The knock came a third time, and then without waiting any longer for his response, he heard the handle click as it opened.

"Nic?"

He registered Christine's quiet voice as she entered, his curiosity peeked slightly at what she had come for, but he didn't respond, wishing she would just leave.

Christine surveyed the room entering slowly. The bed was made, not slept in, and she spotted him over by the closed balcony doors seated in one of the chairs. He did not look in her direction as she approached him, but as she drew closer, she could tell he was awake.

"Nic?" she tried again as she placed a steaming mug of coffee on the small table next to him. "I thought you could use some coffee." He glanced up at her then, and she realized she had never seen him appear so run down before. His eyes were blood-shot, his hair was a mess, and he still wore the remnants of the suit he had on the day before.

"Thanks," he mumbled to her, hoping that's all she came for and would leave him alone now.

But clearly not as her next words to him were, "mind if I join you for a minute?"

He did mind. But he didn't want to be rude, she did think enough of him to bring him coffee after all, and a brief thought crossed his mind that soon, Christine would be his sister.

He lifted a shoulder in a gesture that said "whatever," then reached for the mug taking a sip. He flinched as she opened one of the balcony doors, allowing more light to flood the room. A soft, crisp breeze passed over him. It was a tad chilly, but mildly refreshing, and he felt his senses becoming more alert.

"I wasn't sure how you liked it," she said taking a seat opposite him and pointing to the coffee.

He shrugged. "I'll drink it any way it comes," he replied, his voice sounding a bit course. "Did Derek send you?"

Christine shook her head and gave him a small smile. "No," she answered, "as a matter of fact, he advised me against trying to talk to you. He said I was wasting my time."

"He was right," Nicola murmured.

"You'll be happy to know nothing burned down last night," Christine continued, trying to keep the conversation light, "only a small group of, what seem to be for now, peaceful protesters outside the gates." Nicola raised his eyebrows, knitting them together. "Nothing the guard hasn't been able to handle," she added.

"Is that what you came to tell me?" he asked, hoping that now she had delivered her update, she'd go, but she shook her head again.

"I came to ask you if you were planning on going to see Taya," she stated, her tone confident.

He gave her a confused look. "No," he said as he cast his eyes down into the mug in his hands, "it won't change who she is, nor what she's done," he looked back at Christine, "and it would only make this more difficult for both of us."

"You know," she began, "I don't know Taya too well, but I'm having a hard time believing that she would do something like that to her country. Or to you."

Christine stood and walked toward the balcony. "My impression of her was always one of integrity and loyalty," she looked back at Nicola, "that wouldn't change just because of who her family is."

"Maybe your impression was wrong," Nicola said flatly.

"Do you think it is?" she asked.

He remained quiet. The truth was he didn't think she was wrong. But Taya had lied about who she was. She had been lying to him this entire time.

Christine let out a slow breath as she retook her seat.

"I know what you're feeling," she said, "I know you feel betrayed, and you think it's best to accept what you think you know at face value. You think it's easier to walk away rather than confront something that could ultimately break your heart." He looked at her sharply, considering her words. "But you may discover down the road that there were things you didn't know or realize, and by the time you do realize it, it may be too late. You know in your heart who she is and what she is or is not capable of."

He was quiet for several minutes pondering what she said.

"I…I'll think about it," he finally said, unwilling to relent easily.

"I've been there," Christine added urgently, her voice slightly irritated at his stubbornness, "don't make the same mistake I did. It could cost you everything you care about." She rose to leave and picked up the now empty mug.

He heard the door click behind her as she left, and he stared after her, her message lingering in his mind. He wondered briefly what her own situation had been; she was obviously speaking from some experience.

He sighed, gazing once again out the balcony window knowing Christine was right, but how could he face hearing Taya admit out loud that she lied and betrayed him? What would he even ask her, how would she respond?

As he continued to play out how he imagined the conversation would go, it dawned on him that Taya would never say those things to him. She couldn't because they simply weren't true. He stood now, narrowing his eyes, understanding suddenly why he had been struggling so much to believe what she had done.

She hadn't.

And regardless of how it seemed, she was innocent. She had to be, because he believed she loved him.

It was after 8:00 a.m. as Taya was being led back to her holding cell from the interview room. She had been downtown now for a little less than 12 hours, and prior to that, she had been held prisoner by Bryan in that grimy, little house tied to a chair for all of the previous day. Here, she had at least been given food, water, and allowed to clean up some, but she was exhausted, her clothes were filthy, and all she could think about was how she just wanted to go home.

She had spent the past three hours being questioned by Esposito and Romano, not that they believed anything she said. Which she half expected, now they knew who she really was. But it was her word against Bryan's, wasn't it? There was no actual proof that things happened the way he had claimed they did. And had they even bothered to question him at all? Especially after she made it clear to both of the officers that Bryan was the one behind all this!

In response to her side, they had only given her looks that plainly stated they thought her story only sounded like a desperate attempt to be released. Bryan was, after all, a highly respected political figure. She was a DeGrassi.

Her head was pounding as she re-entered the small cell, hearing the loud *clang* of the iron door close behind her. She had been placed in what could be deemed as a "nicer" cell, not the typical doom-and-gloom tiny enclosure with a single dingy cot. Her room had a cot, but it was clean, with a suitable mattress, and resembled more of a small bed. There was a simple desk and chair, as well as a separate bathroom which contained a new bar of soap and toothbrush. She assumed because of her status within the government she was given such luxuries, and it made her stomach turn as she realized the last person who probably stayed in this room was none other than her own notorious father.

Although she was stricken with fatigue, she could only pace the small room, her situation preventing her from gaining any real rest, as she thought now who would be best to call. She had no family, her friends were mostly among those in her own political party, and once word got out of her true identity, she felt certain no one would be quick to come to her aid.

"You have a visitor," a guard informed her through the window in her door, his voice breaking her out of her thoughts, which were coming up empty anyway.

She looked at him curiously and only nodded as he opened the door for her. He led her back down the hallway toward the same interview room, where she clearly was to receive this visitor.

She couldn't help but be intrigued as to who would come to see her, no one coming to mind that she assumed would want to. But as the guard opened the interview door, and she saw him standing there, (the last person she expected to see), she couldn't prevent her heart from leaping to her throat. He didn't smile, but then, why would he, and she realized he looked as tired as she felt.

Taking a seat in one of the chairs at the long table in the middle of the room, she held her breath waiting for him to speak. Was he here to accuse her? Blame her? Her arms immediately ached to embrace him, but she knew better than to feel that way toward him any longer.

Nicola took the seat opposite her and regarded her with a certain blazing intensity. Unable to meet his gaze, she averted her eyes to her hands in front of her.

"Are you ok?" he finally asked, and she snapped her eyes up to his.

The absurd question surprised her, but not because she was obviously not "ok," but because he actually sounded like he cared.

He sighed at the look on her face. "I know," he said, "dumb question. I guess I meant, are you ok physically, not emotionally." His gaze fell to her neck, where the purple bruise was now turning greenish-yellow.

"What are you doing here?" she said, her voice flat, ignoring his question by asking her own.

He lifted a bag from the floor and set it on the table.

"I went to your house and got you a change of clothes," he said.

She eyed the bag and gave him a perplexed look. Why was he being kind to her?

"I had to promise I didn't hide a file in there," he added, pointing to the bag.

Always joking, she thought, and she even had the notion to give him a small smile, if it weren't for the fact she was in a jail.

"But, that's not why I'm here," he continued, "I wanted to ask you what happened yesterday."

"I find that strange, considering you're the one who had me arrested," she stated quietly, "anyway, I already told Esposito everything I know."

"You lied to me, Taya," Nicola replied, "why didn't you tell me who you are?"

She raised an eyebrow at him. "Why do you think?" she asked incredulously, "because the second you found out, you turned against me! You immediately assumed I was guilty."

He held her gaze with his own, narrowing his eyes slightly.

"If I had already known, because you told me on your own, I wouldn't have jumped to conclusions," he said, "but once a deception is uncovered, it's very easy to believe there are more."

Taya crossed her arms. "Oh really?" she said and half smirked, "now you're passing judgements on being deceptive?"

He spread his hands on the table. "My deception was only to protect you," he replied lowly, "and it ate at me until I had no choice but to tell you everything. But you... Even after I confided in you, you still continued to lie to me."

"And I was only trying to protect me too," she retorted, "why should I live my life under a cloud, not having any opportunities because of who my family is?"

"You shouldn't," Nicola agreed, "but given that you knew Enzo tried to recruit me, that we both know he's trying to overthrow Derek, what's at stake, not to mention what I thought we *meant* to each other, you should have told me."

He didn't raise his voice to her, but his words were strong, and she knew he was right. Regardless of her stubborn nature, which caused her to want to continue to argue her point, she kept her mouth shut instead. The truth was, she hadn't trusted him enough to tell him, and she should have. She sighed, her shoulders collapsing forward.

"I'm sorry," she said earnestly, "I'm sorry I didn't tell you. I was actually on my way to tell Derek everything. About who I am, my connections to Enzo. Enzo told me he wanted to rig the vote. But I was taken before I could say anything."

"Yesterday morning," Nicola confirmed, "that's why you wanted to meet with Derek?"

Taya nodded, and she hung her head, long blond strands of hair falling in front of her face. He reached for her hand lying on the table between them and covered it with his own.

"Just tell me what happened so I can get you out of here," he said, and she stared at his hand grasping hers for a moment before raising her eyes to meet his.

She was reluctant to re-hash everything she had already told Esposito and Romano. What if afterwards Nicola still didn't believe her either. She wasn't sure she could bear it, but she also didn't have any other options.

"It was all Bryan," she said finally with a tone of defeat. "Bryan

240

was the one who kidnapped me, he was the one who called you."

"Bryan?" Nicola repeated blankly, "but, he was with you last night. You mean to tell me he didn't rescue you from Enzo?"

Taya gave a short, bitter laugh. "No, he only made it appear that way, so I would be suspected and not him."

Nicola stared at her disbelievingly. "Why didn't you say something? Anything?"

Tears formed in her eyes. "I was so scared!" she blurted out, and her words were rushed, "he was threatening to kill me, he had a gun. He told me if I 'played along,' I'd live. By the time I realized what he was trying to do, it was too late. He had already told you I was Enzo's sister."

Nicola placed his head in his hands, there was no way she was lying to him now, the intense emotion in her voice made it clear she had been in fear for her life. And he wasn't surprised Esposito and Romano didn't believe her. She was a DeGrassi, accusing one of the most loyal members of their government.

"I'm so sorry, Taya," he said, and he reached for her hand again.

She let him take her hand in his, wanting nothing more than to just give in to the comfort he offered. But not only had too much happened now between them, even if she somehow got out of this, there would be no way they could ever be together in the end.

"Tell me," he said after a moment's silence, "why would Bryan want to use you to rig the vote? And how would Bryan know about us?"

Even if they could someone prove Bryan was behind all of this, that didn't necessarily lead to Enzo. There had to be a connection.

"He saw us together in the garden at your reception," Taya told him softly, "and Bryan is not who we all think he is. Not only is he working for Enzo, he hates the monarchy just as much if not more," she paused as a tone of desperation creeped into her voice, "don't you see? *He's* the one who killed Olivia. He's been doing Enzo's dirty work this entire time."

"Did he tell you that?" Nicola asked.

"No," she said slowly, trying to recall Bryan telling her he was doing all of this because Enzo told him to. The truth was, he hadn't, she had only assumed.

"We need some kind of proof, Taya," he said, "otherwise, Bryan has no motive for doing any of this."

She shook her head, trying to think, her mind coming up blank. "Wait," she said suddenly, "the glove."

"What glove?" he asked.

"As I said, Bryan saw us together in the garden the night Olivia was killed. He dropped his own glove where you had been standing. The glove I suspect he was wearing when he strangled her…," she trailed off as something else dawned on her, and her eyes flew open wide. "Oh my God," she whispered, "I'm such a fool."

Nicola looked at her in confusion. "What is it?"

She covered her face with her hands. How could she be so stupid? "He told me that someone had been 'strangled,'" she recalled for Nicola, lifting her head back up to him, as he continued to stare at her blankly not understanding. "*Before* we were ever questioned by the guards!" she exclaimed, explaining to him, "how would he know Olivia had been strangled specifically?"

Nicola raised his eye brows and let out a slow breath.

"Damn," he said lowly, "do you know where the glove is now?"

She nodded. "It's still in a purse of mine at my house."

He stood and began to pace the room. "Ok," he said, "the glove can potentially tie him to the murder, but it still doesn't give us anything on Enzo." He stopped pacing and placed his hands on the table in front on her. "Think for me, angel," he urged, "there had to be something Bryan said, or something he did that made you believe he was acting on Enzo's orders."

Taya looked into his eyes as he leaned toward her, the beautiful smell of his cologne clouding her brain even more. Why did she believe Enzo was involved? She had actually thought it was the organization from New York at first, until…

"The briefcase," she said slowly, furrowing her brow, recalling now the smooth, brown leather briefcase, the detailing; the same one she has seen in Enzo's office. "Bryan had Enzo's briefcase."

Nicola nodded. "Good," he said, "where?"

"Where Bryan was holding me, in that little run-down house," she recounted, "I saw it sitting on a table. I knew it was Enzo's because I saw it in his office. It was very distinctive looking."

"You were in Enzo's office," Nicola repeated, and it wasn't a question as his blood pressure rose slightly. He had hoped to hear her deny that she was actually the woman seen going into Enzo's building.

Her eyes left his as he retook his seat. "You knew I had gone to see

Enzo," she said.

"You were recognized," he informed her, "Romano had his men running surveillance at Enzo's main office. Why were you there?"

Taya groaned inwardly, and she could only imagine how this made her look. No wonder Romano thought she was guilty.

"I only wanted to help you," she said, "you told me Enzo was relaying information to the organization after you. I just wanted him to stop. But in exchange, he wanted me to convince you to lie about the vote. Bryan must have told him about us. I refused his offer."

Nicola understood now giving her a look of empathy. She had been trying to get him out of his own mess. And as a result, she put herself in a precarious situation.

"Taya…" he began quietly, but trailed off.

What could he even say? That he loved her? That all he wanted or would ever want is for them to be free to be together? He knew that could never happen. He cleared his throat, re-focusing on what mattered most right now: getting her released.

"We need to find Bryan as well as this briefcase," he stated. "I will go back to your house and look for the glove. Esposito can get it over to forensics. Is there anything else you can tell me to help prove you were where you said you were? You said Bryan held you in a little run-down house. Where?"

Again, she shook her head. "I don't know exactly," she said, "It was dark. I think it was on the outskirts of the city. There are a lot of abandoned houses around the city. It probably only had one bedroom, two at most, and I think it was grey, maybe green?"

He shrugged. "All we can do is search," he replied, "try to find anything that indicates you were there. But our best bet is to find Bryan."

"But then what?" she asked, "he'll just deny everything."

Nicola smirked.

"I'll beat it out of him if I have to," he said, and Taya had a feeling he was being serious for once.

He rose to leave, and her eyes followed his. "Thank you," he told her, "for being honest with me. For what it's worth, I'm sorry this happened, and I will do whatever is in my power to get you out of here." He paused weighing in his mind to say something else or not. "I want you to know," he said, needing her to hear from him a decision he had made recently, "when this is all over, I am going to leave

Calina and give up my title."

Taya's eyes flew open wide. "What?" She exclaimed, standing, "Nic, you can't..."

"I have to, angel," he said cutting her off, "everyone's going to know how I feel about you."

Unable to stop it, Taya's heart skipped a beat at his words. How he feels about her? Does he actually still love her? She bit her lip, knowing it was foolish to entertain any hope, especially at this time.

"Regardless of if we can nail Enzo, it won't stop those after me, I can't," he paused, "I *won't* allow this to happen to you again."

"But if you leave the security of Calina, you won't be protected from them," her eyes once again filled with tears. How could she let him do this? He'd die.

"It'll be ok," he assured her, "all that matters to me is that you're safe." He reached over to her face and brushed away a stray tear with his thumb. "I'll contact you as soon as I find anything," he promised, then without waiting for her to reply or argue further, because he knew she would, he turned and walked out of the room.

––––––––––––

It was nearing 6:00 p.m. as Nicola waited patiently to learn news from forensics. After talking with Taya, he and Martino had gone back to her house. It had not been difficult to find the purse she mentioned with the glove still inside it. Instructing Martino to take the glove straight to be examined, he then went to relay everything he had learned to Derek, who had been preparing to announce, along with the prime minister, the real outcome of the vote; to join the European Union.

Nicola had joined his brother to stand by his side, along with Christine, while the statement was made to the public. Once the applause, laden with a large amount of relief, had died down following the announcement, there had been a rapid-fire of questions as to why Nicola had originally stated the opposite.

In a very short comment, he then revealed his reasons: Taya Mariano was being held as a hostage to the voting outcome. Refusing to say another word about it publicly, Romano had stepped forward to share that Signorina Mariano was in custody, being held under suspicion for conspiracy, but the investigation was pending, and it is believed there are others involved. Neither Bryan nor Enzo's name was revealed, and Nicola was relieved to not hear Taya being referred to as a "DeGrassi." He knew it was bound to come out, but at least it wasn't now.

Instead of placating the press, Romano's statements spawned a whole new line of questioning at Nicola. As their cameras flashed in his face, their queries came, relentless to know more details about his relationship with Taya: was she in on the scheme or just a pawn, why would he chose saving her life over the wellbeing of his own country? Again, refusing to answer any of their questions, Nicola was immediately surrounded by Martino and a few other guards. He then was able to make his escape away from the countless accusations and prying eyes to the security of the palace walls.

All the while, as he waited for news throughout the day, no one had been able to locate Bryan LaPointe. Derek had agreed his absence, as well as Taya's account of the events looked suspicious, and Romano had been ordered to begin an investigation from that angle. But although a man-hunt had begun, Bryan had still not been found, nor heard from.

He had spoken to Taya twice more, once letting her know he found the glove and a second to inform her of the voting news. Part of him only wanted to hear her voice, if for no other reason than to reassure his mind that she was still safe. Now that the world pretty much suspected a relationship between them, to say his anxiety had been heightened was a vast understatement.

There was a sudden knock at his study door where he had been trying, in vain, to get any work done, then the door opened as Derek entered followed by Esposito.

"We still have not found Signore LaPointe," Esposito shared, and Nicola set his jaw as a determined look crossed his face.

"The fact that he's disappeared only shows his guilt," he said.

"I tend to agree," Derek stated, "and we were just informed that the fibers from the glove match those that were collected from under Olivia's fingernails."

"It's not conclusive evidence," Esposito put in, "anyone could own a pair of gloves like that, and how do we know it wasn't Signorina Mariano herself who dropped it, and just saying it belongs to Signore LaPointe."

Nicola glared at Esposito. "Why would she give us evidence leading directly to her?" he spat. "What about the house she was held in, did you find it?"

In response Esposito placed a small cardboard box on Nicola's desk.

"Those houses are a dime a dozen," he said flatly, "we searched as many as we could matching her description, but found nothing that indicated someone was being held or living in one. No food, or recently used dishes. Most of them had no electricity or running water." He pointed to the box. "We collected a few items of interest: a coffee mug, pens, broken bits of jewelry, matchbook covers, that sort of thing. But I doubt any of it can be used to prove she was there." Nicola groaned in frustration as Esposito continued, "unless we find LaPointe, as well as the briefcase, we don't have anything except a well thought up story."

"We have this."

The voice belonged to Romano who entered the room holding up a glove.

"Yes, well again, we have no proof that glove belongs to Bryan LaPointe," Esposito said, once again dismissing the glove.

"The one Signorina Mariano gave us, you're correct, we don't," Romano said.

Nicola raised his eyebrows confused and shot Romano a questioning look.

"But this," Romano continued, "this I found amongst Bryan LaPointe's possessions at his home. And it is a match."

Nicola ran a hand through his hair and gave a sigh of relief. Finally, something they could use to make a case against Bryan. Now they just needed to find him.

Sensing Romano had more to share, Derek eyed him keenly.

"What is it?" he asked, and Romano handed him the glove.

"That's the good news," he stated, then took a breath. "The bad news is, we found LaPointe."

Nicola and Derek exchanged a glance.

"He was found across the border of Switzerland," Romano explained, "there was a terrible car accident," he paused, then looked at Nicola, "he's dead, signore."

246

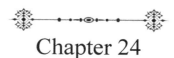

Chapter 24

Dead. Bryan LaPointe was dead. The words echoed in Nicola's brain. The one man who could definitively set Taya free was dead. There would be no confession, and more importantly, he would not be given the opportunity to punch him in the face. Refusing to accept Bryan's unfortunate demise as a set-back to Taya's release, Nicola re-focused on the facts.

"What about the briefcase?" he asked urgently.

It might not matter if Bryan couldn't confess. As long as the briefcase was found in his possession, it would still tie him back to Enzo, which validated Taya's side of the story.

"Taya said Bryan had Enzo's briefcase. It had to have been found, either in his home or in his car." There was a tone of hope in his voice as he looked at Romano, but the expression on Romano's face did not mirror that sentiment.

"There was no briefcase, signore," he stated, then sighed, "and without it, we don't have anything except Taya's word that it exists at all."

Nicola's frustration brought his fist down on his desk hard. "The glove proves Bryan killed Olivia," he declared, "he would have had no other motive to kill her except on DeGrassi's orders. We don't need the briefcase, that should be enough."

"Which DeGrassi are you speaking of, signore?" Esposito asked.

In response, Nicola raised his eyes toward Esposito dangerously. "If I didn't know better, Antonio, it would almost seem as though you are looking for reasons *not* to prosecute Enzo."

Esposito clenched his jaw. "Absolutely not, signore," he responded, "but it is my job to uncover the truth, regardless of how misdirected others may have become due to emotional feelings."

Nicola opened his mouth to retort, but Derek held up a hand.

"That'll do, Antonio," he said, then he turned his gaze to Romano, there was pensiveness in his eyes. "You reported LaPointe was in a bad car accident. What was the nature of the accident?"

Nicola gave his brother a strange look. *What did it matter? The guy was dead.* But he didn't question why Derek cared about the details.

"He ran into a tree," Romano shared, and he opened a file folder he held in his hands. "There was no one else involved in the accident, but there was an opened bottle of alcohol found on the floorboard." His eyes scanned the accident report. "It's been determined he lost control of the vehicle due to intoxication," and he closed the file, handing it to Derek. "He was clearly on the run, knowing we would soon discover he killed Olivia. Unfortunately, we don't have anything to prove he was involved in the voting scheme. Or that he was working for Enzo."

"This is ridiculous!" Nicola exclaimed, reaching the limit on his patience, "of course he was working for Enzo." He looked at Derek for support, but his brother had become engrossed in the accident file. "Derek, it doesn't matter that Bryan is dead. You and I both know he is responsible for both Olivia's death and Taya's kidnapping. Just order her to be released."

"It doesn't say what kind of alcohol was found," Derek replied, looking at Romano again, completely ignoring Nicola.

Romano responded with a confused look. "I can find out for you, signore?" he said, furrowing his brow.

Derek nodded. "Do that now," he instructed, and Romano left promptly, pulling out his cell as he walked out of the study.

Nicola stared at his brother incredulously.

"Derek, what—," but Derek cut off his question.

"Shut up a minute, Nic," he said calmly, as his eyes continued to scrutinize the report.

Nicola looked over his shoulder at the document, curiosity getting the better of his temper: it was the car damage information that had Derek's attention. He finally closed the folder, seeming to have found what he was looking for.

"Just as I thought," he murmured to himself.

"What?" Nicola asked, now bewildered, and he snatched the folder from Derek's hand, opening it back up.

He saw nothing of special note; the front of the car was smashed to pieces which was consistent with the theory of what transpired. *Drunkin' bastard*, he thought to himself.

Romano walked back into the study before Nicola could ask anything further. Derek raised his eyebrows in anticipation.

"Jack Daniels," Romano reported.

Nicola knew his brother well enough to recognize the subtle change in his expression to mean that Derek had expected to hear this information.

"I need to make a call," Derek said, and he immediately began walking toward the door.

"Wait just a damned minute," Nicola stated, stopping him, and Derek turned to face him. "Mind clueing us in? What is going on?" He held his palms up in a gesture that demanded explanation.

Derek's eyes narrowed, and it seemed as though he was considering something. His gaze shifted to Romano, then back to his brother.

"Without the briefcase, it would be in Taya's best interest if there was some further evidence that collaborates her story of a kidnapping," Derek said, ignoring his brother's questions about his behavior, then without waiting for additional protests, he walked out of Nicola's study and down the hall toward his own.

For several seconds, Nicola just stared after where Derek had left, unable to comprehend what he was now facing or what the next steps should be. Without Bryan, and his confession, how would he even begin to prove Taya's side?

Romano cleared his throat, when he spoke, his voice held an apologetic air. "His Highness is correct, signore," he said looking at Nicola. "We cannot release Signorina Mariano on her mere word that LaPointe kidnapped her. Furthermore, we have nothing that says it was all done on DeGrassi's orders. To be honest with you, it is much more believable that she was in on the whole thing."

"I know Taya," he seethed now, his temper finally at boiling point, "she would not do this!"

His angered, dark eyes fell on the small, pathetic box of "evidence" Esposito and his men had managed to scrounge up from the abandoned area of houses where Taya felt she had been held. A surge of rage passed through him; they weren't even trying, he concluded.

In a sudden movement, he grabbed the box and hurled it across the room, the glassware and other random items inside crashing loudly against the fireplace. Romano and Esposito flinched visibly at the piercing noise.

"Find something!" Nicola demanded, his tone sharp. "Something conclusive that says she was where she said she was."

As Esposito and Romano bowed slightly, leaving the study without a word, Nicola sank heavily back into his desk chair. The adrenaline from his anger subsiding, despair once again began to flood through him.

He stared on the phone on his desk. How could he make this call? How could he tell her he failed? What would she say when he told her she would stand trial for conspiracy to commit treason?

Once down the hall, Derek entered his study, then promptly closed the door behind him. He paused for a moment, then instead of walking to the desk, he made his way to the bar instead.

His gaze scanned the rows of alcohol, all of it untouched since he never drank. It was only here for guests, but in his presence, no one had ever accepted an offer.

His eyes now landed on one particular bottle. He picked up the whiskey and watched the dark amber colored liquor swirl within the glass; the black label unscratched. The Jack Daniels had been given as a gift to him, one from 16 years ago, and a ribbon was still tied around the neck.

At least, at the time, he had thought it had been a gift. It had been left on his back porch only two weeks after his mom died. Of course, he had come to realize it was, in fact, a calling card. An indication of a job completed.

Nicola did not know about this distinct bottle of alcohol, and Derek intended for his brother to never find out. Replacing the bottle on the shelf, Derek then took out his phone to make that call.

The morning glow of the sunrise began to fill Christine's studio, and she gave a small smile; the natural light providing the perfect setting as she worked on her current project.

She contemplated the work in front of her, deciding on the color purple, and she began to add layers of various shades, creating texture and movement within the piece. Taking a step back to consider the progress, Christine set down the paint brush and habitually ran her hands over her coat, smearing purple paint down the sides. She inspected her hands now, realizing they were covered in purple, and she gave a small laugh, for in a few moments she was expecting company.

But this is who she was. She was not a pristine and proper queen sitting on a throne, and she had no interest in pretending to be something she wasn't. Derek accepted that she was an artist first, but she was an artist who cared deeply about his country, which was now her country; her people. And she would fulfill her duty as was demanded of her.

She shifted from one leg to another, her back injury still causing pain when she stood for too long. The pain, as well as her slight limp, would be a constant reminder of her past, of what she went through and why. But that was ok, because she understood those events allowed her to become who she was now. She was grateful even, knowing that it gave her the strength to excel in her chosen path going forward.

She would never regret her decision to step in front of that gunman, she would never regret saving the man she loved. And she would never again let anyone believe that her motivations were for any other reason.

A sudden knock interrupted her thoughts and drew her attention from her work to the studio door. She saw Costa enter.

"Isabela Fontaine is here to see you, signora," he said, and Christine nodded, allowing the parliament member to enter.

Feeling the need to put to rest "unfinished business," she had sent word to Isabela the previous day inviting her to the palace.

Isabela was among those most outspoken and reckless during the conference, and Christine not only wished to address this apparent source of possible uprising, but she intended to find out if there was anything more behind the scenes to Isabela's actions. Was she corrupt? Misguided? Or an overly ambitious politician who saw an opportunity for a power grab? Either way, she was on the fence with whether or not Isabela should continue to hold her seat, and Derek had granted her the authority to make the decision on his behalf.

As Isabela entered the studio, her eyebrows raised in a manner that suggested she questioned this meeting location, and Christine waited to see how the politician might acknowledge her. Although she typically preferred informal greetings, that was among friends and those she trusted. Isabela had yet to earn her trust.

"Signora," Isabela said upon approaching Christine.

She did now bow, but she was not required to, and Christine didn't

251

mind. Other than her nose stuck up in the air, Isabela was at least, showing some respect.

Christine picked back up her paintbrush and gestured to a nearby chair.

"You can have a seat if you like," she said casually as she pulled up a stool herself to lean against, then turned back to her painting.

Isabela took the chair she was offered.

"This is quite a bit informal," she said, "aren't you supposed to be a queen in a few months?"

Christine smiled. "A queen can't paint?" she replied. "Well, this is a pretty informal meeting. I thought we could have a chat." When Isabela didn't respond, she continued, speaking as she stroked the canvas in front of her. "I was curious to know, were your actions at the conference your own stupidity? Or were you perhaps bribed by someone else."

She turned back to face Isabela, and the expression the latter's face did not disappoint. Christine realized at that moment this was why Derek always chose to get straight to the point; it was highly effective at throwing people off guard, and her reaction seemed genuine.

"That is absurd," Isabela exclaimed, "I am an honest member of our parliament. I care about our people. And unlike other politicians, I cannot be bought."

Christine nodded. "'Other' politicians?" she questioned.

Isabela shifted in her seat. "Like Taya Mariano?" she answered, and a look of disgust crossed her face, "or should I say Taya *DeGrassi*."

Christine didn't let the surprise show on her face that Isabela knew of Taya's real identity. Apparently, the word was out, and she wouldn't put it past Enzo himself for leaking the information. The more Taya was suspected, the less he was. But she knew better than to voice any opinions in front of Isabela, and at least the politician did not seem to favor the DeGrassi's.

"Well, I wasn't asking about Taya," she said, "I was asking about you. So your decision to call for a vote to de-throne your king was your idea. What was your motive for doing that?"

"There is clearly corruption within the government," Isabela stated plainly, "and it's only gotten worse since Derek Landino came here. He refuses to honor our traditions. So yes, I saw the opportunity to remove him, so I took it."

"Derek is not the cause of your corruption," Christine stated, "nor am I, as an 'American.' Derek has done nothing except weed out dishonest and deceitful politicians since he got here. You think it was better with Marco holding a seat?"

Isabela pursed her lips. "He allows Enzo DeGrassi to continue to infiltrate our government," she stated, "that doesn't make him corrupt?"

Christine blinked at her. "Allows?" she questioned disbelievingly, "honey, if you have evidence to lock up Enzo DeGrassi, please share it." Isabela blew out a breath of frustration and cast her eyes to the floor. "If Derek could put Enzo away, he would, but he can't," Christine continued, "he will not use his authority as a monarch to prosecute anyone without hard evidence. Don't you see how you all have tied his hands with your constant 'power abuse' accusations?"

Isabela didn't answer.

"You can't have it both ways," Christine said sternly, "if you wish for him to not use executive authority because you feel it's a slippery slope, then don't blame him when he can't just lock up someone like Enzo DeGrassi with a snap of his fingers. He is fair, and you need to be fair as well."

The politician met Christine's eyes, narrowing them slightly as though her words had resonated.

"Perhaps, you are correct," she finally consented. "Of course it makes sense to have all the facts before acting, and I admit I jumped the gun," she gave a heavy pause, as though it was difficult to say what she said next, "it won't happen again, signora."

Christine nodded, happy to finalize this matter, at least with one parliament member, and internally she made the decision that Isabela deserved a second chance. Time would tell if she could show support toward the monarchy, but by allowing her to keep her seat would show grace and a willingness to move beyond differences, ignorance, and misunderstandings.

As she and Isabela exchanged words of departure, the latter gave a slight incline of her head before leaving the studio. Christine gave a small smile as she once again returned her attention to her work. She felt content for the moment, and a certain satisfaction that she had done what was needed.

This wasn't the end, she knew, it would never be the end. But she held now a confidence that she was prepared to handle whatever would come next. She dipped her brush again in the paint, mixing it on the canvas, finding new shades of purple to add to her masterpiece.

Early the next morning, Nicola staggered into his study. As with previous nights, sleep evaded him, and last night specifically, he had chosen to deal with his grief through whiskey.

He ran a hand across his face, making his way toward his desk slowly. He didn't even know what to do now or how to move forward, unable to accept in his mind that Taya would stand trial, even though that was exactly what he told her would happen.

She took the news of Bryan's death, the missing briefcase, and the lack of evidence hard. She hadn't cried to him, but he could tell by the absence of emotion in her voice that she was broken, and he had found tears rolling down his own cheeks.

He was still standing by his desk when an attendant appeared in the doorway with a broom and dustpan in his hands.

"*Mi scusi*, signore," the attendant announced, "I was asked by Signora Nucci to clean up in here?"

The young man gestured toward the fireplace where Nicola had thrown the box of items collected from the searched abandoned homes.

Nicola glanced at the fireplace wearily, grimacing, then he strode over toward the attendant holding out his hand.

"It's my mess," he said resolutely, "I'll clean it up."

The attendant furrowed his brow for a second, then handed over the broom. "As you wish, signore," he said, then bowed to Nicola and left the study.

Once the attendant had left, Nicola retrieved the garbage bin near his desk then dragged his feet over to the fireplace, broom in hand. He knelt down, picking up the box and tipping it upright. Reaching first for some broken bits of glass, he withdrew his hand sharply as he accidentally sliced his finger on one of the edges.

"Shit," he muttered, pressing his thumb into the cut to stem the bleeding.

Aware now of the nagging pain in his hand, he surveyed the debris strewn across the floor. He stopped breathing for a second as his eyes fell upon a particular item.

Reaching to retrieve it, he now completely forgot about his headache, the mess, and his bleeding finger. He held it up in front of him, zeroing in on this sole object, his words barely audible as he whispered, "I'll be damned..."

Chapter 25

I t was dusk as Derek and Costa pulled into the public park near the center of town. The normally packed location was chosen specifically for its neutral ground, but since it was so late, Derek had hoped there wouldn't be too many locals hanging around. And he felt certain Costa would ensure the coast was kept clear.

Even with the lateness of the hour, as the sun was setting just below the horizon, Derek still donned a pair of sunglasses as he exited the vehicle and made his way toward the river. He opted to wear a single breasted light weight trench, and although the breeze coming across the water was brisk, he didn't mind. His eyes moved over the area; it was deserted, and he didn't need to look back to know Costa was scanning the perimeter as well.

He placed his hands in his jacket pockets and chose a bench overlooking the river to wait. It wasn't too long before he heard footsteps approaching. He continued to look out over the water as a man took the seat next to him.

"Hello, Jack," he said.

"Derek," the man acknowledged, then paused, "you'll excuse me if I don't address you formally. I feel we go too far back for that."

"I don't care what you call me," Derek replied evenly, "it's not how you choose to address me that insults me."

Jack smirked. "Oh? Then what does, my friend."

"We are not friends, Jack," Derek stated, "maybe at one time we were, when we were kids. And maybe we helped each other out from time to time in the past. But any arrangements between us ceased to exist when you refused to settle with Nicola. *That*," he emphasized, "insults me."

"It's business, Derek, I'm sure you can appreciate that," Jack replied, unfazed. "Your brother got in way too deep. There was no way out for him, and I do have to maintain a reputation. Settling his debt with you would have been insulting to me, you see."

"How is that 'job' working out for you by the way?" Derek couldn't help the jab. He had felt confident that as long as Nicola was within the confines of palace security, Jack's efforts would be in vain, regardless of Enzo's spies on the prowl.

Jack didn't respond, and for the first time since Jack joined him, Derek turned and looked in his direction. For a moment he recalled the childhood friend that he had grown up with in New York, but they had gone in very different directions long ago.

While Derek sought to flex in entrepreneurial ventures, Jack had taken a much more opposing path in life; albeit still successful and powerful.

Although they did not run in the same circles since early high school, Derek had maintained an arms-length connection to Jack. A connection he found useful when he made the decision to eliminate his step-father. He knew Jack had completed the task asked of him when the bottle of Jack Daniels showed up on his back door step. And Dean had never been heard from again.

"You underestimate me, Jack," he now said, "you would have accepted my offer, if it were not for DeGrassi. It had nothing to do with your 'reputation.' You got greedy on DeGrassi's promises of power." He re-focused on the scenic view across the water in front of him, "but unfortunately for you, DeGrassi failed; I'm not going anywhere." He felt Jack tense beside him, giving away that his assumption was correct: it was DeGrassi who ordered the hit on Nicola.

If that were true, Jack was working for DeGrassi, which meant he was also responsible for Bryan's "accident," which Derek had already concluded. He knew Jack was in Calina, and the bottle of Jack Daniels found on the floorboard was too much of a giveaway to those who knew him—it was his way of telling DeGrassi the job was done. Derek was also aware of Jack's methods, and car accidents had occurred before.

"I know someone within your employ ran Bryan LaPointe off the road," Derek continued, "the whole scene reeks of your *modus operandi*; hitting the back bumper to make the car lose control, leaving the Jack Daniels. Sloppy of you really, becoming predictable like that…," he paused, "I want the briefcase, Jack. The one you took from Bryan's car. I only hope for your sake you've not given it to DeGrassi yet."

"I don't know what you mean," was all Jack responded with.

256

"You can waste time if you like," Derek replied, "but the sooner you realize you chose the wrong side, the better it will be for you."

Jack stood, an indication that he was going to leave. He buttoned his overcoat.

"Enzo is… *invested* in my business, Derek," he said, "the side I'm on isn't by choice."

"You always have a choice," Derek replied. Jack stilled, his hands now placed in his pockets. "Why do you let DeGrassi call the shots? This seems out of character for you." After a moment, Jack retook his seat, and Derek knew he had touched a nerve.

"You say he has invested in your business," he repeated, "I'm guessing to the point that he now owns you, doesn't he. Do you enjoy taking orders from him? I never thought I'd see the day when Jack Silvestri took orders from anyone."

Jack didn't respond and Derek couldn't suppress a slight chuckle as he now saw clearly how the hand was to be played.

"I could help you, but you need to do something for me," his tone was all-business.

"Help me?" Jack spat, "did you not request this meeting asking for my generosity?"

"I requested this meeting to give you a chance to hand over crucial evidence against DeGrassi," Derek replied, "but since you won't cooperate, you've left me with no alternative."

"What are you talking about?" And although Jack's voice was firm, Derek knew he would cave.

Jack was most undoubtably someone not to cross. His reputation to those who knew of him and his organization preceded him, and he never failed to deliver. But Derek was not afraid of Jack, he never had been; maybe because of their long-term acquaintance. And up until now, their silent agreement had always been to stay out of each other's way, but unfortunately Derek could no longer turn a blind eye. It was Jack's own fault, he reasoned, involving himself this way.

He removed his sunglasses and met Jack's eye.

"You've forgotten where you are, *mio amico*. DeGrassi may rule over you, but I rule over this land." And as if on cue, Costa appeared by Jack's other side. "You are way out of your depth. You are not in New York, you have no resources or connections here in which you can call in favors. You made a serious mistake by allowing DeGrassi to coax you into following Nicola here."

Jack hardened his features. "You have nothing on me. There's nothing you can do to me."

Derek shrugged. "There's plenty I can do, don't be ridiculous. And as for needing evidence...," he smiled, "well, that only technically matters if you're not the king."

He now regarded Jack with indifference as he drew a cloth from his jacket to wipe off his sunglasses. "You know, there are those within my parliament who fear that I hold too much power," and he paused, replacing the sunglasses back on his face. "Maybe they're right." He let the implication of the words hang in the air for a moment before continuing, "but, you're focusing on the wrong thing, here. Wouldn't it benefit both of us if DeGrassi were out of the way?"

Jack didn't miss the suggestive tone in Derek's voice. "So what are you saying? If I give you the briefcase, you'll help me get rid of Enzo?"

"Thank you for admitting you have the briefcase," Derek mused, and Jack clenched his jaw. "Actually, I only really needed to know that the briefcase existed, why don't you keep it. I think you might need it more. My brother still owes you money anyway, I believe."

"Then what do you want, Derek? I won't be in your debt going forward. I made that mistake with Enzo."

"No," Derek agreed, "once you've fulfilled your end of this bargain, we will not speak again." He paused, "your disagreement with Nicola is settled," he said. "You've been paid and it's done."

"Fine," Jack consented, "but Enzo will not just let me out of the job."

Derek now stood. "No, he won't," he stated, "but, that's not my problem, and I'm sure you'll arrive at the correct conclusion on how to deal with him."

Those were his last words to Jack, and he left him alone on the bench overlooking the river as he and Costa made their way back to the car.

Although he felt a weight lifted with being able to finally free Nicola from his past, he despised the manner in which it was done.

Unfortunately, he was given no alternative in needing to work with someone like Jack, and with any luck at all, he would be rid of DeGrassi as well. Again, not in the way he would have preferred, but where DeGrassi was concerned, he was having a difficult time finding sympathy for the fate of his nemesis. He would make peace with that.

No, what nagged the back of his mind was the thought that he had simply exchanged one enemy for another. As was usually the case when he walked away with the upper hand. There was never really a winner.

As Costa drove back to the palace, Derek concluded his thoughts knowing this was the price of his position. In his role, the obstacles were never ending, and he could solve one problem only to face the next. But this was the life he had chosen, and it was only glamorous to those outside looking in.

Christine knew that too, and he smiled, thinking of her. They would finally be married in a few short months, and that alone, was enough to make him happy.

Taya lay curled up on her cot. She hugged her small, limp pillow because it was all she could think to do for comfort as she contemplated what was to happen next. She was not sobbing or feeling desperate at this time, she was simply hollow. Her thoughts were now on auto pilot, reasoning having no choice but to overtake emotion, as she finally faced the hard truth of her situation.

There was no evidence to collaborate the fact that she was kidnapped. There was, however, much evidence that proved she was Marco's daughter, that she had engaged in deals with Enzo in the past, and that she was seen going into his office days prior to the vote. Not to mention, Bryan's "eye-witness" statements that she was at a residence belonging to DeGrassi the night of the vote, and he had simply picked her up there. Which was a lie, of course, but Bryan was dead, so there was nothing to suggest otherwise.

Today, she would secure a lawyer, and it would be the absolute best one she could get. Although, being labeled a "DeGrassi" may inhibit her ability to find a decent attorney that would be willing to take on her case. Of course, there were also those willing to do it for publicity, and this trial would be huge.

She had come to terms with the loss of her position, her political career was in shambles, and when all of this was over, if she was acquitted, she knew she would have to leave Calina. Even if she walked away from this, there was so much she had to give up: her home, her friends. Her life. And she had already lost Nicola.

If she ended up getting convicted, well…none of that other stuff mattered anyway.

"You need to come with me, signorina," a guard's voice came through her door.

She raised her head to look in his direction; she was not expecting to be going anywhere anytime soon.

"Why?" she asked. Was she being moved? To a more secure cell perhaps?

The guard didn't respond, only opened the door for her.

She rose from the cot, confused, and preceded him through the door. He closed it shut behind her with that metallic sound ringing in her ears.

"Where am I going?" she asked again, but he didn't acknowledge her question, and led her down the hall toward the interview room.

Great, Taya thought, *this can't be good.* And to confirm her thoughts of dread, Romano was waiting for her. They must have found something else, and her heart rate picked up. Maybe she wouldn't even get a trial.

Romano pointed to the chair.

"*Siediti*," he instructed, and she complied, taking the seat offered at the table. "There has been new evidence," he began.

She knew it.

"And, it allows for you imminent release."

She blinked at him, wondering if she had heard him correctly.

"What?" she asked, her voice rather hoarse.

He smiled. "You've been given a full pardon from His Highness," he explained. "Esposito found proof of where you were being held when kidnapped."

"What proof?" She questioned, bewildered.

He slid an envelope across the table to her. She opened the flap and tipped the envelope upside down allowing an item to fall into her palm: her bracelet.

She looked back at Romano with wide eyes. "He found my bracelet? Where?"

Romano nodded. "By chance, yes," he answered, "in the house you said you were being held in. Even Esposito couldn't argue you were there, as he was the one who personally recovered this particular item." He gave a slight cough concealing a chuckle. "Although the bracelet has been confirmed to belong to you, I'm sure he's running DNA tests to make certain."

"It's mine," she said, and she let out a breath she didn't even realize she was holding. She closed her eyes allowing a huge sense of relief to wash over her.

She now inspected the bracelet fondly remembering how upset she was that she had lost it, when it turns out that losing it where she did probably just saved her life.

She noticed the broken clasp, then she narrowed her eyes, looking at the chain links more closely. Was that…blood? Perplexed, she dropped the bracelet back into the envelope. She would have it cleaned and repaired when she got home. And a small smile appeared on her dry lips.

Home. She was going home.

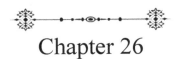

Chapter 26

One Week Later

It was early morning as Nicola made his way toward the main palace kitchen. *An odd place to meet*, he thought, and he had no idea what his brother wanted to talk to him about. But when Derek had sent him the message, Nicola considered now might be as good a time as any to share his own decision and kill two birds with one stone.

It was going to be a sunny day as rays of light began to shine through the windows, and as Nicola neared the kitchen, he noticed a familiar, yet long-forgotten, delightful smell. After surveying the vast space, including the pristine and massive prep area, he followed his nose around the corner and found Derek behind an omelet bar.

He eyed his brother suspiciously, as though he had never seen him before; Derek was wearing jeans and a well-worn, black t-shirt that said "Rolling Stones."

And cooking.

Nicola had no idea Derek could appear so… *normal.*

"You wanted to see me?" he asked approaching Derek, now realizing it wasn't omelets he was preparing, but crepes, and Nicola now understood why the smell of them was taking him back to his childhood.

"Good morning," Derek greeted his brother, not taking his eyes off his task as he twirled the pan over a burner allowing the crepe batter to climb up the edges, perfecting the thin, delicate texture of the dish.

"I had no idea you could cook," Nicola observed taking a seat upon one of the stools in front of the bar.

Derek expertly flipped the crepe over, letting it brown for a moment before sliding it smoothly onto a plate. He then looked at Nicola and gave a slight smile.

"I do possess talents outside of ruling a country," he commented, and Nicola watched as Derek now added scrambled eggs, bacon, and cheese to the inside of the crepe. Then he folded it neatly, and finally drizzled hollandaise sauce on top. He placed the plate in front of Nicola, who stared at the offer for a moment.

"This is how mom used to make it," he said quietly.

"I know," Derek replied, then raised his eyebrows expectantly.

Nicola forked into the dish, taking a large bite, chewing, with a thoughtful expression on his face.

"It's not mom's," he finally said after swallowing, then smirked upon catching Derek's narrowed eyes, "but it's really good," he finished, allowing his brother's expression to turn satisfied.

Derek slung a dish towel over his shoulder.

"I wanted to tell you," he started as Nicola began to devour the rest of his breakfast, "that you are no longer indebted to anyone from New York. They've agreed to a payment, and they no longer pose a threat to you."

Nicola looked up at Derek slowly, replacing his fork on the table. "How?" he asked quietly, not quite willing to believe he was free.

Derek just winked at him. "I made them an offer they couldn't refuse," he said in jest.

Nicola watched Derek thoughtfully as he began to clean up the pan, knowing he wasn't being completely honest. But he also knew if he pried, he'd get nowhere, so he changed the subject.

"I heard the case of Olivia's murder has been officially closed."

"Yes," Derek replied, "and DNA found on the glove confirmed it was Bryan's. He has been named her killer."

"What about Enzo?"

Derek sighed. "There is nothing to prove that DeGrassi paid Bryan to kill Olivia."

"Or that he paid Bryan to kidnap Taya," Nicola finished with a grimace.

"No," Derek confirmed. "But Taya, as you know, has been released with a full pardon. Bryan had motive to kidnap her, use her to coerce you to deliver the vote. He knew what she meant to you."

Means, Nicola corrected in his own mind, although out loud he asked, "what motive?"

"Romano did some digging into his background," Derek shared, "he came from a very unfortunate upbringing as a result of our father's rule. It stands to reason that he sought revenge against us. By delivering a voting outcome to not join the EU, he intended it to cause my removal by parliament."

Nicola shook his head slowly, thinking about everything Taya went through.

"So, Enzo just gets to walk away," he stated, "we have no evidence against him. He caused all of this, and he's free to go about his business."

Derek didn't answer right away, the idea of DeGrassi continuing to slip through the cracks infuriating him. He had to be stopped, otherwise, it was only a matter of time before he cooked up some other scheme to uproot the monarchy. Or hurt someone else.

"I believe in karma," was all he said however to Nicola, who in turn, looked at him as though he were insane.

"Karma?" he exclaimed. "*That's* what you're banking on?" Derek didn't respond and grabbed a cloth as he began to wipe down the bar. "What's going to happen to Taya now?" Nicola questioned, knowing Derek was done talking about Enzo. His heart rate ticked up slightly thinking about her.

Derek smiled. "If you're asking if she still holds a seat within parliament, the answer is: I'd be honored to have her serve our government, as long as she wants to, with my support."

Nicola nodded, satisfied. "A DeGrassi is officially back in the Calean government," he said with a raise of his brow.

"Yes, well, people will just need to get used to it," Derek replied easily.

With Taya's position secure, there was only one thing left to do. Regardless of his new freedom, Nicola still could not remain within the monarchy.

"Derek, I've decided to resign my title," he said, and Derek stopped cleaning the bar, looking at Nicola sharply.

"You are doing this for her," Derek observed.

"I won't put her in danger again," Nicola stated.

"You are no longer a wanted man," Derek replied, "there is no one who could use her in that way again."

"Maybe that's true today," Nicola said, "but I have other reasons as well. Only one of us can serve this government, and it needs to be her. If I remain, there will always be a conflict of interest, and I would not be able to separate my feelings from my duty."

Derek nodded slowly, bracing both his hands on the counter. "You are choosing to step down for the woman you love," he said, his tone thoughtful, knowing all too well what making this decision felt like.

"Does she know you feel this way?"

Nicola shook his head slowly. "Not yet," he said, and Derek gave a half smile.

"Aren't you putting the cart before the horse?"

Nicola shrugged. "It's a risk I'm willing to take," he replied.

"So, what are you going to do then?"

"Well," and Nicola let out a slow breath, "I'd like to stay in Calina. I'm hoping not to get thrown out until I can get on my feet, but maybe it's time I got a job."

Derek was quiet for a moment.

"Whether you serve the monarchy or not, there is a lot of good you can do here," he said, then paused as something began to formulate in his mind. "I've been petitioning the board of Land Corporation for some time now to open a satellite office here. Greg is in agreement it would be a great opportunity for the company, he's just been waiting for the right time, and," he emphasized considering his brother, "he's looking for the right man to run it." Nicola gave Derek a shrewd look. "Besides," Derek continued, "I believe you owe Greg money, and working off your debt would be honorable."

"Yeah…" Nicola said making a face which turned into an embarrassed grin, "I do owe him. You let him know I'm game if he's offering."

Derek nodded. "I'll put in a good word," he promised, "and, I accept your resignation." He then gave Nicola a pointed look. "So you better get going."

Nicola smiled knowingly. Yes, there was something he had to do.

He rose from the bar stool and began walking toward the kitchen exit. He stopped suddenly and turned back to his brother, gratitude filling within him. But how could he even begin to express thanks for all Derek had done? In the end, he decided his "all-knowing" brother knew how he felt anyway.

"Hey, can I borrow your car?" he asked instead, a half-smirk forming on his face at Derek's expression.

"Of course not," he stated.

"Right, got it," Nicola said, then turned again and walked out.

――――――――

"And although it is confirmed that Taya Mariano has been released and cleared of any charges against her for conspiracy or treason,

questions remain as rumors persist that the parliament member is Marco DeGrassi's daughter."

Taya switched off the news. *What a mess*, she thought, and she considered recent conversations she had had with her party's public relations.

Since her release, the press had been relentless, following her around, staking out her home, bombarding her everywhere she went. She had been firm with not making statements or giving interviews, but the pressure continued, and her party thought it best for her to just come clean with all of it, confident they could work with and spin her "DeGrassi" name to her favor. *It was all publicity*, she supposed, and she had nothing to hide really, at least, not more than the next politician did.

She had been surprised at the outreach of support from her colleagues since her release. Of course, she knew what was really going on there. She had received a full pardon from Derek, and since Calina had officially joined the European Union, he had been gaining massive amounts of favor quickly, being hailed as a hero. Especially since it was revealed that Bryan LaPointe was the true culprit, and the monarchy was off the hook in the public eye. So, naturally her ass would be kissed due to her support from him.

Although this revelation made her comeback into her political standing easier, it was also sad knowing that true friends were very few and far between. But did any politician really have "friends"?

Busying herself now with cleaning up the kitchen after breakfast, Taya wondered how she might pass the day. She hated being idle, and especially now, distractions were best. If she sat still for too long, she only thought of Nicola, and thinking about him just hurt too much.

She had lost him in every sense of the word. Not only had she deceived him, but she knew he was leaving; renouncing his title any day, only to expose himself to the life-threats that pursued him. Worse was her guilt, he was only putting himself in danger so that she, herself, could be safe.

She stopped scrubbing the mug in her hand over the sink, realizing that her thoughts had consumed her to the point that she was unconsciously scrubbing the painted pattern clean off.

She dropped the mug in the sink with a thud, and reached for her purse. She wasn't going to let him do it, she decided. And if she had to go to the palace and beg him on her hands and knees to not throw away his life for hers, then that's what she was going to do. She would even offer to give up her position, as long as it meant he stayed within the security he needed.

Determined to make him see reason, she grabbed her keys and rushed out the back door to her car. She stopped in her tracks however and stared at the LaFerrari turning onto her drive. Again, her first thought was that it was the monarch, but she knew better.

No, it was Nicola, and as he parked the car and stepped out, she couldn't help the same sense of confusion wash over her that she felt when he came to her at the jail.

He approached her, his gaze surveying her poised to enter her own car.

"I hope you're not in a hurry," he said, and a slight smile crossed his lips.

She shook her head. "I was…going to try and see you actually," she replied, still caught off-guard that he was here.

His brows came together, and it was his turn to be confused. "Why?" he asked.

She opened her mouth to speak, but her voice caught. She was losing her nerve now that he was standing in front of her so unexpectedly. The increasing upturn at the corners of his mouth didn't help.

"Was there something you wanted to tell me, angel?"

Her irritation at his playful attempt jarred her to her senses. "Yes," she stated, confidence now filling her voice, "you simply cannot leave your position or Calina. I will not let you do this, and I don't care how you feel about it. It's your life at stake, and I will not have that on my conscience."

Her blood pressure was rising now, her words coming quickly, and why—why was he staring at her like that?

"You need to take this seriously," she impressed upon him, a pleading now entering her tone. "I'm prepared to go to his highness and resign. I'll leave the country! I'll—,"

But Nicola never heard what else she would do because he closed the distance between them and placed his fingers on her lips to silence her.

"It's already done," he said softly.

She grabbed his hand. "What?" she exclaimed. "How could you do this? We're going back right now, and you're telling Derek you

267

changed your mind." She moved in the direction of the car, but he grabbed her arm.

"Taya, stop," he said, and she halted, looking up at him, his grip on her not only tightening slightly but pulling her toward him. His expression was suddenly earnest. "There is no longer any threat against my life from New York. It's over."

Her eyes grew wide. "How can that be?" she whispered, and he gave a slight shrug.

"They agreed to be paid," he replied, "so you see, there's no need for you to be concerned either for my life, or your conscience."

She ignored his mockery, this still made no sense.

"But if that's true," she said, "then why did you still renounce? You don't have to do that anymore."

In response, he only nodded slowly and pulled on her arm until she had no choice but to fall into his embrace.

"I had to," he said lowly, "because I love you. And if we are to truly be together, I can't serve as a prince while you serve in parliament. One of us had to leave."

She blinked at his words, furrowing her brow. Together? He wanted them to be together? She opened her mouth to respond, but he continued.

"I came here to beg your forgiveness. For everything I put you through. But even if you can't forgive me, I still needed to resign because I will never stop loving you, Taya."

He brushed his fingertips along her cheek, and it was then she noticed a bandage on his forefinger. She recalled the blood stain on her bracelet.

"You found my bracelet," she realized, a bit dazed. Of course it had to have been him. No one else would have known it belonged to her.

He nodded again. "In a box, yes, that Antonio brought in. He recovered it from the house you were held in."

Tears pricked at her eyes. "You say you came to ask for my forgiveness, but I lied to you about who I am," she cast her eyes down as tears fell from her lashes. "I thought you hated me."

He lifted her chin so she met his eyes. "Hate you?" he questioned. "I wish you had been honest with me, angel, but I don't blame you." He rested his forehead against hers. "I could never hate you," he whispered, "you made me a better man; my reason for everything."

She couldn't stand it any longer, and she brought her lips up to meet his. His kiss was hungry and firm, and he tangled one hand in her hair, refusing to let even an ounce of space between them.

Her lungs burned with needing oxygen, and reluctantly, she broke the kiss, now meeting his gaze with a smile.

"I know this is the part where I'm supposed to say 'let's start over,'" he said, still refusing to relinquish his hold on her, "but the last thing I want to do is forget everything we've shared or everything that I've ever felt for you. So, I guess what I'm asking is if you'll take me as I am."

In response, she threw her arms around his neck, bringing him close again.

"I love you, Nic," she said, "I don't want you any other way."

"I hope you mean that," he replied and laughed, pulling back from her, "because I'm currently broke, and I might need a place to stay until I get a job."

She pushed against his chest, and placed her hands on her hips. "So that's what you're really after here then?" she teased, and she turned beginning to walk in the direction of the back door. "Is that all I am to you? Room and board? You better watch your step 'cause I can always kick you out."

He quickened his stride after her and grabbed her around the waist, pulling her back against him roughly. "You know you're so much more," he whispered against her lips. "You're everything. And I predict very soon, you'll be begging me to stay for good."

As he claimed her lips again, Taya let that wonderful sense of happiness wash over her. Her heart filled with love, and somewhere in the back of her mind she knew for a fact that he was right.

The End

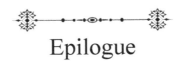

Epilogue

June

"You haven't much time, signore," Costa warned as Derek entered the passenger side of the black Mercedes waiting for him. "It's going to start in 45 minutes," the guard pressed, "and it would look really bad if the king was late to his own wedding. Is this errand really *that* important."

Derek only nodded, not looking anywhere except out the front windshield. "It's important," he stated.

Costa raised his eyebrows, but did not offer any further objection as he placed the car in drive heading toward a predesignated destination Derek had given him.

They drove just to the outskirts of town and arrived at an abandoned factory in about fifteen minutes.

"Stop here," Derek instructed as the car pulled up toward the front entrance, and he glanced at the perplexed look on Costa's face.

"Signore—" he began to question, but Derek cut him off.

"I'll only be a minute," he assured his guard, and he met Costa's eye. "You need to wait here, Vincenzo."

Costa returned a look that stated clearly he did not approve of any of this, but he nodded, following orders. "I will wait ten minutes," the guard stated, "then I'm coming in after you."

Derek exited the vehicle and walked to the front entrance, not surprised to find the door un-locked. As he entered the dark, vacant building he began to hear voices echoing down a corridor.

Slowing his footsteps, he paused around a corner, staying out of sight for the time-being. His presence was expected, so there was no need to remain hidden, but he didn't want to make himself known quite yet.

"Well, where is it then?"

The man's voice was agitated, and Derek couldn't suppress a smile. "I've been patient, Jack, now where is my briefcase?"

270

"All in good time," Jack replied smoothly, and Derek heard the sounds of more footsteps, no doubt Jack's men were circling. "This is your factory, is it not, Enzo?" Jack asked now.

"A ridiculous place to meet," Enzo snarled.

"Well, as you know, I can't be seen," Jack replied easily. "Shame you shut this place down. All those people out of work…" Jack was toying with Enzo, Derek could tell, stalling with the small talk.

"Cut the crap, Jack," Enzo snapped, "just hand over the briefcase. I trust all the money will be intact as well."

Jack barked out a laugh. "That's funny," he said, then paused a moment, and Derek knew what was coming next. He heard the distinct sound of a gun cock and knew Jack had one now on Enzo. "You know, I've decided that a new arrangement is in order between us."

"What is the meaning of this!"

He heard Enzo cry out, and for the first time, there was a trace of fear in his voice. There were sounds of a scuffle and grunting. Enzo would not be able to physically overpower any of Jack's men, and Derek felt now was as good a time as any to make his entrance.

He rounded the corner, taking in the scene: Jack's men having now restrained Enzo, while Jack held a gun pointed at his head.

Enzo's eyes widened in understanding upon seeing Derek enter the room.

"Landino," he seethed.

"Oh, so you do know who I am," Derek replied approaching Enzo calmly, who was now being held by two of Jack's men. "Considering you've never had the guts to face me, I wasn't sure," and he placed his hands casually in his pockets.

Enzo now glared at Jack. "You double-crossing son of a bitch!"

Jack only smiled.

"It's really not his fault," Derek said. "Did you really think you would get away with it all?" He took a step toward Enzo, his eyes piercing directly into him.

"You are done corrupting my country and my people," Derek began taking a measured breath to control his anger before continuing. "You contracted a hit against my brother, exploited my fiancée's hardships practically driving her away, orchestrated the murder of a palace employee, the kidnapping of a parliament member, and the coercion of a false voting outcome, almost causing a coupe. And you know what, DeGrassi?" Enzo clenched his jaw and raised his chin a notch.

271

"I had nothing to prove you did *any* of it."

At this Enzo raised a smug eyebrow.

"You were too good covering your tracks," Derek continued, and he shrugged, his expression suddenly darkening. "I can't put you behind bars. So, I had no choice except to deal with you another way."

"What are you talking about," Enzo sneered, and he saw Derek make eye contact with Jack. "You can't do anything to me!" he tried again, but panic now filled his voice.

Derek only nodded at Jack, then with a last ominous glance at Enzo, satisfied to see real terror in his eyes now, he turned and walked back the way he had come.

Once back outside, Derek opened the passenger door to the car and re-took his seat.

"The person I was supposed to meet didn't show," he informed Costa, and as Costa started the car, the sudden sound of a gun-shot rang through the air. Costa jerked suddenly at the noise and looked immediately at Derek.

Derek frowned. "Did you hear something?" he asked.

"No, signore," he replied without missing a beat.

"Me neither," Derek said, "let's go so we're not late."

As the car took off back toward the palace, Derek thought of his upcoming wedding, and the bottle of Jack Daniels he knew he'd find amongst the gifts.

Jack stood with his arms crossed, now admiring his handiwork. *This had worked out well*, he thought.

"Go ahead and clean up," he instructed his men.

"We heading back to New York now, boss?" one of the men asked.

Jack nodded, a thoughtful expression crossing his face. "Yes, but don't get too comfortable. We will be back soon."

"What do you mean? Back here?"

Jack caressed his beard gently. "I always finish an assignment," he said resolutely, and his man looked at him in confusion.

So Jack clarified.

"Nicola Landino."

272

About the Author

Ace Bryann is an American author currently residing in Romeo, Michigan. False Impressions is a sequel and the 2nd published novel by Ace Bryann. The first, Pictures Don't Lie, was published in 2021, and has achieved a favorable review by Kirkus Reviews, stating the novel is "A thoughtfully crafted tale that will leave romance fans looking forward to more from this promising author." The book was also selected as a finalist by the Global Book Awards in the fall of 2022 in the category of psychological thriller.

In addition to writing, Ace works as a sales process manager for a major financial institution and has worked in the finance industry for over 20 years.

Printed in the USA
CPSIA information can be obtained
at www.ICGtesting.com
LVHW050250180224
772033LV00001B/142

9 798218 343293